Deadly Masquerade

"Before starting out, Joe Pikul made a second call to the cleaning lady, Christine Hamilton, waking her up to tell her the new security code for the house in the Hamptons. Then he grabbed a cup of coffee and a buttered roll, checked on Diane's body in the back of the wagon, and headed north, toward the New York Thruway.

"Joe had spent an entire weekend trying to find a suitable burial spot and failed. He knew he was out of time. The car was starting to smell, the rug was loaded with wet sand, and the ice had melted. Most important he *had* to get rid of Diane before he picked up the kids. . . .

"Once on the New York Thruway, it wasn't long until the Sawoskas' exit. Now Joe was really out of time. With just a few minutes to go, he noticed a small pull-off, at milepost 56.5. He parked the car, opened the rear gate, grabbed Diane's tarp-covered corpse and carried it down the embankment to the edge of a culvert. This was it. After all those years of bickering and fighting, this was good-bye."

RICHARD T. PIENCIAK, working as an award-winning national correspondent for the Associated Press and more recently for the *New York Daily News*, has covered stories including the invasion of Grenada, the South and Central American cocaine trail, America's deadly white supremacy movement, and the Jonestown massacre in Guyana. He lives in Clifton, New Jersey.

MURDEROUS MINDS

DEADLY MASQUERADE

A True Story of
High Living, Depravity
and Murder

RICHARD T. PIENCIAK

A SIGNET BOOK

SIGNET
Published by the Penguin Group
Penguin Books USA Inc., 375 Hudson Street,
New York, New York 10014, U.S.A.
Penguin Books Ltd, 27 Wrights Lane,
London W8 5TZ, England
Penguin Books Australia Ltd, Ringwood,
Victoria, Australia
Penguin Books Canada Ltd, 2801 John Street,
Markham, Ontario, Canada L3R 1B4
Penguin Books (N.Z.) Ltd, 182–190 Wairau Road,
Auckland 10, New Zealand

Penguin Books Ltd, Registered Offices:
Harmondsworth, Middlesex, England

Published by Signet, an imprint of New American Library, a division of Penguin Books USA Inc. Originally published in a Dutton hardcover edition.

First Signet Printing, July, 1991
10 9 8 7 6 5 4 3 2 1

TO CHERYL

CONTENTS

PART · I

A FINAL WEEKEND

CHAPTER · 1

A Cruel Covenant

ON OCTOBER 22, 1987, THREE days after Black Monday, Wall Street's biggest crash since 1929, Sandy Jarvinen flew down from Boston for a rare meeting with her ex-husband. Joseph John Pikul, international vice-president at the prestigious, old-money brokerage house of Arnhold & S. Bleichroeder, sent his limousine driver to meet Sandy at LaGuardia Airport. Soon thereafter, the former college sweethearts met for lunch at an exclusive restaurant in the World Trade Center.

Divorced for thirteen years, the two touched on a variety of subjects at first, but increasingly Joe dwelled on a favorite one: his beautiful blond children from his current marriage—Claudia, nearly nine, and Blake, almost five. Joe couldn't stop talking about how much he loved them, how much he worried about them, and mostly, how much he wanted Sandy to meet them.

Joe had been after Sandy for several months to come to New York to meet the children. But Sandy steadfastly declined, insisting during Joe's late-night telephone calls that she didn't really want to meet Claudia and Blake— nothing against them, she just didn't want to meet them. In fact, Sandy had agreed to the trip to New York only after Joe promised to discuss a settlement of her lawsuit for back alimony, which had skyrocketed to nearly $40,000.

But as he'd always done with Sandy, Joe skillfully kept the conversation on the topic he wanted to discuss—his children—while Sandy, pliable as ever, went along without objection.

After lunch, Joe and Sandy, a matronly woman in her fifties, went to Joe's Battery Park City apartment, the one he'd rented when his present marriage started to fall apart. Looking through some old photo albums Joe had recently discovered, they talked and laughed about old times. Joe and Sandy had a great deal to reminisce about. They'd known each other more than thirty years, and had been through a lot together, good and bad, since their days at Northeastern University.

Joe asked Sandy about her personal life, and she spoke affectionately of her dear friend, an attorney named Vincent Federico. But Joe's interest was merely an opening gambit to bring the conversation around to the increasing problems he was having with Diane, his wife of nine years. He was afraid Diane was going to follow through with her threat to file for divorce and take the children from him. Joe and Diane had been in counseling for the last year, and the sessions had been a failure. Diane was now telling her friends she had something on Joe so devastating he would never see his children. "And there's nothing I care more about than my kids," he said.

Before leaving the spacious apartment, with its view of the Statue of Liberty and New York Harbor, Sandy picked out some of the faded photos from her years as the first Mrs. Pikul. Joe said he was grateful for how nicely she had arranged the pictures in the albums and gave Sandy half of them as mementos of their good times together.

Joe and Sandy then ran a few errands, including a visit to the bank and to Joe's office. Then it was on to the Pikul family apartment at 446 Sixth Avenue in Greenwich Village, where the children had already returned home from school—third-grader Claudia from exclusive Grace Church School, where tuition was $6,900 per year, and Blake from the $3,825-per-annum First Presbyterian Church Nursery School.

Joe released the children's baby-sitter who had been hired to stay through the evening so Diane could attend her writing class at the local Y. Working his persuasive magic of old, Joe convinced Sandy to join him and the children for dinner at Rumpelmayer's on Central Park

South, where she watched Claudia eat a steak and Blake a cheese sandwich.

As the kids were eating their ice-cream sundaes, Sandy presented Joe with a bill for $750. The new black dress she'd purchased in Boston for the trip had cost $300, and the balance of the money was to make up for plane fare and the day's lost wages.

Joe was surprised, but he knew Sandy was telling the truth when she said she didn't have anything nice to wear and couldn't afford to take a day off from work just to fly down and see him. As someone who always carried large amounts of cash in his pocket, Joe paid her—$750 in cash. After all, it had been his invitation.

"Joe, it's wonderful," Sandy said, in appreciation of the fine day. "It's like it never stopped."

Joe returned home to the Village and got the children ready for bed. He also called Carina Jacobson, one of the regular baby-sitters, to ask if she would join the family out in the Hamptons for the weekend. Carina begged off, explaining that she had a previous engagement.

When Diane Pikul arrived home from her job as assistant to the publisher at *Harper's* magazine, Joe didn't have a chance to tell her about the weekend baby-sitter problem. Immediately she demanded to know what had happened to the sitter that she'd hired for the evening. Diane knew she couldn't count on Joe to handle the chore; he wanted all the joys of parenthood but none of the responsibilities.

As usual with failing marriages, it didn't take much to spark a full-scale argument. Diane had a sharp and often abusive tongue, and soon she was not only yelling "faggot" and "motherfucker creep" at him, but Joe had to back off to avoid her attempts to scratch him.

Smartly dressed in a Brooks Brothers suit, Joe—just under six feet and a slightly paunchy 190 pounds—ran down the steps of the duplex and out onto the sidewalk. Diane, all five feet three inches and 115 pounds of her, gave chase past the bus stop, the cleaners, and the deli while continuing to shout angrily at Joe the entire time.

Joe tried to answer back, but he was no match for Diane this night. As dozens of stunned passersby looked on, Joe skulked away and Diane returned home to Claudia and

Blake. She had missed her class, but felt damn good about having humiliated Joe.

Joe eventually retreated to his Battery Park apartment, where he called Sandy and spoke to her for five minutes before going to bed.

The next morning, Joe entered his twenty-eighth-floor office at Arnhold & S. Bleichroeder as he did every day: with a stand-at-attention formality. Bespectacled with a neatly trimmed brown beard, Joe was arrogant and stiff whatever the occasion, perhaps a sign of his lowly upbringing. This was a fast world Joe operated in, one in which he felt the need to always perform perfectly, even down to the simple maneuver of turning over for his masseuse quickly enough. He wanted desperately to belong.

Generally quiet and withdrawn around the office, he also was known for his fierce, impulsive temper. Still, Joe got things done his way. For the most part, that meant he ignored those around him. They didn't exist, unless they screwed up. So long as they fed his ego, Joe was happy.

Joe was a go-getter, a top producer in his work. He had developed an international reputation as the first to zero in on the investment opportunities offered by Scandinavian companies. In addition to carrying on his exhaustive research, Joe traveled the Concorde to Europe once a month to keep abreast of developments in Zurich, Geneva, London, and the Far East. At his current sales rate, Joe figured to gross about $1.2 million in salary and commissions for 1987.

As Joe marched into his office that Friday morning, he grabbed the telephone and spoke with Sandy for six minutes. It seemed the more Joe argued with Diane, the more he called Sandy.

But the arguments were only part of it. It had been a hell of a week for Joe. He'd taken quite a beating in the catastrophic stock-market crash, and to top it off, he'd broken a tooth eating peanut brittle.

Joe called his dentist out in East Hampton for an appointment for Saturday. But Dr. Katz's wife, Bonnie, told him they were going to be tied up at a family bar mitzvah. Perhaps it could wait until Monday, or Sunday if it was really an emergency.

Later that afternoon, before departing for home, Joe also called Diane, and they decided to keep their plans to go to their weekend house in the Hamptons to divide the furniture and other personal belongings. As a first step to dissolving the relationship, both had agreed to sell the house and use the money to help establish their separate lives. The kids would ride out with Joe in the sports car, and Diane would follow later in the family 1986 Buick station wagon.

After getting the kids off to school that Friday morning, Diane walked over to the *Harper's* office to begin her workday.

At forty-three, nine years Joe's junior, Diane had been working at the magazine for just over seven months as assistant to the publisher, her first full-time employment in years. Vivacious and possessed with a wicked sense of humor, Diane had recently started writing again in earnest and had also joined an exercise class.

Her job at *Harper's* had a certain glamorous cachet, but it was not a career-track position. Despite the impressive title, Diane was a glorified secretary, with an annual salary of $22,500. Although she'd always aspired to big things, Diane—an only child from South Bend, Indiana—knew the limitations of her position, and had privately said as much on many occasions.

Still, Diane kept up appearances. The job dressed up her résumé and allowed her to move in the world of famous writers, something she always wanted to be. The job was also a step toward independence, reentry into the workplace, and a start at rebuilding a life with Claudia and Blake that would exclude Joe's tyranny.

Her job and outside activities consumed a great deal of time, but Diane was otherwise dedicated to her children. These days, they were constantly on her mind as she worried about their exposure to her growing troubles with Joe. As Diane had told her colleague Linda McNamara about the previous evening's fight with Joe: "That was the first time I fought back in front of the children."

Diane was concerned about the future. She feared the divorce would be difficult, that Joe might cut off support completely, perhaps even follow up on his threat to quit working entirely and move to Florida to fish for his meals. Just the other day she'd told the director of Blake's nursery school that she was afraid of ending up fifty, alone, and broke.

It was tough to give up the comfortable life she had enjoyed for so long, but as much as Diane had come to treasure the fancy clothes, the dining out, the house in the country, the limousines, the stream of nannies and sitters, the open checkbook, the pastrami-sandwich-thick pile of credit cards, she'd come to realize with the help of a marriage counselor and a therapist that her only hope of salvaging a life for herself and her children meant a break from Joe, regardless of the economic consequences.

Still, Diane wanted every penny she had coming to her, including her share of the furniture in the house out in Amagansett. But that wasn't the only reason to go to the "country." Dividing the household goods would mark her first concrete commitment to a divorce since the summer before, when she had retained famed matrimonial attorney Raoul Lionel Felder, whose clients have included the former Mrs. Alan Jay Lerner, Mrs. Roone Arledge, Mrs. Martin Scorsese, Mrs. Mark Gastineau, and the former Mrs. Mike Tyson, actress Robin Givens.

Hiring Felder had been a bold move, but it turned out to be more show than substance. On and off, Diane had pressed Felder and his legion of staff attorneys for action, but she kept making excuses to delay the filing of court papers necessary to start a formal divorce proceeding. Deep down inside, she hoped the threat of divorce would make Joe change his ways. It hadn't.

This time, Diane promised herself, she really meant it. And the trip to Amagansett to divide the furniture seemed to her to represent the essential first step.

Before leaving to meet the kids at the apartment, Diane telephoned a girlfriend to postpone dinner plans. Diane explained why she and Joe were going out to the Hamptons for the weekend, and she promised to call when she got back to reschedule for either Monday or Wednesday evening.

Diane also spoke to Barbara Weingarden, a friend from New Jersey and the Hamptons, to make plans for Saturday, for their daughters often played together.

With plans unmade and made, Diane grabbed her coat and headed for the $3,003-a-month duplex in the Village.

The Pikuls lived on the east side of busy Sixth Avenue, north of Tenth Street, just a few blocks' walk from New York University and Washington Square Park. Looking south, one could see the Twin Towers of the World Trade Center, home of the expensive Windows on the World restaurant, one of Joe's haunts. The Hudson River waterfront was a short walk to the west, where young boys lean on highway barriers nightly, strutting their stuff for rich, middle-aged men. And at the Meat Market, up by Fourteenth, the daytime beef butchers are replaced in darkness by women living their lives trapped in men's bodies, high-pitched voices with high-heeled shoes. Joe Pikul, a Wall Street mover and shaker, knew of these haunts as well. In fact, his cross dressing was one of the primary reasons Diane wanted to take the children away from him.

After returning home that Friday evening, Diane released the children's sitter and changed out of her workclothes—a stylish, brightly colored red and pink dress by the Japanese designer Kenzo—into a casual plaid flannel Ralph Lauren shirt and black corduroy skirt. Diane then fed the children and changed them into their pajamas.

After kissing and hugging their mother good-bye, Claudia and Blake jumped into their father's silver-gray Mazda RX-7 sports car shortly before seven. Joe drove west to the piers, then south to Battery Park to stop at his other apartment, wanting to get some clothing—women's clothing—and some toys for the children. While he was there, Joe called Sixth Avenue to check on Diane, who said she'd be leaving in about twenty minutes. Then Joe headed for the East End of Long Island, the land of sand dunes, clam bars, and beach colonies—the playground of New York's successful elite.

Diane was in no hurry to make the trip, for she'd grown to hate the ride out to the Hamptons. As anyone who has ever taken the trip from the city knows, traffic can be torturous on a Friday night. Even in October, the ninety-mile trip often takes more than three hours, through backed-up bridges over the East River and then along the "world's longest parking lot," the Long Island Expressway. The final stage, along Route 27, is often the worst. Tie-ups on the two-lane highway frequently appear out of nowhere and slow traffic for hours.

Walking north on Sixth, past the Village Vintner liquor store and Tony Roma's rib restaurant, Diane withdrew sixty dollars from a Republic Express banking center automatic teller machine at 9:36 P.M. At some point that evening, probably after she withdrew the money, Diane also ate a full dinner of steak, rice, and vegetables. Then she walked around the corner to the parking garage on West Tenth Street to pick up the family's station wagon.

Then she, too, headed east.

Joe and the kids encountered little traffic during their journey. It was about ten o'clock—both kids were asleep—as Joe drove by the quaint welcome sign on the main highway:

HISTORIC AMAGANSETT
SETTLED 1680

Once an Indian village, Amagansett is incorporated in the town of East Hampton. For years it had been a quiet haven for artists, but by the 1970's the tiny enclave and the rest of the Hamptons started to liven up as more and more people from New York City spent their weekends there, including celebrities like Andy Warhol, Paul McCartney, Billy Joel, and Faye Dunaway.

It became more difficult to separate the full-timers from the part-timers during the next decade, because the city set started to stay longer and longer. They upgraded their homes or had new ones built. Weekend visits during the winter became more commonplace. As could be expected, the area's old-timers came to resent the fast-lane intruders from the big city.

Joe had long loved the Hamptons area—the rolling dunes and wide beaches, the tranquil bays and deep stands of pine trees, the potato fields, the deep ponds formed by glacial drifts, the art shows. A frequent visitor long before he met Diane, Joe especially liked the tranquillity he often felt in the area, for it reminded him of growing up in Massachusetts along the Ware River.

Turning onto Windmill Lane on the less exclusive bay side of Main Street, and stopping before the renovated nineteenth-century fisherman's shack he and Diane had bought for $237,000 in late 1983, Joe carried Blake in and put him to bed. Claudia woke up, so she walked in un-assisted. She was hungry and wanted a snack. Joe had stopped at the country store for milk and cheesecake, so he let her eat and watch a children's tape on the VCR. Then Joe read his daughter a story and put her to bed.

As he waited for Diane, Joe put one of his tapes into the VCR. As time passed, though, and Diane failed to appear, he grew restless. Inexplicably using a credit card to make the call from his own home, he called the parking garage back in the Village at 11:30. The attendant told him Diane had left somewhere around nine. She was due soon.

But as the minutes continued to roll away—first a half hour, then an hour, then an hour and a half—Joe became angrier. He paced, and paced some more.

By the time Diane pulled the blue station wagon into the pebbled drive somewhere between one and two o'clock, Joe had whipped himself into a frenzy, convinced that Diane had been off somewhere with a boyfriend.

"Gee, Diane, that was a long trip," Joe observed.

"Are you questioning me?" Diane was tired from the solo trip, and was in no mood for any of Joe's crap.

"Not really."

"Fuck you, you're a creep. You faggot," Diane screamed back.

Joe and Diane were at it again.

It was to be their final argument.

CHAPTER • 2

Condoms and Twelve Bags of Ice

THE NEXT MORNING, JOE ROSE from his easy chair in the living room. It was before sunrise, but one of the first things he did, before the kids got up, was call his dentist, Dr. Alan Katz, in East Hampton.

Of course no one was in, so Joe left a message on the machine saying a tooth had fallen out and he needed it fixed. But, Joe continued, he couldn't come in right away because "I have to baby-sit the children. When I woke up this morning, my wife was gone. I guess she's taken off." Joe emitted a nervous kind of chuckle, then hung up.

There was no rational reason for Joe to make the call, given the conversation he'd had the day before with Bonnie Katz about the unavailability of her husband that Saturday. But Joe wasn't thinking too clearly. After a terrible week, he'd had an even more terrible night.

Claudia woke up about seven, Blake about nine. When the children asked where their mother was, Joe explained that she'd gone out to see one of her friends. When they pressed some more, he told them she'd run away.

Joe made the children breakfast, which they ate in the baby-sitter's room while watching children's tapes on the VCR. About ten, Joe walked past the neatly trimmed boxwood shrubs and loaded the kids into the RX-7. He left the station wagon parked in the bushes out back, just off the dirt path running along the edge of Oak Grove Cemetery, on the southern border of the Pikul property.

Several years ago, right along that border, Joe had purchased the last forty-eight empty plots.

Joe made a right onto Windmill Lane, drove past the cemetery and over the Long Island Rail Road tracks toward town. But just as suddenly, he switched gears and headed to the town dump, where he disposed of his household trash and the clothes he had worn the night before.

Once on Main Street, Joe parked across from the Amagansett Hardware Store. With kids in tow, he walked hurriedly into the store and started buying frantically, purchasing a utility flashlight, sponges, three 100-foot-long cords of rope, a blender, birdseed, a knife, a shovel, a bag of rags, a roll of paper towels, a box of garbage bags, two black plastic tubs, a Styrofoam ice chest, five pairs of heavy-duty fishing gloves, a box of Tide detergent, and a wheelbarrow. Several times Joe impulsively interrupted the checkout process to add another item.

The gloves would later prove to be of particular interest. The Hamptons area has a high proportion of fishermen, and every October manager Herbert Kiembock gets many requests for a special kind of waterproof rubber glove: thick, insulated, light brown with red trim. It was those very traceable gloves that Joe Pikul purchased.

At the register, Joe told Kiembock: "I'm stuck with my children. My wife has left me." First Joe pulled out a wad of fifty-dollar bills, then changed his mind and produced his American Express card to settle his $377.64 bill. Joe was asked to give his telephone number on the bottom and instead of 267-3606, he wrote 267-3603. Then Kiembock and another store employee carried the five shopping bags out to the Mazda.

But Joe wasn't done shopping. He grabbed Claudia and Blake and walked down the block to the Amagansett Deli.

Tony Lupo, the man behind the counter, recognized Joe as a regular customer who never looked at prices. "He'd come down the aisle, one of these, one of those. He'd pile it all up on the counter," Lupo would later recall. Often, Joe would pay with a fifty- or a hundred-dollar bill. This day, however, Joe wasn't interested in food. He needed some ice, twelve bags full. Lupo remembered thinking to himself: "The guy must be having a party."

Joe reloaded the kids and drove the half mile home.

Once inside, about eleven o'clock, he called the alarm company to change the security code. Then he called Dr. Katz's office again.

Patricia Sarlo, Dr. Katz's office manager, had come in around nine and listened to Joe's strange message about his wife having run off. She'd tried the Pikul house at that point, but the phone was busy. Joe was a steady customer and had broken several teeth eating hard candy.

On this call Joe connected, but as he'd been told the day before, Dr. Katz was not available. Joe, who was acting more hyper than usual, said he was planning to visit "good old friends" near West Point and was concerned about his appearance. "It looks terrible and I have to get this fixed," he said.

Then Joe said he couldn't come in anyway because he had to take the kids to visit the friends, whom, he said, he hadn't seen in a while. "I have to speak to these people," said Joe. "I think we're getting a divorce. I guess she's left me."

Joe explained that when he had woken up, his wife was gone, and that while he was looking under the bed for one of Claudia's shoes, he'd found some condoms. "She must be seeing someone because these condoms are not my brand," he said. "We haven't been getting along. I guess this has been going on for a while."

Sarlo was concerned about the children, given the fact that Joe told her he'd driven out to Amagansett late the night before and was now saying he was going to drive all the way upstate and then back. "Please be careful driving," Sarlo cautioned.

Joe said he planned to return to New York City or Amagansett by Saturday evening and wondered if Dr. Katz could see him then. Assured that Katz would see him Sunday if necessary, Joe promised Sarlo he would call the dentist's office Saturday evening.

Sarlo hung up the phone and thought to herself: "That was not your ordinary conversation with the dentist's office."

Marshall Weingarden, a friend from New Jersey and the Hamptons, called the Pikul house about 11:45. His wife, Barbara, had been delayed in town, so she asked Marshall to call and finalize the day's activities for the children. The Weingardens—Marshall was an executive at a manufacturing firm and Barbara an advertising manager—had known the Pikuls socially for three years, introduced through mutual acquaintances at a child's birthday party. They also had been over swimming in the Pikuls' in-ground pool several times.

The two men chatted about their children for a minute or two. Marshall mentioned the conversation between the two wives the day before and wondered if the children were going to get together. "There's a story hour at the library at two o'clock," said Weingarden. Joe said that sounded like a good idea but that he was very busy packing. Joe suggested that Marshall pick up Claudia and bring her over to his house to play, but Marshall didn't agree to the attempted handoff.

Then Joe launched into an explanation of Diane's late appearance the night before and their ensuing argument. According to Joe, Diane arrived about 1:00 A.M. but he knew she had left about nine o'clock because he had called the garage to check on her. When he had asked Diane why it had taken her more than four hours to get to Amagansett, she got very angry and left.

"Do you have any idea where she went?" asked Weingarden.

"No," replied Joe. "She left without the car. She's disappeared."

"Oh boy, this is a really bad week for this to happen to you—after all the stock market crashed and everything."

"Yes, and I had a bad report from a doctor also this week," added Joe.

In the course of the conversation Joe also mentioned that he had found condoms in the house, under a couch. He suspected a boyfriend. "You do have a lot of baby-sitters here," said Weingarden. "Perhaps it's one of them."

Joe agreed, "Yes, that could be."

Interrupting the conversation, Joe began talking to someone in the house. When he got back on the line, he mentioned that a man from the alarm company was there changing the security code. Weingarden didn't react aloud to that news but thought that Joe must be changing the codes to lock Diane out.

When Weingarden suggested Joe bring Claudia and Blake over to play, Joe now begged off. "We'll get together another time," he said, explaining that a real-estate agent was coming around in the afternoon to look at the house.

With that, Weingarden said he'd call again to check on how things were coming along.

Agitated, Joe had to get away by himself. But he'd have to get someone to watch Claudia and Blake. Joe thought of Henry Sawoska, his roommate for three years at Northeastern. Henry had been best man for Joe's marriage to Sandy Jarvinen, and in turn, Joe had been best man when Henry married his wife, Louise. But they had drifted apart, especially after Diane entered the picture.

Joe and Diane had attended two football games with the Sawoskas, right after they got married, but attempts to continue those get-togethers failed because Diane didn't like football. One also couldn't help but get the feeling Diane didn't like the Sawoskas either. They lived in upstate New York, in a small town called New Windsor near the Catskills, and just weren't her fast-paced style.

Henry had invited Joe to bring his family up for a visit several times, so it wasn't as if a phone call would be completely out of the blue. And even though the roomies had gotten together only twice in the past few years for lunch in Manhattan, Joe had already involved Henry in his personal life, having called him at home late one night in August when he needed someone to talk to. Joe had told Henry about his increased marital problems and claimed that his doctor had told him he had a terminal illness, with only five months to five years to live. "I've got no one to talk to," Joe had said. "You're the only one who'll understand."

"Can't you tell your wife?" asked Henry. Joe said no, he couldn't.

Henry had understood. And he'd understand today, too, Joe figured. He had kids of his own, just like Joe. And so Joe picked up the telephone and called his old college buddy.

Henry's wife, Louise, answered the phone. Joe said he was upset and told Louise that Diane had left him with the children. Joe said he would like to come up for dinner and also asked if she could baby-sit sometime.

While Henry had met Blake one time in Manhattan, Louise, a soft-spoken, gentle woman, had never laid eyes on either of Joe's children. Still, she agreed to help out as best she could, then handed the phone to Henry for directions from Long Island.

The voice on the phone sounded upset, and as Joe began talking rapidly, Henry became concerned. Sure, come up on the New York Thruway, Henry said. Take the Newburgh exit, Exit 17. Joe said they'd be there about 6:30.

By this time Claudia and Blake were impatient to go outside to play ball. Joe wasn't really in shape anymore, but he would do anything for his children and out they went. Shortly thereafter, a seemingly insignificant thing occurred. The soccer ball rolled into the honeysuckle bushes and Joe cut himself retrieving it. Joe would remember that cut in the months to come.

By five, Joe loaded the kids into the station wagon and set off on the long ride upstate to the Sawoskas.

Joe pulled off the Long Island Expressway in Yaphank and placed a call at 5:22 to Sandy, up in Norwell, Massachusetts.

"I have something to hide," Joe said. "Can I hide it with you?"

Sandy, who assumed Joe was merely referring to hiding an asset—a ruse he'd used quite well during their divorce—agreed to her ex-husband's request.

Joe then said something about coming up to visit. Sandy said, "Sure, anytime."

At 6:11 Joe again pulled off the road, this time at Exit 25 of the Northern State Parkway, to call Henry Sawoska again. "We're running a little late," he explained, telling Henry not to wait for them for dinner.

Joe and the kids wouldn't arrive until about 8:30 or nine. As Claudia later recalled, her father kept getting lost.

Once Joe stepped inside the house, he appeared to be upset. Perspiring, he removed his down ski vest, which he held against his chest.

"Come on. Let me take your jacket. Relax," said Louise.

"No, no, no," said Joe.

When Henry went out to the station wagon to help Joe bring in the overnight bags and stuffed animals, he saw that the back storage area was loaded with paraphernalia, strewn about in no apparent order, right up to the windows. Henry got pretty close to the back of the car, but Joe did the unloading.

Once inside, Joe remarked about how impressed he was with the house and wanted Henry to give him a tour. They had gotten no further than the basement, though, when Henry asked, "What's the matter, Joe? What's bothering you?"

Joe explained that he'd found a condom under his bed that wasn't his. Joe said he had trusted Diane, but that he now knew for sure that she had a boyfriend. As the two men talked a bit about Diane's disappearance, Joe contended that she'd run away several times in the past, for days at a time, without ever making contact.

By the time Joe had finished his tale of woes—he had taken a beating on Black Monday, plus his doctors had sent him confirmation on his short time to live—Henry was deeply worried about his friend. This was not the cocksure, fiery-tempered stock-market executive he knew.

When the two men returned upstairs, Louise had made grilled cheese sandwiches, and everyone sat around the table. The conversation was light and breezy, mostly about children, when Joe suddenly announced that he had to leave. Louise and Henry got very concerned. As Louise would later recall: "We knew he was going through a trying experience and I had already prepared beds upstairs for them to stay. But he just wanted the children to stay, saying that he had things that he had to do and that he wouldn't be staying overnight."

Minutes later, though, Joe contradicted himself, explaining that he had something to take care of and would return to spend the night after completing his task.

The Sawoskas then tried to talk him out of that plan. They didn't know, or ask, what he had to do or where he had to go, but they didn't want him driving around half the night in his obviously distraught condition. "Wherever you're going, stay for the night and come back the next day," said Henry.

Joe agreeably switched gears. "I need some time to myself," he said. He said he had to go back and take care of a few things. Apparently feeling compelled to offer at least one example, Joe specifically mentioned he had chipped a tooth on peanut brittle and wanted the dentist to take care of it. Joe assured the Sawoskas he would be back the next day to pick up the kids.

About 10:15 P.M., Joe got back in his car and started driving.

CHAPTER • 3

A High Water Table

Joe was soon on Interstate 84, headed for Massachusetts. In Hartford, he called Sandy, telling her he was on his way up to see her, but needed directions.

Sandy had been asleep, and it took her a minute to realize what Joe was saying. When he called that afternoon, she hadn't realized that he meant he was coming to see her right away. Still, she gave him directions, then went back to sleep. The last thing she expected was for Joe to actually show up.

At about four o'clock Sunday morning, Sandy's phone rang again. This time Joe was calling from a phone booth across from the Hitchcock Store in town. He was lost.

"I'll come down and get you," Sandy said. She threw on a raincoat and drove to the center of town.

There was no one around but a lone car parked just across from the fire station, a station wagon with wood paneling on the side and a car telephone antenna on the top. Sandy pulled alongside and noticed a man seated behind the steering wheel with his back turned. Sandy beeped the horn lightly and the man turned around. It was Joe.

In the back of the wagon was a big pile, high up in the window, covered by something brownish, perhaps an old blanket. There were little things piled up around it.

Sandy made an illegal U-turn in the police department parking lot and headed back home. Joe followed in the station wagon, but kept a considerable distance behind, perhaps spooked by where Sandy had made her turn. Several times along the way, especially at key turns, Sandy was forced to stop and wait for him to catch up.

Both cars pulled into Sandy's long driveway at about 4:30. Sandy maneuvered her car around the circular section at the drive's end, got out, and walked toward Joe's car, which he stopped about twenty feet down the drive. As she approached, though, Joe waved her off, so she turned and entered her house.

Joe came in a few minutes later, carrying a canvas bag and a shoulder bag. He began pacing back and forth, back and forth. Seeing how jittery he was, Sandy made him some coffee and they sat down to talk.

"Where can I bury it?" Joe asked.

Sandy was confused. She had thought Joe wanted to hide some assets, but now he was talking about burying something. "Bury what?"

"Where can I bury it?"

"Joe, you're going to have to tell me what it is you want to bury," Sandy responded. Assuming Joe wanted to hide some documents—securities of some type—she suggested a safe-deposit box.

"It's too big for a safe-deposit box," he replied.

Joe was really getting on Sandy's nerves now. Leaving the room, she sat down on the floor of her library area and snapped, "You know, you're really going to have to tell me what it is you want to bury."

But Joe continued to pace, back and forth, back and forth. Then he walked over to Sandy and slumped down in the wing chair. For long moments he just sat there, chin on his hands.

Finally, he looked up and blurted, "I had to eliminate her."

Sandy was stunned: Joe was talking about Diane. She realized now what it was he wanted to bury.

Sandy became more frightened than she had ever been before—no small feat given the many beatings Joe had given her during their married life. Nervously she told him that her property wasn't a good place to bury anyone, being right next to a brook. "I have a high water table."

Joe didn't say a word. He just sat there.

"Where are the kids?" Sandy asked. Joe told her he

had left them with Henry Sawoska, their old friend from college.

Sandy, who always looks at things analytically, pretended to discuss alternatives with Joe. She figured she had to come up with something to send him on his way. She mentioned several parks in the area, one in Norwell and another in nearby Hingham, but she said that burying someone in either of them wouldn't be a good idea since the parking lots were considerable distances from the wooded areas. Someone might notice the New York license plate.

Sandy also suggested that Joe consult a lawyer and mentioned her friend, Vincent Federico. Grudgingly, Joe let Sandy call him, but she got his answering service.

Sandy then suggested that Joe head out toward the Berkshires, where many years before the two of them had rented a variety of summer and winter cottages. Joe said he would consider that suggestion, then got up and walked out.

It was about 5:30 A.M. now, and with the clocks being turned back an hour, it would be light soon. It wasn't cold, but Sandy sat in her library feeling frozen, just staring out her window. Even for a woman who spent all those years with Joe's craziness, the past sixty minutes had been excruciating.

About an hour later, Joe's car stopped at the end of her driveway and stayed there for a while. Obviously, he was thinking about taking another crack at getting Sandy's help. But he thought better of it and eventually drove off again.

As the morning wore on, Sandy came out of her shock and wondered if the best course of action was to go to the state police barracks nearby in Norwell. But then, by her later account, she realized she "didn't have anything to tell them." More to the point, she was scared that she, too, was in trouble. Not only had her former husband just tried to convince her to let him bury a body in her backyard, but just a couple of days ago she had flown down to New York to meet him and the kids. Then she remembered a conversation back in the summer, when Joe told her that Diane might have to have an accident, that he was dying of AIDS and there was no way he wanted Diane to get the kids. But even that wasn't all of it. Joe had beat the shit out of Sandy for years. She knew the violence he was capable of if he found out she'd squealed on him. No, going to the state police barracks was not such a good idea.

Instead, Sandy drove to Federico's apartment complex in Weymouth. He was a lawyer. He would know what to do. But when she got there, Federico wasn't home, and the security guards wouldn't let her in.

Getting more frazzled by the minute, Sandy drove back home.

Joe headed toward Norwood, another South Shore suburb, to visit the graves of an aunt and uncle he'd been close to while attending college. Joe frequently sought solace in graveyards. "I often did when I had problems and troubles. I got a certain peace and some thoughtful insights," he later explained. This morning, however, he was much too overwrought to think anything through straight.

About 8:30, after driving west for an hour, Joe once again reached for one of his favorite conveniences: the telephone. He dialed the Sawoskas, who were at that moment a long, long way away.

Joe told Henry he'd be coming shortly to pick up the children. Henry didn't ask, but he figured Joe was back in Manhattan and that the trip north would take an hour and a half. The Sawoskas were on their way to church—services were at 9:30—so it was agreed that Joe would come about eleven o'clock.

A few minutes later, Joe reached out to Sandy again, asking if she'd been able to contact her lawyer friend. Sandy said she'd reached his answering service again, so Joe said he would call back.

Eleven o'clock came and went at the Sawoska house with no Joe. He called, though, at noontime, apologizing for being late. He explained that he didn't feel well and had taken medication that was making him drowsy. Louise suggested Joe stay where he was and get some sleep.

But Joe insisted, explaining that he was already on the Thruway. "No, I'm on my way. I'm going to come up and get the kids."

Then Claudia got on the phone. "Daddy, I love you and

I miss you," she told her father. He assured her they would all be together again real soon.

At this point Joe was near Ware, Massachusetts, his hometown. He drove by the senior citizens complex where his mother, Bernice, resided, but he never rang her bell. Joe also went to the cemetery in nearby Three Rivers to meditate over the graves of his father and grandmother.

Then he called Sandy and asked if she'd contacted her lawyer friend. This time she had good news and gave Joe a couple of telephone numbers. All the same, it was obvious that Joe was still very agitated and confused. He said he couldn't leave "the package" in Ware because it was too close to the road. Clearly, he had no idea how to handle the situation and was begging Sandy for advice.

"Why don't you go turn yourself in?" she suggested.

The phone line went silent, then dead.

Joe continued to drive westward, back toward the New York State border. Soon he was in the Berkshires, and he turned off and headed toward the tiny ski house he and Sandy used to rent near Lenox, hoping to find someplace to dump the body. But again he struck out. It was hunting season, and with so many people walking around, Joe was afraid someone would see him.

He called Sandy again, but he only got her machine. When she returned from shopping and looking in on her elderly mother, Sandy heard Joe's recorded voice tell her that he'd gone to "the winter house," but couldn't do anything because it had been too crowded.

Late that afternoon, Claudia began to worry about her father. During his last call, Joe had said he was on the Thruway. Surely he should have arrived by now. Claudia said she wanted to call the apartment in the city, but Louise resisted. "Why don't we wait? Maybe Dad's resting," she said. And Claudia relented.

By six o'clock Louise also was growing concerned. So when Claudia again requested permission to call home, Louise approved.

Louise dialed the apartment on Sixth Avenue, but of course Joe was not there. Claudia said she had a second number, for her father's other apartment. "I can get Dad at this phone number," she said. But again there was no answer.

Louise Sawoska fed the children and got them ready for bed. "Don't worry," she told them. "Daddy must have been detained somewhere and he'll probably call us later." She assured the youngsters that if their father did come to pick them up during the night, she would wake them and they'd be all ready to go home in their pajamas. Louise then put the two motherless children to bed.

With the arrival of night and Diane still not buried, Joe drove down the New York Thruway, past his children, and back into New York City. He would later relate that he spent the night sleeping in his apartment at 446 Sixth Avenue.

Diane spent the night out in the cold, on the curb, in the rear well of the station wagon, wrapped in a green canvas car cover.

The next morning, an utterly exhausted Joe Pikul headed north to pick up his children. Out of time and opportunity, this arrogant, extremely bright businessman who didn't know the first thing about being a criminal, dumped Diane's body in one of the most obvious places imaginable.

PART·II

LIFE AND DEATH

CHAPTER · 4

A Southern Belle
from Indiana

ALL OF HER LIFE, DIANE Jackson Whitmore Schnackenberg Pikul dreamed of glamorous things: her name in
lights, a successful knight in shining armor, breathtaking
surroundings, and hobnobbing with important people. But
all she ever ended up with were impressively titled secretarial jobs and lonely nights when she bemoaned her
lack of stature.

Born on May 20, 1943, Diane was spoiled from birth.
Part of the coddling resulted from her chronic asthma,
which almost killed her as a toddler, but the pampering
continued throughout her later years. To Don and Jane
Whitmore, Diane would forever be their little princess.

Her parents' decision to have one child was a conscious
one. "When we wanted to go out Saturday nights, we were
lucky to have a dollar bill between us," Don Whitmore
recalled. "We married in 1937 and didn't have a child until
1943. From a financial aspect, we didn't feel we could have
more children and raise them properly. And by the time
our finances grew, it was too late."

A graduate of Purdue University, Donald Eckman
Whitmore had been working as a plant engineer for Studebaker, one of the major companies in the South Bend
area, when sensing that the company was going downhill,
he moved the family to a new job in Birmingham, Michigan, when Diane was twelve.

The Whitmores, both Protestants, remained in Michigan
for only two years, when a former Studebaker vice-

president called with a job offer from Mack Truck in New Jersey. So in July 1957 Don Whitmore switched jobs again. Mrs. Whitmore, who had attended St. Mary's College and Milwaukee Downer College, followed with Diane after the house was sold, just in time for school.

These moves, coming in the fragile years of early adolescence, played emotional havoc on young Diane, and insecurity would continue to dog her throughout her life.

Nevertheless, Diane's star sparkled brightly at North Plainfield High School where she received a Merit Scholarship letter of commendation. She already liked to write, was president of the Spanish Club, treasurer of the Dramatic Club, had the lead role in school plays, and was a member of the senior-class cabinet. Diane also won a countywide American Legion public speaking contest, a New Jersey state Junior Chamber of Commerce speech contest, and came in second in the state Jaycees local radio script contest.

The Whitmores' New Jersey home was a bustling place, often filled with six, eight, even ten classmates playing and working on projects together. The door was always open after school and on weekends.

For all her seeming success, Diane was perhaps trying too hard to gain approval. Following an essay contest, she was one of four seniors in the Class of 1961 selected to speak at graduation. She also finished in the top ten of her class. But in later years Diane told her friends in New York that she'd graduated class valedictorian, and the boast was even printed in one of the stories following her death. That was the way Diane operated—always putting an extra spin on things to make herself appear better than she really was.

In the fall of 1961, Diane enrolled at Mary Washington College in Fredericksburg, Virginia, the women's branch of the University of Virginia. She continued to pursue her love for the Spanish language and also studied two semesters of French. But she found the school wanting. "I know as much as the teachers know, and the teachers told me so," Diane told her father one day, desperate to transfer. Soft-natured and pliable, he consented.

Diane decided to attend one of the Seven Sisters schools, feeling the prestigious colleges were more appropriate for her needs and stature. She decided on Mount Holyoke, in South Hadley, Massachusetts, which incidentally was a short drive from the hometown of her future second husband, Joe Pikul.

In the fall of 1962, Diane arrived at the all-girls campus ready to pursue her English major and to continue her acting and writing. Mary Beth Whiton, another transfer student with midwestern roots, was assigned as Diane's roommate, and the two lived together for the next three years, becoming close friends.

During her Mount Holyoke years, Diane participated in theater productions and worked on the college newspaper and for the college news bureau. Sometimes her stories appeared in the local *Holyoke Transcript-Telegram*. She could speak and read Spanish fluently, read French, and type fifty words per minute. Diane also liked to listen to Edith Piaf records, bluesy songs of love and despair sung in French.

Throughout her school years, Diane worked summers to help with college expenses: secretary-receptionist in Detroit, restaurant waitress, "Girl Friday"—her description—at a photo studio, and cocktail waitress on Cape Cod, a job Diane felt beneath her. She also spent part of one summer doing volunteer work at the Pontiac State Mental Hospital in Pontiac, Michigan.

More important, Diane developed a reputation as a fast mover at Mount Holyoke, the kind of person who flirted with the forbidden, with life on the edge. In the mid-1960's that meant cutting classes, drinking off-campus, being sexually active with different guys. Diane didn't just break the rules, she made it clear she was breaking them to show everyone she knew how absurd they really were. If the dormitory doors closed at 10:00 P.M., Diane showed up at 10:05. Most of all, she made other girls feel silly for being so prim and obedient.

Mount Holyoke students were pretty sheltered back then: dorm doors were locked by ten o'clock during the week and eleven or twelve on the weekends, there were sign-in sheets, and dormitory parents guarded their brood. Diane made fun of all those rules. She stayed out all night on weekends, signing out for home or concocting a convincing excuse. She attended Ivy League mixers, almost always dating older men—potential doctors and lawyers—then returned to the dorm to talk of her exploits.

Whiton recalled that when Diane first arrived at Mount Holyoke, she presented herself as a southern belle, making jokes and talking with a southern accent. "But she grew up in the Midwest. She grew up where I grew up. . . . She was chameleonlike in taking a lot of that on. That was her sort of ticket of identity, like she was not a midwestern girl."

Almost everyone remembers Diane, southern or not, for her humor. "She had a kind of acid wit, which probably covered up a lot of vulnerability," said Whiton, now a clinical psychologist. "At the time I just thought she was advanced socially and able to stand back and laugh at things that were much more painful for me. She was not particularly reverent about her studies nor did she work hard. She was very quick. She got good marks."

There was a wicked side to Diane's humor as well. She would try to be entertaining at a friend's expense, callously zeroing in on a foible with devastating accuracy, making sure it really hurt.

Nevertheless, her friends thought she had a special quality. "She had a magnetic attraction," said one man who dated her in college. Others cited her generosity, for she was known for giving impressive and expensive presents. Whatever the gift, say a sweater or a blouse, it would be just the right style. "It told me there was a lot to her," said Whiton. "She wasn't just flip and shallow by any means."

Underneath Diane's attempts at worldliness, however, remained the insecure, lonely girl. "She did not feel particularly pretty. She wore makeup. She worked at it, a lot," said Whiton. "She wouldn't like people to see her without her face on."

Whiton sensed that behind the facade was someone who hurt and worried just like everyone else, someone who really cared about her intellect and what other people thought of her. "She was slick, even in college," Whiton said of Diane, adding that if someone who'd met the both of them in college said one of them was going to be murdered, "I think they would have picked Diane rather than me."

Kathy Becker, another English major and dormmate, said Diane was an unknown quantity. "There was part of Diane that you just didn't get to know. She struck me as being somewhat introverted, self-contained, a guarded person. Not your typical happy-go-lucky, outgoing college kid."

One of Diane's ways of being worldly—her drinking—had a dark side. Whiton, who said she "really admired" Diane back then, recalled that she had her first drink with her roommate when they were twenty-year-old juniors. They used fake IDs. "It seems silly to people now, but back then she was leading me into a quasi-adult world of pleasures, to get absolutely drunk with her," said Whiton. It wasn't as if Diane drank in her room or alone at a local saloon every day. She just found occasions to get drunk all too often. "It was more going out with the guys or taking me or a friend out. She would take the leadership, getting our fake IDs. She would say 'This is what you do' or 'This is the place to go.' "

Diane's drinking did not spring out of nowhere. Both her parents liked to drink, Diane's mother more than her father, and every day at five o'clock, without fail, one of them would announce: "It's cocktail hour." It was a ritual Diane grew up with and adopted for herself in later life.

What's more, in the latter half of her junior year, Don Whitmore switched jobs once again, this time moving to Longmeadow, Massachusetts, just fifteen minutes from the Mount Holyoke campus. Leaving Diane's mother behind to sell the house, Don Whitmore stayed at a nearby Hilton. Starved for company, he frequently stopped by the campus to take the underage Diane and Mary Beth out for a couple of drinks.

At the time, none of the behavior seemed inappropriate. Don Whitmore was an enjoyable guy, and the girls liked being introduced to new, exotic drinks. The young sophisticates liked cocktails with names—Manhattans and martinis were high on the list.

Once the Whitmores settled into their new home in the suburbs of Springfield—color-coordinated from top to bottom in aqua—Diane and her girlfriends often visited for the weekend. And when cocktail hour rolled around, the girls joined in.

Another important trait that emerged in these years was Diane's desire for money. She let it be known that she wanted a fancy house, fancy cars, maids, and all the other symbols of wealth. To Diane, it was important to marry someone rich and influential.

This was partly a sign of the times, of course. Known as "uncommon women," Mount Holyoke students were expected to do it all, combine satisfying careers with fulfilling marriages to the Ivy League elite.

Many of Diane's Mount Holyoke classmates did marry pretty well, but they married men who were in law school or medical school and endured the struggle of eventually making a comfortable professional existence. Diane, though, wanted the rewards without the challenges. "She'd say, 'You can marry rich and you can marry powerful—that's good. And you can still do your writing or have your own work,' " Whiton recalled. "She wanted to have a place in the world that way."

Diane met a Yale University School of Medicine senior at a mixer during her junior year, and before long they were seriously dating. By the spring, when he graduated and set off for his internship in the Midwest, there was talk of marriage.

"Diane was a great girl," said the man, now a successful surgeon. "She was a very special person, she had a great ability to look at things. She could take a thing in the conversation and turn it over and see so many facets. She had a wonderful mind, highly unique. I thought she walked on water." Diane was fascinating to listen to and would draw people in with her humor and spontaneity, according to the man. "No way was she ever blasé."

Midway through Diane's senior year, Don and Jane Whitmore announced that their daughter was engaged to be married on July 10 to the doctor-to-be from Yale. They were very proud of their daughter's catch, for the prospective groom's credentials were most impressive.

But the wedding never took place.

While the prospective groom was working eighteen-hour days on his internship, Diane was busy cheating on him, and not with just one guy. Once her fiancé found out, the two began arguing frequently and the battles grew increasingly intense. The doctor repeatedly told her how unhappy he was that she'd been unfaithful, and expressed a fear that she might continue screwing around after they were married. Diane struck back with a vengeance, picking on him with her combination of perverse humor and viciousness. "If she wanted to get back at you verbally, she could do it in a tremendous way," the man recalled. "She could be mean, almost sadistic. She would find your soft spot and attack very viciously."

Infidelity wasn't the only problem with the relationship, according to the doctor. Diane wanted to preserve her career options as well as family life, but the doctor wanted to have children soon after marriage. There was no persuading Diane. "She was just a spoiled brat at times. She was going to do things the way she wanted and that was it. Her philosophy to others was, 'If you don't like it, lump it.'"

The wedding was called off, although it was Diane who made the final decision. If she had been willing, her fiancé would still have had her. Fascinated with Diane, he in fact continued to date her for twelve years, until 1977, when he met the woman he eventually married. He said he thought a lot about Diane when he wasn't with her, but time and again when they saw each other, she would turn things bitter. "It was a repetitive cycle. It was kind of a love-hate relationship," he said. "She wasn't vicious all the time, but then ultimately the other side would come out."

A pattern of relationships had been established.

After rejecting her first fiancé, Diane headed for Manhattan. She wanted the fast lane and bright lights, said Whiton. "She wasn't going to end up being the wife of a professional in a small town. She was going to go to New York."

Following a trip to San Francisco—a requested graduation present from Mom and Dad—Diane began working for Time, Inc., first as a business trainee, then as a secretary to the editor of the Modern Living section at *Life* magazine. During her stay at Time, Inc., Diane dated Tommy Thompson, a *Life* magazine writer who went on to write *Blood and Money* and several other best-selling true-crime books.

Though her former fiancé moved to New York in 1966 to do his medical residency at a hospital, he was no longer "the right person," the one who would give her entrée into a world of influence, international locales, and money.

Enter Ralph Erik Schnackenberg, a photographer with a mysterious background.

As Schnackenberg told the story, he and Diane were on a train going to visit their parents—his in Connecticut, hers in Massachusetts. It was in 1967, when Diane was twenty-four. "I hit on her, simple as that," he said. "There was an empty car and there was this attractive woman sitting by herself. It was very clichéd stuff. 'Is this seat taken?' and we had a conversation. . . . I played at the intellectual bit. We started talking about Existentialism, of all things, as a goof. Instead of hitting on her with the usual nonsense, the intellectual approach seemed to work. I had no idea what I was talking about but we laughed about it."

"That would be grand," Schnackenberg remembered Diane saying when he promised to call for dinner. "Her use of the word 'grand' just stuck. It was something out of F. Scott Fitzgerald."

Back in New York, their relationship started off casually, with a couple of dinners, but it quickly led to bed. All the same, both kept up with other relationships, and Schnackenberg had this habit of suddenly disappearing for "foreign assignments."

Asked to explain his background, Schnackenberg contended that he was a commercial photographer for advertising agencies. "I did a lot of location work in South America, the Middle East." He certainly wasn't interested in Diane for more than an occasional dalliance, for within months he married another of his girlfriends.

In tandem with her failure at romantic bliss, the rest of Diane's life took a tailspin as well. After arguing with a higher-up at *Life*, she departed the Big Apple in November 1967 for Vail, Colorado, which was then just starting to bloom as a big ski resort. Diane hoped the change of scenery would have a positive effect on her mentally, and afford her an opportunity to ski and meet men.

According to her résumé, Diane was hired as "secretary

to the president" of Vail Associates, which grew into the major developer of the region. Years later, Don Whitmore was still under the impression his daughter had been hired by some big shot to "help run the hotel." Many of Diane's friends, though, said they'd never heard about her office job and were under the impression she had worked as a cocktail waitress. In any case, the job lasted only seven months, basically the ski season.

It was during this period that Diane's drinking began to appreciably affect her on a day-to-day basis. One day while skiing in a drunken stupor, she sustained a severe spiral break in her left leg. Eventually, she returned east for treatment, undergoing special surgery in Boston.

The post-accident period was a very low time in Diane's life. Some of the surgery was cosmetic, to remove a bump that had formed on her leg. She walked with a limp and a cane. She was understandably depressed, which in her case led to more drinking.

Convinced by her father not to return to the mountains, Diane went to work briefly as "personal secretary" to TV producer Allen Funt. Ever the expert at stretching the most out of little, Diane's résumé listing for Allen Funt Productions read: "Production assistant for United Artists feature film and television commercials, scheduling locations, crews and candid subjects." The last item was a less-than-subtle reminder of Funt's popular creation, "Candid Camera."

In September 1970, Diane began working for the New York City Parks and Recreation Department, first as a provisional typist, then as a provisional recreation director. She performed well for government. It wasn't the bright lights of Broadway, but it paid the bills. In June 1973, when the financially strapped city began hiring for the first time in a decade, Diane was among fifty who received a permanent position, at a salary of $8,100. Eventually she served as an assistant to high-level officials in the department and as special-programs coordinator, developing and running privately funded recreation events at city facilities. Over the years she wrote letters, speeches, newsletters, and annual reports.

"She was a professional recreation person. She was an executive assistant and handled a lot of correspondence, incoming calls, information, communications that came through the system, and from time to time I even put her on special projects," said Joe Davidson, who, as the city's commissioner of recreation, was Diane's boss from 1973 to 1976. "She was quite knowledgeable, quite capable of working out problems and issues." Diane also served as Davidson's advance staff when, filling in for the mayor, he would award plaques or keys to the city to dignitaries like soccer legend Pele or swimming great Johnny Weismuller.

Here again, Diane tried to make more of her position. Her 1987 résumé listed her experience as "assistant to three commissioners," but she actually worked solely in the recreation division. The title "commissioner" is used quite liberally in the Parks Department bureaucracy, by as many as twelve people.

Diane sometimes gave her father the impression she was practically running the place. He remembered his daughter telling him she got along so well with her bosses that she kept getting promoted. Whitmore had the impression that one particular boss liked her so well "he even sent her home in his limousine." Around the office, there was another well-traveled version of that story, indicating an illicit romance.

And so it went with Diane, never able to face up to her true position in life. "She liked titles," said Diane's first fiancé, explaining that he had sometimes called her a "short-ball hitter," a term Diane despised because it struck home. "She didn't have the incentive to follow through. She would just drift along," he said. "She never put the effort in that was needed to succeed. The fact that the jobs she ended up in were all menial was part of her personality."

Others agreed with that assessment. "She always was resentful that she wasn't literally born with a silver spoon in her mouth, which is possibly one reason she wound up with Joe Pikul," said Schnackenberg. "She was resentful that she wasn't CEO of something or other. On the other hand, she didn't try. I think she was trapped in her own fantasies."

Whiton said she had an image of Diane "being immaculately dressed, working in fancy places but in very low-level jobs." She said Diane really enjoyed rubbing elbows with important people and the string of impressive-sound-ing job titles. "Except I believe in her heart she knew that she was an assistant, and particularly as you get into your forties, you realize that you're going to have to stand more on who your character is and who you are inside to feel good about yourself."

With a tinge of sadness, Whiton said she was convinced Diane could have been a successful writer, if only she had applied herself. "This is somebody who took all their personal power and intelligence and warmth and built a facade instead of working hard and trying to get different jobs and submitting stories as you went along, getting your rejection slips and all that stuff."

According to Schnackenberg, no matter what Diane did, she was unsatisfied. "She always felt that she was meant for better things. She'd been to one of the Sister schools, and she resented the fact that she'd had less than glamour jobs. Yet on the other hand, she never pushed hard enough to get the kind of work she wanted. She would bitch about it, but that was about it."

Diane's lack of dedication was most apparent whenever she shifted into her "I want to be a writer" mode. "I think it was the sort of thing of being half-shitfaced and saying, 'Well, if I got my act together, I could write the Great American Novel.' But she never sat down to do it," said Schnackenberg. "She did write in a diary every night, but I think that was that romantic stuff of whining into a diary, kvetching, you know, 'why hasn't the world discovered me yet?' "

Ralph Schnackenberg should know. While working for the Parks Department, Diane renewed her relationship with Ralph, who by this time was divorcing his first wife. "Our relationship was unconventional," said Ralph, explaining that he was still traveling a great deal. But when he and Diane did get together, the relationship was "incredibly intense and very physical."

Intense it may have been, but apparently it was not satisfying, for throughout this period, Diane's drinking worsened. She attended Alcoholics Anonymous meetings once in a while. But like so many other things in her life at that time, the AA sessions were borne of momentary impulses. Things were going to have to get a lot worse before they got better.

Once or twice a year, Diane would disappear from work for a week or so, and when Parks Department co-workers would finally reach her at home, it would be obvious she was on another bender. Like so many people who were young in the late sixties and seventies, Diane dabbled in marijuana, but her drug of choice was booze. Some mornings she would get up and pour herself a glass of straight vodka, then head off to her job at the Parks Department. "I said, 'This person has a problem,' " said Schnackenberg. "And I think part of it was to piss me off. She made sure I would see her drinking the vodka."

At first, he believed the drinking was based on Diane's "romantic notion of the charming, dissolute drinker, that southern-writer mystique. Her friends always thought it was amusing, and that always annoyed me, all her quote 'friends' never took her aside and said, 'Diane, you're killing yourself.' " Schnackenberg claims that from time to time he tried to talk to her about her problem, but acknowledged he didn't push too hard either, for he was known to tipple a glass or two himself.

As the drinking problem continued to worsen, Diane's peculiar relationship with Schnackenberg ran hot and cold. Ralph would blow into town, move in for a couple of weeks, then vanish for another assignment in some exotic location. Three or four months later, he would return to renew his relationship with a willing Diane.

Schnackenberg's disappearances obviously prompted questions. As one of Diane's friends put it, "Ralph was a mysterious photographer," with a "who-knows-what-he-did kind of life." Diane liked that at first, but over time she professed to have become terribly afraid of him, telling people that he worked for the CIA. Thomas Kenney, one of Diane's co-workers from the Parks Department, remembered one story in particular, when Diane explained that Ralph was supposedly off "doing a job for somebody," flying a DC-3 over the jungles, making a drop somewhere. She even brought in a photo of a DC-3 making a pass over a rain forest.

Schnackenberg, however, insisted that he never worked undercover for the government. He said the issue would "crop up every now and then, but it's just not the case." He characterized the story as another one of Diane's romantic notions and suggested she used the yarn in an attempt to cover his absences: "Why isn't he with you?" "Well, he works for the CIA."

Whatever the truth, Diane didn't end the relationship. She liked the glamour of Ralph's trips, and accompanied him on several of them, including one to Bogotá and Leticia, Colombia, a lawless Amazon bush town bordering Brazil.

In the Colombian capital, according to Schnackenberg, he usually waited for a tardy Diane in the lobby of the exclusive Hotel Tequendama with his driver, interpreter, and equipment. Every morning, the desk clerk, who had been led to believe Diane was in the movies, had to call upstairs to the room. "She would make a grand entrance into the lobby and this whole entourage would stand up, we'd get in a car and go someplace. And she loved it. She'd say, 'Ah, Christ. This is what it's supposed to be like.' "

The side trip to Leticia, though, marked one of the low points in their relationship. "Everybody was involved in coke. And I had to put the word out that I wasn't with DEA—people had to know who you were," he explained. He said they stayed at a place owned by Michael Tsalickis, a prominent American businessman with alleged ties to the Cali Cartel, the second-largest cocaine distribution network in the world. When asked why he and Diane went to such a backwater drug haven, he said that he'd gone to Leticia to take photos for a number of clients, including black-and-white advertising shots for a foster child plan group back in the States.

Diane, bored stiff in the remote village, resorted to drinking. "Once she got just drunk on her ass, and we'd had a huge screaming fight—I think it was about her drinking, in fact. She tore off all of her clothes and went staggering off into the goddamn boonies, literally into the jungle, howling and screaming.

"This is after the town generator is off, so you can hear every sound. It was incredible. And I knew that everybody in this little piss-ant village was listening to the crazy gringos," Schnackenberg claimed. "I was pissed. I figured if she's going into the jungle, fuck it." Schnackenberg, by the way, was pretty drunk at that point himself.

The next morning, he and Diane sobered up. Diane had cut her foot badly, and after thrashing around in the brush, her face was battered. She looked "beat up really bad, as if I had whacked the shit out of her." At breakfast in a small café, "the two of us pretended that nothing had happened. We were hyperpolite with each other. And that's when she came out with this Dick and Liz act—you know, where Liz Taylor always had sunglasses on, hiding the shiners after a fight. Diane loved that image."

Back in New York, the two of them saw therapists and told friends they were "working on making commitments." But the fighting continued and the drinking continued. Diane bugged Ralph unceasingly about his divorce, demanding the case number at one point so she could confirm that the papers had at least been filed in court.

Despite every warning sign imaginable, Diane and Ralph exchanged wedding vows on a dreary day in June 1975 on the docks of the Seventy-ninth Street Boat Basin in Manhattan.

For Diane, the marriage was something she *had* to do for her emotional well-being. Over the years she had grown worried about becoming an old maid. She'd even taken to joking about the fact that many of her college classmates were already divorced or working on their second marriage. Despite her parents' unhappiness with her choice, she viewed ending her spinsterhood as more important than the social status of any future groom. So she told herself that Ralph *was* her knight in shining armor because of his exciting work in far-off places.

It rained heavily all morning before the ceremony, but the skies cleared in time for the service by a Lutheran minister. Then everyone boarded a large boat and took a ride up and down the Hudson River, regaled with wine, cheese, and Janis Joplin music.

No sooner had they made the union official than Diane and Ralph realized it was a mistake. They just weren't right for each other. "When I was mad at her one time, I called her the only WASP JAP I ever knew in my life. I think she was the classic only-child princess. Her mother and father doted on her. Yet she was resentful of them, which I never understood. There were things that were there that were hidden, that I could never get out of her," said Schnackenberg.

After returning from a honeymoon in Jamaica, the two began arguing more frequently over the most mundane things. More serious was Diane's eavesdropping on Ralph's telephone conversations, no doubt prompted by her suspicions about his job and possible extramarital activities. When she went as far as opening his mail, he blew up.

Don Whitmore said Diane later told him that Schnackenberg grabbed her, pushed her over to the window, and told her: "If you ever open my mail again, I'll throw you out the window." Schnackenberg's version was different: "I'm a very private person. And when she opened my mail—she was either paranoid or jealous about God knows what—I *was* furious. But as far as taking her to the window, I don't think so. I know I was mad. I don't deny that. I had every right to be."

That's not to say there weren't some physical confrontations in the Schnackenberg household. "We probably had pushing sessions, but there was never beatings or that kind of craziness," Schnackenberg stated emphatically. He contended that he instead took to putting a fist or foot through a wall rather than punch Diane. "It wasn't that kind of gratuitous smacking Diane around. She was pretty delicate. But when she was drinking, she would get nasty, goading me, *Who's Afraid of Virginia Woolf* kind of stuff, really foulmouthed. It went both ways. I woke up one time, opened up one eye, and there she is sitting at the edge of the bed with a knife in her hand and drunk as a skunk. I had no idea what she was thinking of. I promptly dressed—I had the whole Freudian nightmare—and I left. I didn't attempt to take the knife out of her hand."

One last incident exemplifies the drunken misery of their marriage. As Schnackenberg related, "I was sleeping and she was spending her evening drinking—the usual stuff: I'd hear the ice cubes clinking into the glass and I knew she was quietly getting wrecked. And she was playing a record over and over and over again. It was a country-

and-western thing, Kris Kristofferson and Rita Coolidge.
It was maudlin C&W stuff, and it went on and on and on.
Finally I flipped out. I came in from the bedroom and took
a chair and simply smashed the stereo. And I went back
to bed. And that was it."

The insecure child had grown into a capricious, venom-
tongued alcoholic, alone again and still in search of the
man of her dreams, someone who would give her the life
of the rich and the genteel.

CHAPTER • 5

The Lightning Rod

GROWING UP IN ROUGH-AND-TUMBLE blue-collar surroundings, Joseph John Pikul never had anything handed to him. Joe was a poor Polish kid trapped on the wrong side of the river that splits the old mill town of Ware, located in the center of Massachusetts. Forced to do without, Joe was determined to make something of his life. He was a survivor.

During his childhood, his family moved several times, but always remained within spitting distance of the Ware River. In his youth, the waterway was the heartbeat of Ware, lined with a wool mill, a carpet mill, and a cotton mill.

Michael and Victoria Pikul, Joe's paternal grandparents, came to the United States from Poland in the late nineteenth century during a wave of Polish immigration. To this day, Ware is predominantly Polish. Michael Pikul was employed by the mills that proliferated along the riverside, and Joe's father, Joseph Paul Pikul, born in Ware in 1911, was working at the Ware Woolen Company by his late teens as a weaver and later as a blocker.

Joe's mother, Bernice Ann Topor Pikul, was born in Czechoslovakia and came to the United States when she was four years old. She worked at the Ware Shoe Company until her retirement in 1970. A devout worshiper at St. Mary's Roman Catholic Church, she couldn't read or write or handle money. As a result, Bernice looked to her husband to make all the decisions.

For several years Joseph and Bernice lived with his parents, but it got crowded when Joe's sister, Janice, was born in 1932, so they set out on their own. Joe was born two years later, on December 3, 1934.

Physical abuse was common at the Pikul homestead, according to Joe, who said his father, a heavy drinker, often beat him and other family members. Joe recalled that even at the tender age of five, "My father punched me in the jaw and knocked me around the room. He used to chase us out of the house at night, stuff like that. In the alcoholic household, usually one kid gets the brunt of it. He's kind of a lightning rod. I was the lightning rod."

Joe was thought to be an oddball during his high-school years. It wasn't anything particular; he just didn't mesh socially with the "in" crowd. Viewed as a recluse, he never dated and rarely attended Friday-night dances at Ware High or Saturday-night roller skating at Town Hall. "He just wasn't a mixer," said classmate Billy "Buff" Phillip, who now runs a liquor store in town. And when Joe did show up at the dances, his clop-clop inadequacies often drew snickers from the more "sophisticated" Ware Maidens, as the girls were called. Little did the young ladies know of Joe's more private burgeoning interests; he'd already been caught rummaging through his sister's underwear drawer.

Joe was a brilliant underachiever in high school. He often directed his brainpower at his teachers, sparring with them on points that had no relation to the day's lesson. More telling, however, is that even at this age he displayed an arrogance his instructors found exasperating.

"I remember Pikul came to school one day and answered every question there was from the teacher, every goddamn thing. He was a brain," recalled former classmate Ronald Luszcz, who now runs a lawn-mower repair service in town.

"He was as smart as a whip. He could read it once and it would stick with him," said Phillip. "I used to copy his notes. In fact, he helped out a lot of guys."

James Roach, a Ware High contemporary, said he was not surprised Joe became a stockbroker. "He was always into math. He was into numbers. The main thing was that he was an intellectual type in his teens, compared to everybody else. That, I think, is really what set him aside from most of us." Joe seemed too smart for his surroundings. As a result, many contemporaries were intimidated by him.

Roach, now the town clerk, treasurer, and tax collector, remembered Joe as a loner, completely out of step with the typical Ware teen. "Say there was forty-eight people in a class? Then there was Joe Pikul. If he had been from Long Island or someplace like that, people wouldn't have even noticed him. He just seemed to be out of touch with our crowd."

Nonetheless, Joe tried to fit in. He played lineman on the Ware Indian football team and served as manager of the basketball team. He also belonged to the Warriors Club, a service group, for two years, and was a member of the Glee Club and Latin Club in his senior year. More notably, for three of his four years, Joe handled the homeroom banking, collecting his classmates' passbooks—nickels and dimes for weekly deposit at Ware Savings.

All in all, it is not surprising that over the years Joe had little contact with his roots, returning only infrequently to visit. Still, his parents were very proud of their New Yorker son. His father would invariably bring up his rich, successful boy during coffee-shop chitchats, telling of all the killings he was making in the stock market.

One incident, perhaps more than any other, served to magnify Joe's hometown image of "local boy makes good in the big city." This is the time he dispatched a limousine to pick up his mother and father for a special event in Manhattan involving one of his children. "That certainly makes an impression in a small town, to see a twenty-foot limo pull up," said Floyd R. Maynard, editor of the *Ware River News*.

When Joe was growing up, money was tight in the Pikul household. Joe's parents were lucky to pull in eighty dollars a week between them, and financing a college education was out of the question. So after graduating from high school, Joe worked two jobs for a year to raise tuition money.

His workday started with the graveyard shift in a Ware textile mill, where the humdrum, sweatshop existence served to further motivate him to find a better way of life. In the morning, he stopped off at home for breakfast, then got in his car and headed for his second job, working construction for the Ware Water Department. He also was a member of the Massachusetts National Guard from 1951 to 1953, attending summer boot camps. And when he enrolled at Northeastern University in Boston in the fall of 1953, he joined a five-year cooperative program that allows students to split their time between working and taking courses.

According to Joe, throughout his entire education he only received $1,000 from his parents, but he did receive many scholarships. In one outside job that lasted a year, he worked as a student technician in the Instrumentation Laboratory at the esteemed Massachusetts Institute of Technology. He briefly dug graves and got fired from a job at a deli because he ate too many pickles from the barrel.

Joe was always running around, trying to get ahead during his college years, often too busy for more than a quick hello to old acquaintances from Ware. His determination paid off, though, for he graduated from Northeastern in 1958 with high distinction—the equivalent of magna cum laude—majoring in finance and insurance. He was also a member of ROTC and after college spent six months' active duty in the Army Finance Corps, being honorably discharged as a lieutenant.

During his second year of college, he met Sandra Mae Jarvinen, and they soon fell in love. He beat her once during their college years. On September 5, 1959, following his discharge from the service, Sandy and Joe were married.

They set up residence on Beacon Street in Boston. According to Joe, he enrolled in Harvard Business School several weeks later, but injured his knee playing touch football soon thereafter. Following an operation, the Harvard athletic surgeon recommended physiotherapy before returning to school the following year. To get-ahead Joe, a year might as well have been eternity. He was anxious to get started with his life. Because of this, when Standard & Poors offered him a fellowship at Columbia, he decided instead to start working full-time for them as a securities analyst. He moved to New York City in January 1960, and Sandy followed a few months later. They set up shop in an apartment in the eighties on the East Side, eventually moving down to Greenwich Village.

At first Sandy worked for MacGregor Sportswear, then served as administrative assistant to the office chief for a Canadian brokerage firm on Wall Street. She was an invaluable help to Joe, assisting him at night with reports and the like.

Joe worked at S&P until 1966, when he joined Picard and Co. to "manage money." Two years later, he left that position to open his own business, Sage Associates. Again, Joe was managing money. And again, Sandy was of invaluable assistance with research and office work. She traveled with him extensively, kept charts, and helped him raise funds.

Located at 80 Wall Street—it was important for Joe to be on *the* Street—Sage Associates was a limited partnership, set up so Joe had complete control. In addition, he took to calling himself Joe Pie-kul, instead of the traditional pronunciation, Pick-le, thinking it sounded more distinguished. He did so well that by the end of November 1969—a terrible year for the stock market, with the Dow Jones Industrial average off about 17 percent—Sage was up 13.44 percent, before normal operating expenses. Other, much larger funds were down 25, 35, even 40 percent. Joe, who invested more than $400,000 of his own, was on a roll. He even got his sister's husband, Lt. Col. Edward Pawlowski, to invest $50,000.

Full of confidence, Joe informed his partners that the minimum participation would be increased from $50,000 to $100,000 by December 31, 1969. Underinvested partners were instructed to send the additional funds by then or withdraw. The ploy didn't work, however, as many partners balked. Two investors pulled out and launched a lengthy lawsuit over unrealized profits. Joe and the former partners eventually settled, but the battle consumed several years and tens of thousands of dollars in legal fees.

Regardless, Joe was doing so well that his exploits at making money in a bad market were detailed in a 1970 *New York Times* business-page column. "If you asked 35-

year-old Joseph J. Pikul the secret of successful money management in a bear market, he might give you a one-word answer—travel," began the "Market Place" article.

For in 1969, when go-go fund managers tended to swap stories on stocks, then watch in despair as their favorite "concept" companies got clobbered in the bear market, Joe Pikul logged 100,000 miles to check out stories for himself. As a result, in the 1969 disaster year for the go-go funds, Joe Pikul managed to show a gain of two percent on $9 million worth of the $18 million portfolio of Mid-American Mutual Fund. Meanwhile, the Dow-Jones industrials were down 15.2 percent and Standard & Poor's average of 425 industrials dipped 10.2 percent. The average mutual fund showed a loss of 14.47 percent in darkest 1969 and the go-go funds had losses that often exceeded 25 percent.

There was a cautionary note in the story, though, providing insight into Joe's insecurities as well as his true business acumen.

Does this mean then that Joe Pikul has all the answers, that he is impervious to bear markets and mistakes in judgment? He'd be the last to claim this, though he is understandably proud of his record. He's wary of his ability to turn in the same kind of record with substantially more money to manage. He was once asked by a prominent figure in the mutual fund industry if he thought he could manage $100-million and he said he honestly couldn't say. The man commented: "You'll never make the big time if you can't."

On the surface, his success was heady stuff for a poor boy from a Polish mill town. But on the domestic front, the strain of being an upstart in the well-heeled world of Wall Street showed in virulent form. Not only was Joe drinking heavily, but the old adage "The sins of the father are visited on the son" came forcefully into effect in Joe's case. When he drank, he lashed out. Only in this case, the target was his wife.

If ever a woman fit the description of a battered wife,

drawn like a magnet to the violence of her man, it was
Sandy Jarvinen. She fled several times over the years, only
to reconcile. The bad times were terrifying, certainly; but
Sandy loved Joe like she loved no one else. She tried
always to focus on the good times and forget the bad times.
"Joe had mentally and physically battered me down so
much I felt I had no self-worth, that he was the most
important thing. His work was important. His life was
important. And mine wasn't. He was such a charmer on
one hand, and could move so quickly from one mood to
the other that he kept you continually off guard. You just
never knew when he was going to blow—and you never
knew why. And so you never had a chance to develop your
own personality."

Joe was master of the household. "He had the right to
live his life. I had the right to serve him," said Sandy.
"You did not question him. You did not go in his study.
You did not answer his private telephone. You did not go
through his pockets in his suit. You didn't read his mail
or open his mail; you put it on his desk and left it. You
could write the checks but could not know the balance.
Those were the ground rules. You didn't step over them.
If you stepped over them, you got beaten."

Sex with Sandy was of little interest to Joe. Intercourse
was confined to once or twice a year with her, though Joe
had several girlfriends on the side. "Sex was a small part
of our relationship," Sandy explained. "We were business
partners. We worked together. We traveled together. We
were best friends. I just didn't think about it."

But looking back years later for incidents that would
put things in better perspective, Sandy recalled the time
in 1965 when she walked into the summer house on Lake
Garfield in the Berkshires in the middle of the week. There
was a camera on the kitchen table. Walking through the
house, she noticed that some pillows had been moved
around. Upstairs, there was shaving cream on the walls of
the bathroom. "When I went into our bedroom, someone
had gone through my dresser drawer and had taken out a
black lace bra and black lace bikini panty. If I were lying
on the bed, they were in the exact location of where they
were supposed to cover."

Upset, Sandy called Joe in New York. He blamed it on

a male neighbor and told her to leave the house immediately. Sandy got a hotel room and Joe came up from the city. "He took the camera, which did not belong to us, and someplace he got the film developed. It showed two men and one woman, but none of them recognizable to me—I mean the parts that were showing I could not recognize. But Joe got all excited about this. He was happy and laughing . . . all lighthearted about it. It didn't arouse him for us to have sex. It was just sort of exciting to him to think that someone had done this and he could see it."

Joe assured Sandy he was going to investigate the identities of the ménage à trois but he never did, concluding that the people had merely broken in to use the house. "I never questioned it. I just let it go," Sandy said. "Now that I look back, I'm a little older, a little wiser, and I've grown up a little bit, I would say that Joe was there."

Back in those days, Joe was too busy to have kids. "He was very involved in his business. He just wanted me to be around for him all the time. When we finally did decide to have children, we found out he couldn't." Or at least that's what Joe told Sandy, attributing his low-sperm count to years of drinking. As the relationship gradually deteriorated, children became a nonissue.

And the relationship deteriorated in dramatic fashion. Joe verbally and physically assaulted Sandy to no end. "The whole atmosphere was one of a war zone, whether it was the beating or the mental pressure that you never knew what he was going to be like at any particular moment." Sandy usually knew when to pull back during the verbal duels, pushing Joe only so far. She would flee to neighbors or sleep in the backseat of the car. But sometimes, the abuse turned violent.

Sometimes Joe's outbursts were triggered by a bad day at the office. "I used to check the stock market to see what it closed at and checked all of our stocks just to know what he might be like when he came through the door—if he came home that night," said Sandy.

Over time, the incidents became more and more ferocious, the brutal attacks more and more frequent. During one incident, Sandy fled to her bathroom off the master bedroom, locking the door behind her. Joe kicked the door in and started beating her. "I remember being on the floor, the coldness of the porcelain of the toilet and the tub, and he was kicking and hitting me with the bath brush and his fist."

In 1966, Sandy was in a major car accident when the brakes on a new car she was driving suddenly failed. She spent several months in the hospital and underwent extensive reconstructive surgery on her face. Suspicious of the origin of the brake failure, she wanted the car thoroughly checked when she got released from the hospital. But the car was gone; Joe had taken care of that. The beatings stopped for a while after the accident, but several months after Sandy's release from the hospital, a neighbor overheard her screaming one evening, "No, no, no, Joe, not my face."

Joe's behavior continued to grow more bizarre. He turned up one day in 1968 with a stab wound, which he blamed on "a girlfriend." And in 1969, he beat Sandy on the head with a statue. Tumbling down the stairs of their duplex, she was temporarily knocked out. Bloodied and bruised about the head and upper body, she crawled up the stairs to retrieve her car keys and some money. Joe was fast asleep, without a care in the world. Sandy fled New York, driving toward her parents' home in Massachusetts. But she only got as far as Connecticut when the concussion sapped her strength. She called her parents, who came and rescued her.

As she had done before, however, Sandy came back for more. Joe called and asked her to meet him at the Ritz Carlton in Boston. "I didn't want to, but I finally broke down and I went to meet him. He started telling me the business was having this problem and that problem and we had a meeting in the Midwest and I had to go out because he'd hurt his arm. I ended up getting on a plane, and as soon as we got to the Midwest, into the hotel room, he started the crap all over again, yelling and screaming. I just went down to the desk and got another room. It was a very bizarre life."

As her marriage disintegrated, Sandy felt alone, with nowhere to turn. "You have to remember in that particular time, no matter who you went to, as a female, you were wrong, it was your fault. The courts told you it was your fault. The police told you it was your fault. The psychiatrists told you it was your fault. Everybody told you, 'It's your fault. You're the female. You're responsible if he's upset.' No one would protect you. There was no place to go. There was nothing you could do. You were trapped, and after a while, you began to believe it."

In 1970, the same year as the glowing article about Joe appeared in the *Times*, Sandy and Joe legally separated, and she returned to Boston. In a separation agreement dated October 9 of that year, Joe consented to pay Sandy $1,000 per month until she died or remarried. Joe's attorney drew up the legal documents; Sandy did not have an attorney of her own.

Despite the years of abuse, Sandy and Joe were not through with each other. In 1971, she accompanied him on a two-week trip to Spain, Portugal, and Ireland. During that same year, Joe agreed to modify the separation agreement so that the $1,000-per-month payments would continue in the event of a divorce, a convenient loophole in the original paperwork. In March 1972 she traveled with him to California and Mexico. On a later trip together to Portugal, Sandy had "an accident," a fractured wrist.

The year 1972 was sour business-wise as well. After expenses Sage Associates barely managed a 4-percent profit, and several investors made as little as 1 percent. As a result, certain Sage partners, accounting for 23 percent of the operating capital, withdrew their participation. Even Joe's brother-in-law pulled out. Instead of drawing new business, Joe was starting to lose the old. A look at the books also shows that Joe owed the company $261,704 from a loan and owed brokers $443,149.

Things got worse in 1973 in all corners. Without the stabilizing influence of his wife—odd as that might sound in the context of their marital battles—Joe took more and more to drowning his sorrows. By now he was drinking on the job as well.

A particularly disturbing incident occurred on August 14, when limousine driver Malcolm Rattner took the elevator to Sage Associates' fourth-floor offices to pick up a package from Joe.

Rattner was met by a pair of glazed, gleaming eyeballs. "I know you're here to kill me and were sent by my wife," Joe told him. It didn't matter that Sandy had long since moved back to Boston. Joe was convinced Rattner was Sandy's boyfriend.

The driver denied the accusations, but Joe didn't believe him and pulled out a loaded .38-caliber revolver. Playing with his penis through his pants, Joe put the gun to Rattner's head and ordered him to write on a pad: "I came upstairs to kill Pikul because I'm going out with his wife, but I changed my mind and committed suicide."

Instead, Rattner wrote in a note later found by police: "I am sitting in Mr. Pikul's office, he has a gun to my head, and I think he is going to kill me." According to Rattner's subsequent sworn testimony, Joe went into a tirade and proceeded to pistol-whip him. When Joe was distracted by a noise, Rattner grabbed a telephone set from the desk and started beating Joe with it. He then raced to the fire door and ran all the way down to the lobby. But when he got there, much to his alarm, the door was locked and he couldn't get out. Close behind, Joe spotted him, got down in a combat stance, cocked his gun, and took aim. Just at that moment the building super appeared and opened the door to see who was banging so wildly. Joe quickly returned upstairs and Rattner fled. He got in his car and drove to the fire station located by the ferry to the Statue of Liberty.

Police responded and recovered the gun—it was loaded with six rounds—along with Rattner's note. But when it came time for trial, Rattner was "no longer able" to remember if Joe really had a gun.

Rattner's bosses had threatened to fire him if he testified against Joe, one of the firm's good cash customers. Joe gave him $1,500 for medical expenses, and charges of assault with intent to cause physical injury, reckless endangerment, and possession of a loaded firearm were dismissed with the proviso that Joe undergo psychiatric treatment. If Joe kept his nose clean, the system would forget about the charge. And that's exactly what happened—the system forgot. Joe Pikul was on the road to larger tragedies.

The following year, 1974, was even worse. After six roller-coaster years with Sage Associates, alcohol drowned both Joe and his business. More partners pulled out, several additional investments went sour, and then Sage was gone. Joe stopped sending Sandy her support payments, and he was arrested for criminal possession of a controlled substance, a pharmaceutical drug. Police found a shotgun in the trunk of the car and $1,300 in fifties and hundreds in Joe's pocket. But Joe again avoided trouble, as the charge was plea-bargained to a simple violation.

After fifteen painful years of marriage, Sandy and Joe were divorced that summer, but not until Joe made several death threats against her.

Joe needed help, and he needed it badly.

CHAPTER • 6

Addiction
Dating

AFTER A YEAR OF KEEPING a low profile, during which time he received medical and psychiatric help for his health problems, Joe reentered the work force in September 1975 as a securities analyst for a small firm in Manhattan.

The key to Joe's turnaround, though, came in April 1976, when he started attending Alcoholics Anonymous, usually in the Wall Street area. He marked May 11, 1976, as his first day of sobriety. In a diary he kept as part of his recovery efforts, Joe wrote: "AA is the greatest thing that will ever happen to me on this earth—I have it today—why not enjoy it more and more. There's no rush really. I can live on what I'm making now if I slow down and take it easy."

Joe seemed soft-spoken at the meetings, yet in possession of "a great propensity for anger" and "a volatile temper," according to one fellow attendee. "He was like somebody who was always holding on to himself, trying to keep control. When he got annoyed about something, he would almost talk through clenched teeth."

Joe was also addicted to food, sugar especially, and belonged to Overeaters Anonymous for a time. He wrote in his diary, "Food, compulsively eaten, makes me sick, and prevents me from growing, feeling very good about myself. Most of my life (even before alcohol) I ate compulsively. Today . . . I didn't. I must get better. Jesus help me stay sober and abstinent."

If Joe didn't get drunk on booze, he got drunk on food.

And if he didn't get drunk on food, he got drunk on pills. In his writing, Joe said he recognized that all three were poisons whose use represented "running away from reality."

Recovery wasn't easy. Some days Joe woke up ill, or spent a sleepless night tossing and turning, sometimes vomiting from excessive overeating. He had trouble being with people, sometimes just looking at them. He hated the taste of his food. Even water tasted bitter.

Joe went from one bad habit to another. "If sugar has done this to me all my life I have been (am) one sick person," Joe wrote on August 31, 1977. He vowed to abstain from sugar, "or eat compulsively, which leads to sugar, or of course drink or take any pills. God please give me the courage to be honest about sugar and overeating."

On occasion, Joe became obsessed with his diet, cuting down to 1,000 calories a day, taking pills to flush out his system. Again he made himself ill. In one diary entry, Joe said he feared that the only way to refrain from one vice was to take on another. "Today is filled with pain and horror," he wrote before adding the following formula for failure: Sugar = Drunkenness; Sugar = Drugs; Sugar = Booze; Sugar → Booze → Pills → Disaster

Joe left the appearance of someone fighting to change for the better, but he also projected a feeling of hopelessness. It was in this state that he met Diane Schnackenberg.

Diane was having problems of her own during those years. Reeling from the failure of her marriage, she continued drinking, heavily at times. She would show up for work on a regular basis, perform her duties enthusiastically, and then all of a sudden disappear for several days, or even a week, according to a former co-worker.

Conditions worsened when Diane's mother died in September 1976. After the funeral she spent a great deal of time in Florida helping her father through his loneliness. Don Whitmore sensed an extra closeness during that period, but his daughter never told him her innermost secrets, like her addiction to drinking. And he never opened his eyes enough to see. "Diane never had a drinking problem. She would drink socially," Whitmore claimed.

Starved for a male friend to talk to in the aftermath of her mother's death, Diane called her first fiancé, who was shocked at Diane's state and the adverse effect the death had on her. "She seemed to have gone downhill," he said. "She was wondering what she should do—take Valium or drink—in order to cope with the grief." He said she did both.

Diane subsequently came to visit the doctor, and one day when they were out for a walk, "all of a sudden she looked at her watch and said: 'It's cocktail hour.' " Sure enough, it was five o'clock.

Haunted by what could have been, Diane noted in her diary on July 10, 1977, that the day would have been her twelfth wedding anniversary.

That fall, a year after the death of Diane's mother, Donald Whitmore married again. Technically, Diane was still married to Ralph. Save for an occasional one-night stand, she was very alone.

And so they met, these two addictive personalities, at an Alcoholics Anonymous meeting. Both were suffering from symptoms that often bring on alcoholism: a history of troubled relationships, low self-esteem, and depression. They also appeared to be victims of "Adult Children of Alcoholics Syndrome." It was not the best way to start a relationship.

Joe and Diane didn't date at first, for Joe was further along in recovery and was afraid to get too close. "She was having trouble staying sober," Joe later explained. "I was very newly sober and they say in the program not to have emotional involvements for the first year."

There were other romantic possibilities, for AA meetings were a great place to meet singles. Joe rejected several women he impressed, but for most, Joe's uncanny ability to make money was not enough.

Diane and Joe began dating in January 1978. Joe spat at Diane's face during their second date. The relationship quickly blossomed. Diane was impressed with the way Joe threw money around and told friends he spent it "like a drunken sailor." Before long, the theme of marriage was Topic A on a very short list. This was to be a love affair of necessity. Time was running out; it was now or never. True love could come later, if at all.

Although the man she hoped soon to wed was divorced, Diane was resolute about obtaining an annulment from Ralph. These were still the times when most Christians, women especially, frowned on divorce but somehow felt understanding and forgiveness for anyone who had obtained an annulment. It meant a mistake had occurred. "I got an annulment" meant "I'm a victim." Diane certainly felt she was a victim, and therefore had to avoid the stigma of divorce. Her unrelenting pursuit met with success on April 3, 1978. The annulment decree was uncontested.

Six months after they began dating, on July 14, 1978, Diane and Joe became Mr. and Mrs. Joseph J. Pikul. In what seemed no mistake, Diane was already more than two months pregnant. Precious little time had passed between annulment and conception.

The ceremony was held at the Dreamworld Inn, in Carmel, New York. There was no best man, no maid of honor. The fathers of the bride and groom served as official witnesses. The only other attendees were Pikul's mother, Bernice, and Diane's new stepmother, Gretchen.

Diane wore a very romantic scooped neck, antiquey-looking outfit, "sort of brocaded looking, with a cameo on a velvet ribbon around her neck," according to a close friend. Her hair was set in a curly Julie Christie–type wave.

During the post-ceremony dinner, Joe announced that he would be the breadwinner and Diane would stay home. The newlyweds honeymooned in Montauk.

Joe first moved from his apartment in downtown Tribeca to Diane's place on Riverside Drive on the upper West Side, but with the baby due in a couple of months, they moved to larger quarters downtown, to 201 West Eleventh Street, in Greenwich Village—complete with an elaborate walnut, canopied waterbed with mirrors.

Diane and Joe knew they weren't youngsters anymore, and they rationalized the pregnancy by telling everyone they wanted to have children right away. But the pregnancy gave the relationship the air of a shotgun romance. "I don't know if they would have gotten married at that point had she not been pregnant," said one of Diane's longtime friends. "What Diane said to me was: 'We decided we were going to get married anyway, so we might as well get married now.' Diane was thirty-five at that point, Joe was forty-three, and I think they both decided that this was their shot."

Claudia Whitmore Pikul was born by natural birth on February 1, 1979, and both parents were enthralled. Neither of them was drinking. Both had quit smoking. Drugs were out. The baby was the hot glue fusing them together. Claudia was baptized Roman Catholic, Joe's religion.

From the first, Joe was a good father, doting on his offspring. But his sobriety was not enough to curb his violent temper. Nor was Diane the meek spouse Sandy had been. Temperance and motherhood did not cure her emotional problems. All too quickly Joe's ugly propensity for lashing out at his wife surfaced again.

One day in a fit of anger Joe started picking up pieces of china from Diane's deceased mother's collection, and one by one he smashed the treasured pieces onto the kitchen floor as newborn Claudia lay crying amid the debris.

Joe also started pushing Diane around. Diane told friends of one incident where Joe suddenly put Claudia down on the floor, grabbed Diane's hair, and dragged her around the room.

His fits of rage were not limited to Diane, but widened to include her acquaintances. Once, when Joe didn't like what the husband of one of Diane's friends had said about him, he went down to their loft and banged on their door all night long, threatening to kill them. Joe harassed another male acquaintance merely because he'd had coffee with Diane.

Diane began to confide in her father, telling him about Joe's temper and vindictiveness. "Claudia had just been born when she came to me and told me she couldn't continue to live with Joe," recalled Whitmore. "She said he would have these ornery tantrums. It was mostly verbal abuse. Things got a little better, but about every other year she'd tell me she didn't know how long she could take it. She wasn't happy at all." Anything that went wrong, Diane was to blame, according to Whitmore.

Whitmore said he told his daughter: "You have a baby here. You have to try to make this thing work."

In September 1980, Joe obtained an analyst's job at the prestigious Arnhold & S. Bleichroeder brokerage house. He impressed quickly, and found himself on the fast track in no time.

Word of Joe's success spread swiftly, and it wasn't long before he received a call from his ex-wife Sandy, who had remarried in June 1976. Under the terms of their separation, Joe wasn't responsible for the $1,000-per-month alimony anymore. But Sandy was still owed more than $28,000 in back payments. Over the years she had tried to get Joe to pay, even hired a Manhattan attorney at one point. But besides a payment of $1,400 he'd sent in 1975, Joe had steadfastly avoided contact with Sandy.

Sandy called under the guise of congratulating Joe on his new job, having been alerted by a mutual friend. They chatted like old times. Joe said he'd remarried and had a girl named Claudia. Sandy brought Joe up to date on her new life. It was all very pleasant.

The first call was followed by a second, and a third. Occasionally, Sandy asked Joe's advice on a specific security. After all, he was the master. Eventually, though, she got around to what she really wanted—the back alimony.

With his years of experience with her, Joe easily held Sandy at bay. He pleaded poverty: the baby, the wife, the new job. "You should be more thoughtful of my new responsibilities," he instructed.

The conversations nonetheless stayed friendly and begot more conversations. Whenever she could, Sandy brought up the money, saying she was broke or involved in a new business venture or whatever she could think of to get Joe to pay up.

That summer, Joe relented and sent Sandy a $500 personal check. He enclosed a brief note with it: "Well, it's a start. When and as I can, we will continue. This market is hell! Every wish for success in your business, J."

Once she got the check, Sandy started calling Joe's office on a more frequent basis. She wanted more.

Joe stopped taking the calls.

In January 1981, Joe, Diane, and Claudia, almost two years old, moved into a larger apartment in the heart of Greenwich Village. The apartment, at 446 Avenue of the Americas, had two stories and an attic area with a slanted ceiling. Located above a dry cleaner's, the duplex featured a living–dining room, kitchen, powder room, and a smaller area with a pullout sofa on the second floor; three bedrooms and a bath on the third and a small attic area on the fourth floor that Joe converted into an office and declared off limits.

They also began renting a summer home on Windmill Lane in Amagansett, which they would later buy. The property had a beautifully landscaped backyard that was more than 200 feet deep, with tall stands of pines and the pool in the middle, separated from the house by a large patio and sliding glass doors. All this was enclosed by ten-foot hedges.

Their marriage continued to deteriorate, but instead of making a clean break, Joe and Diane decided to have a second child.

"I don't want to leave one child in the world. I want the child we have to have someone else so that if anything happens to us, that child won't be alone," Diane told her father one day. But by now even easygoing Don Whitmore was convinced that Joe was bad news. He kept hearing, and seeing with his own eyes, his son-in-law's bizarre behavior. Child or no child, Whitmore told Diane, she ought to leave.

"I said to her: 'I don't know why you'd want to have another child married to him.' He was so obnoxious. I told her: 'You don't have to take this. When you make up your mind, let me know and I'll help you financially.' But she never left him."

Seven months pregnant, Diane accompanied Joe on a business trip to San Francisco in October 1982. One night as they rode back from dinner outside the city, they got into another of their senseless arguments. As Diane later related, Joe got angry when she said the word "fuck." In the pouring rain, he stopped the car on the highway and told her to get out. He left her there, forcing her to hitch-hike back to the hotel.

Diane checked out of the hotel immediately and went undercover for a few days. During her disappearance, Joe called Don Whitmore in Florida to check if she was there. Whitmore said Diane wasn't with him and told Joe that he and Diane needed to solve their problems by themselves.

"Tell her she'd better get home right now or I'll have nothing to do with the new baby," Joe threatened. Always one to calmly absorb the worst, Whitmore recalled years later in a flat, unemotional tone: "I thought that was a pretty cheap shot. You don't dump a pregnant woman alone on a lonely road in the dark."

Matters had reached such a state that when Diane was rushed to an emergency room with an asthma attack in her eighth month, Joe complained because she upset his plans to go to a football game. "You're ruining my day," Joe told his wife. Because of this, he refused to go to the bank machine to get her some cash.

On December 28, 1982, Diane gave birth to Blake Joseph Pikul. Diane jokingly told her friends her children were named after characters on the TV soap opera "Dynasty."

Joe was ecstatic about the baby, especially since he now had someone to carry on the family name. But it wasn't long before he erupted again. One day when Blake was several months old, Diane brought him into the master bedroom to nurse. When Blake let out a whimper, Joe began screaming at the both of them. He started tearing Diane's hair out, then chased mother and baby out of the room.

Diane again told her father and friends that she was going to get a divorce. But she stayed and continued to put up with Joe's abuse. When a friend offered her a book on battered women, Diane erupted in anger and banished the woman from her life.

By now Joe was making a solid six-figure income. It was money that he and Diane both had no problem spending. They dined out frequently and enjoyed the theater.

There were maids, massages, baby-sitters. Limousines became the mode of transportation in the city, especially for Joe. There was live-in help, hired after Claudia's birth and increased after Blake's. This afforded Diane frequent breaks from the children and gave her the time to pursue her own interests. She liked to shop, and her taste in clothing, which was exquisite, was also expensive. For his part, Joe would get his imported suits dry-cleaned after a single wearing. If his shirts weren't perfectly starched, he'd send Diane back to the laundry in tears to request that they be redone.

For the most part, Joe asked few questions about expenses. Everyday pin money was no object. An incalculable amount of cash was frittered away. Money was roaring in and roaring out; there was more where that came from.

That's the way it was supposed to be with royalty, and sometimes Joe viewed himself that way, with Diane serving as a cross between a subservient queen and a lowly servant. After all, she didn't work the way his first wife had. On several occasions, Joe rode to dinner in a chauffeur-driven car while Diane followed in a taxi. One notable example of his chauvinistic arrogance occurred at the end of a family visit to Florida. While Diane and her father were running after the two kids, waiting for the plane at the Tampa airport, Don Whitmore noticed that Joe was down at the other end of the terminal jabbering away on the telephone, without a parental care in the world. Whitmore couldn't understand why Diane put up with such insolence. "He's my Superman. He can do whatever he wants," she said with sarcasm.

But that was only half the story.

Over the loudspeaker, the flight was announced, starting with the first-class passengers. Suddenly Joe hung up the phone and boarded the plane. Diane kept running after Claudia and Blake; it wasn't time for them to board yet.

Whitmore was flabbergasted as Diane explained that Joe was flying first-class while she and the children were flying coach, *on the same flight*. "This is a great life. I have the two children and he gets on first class. He takes no responsibility," said Diane.

There were limits to Joe's largess when it came to his

mother and father, too. During one visit Joe's father requested money to buy a car, and Joe obliged. Before long, the father asked for another new car, and Joe obliged again. A year or two later, when his father requested another trade-in, Joe told him to go to hell. He also told him not to come visiting anymore to the Hamptons. Then he went into a tirade about how his parents had mistreated him all his life, how they didn't care about him until they wanted something.

When Joe's father died in late 1983, Bernice Pikul moved into the Valley View senior citizens apartments near the Ware River. Joe rarely visited.

At about the same time, Sandy started threatening to sue if she didn't get her money. She hired another New York lawyer and finally filed papers.

Joe's lawyers quickly sought to dismiss the civil suit as frivolous, contending the six-year statute of limitations had long since passed. But Sandy's attorneys produced the $500 check and letter from Joe dated August 31, 1981, to show that the legal time clock had begun to tick anew. Joe then contended the money had been "a gift" to help Sandy in a new business venture. He decided to fight the lawsuit all the way.

In the meantime, Joe became a man obsessed with his work. He frequently walked around his property in Amagansett with a telephone cemented to his ear. He didn't know the word "relax," even on weekends. After five years at Bleichroeder, Joe proudly revealed to his family that he was now international vice-president with an equity interest.

Joe traveled more than ever. On many a Sunday afternoon, he would suddenly get up from his chair by the pool in Amagansett and announce that he had a 6:00 P.M. flight to Zurich or wherever. He'd call for a limousine and depart just like that.

Never a mixer, Joe now hardly talked with anyone unless it involved the stock market. When the family went to Florida to visit the Whitmores, if Joe wasn't pinned to the telephone, he would often suggest to his father-in-law that they take a ride down to the broker's office to see what was going on. With Don Whitmore sometimes in tow, Joe would sit and watch the tape for hours. Only then would he loosen up and come to life.

Whitmore claimed there was another side to Joe's Wall Street dealings—insider trading conducted from his fourth-floor attic office at the apartment on Sixth Avenue. Aided by his computer and telephone, Joe would trade tips for hours into the night with a half-dozen associates from other firms. As Whitmore told the story, which he said he was told by Diane, Joe would place his orders through his confederates at other brokerage houses and vice versa. "He couldn't do it through his own company," said Whitmore. "If you work through your own company, they think you have inside interests. He was making a lot of money." Shortly after the culmination of one successful tip, Diane proudly told her father: "Joe made $50,000 last week on Reebok Shoes."

Of course, the stock market is no different than the poker table or the ponies. An obsessive gambler talks often about his winnings and rarely about his losses. Joe Pikul was no different; he had more than his share of losers.

In Amagansett, the Pikuls were viewed as a quiet couple who kept to themselves, except for their battle against the town fathers in 1984, when Liz Hotchkiss, owner of Stony Hill Stables, the horse farm behind his house, sought permission to build a 100-foot windmill on her grounds.

At the town council meeting, officials explained that the noise level was very low, only sixty decibels at 100 feet. The Pikul home was more than 500 feet away. But Joe was not impressed and objected vociferously. He contended that the windmill would destroy the peace and quiet he and Diane had hoped their Hamptons home would provide. No one else objected, though, and the town council granted the necessary permits.

The windmill dispute rekindled the decades-old rancor between longtime year-round residents and outsiders with weekend or second homes. Some residents saw Joe's protests as an attack not only on the horse farm but on their way of life. As one Amagansett citizen, Michael Light, wrote to the *East Hampton Star* weekly: "Our upstanding new resident is pleased with his fine buy and proud of his serene retreat, until one day the gauche farming types next door have the gall to erect a modern windmill.''

Alexander Peters, another local resident, said Joe was "perceived as this total city investor nut who came out here, bought land right next to a stable that's been there forever, and then started screaming about what's going on there.''

It was at this time that Diane noticed Joe had developed a marked disinterest in lovemaking. When she asked him why, Joe replied: "Maybe if you had a career you'd have something else on your mind besides sex.'' He told Diane that her lack of creative productivity made her unattractive to him and he suggested she get a job.

To rub it in, Joe would come into the bedroom some nights, put his foot up on the mattress, and proclaim: "What have you done to be tired?"

Joe also accused Diane of having a boyfriend, given the fact that she had cosmetic eye surgery. Since their relationship was going nowhere fast, he said he knew she hadn't fixed herself up for him. But was it really that? Or was he jealous because he couldn't be as pretty when he dressed up as a woman?

To Diane, Joe's behavior was growing more and more bizarre. He was threatening her now, and she thought about seeking a temporary order of protection. But she never followed through. He started keeping guns at the house in Amagansett, often taking target practice at a sheet of paper attached to the fence bordering the horse farm.

One Friday night Joe entered the house screaming: "Where's that little tree that was in the corner?" Diane said the gardener had removed it during his trimming.

"God, can't you tell the difference between what's good and bad? I give you money to run the house, can't you even run a house?" Joe demanded. The bush had been no higher than four feet. To the untrained eye, it was a bush, a no-big-deal kind of bush. But Joe was in an uproar. He said it would cost up to $3,000 to replace. For the life of him, he couldn't understand how Diane had failed to re-alize that the gardener was removing such a valuable commodity. For the entire weekend Joe talked about nothing else—the bush in the corner, the missing bush, where's the bush, how could you let him do that?

Terrified, Diane called the gardener when Joe wasn't around, and the man said he knew exactly where he'd put the bush in the town dump. Sure enough, the man retrieved the bush and came back Monday morning to replant it.

Then there were the lavish dinner parties Joe organized, for example at the River Café in Brooklyn. At the last minute, he would make Diane call the twenty or so of his friends to cancel.

Diane started to complain to friends that Joe was becoming antisocial, that they didn't go out enough. So on many weekends in Amagansett, she went out without him. Then, when she returned, Joe would demand: "Which guy were you with?"

Diane's friends were no longer welcome to visit. When one of them didn't leave fast enough one day, Joe punched her in the stomach and told her: "You have enough hair on your face to be a man."

Another time, Diane considered hosting a craft fair at the Windmill Lane home with some people who'd been featured in a *New York* magazine article. Joe told her to forget it and threatened to drive out from the city and physically remove all the guests if such an event was ever scheduled.

The spouse of another friend accidentally erased a floppy disk that Joe needed for work while he was showing Diane how to use Joe's computer. Joe retaliated by stealing Diane's appointment and address books and threatened to fracture the man's bones.

Money began to vanish from Diane's pocketbook. One night Joe made believe he was going to shoot Diane with a toy rifle; on another night, he shot a rat at dinner.

His worst behavior would follow their fights. According to Diane, Joe would sabotage her car, releasing air from the tires or removing engine parts so she couldn't go anywhere. Joe also often broke the door lock to the room where Diane had sought retreat. Once he couldn't break the lock, so he removed the hinges. He even knocked her down a few times while Claudia and Blake watched. On occasion, he would fart loudly when Diane entered the bedroom.

In his mind, Joe was no doubt blaming Diane for each

outbreak. Her acid tongue brought out the worst in him. She would scream and yell, he would do something crazy. No sooner had he exploded, though, than Joe would be trying to make up, sending her huge bouquets.

All of these outbursts paled alongside the discovery Diane made in February 1986, however, shortly after Joe had returned from a business trip to Singapore. While trying to reconcile their various bank accounts, she discovered a check for several hundred dollars that Joe had written to a lingerie store. Since she hadn't received any sexy presents lately, she feared the worst—another woman.

Inspecting one of Joe's suitcases for evidence, she discovered to her horror dozens of bras, panties, and pairs of pantyhose. Her curiosity aroused, she searched the Amagansett house and found ten more suitcases filled with female attire, falsies, anal vibrators, homosexual books and tapes, hair pieces, and about sixty Polaroid pictures of Joe dressed as a woman. Worse, she discovered a half-hour-long video of Joe dressed in drag, prancing around the house while masturbating.

Some of the clothing, mostly lingerie, belonged to Diane.

Shocked and frightened, Diane stored the photos and the videotape in a bank safe-deposit box. Shortly after Joe discovered his photos missing, Diane's bank key disappeared. Then she learned that he had gone to the bank and told officials that his wife had died. The bank people didn't give him access to the vault, though, thereby denying him an opportunity to retrieve the incriminating materials.

Instead of leaving at that point—more than eighteen months before her death—an emotionally paralyzed Diane stayed, trapped by the covenant she'd made with Joe and their grand style of life.

It was a pitiful game of three-card monte Diane was playing, and she kept turning over the wrong card. She still tried to present herself as happily married to a rich, successful man of Wall Street. But underneath she was a bundle of misery. She wanted out, but hadn't figured out how to act.

She was in psychotherapy now. But if she was gaining any insight from the sessions, it wasn't making things noticeably better. When Joe was in one of his moods, he was unbearable; other times, he was a great guy. Too often Diane chose to focus on the bearable and rationalize the unbearable. It was no wonder she had shunned the book on battered wives. Like so many women trapped in a marital nightmare she was dependent on her man for money, for self-esteem, for almost everything.

So Diane stayed. She wasn't at bottom yet.

CHAPTER • 7

"I Have Something on Him"

THE SUMMER OF 1986, JOE stayed in the city and worked. He didn't feel well and gradually became convinced that his poor health and swelling were symptoms of AIDS. By this point, he knew he was HIV positive and feared the worst. "The first encounter was five–six years ago. Could that have been a one in a million?" Joe wondered in a diary entry.

Diane and the children set up house full-time in Amagansett. Diane managed to draw considerable attention to her bikini-clad body on the sands of the staid Amagansett Beach Association, the swim club on the richer side of Main Street, the ocean side, where the Pikuls were interloping members. Suffice to say the old-money men liked the view, their wives did not.

Inexplicably, Joe changed the locks on the Sixth Avenue apartment one day without telling Diane. Then he told her that if she and the children came into Manhattan, he would close the Hamptons house, fire the nanny, and bring everyone back into the hot and muggy city. "The summer will be canceled," Joe warned.

But that was the last thing Joe wanted to do. He merely wanted to guard against surprise visits. He was back up to his old tricks, and being careless about it to boot. After Diane's death, one of his masseuses realized that those strange red marks on his back had been made by bra straps.

In a June, 1986, diary entry, Joe questioned how he could have been so careless with his suitcases. "I feel like it's hopeless. Can't get high. Can't forgive myself. Is there a way out? I didn't protect the thing that gave me this rush. . . . D is really a selfish lady. . . . Now I feel she's beat me. . . . Dressing is fun but lonely. A laughing matter for most people—what humiliation. I'm feeling suicidal."

Joe felt as if Diane had gained the upper hand. "Boy am I a jerk," he wrote. "She beat my ass completely . . . Women—How can I be so stupid? I offered myself to my enemies. Have to be the chump of '86! I'm a fucking joke . . . Why don't I just kill her—and stop fucking around. Sure, I was so stupid. Why not kill me? . . . I knew what she knew, dismissed it from my mind. . . . Said I was alone, and 'Why are you picking on me?' (She has) absolutely no fear." Joe wrote of trying to poison Diane at one point, but said she had detected the bitter taste in her morning beverage.

In another entry, Joe wrote: "Niceness leads to vulnerability, passivity. A defeated wimp-slave is what's required . . . The children!—Wait and bargain. . . . I became sloppy. . . . How could I have been so blind? DENIAL—EGO—ANGER—STUPIDITY—MADNESS—UNDERESTIMATION. Signs all over the place. LIES, HOSTILITY, FACTS, ATTITUDES, TORMENT, COMMENTS. . . . Never analyzed repercussions . . . not enough meetings."

On other pages Joe wrote "Blackmail is blackmail" and "D Must D," as in Diane Must Die. And in yet another entry, Joe observed: "D/ANN controls DICK . . . D/ANN controls."

Finding herself unable to flee from Joe's oppression entirely, Diane increased her threats of divorce as the summer drew to a close. Joe threatened right back: he'd leave her penniless, or worse, he'd kill her and dump the body where it would never be found.

That August, Diane decided enough was enough. Convinced that Joe was in a very vulnerable position because of the lingerie and videotape, Diane sought out Raoul Lionel Felder, divorce attorney to the stars. Even in her misery, she was seeking to rub elbows with the high and mighty. But Diane was not one of Felder's big clients, and as a result she didn't get the treatment she thought she deserved.

Family and friends later alleged that Felder, who charged up to $450 per hour, merely recommended that Joe and Diane get counseling for a year, then proceed with the divorce if need be. For this, Don Whitmore claimed, Diane paid Felder a $46,000 retainer.

Felder denied that he recommended marriage counseling. "You can't do both together," he insisted. "What you do with the lawyer undermines what you do with the counselor." As for the retainer, Felder said it was half of what Whitmore claims, "if I'm lucky."

In fact, Diane withdrew $40,000 from a joint checking account that August, and by her own admission kept $15,000 of it for an emergency fund. Above all else, she was determined to withdraw financially whole from the mess with Joe. She told Felder the $15,000 would pay one month's worth of bills if Joe cut off the money flow completely. That was $180,000 a year, net, for household expenses.

Several days after being retained, Felder sent Joe an initial letter. Not long after, each side hired private investigators. Joe also started pleading poverty—that was part of his reasoning for telling Diane to get a job. But Diane didn't believe him; she was convinced he was hiding assets somewhere. And Sandy Jarvinen, Joe's first wife, still wanted her money. It was starting to look like Sandy's lawsuit might actually go to trial.

On one level, the break was starting to be made. But on another, Diane still desired reconciliation. If Joe would only change, she could continue with her dream life. She and Joe did start going to marriage counseling once a week, agreeing to give it a year. The incriminating photos, though, remained in a bank box.

Faced with the prospect of a humiliating divorce case, Joe, of course, did his best to appease his wife. Diane and the children joined him on a business trip to Vail. Then he brought Diane along on a month-long business trip to the Orient and Scandinavia. In addition, Joe bought her lavish gifts—jewelry, a fur coat, and basketloads of flowers.

But as usual, the newfound bliss didn't last long. The arguments soon resumed in earnest, especially about money and her continuing outside social life. Every chance he could get, Joe berated Diane for what he considered her wanton wastefulness. As for her parenting techniques, even Joe's mother, who liked Diane, remarked, "The children were a bother to her."

None of this was doing Claudia and Blake any good. A confused Claudia told her mother that she'd noticed Daddy looking at women's makeup displays while shopping. Blake was slow in his speech development and at least one of his therapists suspected his home environment as the cause. That opinion only made Joe more angry.

In the fall of 1986, Blake failed to qualify for admission the following school year to Grace Church School, which Claudia attended. Joe stomped out of a meeting with Marjorie Goldsmith, Blake's nursery-school director. When he returned home from work, he sent his sobbing son to his bedroom and forbade him to leave for several hours. Joe couldn't accept failure.

For every action there was a reaction with Joe and Diane. Joe spent New Year's Eve 1986 on a business trip, later claiming he lost more than a quarter of a million dollars gambling in Monte Carlo. Diane could never confirm whether he really had gambled the money away, or if his story was just an excuse to hide more sinister expenditures—drug use, sex purchases, even market trading losses.

As a result, on January 7, 1987, she sent a packet of forty-eight Polaroid photos and the videotape to Felder's office, asking that the materials be placed in the lawyer's vault and instructing that if anything happened to Felder, the materials were to be returned to her in private. Diane ominously told Felder that if she died, the materials should be returned to Joe, "Unless I die under suspicious circumstances."

Diane knew she had Joe where she wanted him, but instead of using the photos immediately, she was still looking for her own form of leveraged buyout; she wanted to make sure Joe supported her and the children in the style to which they were accustomed. So the photos stayed under wraps. It wasn't until months later, following another blowup with Joe, that she even let Felder review the material.

According to the attorney, when he did look at the photos, he told Diane she should go to court immediately to obtain an order of protection. But she declined. "People like this are very clever. They never say no to you," Felder said. Instead they come up with "one round of bullshit excuses after another," including "Let me think about it," "What about the kids?" "What will his reaction be?"

"It's called humanity," said Felder. "They don't want to do it; they do. Then they don't. Their husband will hit them one night, then they'll want to do. Three nights later, they're doing great, and 'forget about it.' "

To Felder, Diane was "basically a doomed person, preordained for destruction one way or another." He said if Diane had followed through with the divorce, she probably would have gone on to another "unproductive, unhappy life," "some other destructive relationship. There were basic personality flaws within Diane, pathetic personality flaws." He said Diane had "no ego strength, was frightened of life, frightened of herself, no self-assurance in terms of worthlessness, a sense of not deserving more in life, a sense of not wanting to be helped, a kind of person who curses the darkness and doesn't light candles."

While Diane struggled with her lonely internal battle, Joe secretly rented an apartment in Battery Park City. The four-figure monthly rent further drained the Pikul cash flow, but Diane had no idea that Joe was heading toward fiscal ruin.

Several friends told her to leave without waiting for a financial settlement, but she was determined to get out whole. Diane didn't say what she had up her sleeve, but frequently expressed confidence in between her moods of fear and depression. Some days she was fearful of Joe's threats to make an issue of her having hired too many baby-sitters too often; other days, she confidently exclaimed: "He'll never get the kids. I have something on him."

Even though she had still not officially filed for divorce, Diane thought she'd worked everything out at one point: she and the children would move to a Long Island suburb; Joe would pay the rent and full-time child-care help. But the next thing she heard, Joe said he was broke. It didn't help that his net-worth statement for Felder was months overdue.

During this same period, Diane also started looking for a job, but even that was not a simple chore. It turned out that she had never resigned from her Parks Department job, which now carried a $24,030 annual salary. The maternity leave for Claudia in 1979 had run into a maternity leave for Blake in 1982, and from there Diane had somehow managed to stay on the employee roster. Whether it was an accidental oversight in a city not known for its efficiency or a deliberate act, Diane had not followed regulations regarding such leaves. Rather than be terminated, she was forced to resign on February 3, 1987, following an internal investigation by the Parks Department's inspector general's office. The same city bureaucrats who confirmed the resignation were less than forthcoming when asked whether Diane had ever collected a paycheck during those eight years she was "absent without leave."

That March, Diane reentered the work force full-time, as assistant to the publisher at *Harper's* magazine. Basically a secretary, Diane was earning less than if she'd returned to the Parks Department. As usual, other factors came into play. Diane was back with an important-sounding job, rubbing glamorous elbows. She was talking about becoming a writer again.

"You should be happy now, Joe. I got a job," she told her husband.

"Now you screwed up our income tax," he snapped back.

That summer, a summer Joe subsequently described as the best of his life, Diane stayed in the city for the most part, concentrating on her new job and her personal life. She enrolled in an exercise class. She also kept busy writing short stories, having been accepted into a writers' workshop at the West Side YMCA, one of twelve chosen from seventy applicants.

Her sometimes amateurish writing was highly autobiographical. The main female characters in several of the stories—whether sophisticated New Yorkers or schoolgirls from Indiana—were depressing, scheming souls, lacking in self-esteem, mired in sad relationships with cruel, violent men.

It didn't matter to Diane that she was just a student in a YMCA workshop; she was ready to be published. She wrote to a magazine trying to get her work into print.

With the job and her other activities, Diane didn't have much free time. To Joe, that meant she was abandoning the children. No matter what else could be said about Joe, there was no doubt he dearly loved Claudia and Blake. In many ways, they were his reason for living. He insisted that the children once again spend their vacation out in Amagansett. Then, expressing concern over the prospect of the kids being wholly in the care of a live-in baby-sitter, he proceeded to take most of the summer off himself to stay in the Hamptons.

Joe's decision was an especially irrational move, given that in the summer of 1987 the stock market was going wild, with the Dow setting a 2722.42 record that August. Everyone on Wall Street was making a bundle, and here was Joe taking it easy out at the beach.

Joe's absence from work only served to make Diane more angry. He made "only" $90,000 in commissions during May, June, and July. She started to call him lazy, and Joe realized he could generate considerable irritation by threatening to quit his job, move to Key West, and live off the sea.

Despite his claim of total parental dedication that summer, Claudia and Blake were sent off to the ritzy Pathfinder Day Camp in Montauk. (With video camera in hand, Joe made quite an impression at open house as the dedicated father—Hamptons, 1987 version.) Although some locals attend the camp, most of the slots are filled by New Yorkers who bring their kids out to the Hamptons to escape the city, then ship them off to camp all day. As one local law enforcement official put it: "It's the kind of place where you put your kids on the bus and be done with them." So Joe was enjoying his children in the same detached manner as Diane—all the while poisoning their minds against their mother.

Joe repeatedly told Claudia and Blake that if Diane really loved them, she would be out in Amagansett instead of working in the city and hanging out with her friends and going to exercise class. "She's only interested in herself," Joe harped, explaining that he'd rescued their mother from the gutter. If not for him, Joe claimed, Diane would still be living in filth and rodent-infested squalor.

When Diane did come out to visit, Joe would say nasty things to her loud enough to be heard by the children in the next room. "You don't want these children. They'll see you for what you are and hate you even more." Other times, Claudia quoted her father as saying that her mother was slow and always late. In addition, Joe told his daughter that her mother was jealous of her, because she was growing more beautiful while Mommy was growing older and uglier.

The children were being used as weapons in the marital battle. "Mommy, I don't know who to believe," Claudia told Diane one day. "Daddy says all these bad things about you."

Diane subsequently sought to explain some of her parenting methods to her divorce lawyers by claiming Joe "encouraged me to have extensive baby-sitter coverage when he was home." She criticized Joe for currying favor with the children by allowing them to stay up too late, overindulging them with junk food and gifts, and failing to discipline them properly, such as asking them to pick up toys.

Explanations notwithstanding, Diane saw little of her children that summer, coming out to the Hamptons only for brief weekend visits. True, she was keeping her distance from Joe. But in doing so, burying herself in her job and social activities, she virtually abandoned her children.

Even in separation, Diane made knee-buckling discoveries about Joe that summer. Perplexed at how he had learned certain aspects of her strategy for the divorce case, she came to the realization that she'd discussed the subject on the telephone with her girlfriends. So, on July 30, 1987, Gaetano Capolupo, a retired New York City police detective, was summoned to conduct an electronic sweep of the Sixth Avenue apartment. First, Capolupo detected an "off voltage" on the telephone line. Then, by going phone line to phone line, he found a tape recorder in the attic "hidden under some clothing up against the wall, and hooked to the telephone line. The telephone line was hidden behind the cushions and a wicker basket was placed in front of the telephone jack box, so that you would have to move it to see it."

Capolupo wanted to remove the device, but terrified of what would happen if Joe found out she knew, Diane insisted that the machine be left in place. At least now she knew to watch what she said over the phone.

The cross dressing remained the most upsetting issue to Diane. When confronted with her discovery and the threat of divorce more than a year prior, Joe had promised to change his ways. But one day, while sorting through a load of his laundry at the Amagansett house, Diane discovered one of her bathing suits, the stitching severely stretched and ripped, as if someone much larger had worn it. When she confronted Joe, he explained that he had "just wanted to wash a bathing suit."

The stretched bathing suit prompted her to probe deeper. She realized that her sanitary pads were missing in large quantities and that her lingerie and bathing suit drawer had been rummaged through. Several of her nightgowns and dresses were lying on the floor, or hung up inside out. She found two shopping bags filled with women's lingerie, bathing suits, and falsies in a basement closet.

Confronted once again, Joe removed the clothing. Simultaneously, though, he began keeping a rental car hidden in the bushes of the cemetery bordering their property.

Looking through Joe's wallet one day, Diane discovered a photo of two people dressed like women. One of them had an erection, the other was performing oral sex.

Diane also discovered pills on the floor of the Amagansett house. She confronted Joe, who gave a variety of explanations—his stomach, his knee. But Diane looked up Didrex in a prescription drug guide and found the pills listed as an appetite suppressant in the amphetamine family. She was especially concerned in light of Joe's previous dependence on uppers and the possibility that such abuse could trigger violence.

All the while, the war between the two continued to escalate. Like many couples in the death throes of a failed marriage, Diane and Joe argued over just about anything, and just about anywhere. During a fight after dinner in the Hamptons one evening, Joe threw Diane out of the car and failed to return for her. She had to walk back to the restaurant and summon a taxi.

Joe returned to work that August, earning $165,591 in commissions that month alone. Of course, being back in the city meant more run-ins with Diane, whose friends were now not allowed in the Sixth Avenue apartment even if Joe wasn't present. He didn't like any of these people, claiming they were all from AA.

Joe's head was unraveling, piece by piece.

Some days he would act as a personal wrecking crew, sifting through Diane's personal property. He threw out files she had categorized, explaining that anything in the house was ultimately his, so he could do whatever he pleased with it. He also started reading Diane's appointment book and combing through her purse before she left for work. He denied her access to bank accounts and failed to return all night without alerting Diane to his whereabouts.

If Diane was on the telephone and Joe wanted to make a call, he loudly walloped the extension phone, making it impossible for her to carry on a conversation. Claudia took to telling baby-sitters: "Be careful what you say in the house, my father has it bugged."

Diane told of one weekend when Joe spent virtually every waking minute shouting insults and harassing her, throwing things at her and bumping into her. In front of business associates one evening, Joe referred to Diane as a lesbian, a failure, and a drunk.

Upon hearing that one of Diane's closest acquaintances had had a malignant tumor removed, Joe proclaimed: "Maybe you'll all get cancer. You richly deserve it."

In one particularly bizarre incident, Diane arrived home one night at the Sixth Avenue apartment only to find Joe propped up on his elbows and knees, eating out a piece of watermelon, his pants pulled below his knees.

The Tuesday after Labor Day, Joe lost his cool with Bernetta Seegars, a twenty-six-year-old accounting student who'd worked for the Pikuls since Claudia was two. Diane was back in the city, and Bernetta was in Amagansett taking care of the two children. Apparently anxious to get the house to himself, Joe sent the sitter and children into town with specific orders not to come back before a certain time.

But it was raining out, so Seegars directed the taxi to return to the house a half hour early. When they arrived, Joe went berserk, yelling at Bernetta, then running around the house mumbling under his breath. Bernetta, who had quit once before following an argument with Diane, had never seen Joe act like this. Sure he was weird, always demanding things go his way. But this time Joe was acting like a lunatic.

Bernetta told him to stop yelling, but he didn't. And when he got angry at her for using the washing machine, she quit right on the spot, after working there nearly seven years.

When Claudia sided with Bernetta, Joe angrily locked his daughter in her room until she changed her mind.

Two days later, Diane took a significant step forward, writing a note to one of Felder's associates—her first attempt at documenting her concerns. But it was clear from the memo that she still had mixed emotions. She said it was important that Joe get out of the house promptly, but then wondered if she'd be better off waiting until her tenth wedding anniversary, nearly a year away, in order to obtain increased Social Security benefits. "Order of protection? Backup detective work desirable?" Diane wondered in her note. "How far away can I move? Pay for graduate school for me? House in country?"

Commenting afterward about Diane's reason for staying around for another ten months, Felder said he felt it was "a ludicrous excuse, a clutching-at-straws excuse. You're going to sit there with a lunatic because maybe when you are sixty-five, or whatever it is, you'll get forty dollars a month more? I mean, just think about that."

Diane was a tragic figure at this point: externally she claimed new-found strength, but inside her emotionally battered shell there was an insecure woman terrified of Joe's threat to fight for custody of the children by making her look like a neglectful mother too occupied with her social life and job. Yet Diane also wanted to know if Joe could be forced to pay for her additional schooling.

The money issues were important to Diane, but what she didn't know was that she and Joe were going broke. Not only had several of Joe's personal Wall Street tips failed, but as the market began to drop from its record peak, he was hit with several margin calls. For example, on September 24, Bleichroeder officials notified him that a $28,344 margin call was due in the morning.

Suddenly, he wanted to sell the house in Amagansett and all the furnishings as soon as possible. He told Diane if they didn't sell, the IRS would put a lien on the house for the $248,000 in back taxes they owed. The monthly rent on the apartment in the city—$3,000 plus—and the monthly mortgage out in Amagansett—$2,161—were continually late. The landlord from Sixth Avenue was threatening to sue. Then there was the other apartment in Battery Park City, the one Diane still didn't know about, the rent for which was another $1,650 per month.

Between Joe and Diane there were nearly $2,000 a month for psychiatrists and psychologists. The pressure had built to the point where Joe started taking cocaine in large quantities, so thousands were going up his nose.

On top of everything else, the kids' tuition was due, another ten grand. To say nothing of the extra cost of Joe's dressing for two.

Diane had too many other problems to see the obvious signs. She had believed Joe all too easily the previous year when he had promised to change. The fancy coats, the jewelry, the trips, the flowers, and the sudden attention had, unfortunately, worked their dazzling spell.

Entangled in a frightening dilemma, Diane didn't know which way to go. She wanted out, she didn't want out. She wanted to keep her rich life-style, she didn't care about the life-style. She wanted out, she didn't know how to get out. She wanted to show she was strong enough to make it on her own, she was too afraid to try.

Diane wanted revenge, too. She was angry and hurt. Joe was going to pay, especially for his sexual betrayal.

And the alternatives—what were the alternatives? Diane feared she might end up living in a shelter, only to be sued for abandonment and having to defend her actions. Like many women, she decided to stay through the divorce figuring it was the best way to keep track of the children and make sure Joe didn't inflict worse damage on them. To Diane, there were no alternatives.

CHAPTER • 8

Of Maids and AIDS

OF ALL THE PENDING ISSUES of dispute, selling the house in Amagansett caused the least friction. Diane had grown to hate the place, and the sale would also psychologically get the divorce moving, although Diane and her attorneys still had not filed any papers in court.

With the money crunch looming, Joe, Diane, the children, and a new live-in helper journeyed out to Windmill Lane in mid-September 1987 to clean up the property for a real-estate appraisal.

The two combatants argued as usual, mixing important issues with the innocuous. Their hatred for each other had grown so bitter that both could suddenly calm down at the peak of battle to discuss things rationally, as if other personalities had taken over. Then they'd go right back at it.

Diane now knew to watch her words on the telephone, but she had no idea that Joe had also begun to secretly record their arguments—as well as fellow speakers at Alcoholics Anonymous meetings—with a microcassette recorder hidden in his pocket. He now restrained himself for the most part, acting the role of henpecked husband as an untethered Diane worked herself into a frenzy of obscenities and threats.

"What about saying the cats are more important than your daughter? Who was doing *that?*" Joe asked as the argument began in earnest.

"You want custody?" asked Diane. "You want 'em? You want 'em? Why not? Why *don't* you want custody?"

"Can't you talk quietly?" said Joe.

"Why not? Too much of a burden?" Diane continued. "Can you talk quietly?"

"No," said Diane. "Don't tell me how to talk. I can't talk quietly. I have no intention of talking quietly. You fucked me good. And now you're trying to turn my children against me."

Diane cited Joe's having told the children she didn't care about them and that she wasn't around because she wanted to work instead. Joe claimed he'd never said that.

"Oh, you—yes, you did!"

"Never," insisted Joe. "Diane, you, you know you're in very heavy denial about those things, Diane."

"Fuck off!" she snapped back.

Then they argued about why Diane picked that particular weekend to clean the porch, which often looked like a jagged pyramid of toys, pool furniture, and odds and ends. "You said, 'Clean the porch, clean the porch.' I'm cleaning the porch. You tell me to do things, and I do it, Joe, because I need your money and I need you to let me sleep at night."

"You're doing this because Daddy's coming and you don't want him to see," said Joe, alluding to an upcoming visit from Don Whitmore. "That's what you always did."

Letting the conversation drift, Joe demanded: "What about letting your daughter choke to death?"

"Oh, shut up! I'm so sick of this bull," said Diane as she threatened to expose Joe's psychiatric problems by bringing one of his therapists into court if he fought the divorce. "You want this in court and you're gonna be really sorry."

Joe claimed he was working hard on solving his problems and accused Diane of doing little more than make noise about hers. "I mean, a little bit of work brings out the beast in you, doesn't it?" said Joe. "Retaliate, Diane. Kill me. I don't care what you do. You don't scare me. You don't scare me, Diane! I'm gonna tell you something. I don't care what you do. You can't scare me, you can't hurt me, Diane."

"Why don't you just leave?" she replied. "I don't want to talk to you anymore. Are you afraid you can't get in the last word? Why don't you hit me, Joe? Why don't you knock down the door?"

Inevitably, the argument turned to the troubled marriage. "You can forget any kind of separation," said Diane.

"You're in command, Diane," said Joe.

"*You're* in command," Diane answered back.

"You're working," said Joe.

"*You* never want to make any money," said Diane. "You don't want to make some money and you're the one with the brute strength that knocks people down and you step on 'em, right? And you're the nastiest prick I ever met."

"I'm a faggot. I'm—"

"You *are* a faggot," said Diane. "You're worse than a faggot. You're a nasty, cowardly bully. You're a liar. You're a cheat. You're dishonest, you're dishonorable. You're mean. You're nasty. And you're psychotic. And I don't want to live with you and I want to see you as little as possible. I don't want any kind of agreement where we have to talk about this."

"What are you doing here?" asked Joe.

"What am *I* doing here? I'm here telling you," said Diane. "I haven't told you this before: I don't care about you. I hope you die. And I hope you die soon. . . . You're dying of AIDS, aren't you? You're dying of AIDS. Your stomach is getting bigger every day. And you know, you probably haven't noticed but you look pathetic from the back. There are sags at the crack. Look at yourself in the mirror sometime. You're really unattractive. Are you suffering? . . . Are you gay? Are you gay? . . . I'm living a bad life. I've had a bad decade, Joe. I had a real bad decade."

Next, Diane complained that Joe was spending too much time with the children. "I think you're a very bad influence on them. And I don't want you anywhere near me. . . . I'm gonna have to get rid of you. I'm not living with you through this divorce."

"Have I—" Joe attempted to ask, but Diane cut him off.

"I want you out of the house. I want you out, baby."

"Have I ever—"

"You know that? I'm not repeating myself. I don't want

anything to do with you. I mean, I'm gonna hang you if you don't cooperate. You, you, you've threatened me."

The argument petered out, and Joe and Diane proceeded to spend part of the day working together getting the house in order for the appraisal. But late in the afternoon as they were sorting through a disorganized pile of family pictures, the verbal warfare resumed.

According to Joe, not only had Diane neglected to put the albums in order, she was now stealing the best shots.

"So what?" she responded before denying she'd removed any of the pictures. "That's like a lower form of life," she said. "Take our children's pictures and hide them."

Joe cut her off: "You had full time to put 'em into albums. You never touched 'em. Never." He also accused her of never having bothered to snap any photos of the kids. "You're too busy."

"So you deserve to steal from me?" asked Diane.

"I've had the best summer of my life," said Joe.

"I hope that—"

"Except for you. Except for you."

A child began talking in the background and the arguing stopped so that parental duties could be attended to. Within moments, however, Joe and Diane were at it again, arguing about the new live-in helper: whether Diane should apologize for being rude to her the day before and whether Joe had improperly offered her a raise and use of a rental car not to quit.

"You were rude talking like that in front of people, in front of your girlfriends," said Joe.

"I'm not gonna apologize to a single soul. No. I apologize to people when I apologize to people, and—"

"Oh, I've stopped," Joe interrupted. "I've given up."

"You never did apologize!" snapped Diane.

"Oh, look at her go. Look it, look it, look at Miss Powerful," said Joe. "Oh, look it. Look it, look it, look it, look it, look it."

There was a crash. "Look it, she's throwing the chair outside," said Joe.

"You better believe it," said Diane.

"Look at this," said Joe. "She's so powerful, so controlled."

"This is *my* house," said Diane.

"Feel better now?" asked Joe.

"None of this shit makes me feel better!"

Joe turned to the nanny and instructed, "Get the kids in the car. Let's go."

Claudia asked: "Daddy, are we going?"

"We're gonna go for a ride," said Joe.

"Oh, you go for a ride," said Diane. "I'm going to New York— Did you take the pictures from New York, too?"

"I haven't taken anything from New York," said Joe. "I haven't taken anything."

"Oh, yes, you have," screamed Diane.

"Get hold of yourself," said Joe.

"No, I will not get hold of myself," said Diane, the day-long series of skirmishes taking their toll. "Stop stealing from me."

"I'm not stealing from you, Diane."

"Yes, you *are* stealing from me."

"I am not," said Joe.

"You don't call that stealing?" asked Diane, showing Joe an empty box.

"No."

"Stop stealing my sanitary pads!"

"Let's go, people. Your mama's having another bad day," said Joe, heading for the driveway. "Let's go. Let's go. Let's go, let's go, let's go. Let's go. Let's go. Let's go. Let's go. *Let's go!* Go, go, go. Get in. Get in. Get in."

Turning back to Diane, he baited her one more time. "Go ahead, yell. Yell. Show me how strong you are. How much vocal power you have. How nasty you are."

Diane was only too happy to oblige. "Faggot, faggot, faggot, faggot, faggot. Want to wear this thing out? Or did you want to wear this?" asked Diane, displaying several items of women's clothing. "Liar, liar, liar, liar, liar. Shut up, Joe."

As Joe tried to get a word in edgewise, Diane cut him off: "Joe, why don't you get your prick cut off? Why don't you get your cock cut off, huh? And shave off your hair and take hormones so you don't have to wear falsies. Huh? Why don't you? How can you do this to the mother of your children? And don't even begin to tell me that it's because I had a variety of men fucking me in the ass. Because it has been eight years—that's the maximum amount of time that I have been successful in the last eight years, baby. Your daughter would have AIDS. You're lucky your son doesn't have AIDS. You took the chance of infecting him with AIDS. You, you went around and had a homosexual affair when I was nursing Blake, you cheap cunt! I don't need an audience to say that. Just you."

Diane paused only to catch her breath before she screamed, "Get out of my underwear, Joe! Stay the fuck out of my clothes! Buy your own underwear! You think I believe you threw that stuff out. I don't believe it for one minute."

She went on to say that the marriage counseling was a waste of time because "I firmly believe you're psychotic and I also believe you're on drugs. I gave you an extra year, and you were gonna prove what a nice guy you were, and all you did was use this time against me. But I'm right on your ass, baby. I know everything you've done. And that has just made the case against you worse."

"You don't know everything I've done," offered Joe.

"I know a lot of what you've done," said Diane. "I'm sick to my stomach with you!"

Joe accused Diane of spying on him.

"You better believe it! And I'm gonna use it all. I wasn't gonna use it all, but now I am going to, Joe. I don't care. You kill me, baby. You go ahead and kill me. Try and kill me."

"Why are you hysterical?" asked Joe. "Why'd you have to do all that yelling and screaming and abusive language?" asked Joe.

"Because it's my job, baby," said Diane.

Diane let Joe know she knew about the telephone tap back in Manhattan. But Joe didn't appear the least bit concerned about his actions. Cognizant of her strategy sessions with her girlfriends, he instead wanted to know what she was so worried about. "What could you possibly have that you want to hide on the telephone, Diane—a good soul like you?"

"I'm gonna crucify you for that," Diane screamed, before switching the conversation to the incriminating videotapes and photos. "You know something, I don't give a fuck what you do. And you know something, you're right. If you go to court with me, they're public record. That's exactly what they do at *Harper's*." She then explained how certain items in a messy Joan Collins divorce case had come to light. "I asked, I asked."

"You feel very powerful, don't you?" asked Joe.

"No, I don't feel powerful. I don't feel powerful at all," said Diane. "You have never enabled me to be behind any locked door, although you consistently lock me out. The only reason you didn't knock the door down last night is because Ruth was there and you were embarrassed in front of Ruth," she said, referring to the new live-in.

"How do you know my motives in all these things, Diane?" asked Joe, setting the tone for another blowup.

"Because I know you better than anybody in the world."

"You don't know me at all," said Joe.

"I know you much better than anybody," said Diane.

"No, no," Joe protested.

"You don't know yourself at all," said Diane.

"No, that's—"

"I know you better than anybody in the world," Diane said, cutting him off.

"No, no, you don't," said Joe. "You're not smart enough to know me. I've known smart women, but you're not one of them."

"Joe, I have been very— Shut up," Diane scolded. Joe tried to protest that he wasn't interrupting.

"Yes, you were. You were interrupting me."

Back and forth. Back and forth. "Fuck off," yelled Diane. "You were doing it all. I was giving you a second chance to try to rehabilitate yourself and you fucked me good. You're always trying to fuck me, Joe."

"How did I fuck you?" he asked.

"And you're hiding your AIDS from me."

"How, how did I fuck you?" asked Joe, avoiding the second question.

"You don't treat me decently. And I don't care what you do."

The conversation then turned to money and whether Joe was lazy for having taken part of the summer off. "You make twenty-two-five, I make a million-two—and *I'm* lazy, right?" said Joe. "It's that mouth that makes you so mediocre."

The poison darts were flying back and forth. "By the way, I can have lunch with men, you know," Diane said. "There's nothing against that."

Joe stuck with money issues. "Why do you make twenty-two-five for?"

Diane explained that it was an honor to work at "one of the most esteemed magazines in America."

"Certainly should be happy living on *that*," said Joe, sarcasm dripping.

"I don't have to live on that."

"Yes, you do," said Joe firmly.

"Well, I have to, but I'll get child support for them," said Diane. "I want the money from the time that I helped build up your career, by staying at home taking care of the children."

"You helped me build my career?" asked Joe.

"I sure did."

"By giving me what kind of support?"

"I took care of the children," said Diane.

"That's all you did. Well, you get baby-care help," said Joe. "That's all, because you didn't give me any emotional support."

"I sure did," said Diane.

"You did not."

"Well, you're psychotic, you know," added Diane.

"The point is, all our stuff was hanging around, you did nothing with it for years." Now Joe was back arguing about the photos, contending that Diane only became interested in the children's pictures when he started putting them into albums. "You become competitive. That's the reality of it," he said. "Give me a break. You haven't put one picture in order. You never did one single one. Not one single one."

"You know what I was gonna do for you?" said Diane.

"What?"

"I was gonna make two of each so that you would have one."

"Yeah?"

"I told my friends a year ago," said Diane.

"Oh, yeah?"

"Yes! So it would be fair."

"A year ago!" said Joe.

"I was also gonna buy you a Rolex watch with the money I make. I couldn't believe it. I found it on my calendar that I was gonna do that," said Diane.

They then argued about the photos again. "Joe, don't argue with me," said Diane. "There is nothing you can say to me. You are the lowest of low. I think you're a psychotic man. There's no way to get through to you. . . . To think that, you know, you don't have friends, you don't have family. You have a record. You didn't pay off people. . . . I don't care if you kill me. I don't care if you blame me. I don't care if you take my children. I don't care if you don't . . . kill your-yourself, or run off with seventeen women, or cut off your prick. I don't give a shit what you do. Leave me the fuck alone! You have gotten me so mad. Nothing you say matters, so save your breath. . . . I don't care if I go to jail. I'll kill you if I have to!"

"Okay," said Joe matter-of-factly.

The conversation returned to the children, and Diane complained about him trying to turn them against her. "That is the last straw. . . . I mean, that is really so low. You know, I am mad and I am brokenhearted. I tried as hard as I could. And you know in your heart that I did."

"I don't believe you did," said Joe.

"Well, that is too bad," she continued. "I was not always—"

"Behind my back you were always talking about me from the beginning, Diane. And you continued—"

"I don't want you to have access to them," interrupted Diane. "You will have minimal access."

"You must feel very powerful."

"I don't feel—do I look like I feel powerful?" Diane asked. "I don't feel powerful at all. If I were powerful, I wouldn't have to act this way. I make 22,500, and I'm an old lady. I'm not like somebody that everybody wants to marry. And I probably have the AIDS virus. I'm too scared to go and get a test. I'm sure I do. You do, too."

"Why?" asked Joe. When Diane didn't respond, he asked again, "Why?"

"Why?" Diane finally answered. "Because you had a homosexual encounter."

"Well, how do you know?"

"Because somebody told me."

"Oh, really," said Joe. "That—that—that is, of course, ridiculous. And you know it is."

"Well, I don't care. I don't care," said Diane.

"That's absolutely ridiculous," added Joe.

"Well, if it's ridiculous, then you go have a test," pressed Diane.

"Absolutely ridiculous," said Joe.

"Why won't you have a test?" asked Diane.

"Why don't *you* go?" Joe shot back.

"Because I don't want to know," said Diane. "I was going to and then I couldn't go because you were—"

"You haven't seen anything yet, Diane. . . . Diane, you've got your finger between your crotch, that's what you have. Tell the whole world, Diane, I'm not afraid of you. Tell everybody."

"I will," she promised.

"Well, go ahead. Go ahead. You'll be left with your memories," Joe warned. "Nothing. Zero. Zilch. Go. Go ahead, Diane. Diane, you're powerful. You've got a chance. Come get me."

CHAPTER · 9

"Don't Worry, I Can Handle Him"

As HIS MARRIAGE TO DIANE teetered on the edge that September of 1987, Joe began cultivating a new confidante: his ex-wife Sandy Jarvinen.

The calls to Massachusetts started innocently enough; Joe said he'd found some old photos of their life together while going through boxes in the cellar at the Amagansett home. But as the weeks progressed, and the calls escalated in number and length, the subject matters jumped all over the lot: he'd met some old friends of theirs, Diane wasn't taking care of the kids, she was never around, he wanted to settle Sandy's alimony suit, he was very unhappy, he was dying of AIDS, he was getting a divorce, his wife was cheating on him, he didn't know who was watching the kids when he was out of town, Diane was blackmailing him, he was concerned about the welfare of his kids, he wanted Sandy to come to New York for a visit.

In contrast to his disappointment over the condition of his photo collection from his years with Diane, Joe told Sandy their old photos had been "wonderfully put together in albums and showed a lot of love and concern about our life together."

Sandy, always trying to figure out a way to get her alimony, was willing to talk on the telephone, but continued to decline Joe's invitations to Manhattan.

While Joe worked his back-channel diplomacy with Sandy, Don Whitmore and his wife Gretchen flew in for their visit to Amagansett. Joe went out of his way to harass

Diane, calling her a bitch and a cunt. He tried to keep her up all night, haranguing her from room to room. He promised to break her while the in-laws were visiting so they could see "the real" Diane, "so they can see what you're really like."

This time Diane had something to shut Joe up with, informing him that her private eye had turned up evidence of a previous felony arrest for assault with a deadly weapon.

That news calmed Joe down, enabling Diane to enjoy her weekend. The following week, though, he repeatedly demanded to know if Sandy had supplied her with the information. It wasn't an unfair guess, given that Sandy's alimony suit had finally moved center stage. Unable to resolve the dispute, the judge ordered a trial conference for October 1. Now there were two women officially clawing at what they thought was Joe's fortune.

As a result of the judge's ruling, Joe grew more adamant about seeing Sandy in person. When she refused to fly down to New York, he tried to convince her to meet in Boston. Again she refused. They finally agreed to meet on Cape Cod, and Joe made plans to fly into Hyannis Airport.

Within moments of meeting, Joe explained that he wanted to change his will. He asked Sandy to review his plan because of her expertise in estate planning. He wanted to establish one-third trusts for each child and for Diane. He wanted Sandy to control the plan as trustee. Diane would only receive her interest. When she died the principal would go to the children.

Sandy asked him why he wasn't giving Diane her proceeds outright. "It'll drive her crazy that she won't be able to get at the money," said Joe.

He then began reciting his litany of domestic problems, insisting that he did not want Diane to get custody of his children under any circumstances, that she was too irresponsible. He asked Sandy to be their guardian.

"I can't be the guardian. Your wife is their natural guardian. She'd be the guardian if you passed away," Sandy explained.

"Well then, she'll have to have an accident," said Joe.

"Don't be ridiculous," Sandy answered back.

That night Sandy tried to figure out what the hell Joe was up to. If he was to be believed, he was dying. But he had lied and cheated and misled her so many times in the past, she was skeptical, to say the least. One thing was certain, she wasn't about to drop her lawsuit that easily.

Diane wasn't about to give up either. The day after Joe's visit with Sandy, she typed out a five-page letter for her attorneys, detailing Joe's recent and past behavior, including his references to her as a lesbian, his resumed cross dressing, and his use of amphetamines. Diane asserted that Joe had "habitually tried to control my behavior by withholding money, a habit which I fear would continue after divorce."

She described Joe as "controlling and abusive" throughout the marriage, "occasionally physically, and frequently in speech and manner. He was an abused child and is a recovering alcoholic. (Me too.) He is prone to extreme mood swings and can be generous and lavish with praise, in between the angry times. But his moods have been more consistently negative in recent weeks."

According to Diane, Joe denigrated her job and the salary, and told her "my youngest child was not ready for me to work and my father (who is 80 and living in Florida) would most likely die before I had vacation time to see him again." She complained that Joe "took off a great deal of time from work to spend in the country" with the children that summer. "Until this time, he had worked long hours and frequently traveled internationally."

Diane also wrote that Joe had promised he was "definitely planning to kill" her and had told her that "he probably wouldn't survive it either, but that was okay."

Presumably Diane didn't believe the death threats because she stayed. But Diane didn't know the half of it. Joe was busy during these months making more sex tapes, taking the roles of other personalities—Chloe, Jasmine, and Adolph—in the videos.

One of the home-movies scenes began with several cracks of a whip off camera. Then Joe came into view, dressed in a red bathing suit—a woman's bathing suit—and a string of pearls.

He went through more costume changes than a headliner

in Las Vegas as he pranced around to several pounding, thrusting Rolling Stones songs performed by Tina Turner. "I just love dressing," Joe said. "Drag queen. God made me this way."

Applying makeup, he complained about Diane. "She wants to see if I'm still a faggot. She wants more money. I'm a drag queen, fuck it," he said. "I must be macho to my wife. She doesn't like faggots. My legs aren't shaven because I have to appear macho. I love shaving legs. I love wearing bras and panty hose."

During his clothing changes, Joe refused to acknowledge the existence of his penis, using sanitary pads to cover it up.

To aid in his pleasures, he took a sandwich bag filled with white powder from a bureau drawer and snorted several times. He also consumed from a tiny bottle, presumably amyl nitrite. "Coke. I am what I am, I'm both . . . I'm so high."

Wearing a black camisole with a shotgun in hand and a German military helmet on his head, Joe took the role of Adolph. Then he switched from Chloe to Jasmine, with Chloe violently hating Diane and Jasmine wanting to be the real mother for the children.

Joe didn't confine his theatrics to the indoors. The camera rolled in the backyard, in the wooded area leading to the cemetery. He was dressed in a black lace teddy as he carried a shotgun. "Let's get on with the show," he said as he walked off camera. A shotgun blast followed a few seconds later.

At one point, a nervous and agitated Joe picked up the camera and ran through the wooded area. "They're coming. They're coming. Who the fuck cares? Diane knows all about this shit. She's got some pictures and she's taking me to court and taking the kids. Let me just enjoy this."

At another point, he popped up poolside, wearing a woman's bathing suit and an old-fashioned rubber bathing cap. It was a cool night and vapor drifted off the water's surface. Joe grabbed a couple of the children's toys and took a dip.

As the Long Island Rail Road train whistle blew in the background, Joe proclaimed that he was "feeling pretty sexy. This is just some family fun. . . . Oh, Diane. How I hate you."

Joe was quickly losing what little claim to sanity he had left.

Perhaps to counter the visit from Diane's father, Joe's pregnant niece, Edleen Bergelt, and her husband, Keith, were invited to spend the last weekend in September at the Amagansett home. Joe and Diane had been embroiled in yet another bitter dispute the night before. The confrontation had ended with Diane saying she was too tired to drive to the Hamptons in the middle of the night and Joe taking off in a huff with the children.

When the Bergelts arrived that Saturday morning neither Diane nor Joe was there. When they called the Pikul apartment in Manhattan, they were surprised to hear Diane's voice. Diane in turn said she was surprised that Joe and the kids weren't out in the country. Since Joe wasn't in Amagansett, Diane said, she had no idea where he'd gone off to.

Calls by Diane and Edleen's husband to local and highway police failed to yield any clues, and it wasn't until Sunday morning, thirty-six hours after Joe vanished, that Diane heard from him again, and that was by telephone.

Joe said he'd be bringing the kids home in an hour. Instead he called again in midafternoon to tell Diane he now wanted to pick up the children's swim suits. When Diane demanded to know where he'd taken the children, he hung up.

Diane went to the attic to remove the tape from Joe's recorder. She didn't want Joe to know what she'd be up to. In her panic, Diane was afraid she'd disconnected something. Capolupo was performing a countermeasure sweep at a Wall Street brokerage house when his beeper went off. The "security consultant" rushed over to the Pikul apartment and reinserted the tape into the machine. He put everything back like it was supposed to be.

As the afternoon wore on, Diane grew more frantic. One of her friends told her to call the police. Terrified of what Joe might do to her afterward, she declined. It wasn't until 8:30 that Joe finally showed up at Sixth Avenue with Claudia and Blake, who later explained they'd spent the weekend in an unfurnished apartment with a view of the New York Harbor, eating junk food and sleeping on the floor. They'd been at Joe's secret apartment in Battery Park.

Over the next several weeks, Joe continued to take off with the children, unannounced, or neglected to bring them home at the prearranged time. His allegiance to his father growing more by the day, Blake told Diane that Daddy was going to fight to keep the house as well as him and Claudia. For her part, Claudia had started to act out, hysterical with crying fits over the pending divorce and fear she would never see her father again.

In the midst of this turmoil, Joe and his young associate, Jean-Jacques Sunier, departed October 6 on Swissair Flight 101 from Kennedy Airport. It was a frantic-paced trip to Zurich, Amsterdam, and back to Zurich, meeting with top officials at several banks and businesses.

Every night, Joe called home. And every night, by his account, Diane wasn't there. He said he was particularly disturbed that a different baby-sitter was on duty each time, people he did not know.

Most nights after Joe tried to reach Diane, he also called Sandy. She would pick up the phone and mostly listen. "She's out again," Joe complained the night before he returned to the States. "I don't know where the children are, she's been out five nights now, different baby-sitters every night. I don't know who they are. You just can't leave kids with someone you don't know in New York City."

Upon his return, Joe decided he would no longer attend or pay for additional marriage-counseling sessions, at $100 a visit. He made this announcement after the therapist expressed concern that each parent had to know where the children were at all times.

The following Saturday, October 17, 1987, Joe again took off with the children and failed to bring them back when promised. By late afternoon Diane headed for her office, where she spent the evening working on another lengthy letter to her attorneys.

In this missive, she detailed Joe's abusive behavior and accused him of being a drug-using homosexual. Diane said she couldn't figure out if Joe was spending his nights with other women, other men, or alone with his lingerie. She expressed concern about the mounting bills and said she wanted to change her name back to Whitmore. It was time to end the misery for Claudia and Blake, Diane said, begging to be rescued.

For once Diane was confiding her innermost thoughts to her legal representatives, but she still showed ambivalence. In the notes she'd used to prepare the lengthy letters, she mentioned the AIDS issue, and that she'd caught Joe in bed with Claudia, but she didn't mention either point in the actual documents.

The next Monday was Black Monday, the second-worst day in the history of Wall Street. Joe took a beating, and the pressure helped push him to the emotional brink.

During that week, Diane told several acquaintances that she was going to meet Joe in Amagansett for the weekend to divide up the furniture. Friends and co-workers responded with a barrage of advice that she not go. But she would hear none of it. There was an eerie newfound confidence in her voice. "Don't worry, I can handle him."

That Wednesday, the couple headed over to Blake's nursery school, having been summoned by director Marjorie Goldsmith, who wanted to discuss several important issues: where Blake was going to go to school the following year, the sudden switch of his speech therapists, his need for additional speech therapy, and the stress the impending divorce would inflict on the children.

Goldsmith was well aware of the divorce plans. Diane had told her about her rocky marriage as far back as 1985, during a conference the school official had called to discuss Blake's disruptive behavior when he first enrolled. Goldsmith explained that both parents had to be more available to the children, that they had to be on the lookout for regression, and that the children had to be reassured that they still had two parents who loved them, even if one of them was moving out. Both Joe and Diane expressed a willingness to consider Goldsmith's suggestion of joint custody, but when Joe left the room, Diane said without explanation that she didn't expect that to happen.

After the nursery-school meeting, Joe headed to his office, where he promptly placed another call to Sandy, his safety net. With all the pressures building, he told her she *had* to come to New York. As always, Sandy wasn't interested, but gave in when Joe assured her he wanted to discuss settling her alimony suit.

Diane, meanwhile, had personally dropped off her latest letter at Felder's office. Felder subsequently said he confronted Diane in the hallway, expressing special concern over her additional allegation that the children had been blindfolded during their weekend visit to Joe's Battery Park apartment, an allegation contained in neither of her five-page letters.

Felder said he begged her to give the go-ahead for filing a formal order of protection. "To me, this was a bizarre, crazy act. The children were in danger now. If a crazy woman wants to subject herself to it, there's nothing you can do; she's an adult. But I was worried about the kids. Anyone who would blindfold kids—I mean, how many times in your life has anyone said their kids were blindfolded in a car and driven around the city?"

But Diane once again refused to go to court—or cancel her weekend plans. "Don't worry, I can handle him," she assured Felder.

Although her friends later questioned the lawyer's inability to take action, Felder said there was nothing more he could have done. "I'd been through it before with her," he said. "You can't break somebody's arm. She was burdened with a real screwed-up psyche. . . . People like her, they're very fragile people. You've got to be very careful with them. I'm a pretty good judge. I see these people all day. I think she was the typical former alcoholic—masochistic, insecure, with no ego strength." Instead of alcohol, he continued, "the relationships are addictive. These women who come in and say, 'I'm thinking of getting a divorce, what will I get?' They're looking for reasons not to get divorced whenever they ask that. Somebody who really wants to get out says, 'Do the best you can for me, go to court, whatever, I gotta get out of there. In fact, I can't even wait. I'm gonna move out tonight with my kids.' "

But Diane couldn't, or wouldn't, remove herself from Joe's control. "She needed him for whatever reason— some crazy, twisted reason in her head. He must have been at some point a structure for her in her life, which is an indication of the sickness she had, too," said Felder. "It was a misbegotten marriage: two drowning people clutching each other, and they both drown at the end."

After Joe put Claudia to bed in Amagansett that fatal Friday night, he waited for Diane in the baby-sitter's room, watching a tape on the VCR. When Diane came in, he asked her where she'd been so long. They argued. Inside the house, outside the house.

Then Joseph Pikul, father of two, took a blunt object and began smashing his wife's face and head, again and again and again—at least ten times. He struck her in the left cheek, twice above the left eye, twice on the right temple, once on the left temple. Her eyeballs popped. He whacked her on the left side, creating a ten-centimeter hemorrhage on her rib cage.

Then he began strangling her. He choked her for at least thirty seconds, the minimum time for killing a person. In the process he broke a bone in her larynx. Diane became light-headed, then unconscious. Then she slumped to the ground, never to rise.

At some point during the early-morning hours, Joe put Diane's body into the Mazda and drove the one-tenth of a mile to the end of Windmill Lane and onto a potato patch. He looked around for a place to bury her, found none to his satisfaction, and departed, leaving tire tracks in the process. He then headed northeast toward the bay side of Long Island.

At Alberts Landing Road, he made a right turn and headed for the lower portion of Gardiners Bay. As he would later recount in his most consistent version of events, he then made another right turn, onto Little Alberts Landing Road, and stopped the car in the small parking lot at the edge of the beach.

He carried his wife's body, one hand on the collar of her Ralph Lauren shirt and the other on the waistband of her corduroy black skirt. The shirt collar ripped and the metal clasp on the waistband bent open. He knotted the ripped portions of the shirt to form a handle.

He then tried to bury her in the sand, but her legs ended up sticking out. No doubt terrified by the sight, he dug her back up, put her body back into the Mazda, and returned to the house.

After Joe transferred Diane from the Mazda to the rear well of the station wagon, he went inside and fell asleep in his favorite recliner.

The next day, he wrapped her body in the green tarp he used to cover the sports car whenever he left it out in Amagansett. Then he used the ice he purchased at the deli to preserve the corpse. Between the tarp and the body, he laid out two plastic sheets that he and Diane had used to protect their pool chairs from the elements.

There was a long cord, much like telephone wire, that Joe had used to cinch the tarp around the Mazda. Now he used it to keep Diane in place.

He grabbed the belt from his peach terrycloth robe, the one with the words "Hotel Ritz, Paris" sewn in next to the establishment's insignia, and tied Diane's wrists together.

He got some white clothesline and pink cord out of a utility closet. He tied a knot around Diane's neck, then her feet. He stuffed the inside of the tarp with beach towels, a small beach blanket, a pink throw rug, and a multicolored terrycloth bathrobe. Then Joe wrapped the tarp closed.

With Diane stored in the rear well of the Buick wagon, he loaded the top of the back storage area with suitcases and kids' sleeping bags, blankets, a kitchen knife, his 20-gauge pump shotgun, and the rest of the stuff he bought at the hardware store.

The Pikul family was finally set to visit Henry and Louise Sawoska.

PART · III

THE
INVESTIGATION

C H A P T E R • 10

A Shower and a Shampoo

THE MONDAY AFTER DIANE'S DISAPPEARANCE, October 26, 1987, the phone rang at 5:58 A.M. in the Sawoska house. It was Joe calling about his kids from a phone booth at the corner of Sixth Avenue and Eleventh Street in Manhattan. He was too paranoid to use his home phone, so he went out into the street—where he proceeded to use his company telephone credit card.

The Sawoskas were in the process of getting their children ready for school and themselves ready for work. Louise was also in the process of trying to get a neighbor to baby-sit for Claudia and Blake because she had no idea where their father had disappeared to. "You know, I've got to go to work," she curtly told Joe when he called. He apologized and said he was definitely on his way. Louise was relieved since she and Henry had decided that if Joe didn't surface that morning, they were going to call the state police and report him missing.

Before starting out, Joe made a second call, to the cleaning lady Christine Hamilton, waking her up to tell her the new security code for the house in the Hamptons. Then he grabbed a cup of coffee and a buttered roll, checked on Diane's body in the back of the wagon, and headed north, toward the New York Thruway.

He'd spent an entire weekend trying to find a suitable burial spot and failed. He knew he was out of time. The car was starting to smell, the rug was loaded with wet sand,

and the ice had melted. Most important, he *had* to get rid of Diane before he picked up the kids.

At a quarter to seven Joe stopped on the Palisades Interstate Parkway in Englewood, New Jersey, and tried once again to reach Sandy's lawyer-friend, Vinnie Federico. Just as he had the day before when he'd been riding around Massachusetts, Joe got the answering machine.

Once on the New York Thruway, it wasn't long until the Sawoskas' exit. Now Joe was really out of time. With just a few minutes to go, he noticed a small pull-off, at Milepost 56.5. He parked the car, opened the rear gate, grabbed Diane's tarp-covered corpse, and carried it down the embankment to the edge of a culvert. This was it. After all those years of bickering and fighting, this was goodbye.

The five-pound weight was still attached to the cord, so Joe placed that on top of Diane, then grabbed a nearby tire and positioned it atop the canvas as well. He climbed back up the side of the hill and back into his car. Within a couple of minutes he was paying his toll at the Newburgh exit.

Then using a public telephone outside a Denny's Restaurant, Joe called the kids' schools back in Manhattan to tell them Claudia and Blake would be absent. Seven miles later, he arrived at the Sawoskas, where Louise, who by now was upset and scared, was waiting anxiously. Henry had already left for his job in the city.

It was just nine. At first Joe didn't come into the house proper; he sat on the stairwell in the front foyer, with his head down, looking nervous and haggard. After a few minutes he rose and entered the family room, plopping himself on a couch. "We were so worried about you," said Louise.

"I'm sorry," he answered. Claudia and Blake ran to their father and hugged him, kissed him, and hugged him some more.

Joe was carrying the children's things out to the car when the phone rang. It was Henry, wondering if his long-lost roommate had shown up to collect his children after disappearing for thirty-four hours. Louise ran outside to get Joe, but he was in no mood to talk to anyone, especially a friend who could reasonably be expected to ask some tough questions in the wake of the weekend's events.

Joe said he'd call Henry at his office and hurriedly drove off.

Christine Hamilton headed over to Windmill Lane about eight that morning. Inside the house, she found a scrub brush and cleaning supplies strewn along one of the sliding glass doors, an unusual situation since the Pikuls were very careful about keeping such household goods locked in childproofed cabinets. Two of the products, a window cleaner and a scouring cleanser, were open, and Hamilton couldn't find the bucket she usually used for mopping the floor.

Hamilton also found some bed linen in the washer and dryer, and noticed that the green tarp cover was missing from Joe's Mazda. She dusted, vacuumed, cleaned the bathroom and kitchen, then departed about midday.

As Joe drove along Route 32 in the Vails Gate section of New Windsor, Claudia and Blake started clamoring for fast food, so he pulled into a McDonald's for breakfast. As the children enjoyed the playground, Joe called his office from a public telephone to check for any messages and to tell them he'd been delayed. There *was* a message, in fact, left by a fellow named Doug Ellis from *Harper's* magazine. Joe wasn't in a hurry to return that call; he decided *Harper's* could wait.

Instead, Joe called Henry Sawoska at New York University Medical Center, where he worked, and apologized for his disappearing act. He claimed he'd taken some sinus pills and fallen asleep on Sunday. "The children had a very good time," he said. "We should get together again sometime."

After breakfast, Joe hit the phones again, trying unsuccessfully to connect with attorney Federico at his home in Massachusetts, then at his office. He left messages both times. At eleven, he also placed a call to *Harper's*. Doug Ellis, vice-president and general manager, wasn't around at that moment, so he talked to the receptionist.

"Has Diane come in yet?" he asked. The receptionist said she hadn't. Joe explained that he and Diane had fought over the weekend and that she had left him. "I think she ran off with a boyfriend," he said before hanging up.

When Ann Stern, assistant to the editor, arrived in the office, she was informed that Diane had failed to appear for work and was not answering at any of her phone numbers. Since joining *Harper's* in March, Diane had never been absent without calling in. Given their knowledge of her tumultuous home life, Joe's threatening behavior, and her plans for the weekend, Stern and her co-workers became very concerned. They reached for Diane's Rolodex and started calling around.

Randi Warner, another of Diane's co-workers, called First Presbyterian Nursery School, where no one had seen Blake or his mother, but someone in the office had taken a call about Blake still being in "the country" with his family. Claudia was likewise absent from school.

Stern then called the Sixth Precinct, the police station that covers the Pikul duplex in Greenwich Village. She spoke to Detective Eddie Ambrositis. Ambro, as he is known, went over to 446 Sixth Avenue, knocked on the door, rang the doorbell, but no one answered.

Ambro returned to his business, for in New York City missing-persons calls are routine, literally by the thousands citywide, and almost always the "missing" person shows up. Essentially, all Stern reported was that a co-worker mired in a marital breakup had failed to show up for work, on a Monday no less. The department would need 10,000 extra cops to check out every call like that.

At 12:38 P.M. Stern placed a call to the East Hampton Police Department, which covers Amagansett. She told the dispatcher she was concerned about the welfare of a colleague at *Harper's* magazine, Diane Pikul, who had failed to report for work after supposedly spending the weekend at her home on Windmill Lane.

Police Officer Richard Faulhaber, dispatched to the Pikul residence, arrived there ten minutes later, noticing a Mazda parked in the driveway. He looked around the grounds and tried all the doors. He then radioed back that the house was secure and that no one was home. Since everything appeared to be in order, Faulhaber departed. Within the next half hour, a guard from the Holmes Protection Service arrived, entered the house, and looked around. Finding the house empty, the guard locked up.

At 1:44 P.M., the East Hampton PD called Stern back to tell her Diane was not inside the house. Stern said she wanted the area around the house searched and the inside of the house investigated further, but was told that Diane would have to be reported missing in New York City, her official domicile.

By midafternoon, the phones were ringing off the hook among Diane's circle of friends. They sensed that something terrible had occurred, and not being versed in the ways of bureaucracy, they couldn't understand why the cops weren't jumping into high gear. At three, Stern again called the East Hampton authorities, who this time somehow got the impression Diane was an editor. Stern was again told to call NYPD.

It was a nice day that Monday, hot for late October, and manager Steve Frank and a couple of his men were making small talk near the pumps at the Exxon station on Route 17K in the town of Newburgh, less than a mile from the Thruway exit, when Joe's blue Buick station wagon with wood-grain side panels suddenly came screeching in. The car slid on the gravel as Joe jammed on the brakes, almost hitting Frank and co-worker Larry Curfman.

Joe jumped out and anxiously requested if there was a car wash around.

"You just passed one," said one of the men, pointing to a large Texaco sign several hundred yards back up the highway.

Joe said he wanted a place that would vacuum his car as well. He didn't explain why, but Claudia had complained about the strange smell. Assured that the Stewart Car Wash would do the job, he took off as fast as he had arrived.

Car-wash owner Otto Rusch and employee Davey Joe Moshinski, Jr., were working out front when they noticed an older bearded man drive in about 11:30, accompanied by two kids—a young girl and an even younger boy. Joe was dressed like a businessman on vacation—wearing a light pullover sweater, corduroy slacks, and white boating sneakers—but he looked terrible, like he'd slept in the clothes. Joe was in need of a shower and a shampoo. More importantly, so was his car.

"Can I have four dollars in change for the vacuum?" Joe asked Moshinski.

Joe drove the Buick onto the automated conveyor system, staying in the car with the kids for the enjoyment of going under the huge powerful sprays. Claudia and Blake were ecstatic to be back with their father. They were having fun again.

Attendant Michael Gordon wiped the car dry, and Joe asked for a couple of extra towels for the interior. He then drove the car to the vacuum area, where he opened the rear gate, removed a large plastic trash bag, and headed toward the rear of the large property, to a giant green dumpster. Joe pushed some of the garbage to the left and some of it to the right, then placed his bag in the middle. Before leaving, he threw some garbage on top to cover up his deposit.

Returning to the car, he began stripping it, right down to the mats. There were sleeping bags, shopping bags, plastic garbage bags, a gym bag, pillows. Joe laid it all out on the center island of the vacuum area at breakneck speed. The low, center aisle wall, about twenty-five feet long, was literally covered. It looked like a rummage sale.

Suddenly Joe walked back to the dumpster and started digging through the debris. Car-wash manager James Mitchell, exiting from the bathroom nearby, looked over at the dumpster and thought someone had wandered in off the street to search for returnable soda bottles. But as he looked closer, Mitchell realized it was the guy with the Buick. He turned to Gordon and gestured: "What's this guy doing?" Gordon shrugged his shoulders and smiled.

Joe had returned to the dumpster to retrieve a small cassette player he had discarded in his frenzy to rid himself of Diane's belongings. Mitchell watched Joe walk back to the vacuum area with the tape deck, place the machine on the back floor of the car, then begin tossing items into a nearby garbage can—a curling iron and women's underwear, among other things. Moshinski razzed Joe about the female gear.

"Is that your stuff?"

Joe was far from amused. "It's not mine."

Cognizant of the fact that he needed an extremely thorough cleanup and realizing that the wall vacs weren't doing such a great job on the sand and water, he asked for assistance. Moshinski said he'd help out as soon as he could.

But Joe was impatient, and after several minutes he walked over to Moshinski and stepped on his foot. "When are you going to start working on my car?"

Davey Joe hastened over to Joe's car immediately. Then, just like that, Joe started talking. "My wife left me. I found a box of someone else's condoms underneath the bed. I took the children and I left."

As he chattered on, Moshinski worked his way to the rear of the car. But before he could get to the third seat in the back, Joe put it down and locked it into place. That area remained unvacuumed.

Moshinski went off to get his change supply replenished. "That guy just cleaned me out of quarters. I need more," he told Mitchell.

Joe entered the office area as well and asked Mitchell's wife, Lori the cashier, if he could use the phone. She immediately noticed that he was missing an upper front tooth. Joe explained that someone was expecting a call from him at noon. It was now 11:50. Lori, who'd been read the riot act by Rusch recently for letting too many customers use the private phone, told him he would have to ask the owner, who had gone off to the bank.

Joe waited impatiently. When Rusch returned, he raced over to ask permission to make a long distance call. At first Rusch said no, but relented when Joe promised to use his credit card.

Instantly, Joe was in action—elbows planted on the counter, telephone to his ear, briefcase opened on the counter. It was now 12:12 P.M. First Joe tried to reach Vinnie Federico, "Could you have him call me back?" he said, leaving the car-wash telephone number. Then he called Sandy, but she, too, was out. So he left a brief message on her answering machine: "The package is down."

Joe turned to Lori Mitchell and explained he was expecting a callback. "Okay," she said. "What's your name?"

Silence.

"So I know the call's for you when it comes in," Lori insisted.

"My name is Joe."

"Are you moving in here?" she asked, having noticed the bags spread out in the vacuum area.

"No. I've been away with friends. My wife left me—again—so I took the kids to clear my head," he said. "She was screwing around. I found condoms under the bed and they weren't mine. I took the kids upstate to be with friends." He also mentioned that there'd been a "big drop" in the stock market—which made no sense since Lori Mitchell would never have guessed that the disheveled customer was vice-president of a major Wall Street firm.

Lori felt sorry for Joe. She also felt embarrassed by his bizarre candor.

Joe returned to his car and decided that he needed a bucket to shampoo the interior carpet. Gordon checked with Rusch, who turned down the request. "We can't give you a bucket to shampoo because we do it and you'd be taking our business away," Gordon explained. "We'll do it if you want."

"Great," Joe answered as Rusch came over to chat. After several minutes of small talk, Rusch went inside to ask Jim Mitchell if he was interested in shampooing the car of some rich guy from the Hamptons. Mitchell said he was, and after he finished totaling up the previous day's gasoline and car-wash sales, he stepped outside to speak to Joe. "How ya doing? You need an estimate to get your carpets cleaned?"

"Yes," said Joe. "I've been away, upstate visiting friends. And I haven't had the car cleaned since I bought it"—more than a year ago. Joe explained that the car was loaded with sand. "I want the sand out of here no matter what." He said he didn't care how long the job took or what it cost. "Just do it," he said.

As Mitchell surveyed the car, Blake began talking to him. But Mitchell, whose daughter was about a year older than Blake, couldn't understand him. He couldn't understand Joe that well either. He thought both of them seemed to be stuttering.

"I don't care what it costs. I gotta get it clean," said

Joe, launching into another speech. "I had to get away for a while. I was looking for a pair of shoes under the bed at home and I found rubbers." At first, Joe's story didn't click. Mitchell thought he was talking about galoshes.

Joe repeated: "I found rubbers under the bed. She's screwing around on me." And again Mitchell gave him a puzzled stare.

"My wife's screwing around on me. She has a lover. She must have run off with him. She disappeared. I haven't seen her."

Now it sank in. Standing there next to the vacuum-cleaning unit and the water bucket and an aisle full of belongings, Mitchell didn't know what to say. He was taken aback by this total stranger exposing his personal life. So he said nothing.

"Come on," Joe told Blake. "Get out of the car. He's gonna take it and clean it." Blake got out and Mitchell drove the Buick inside the building. Joe stood in the door-way between the office area and the garage, staring at Mitchell as he labored over the backseat area. There certainly was plenty of sand stuck between the sides of the seats. Joe eventually approached for a closer inspection. "Is it really messy?"

"No," Mitchell replied as he continued to shampoo the backseat area. "You just have a lot of sand."

Joe left the garage, but it wasn't long before he reentered, this time through the front overhangs. Having reconsidered his earlier reluctance to have the rear well cleaned, he opened the back gate, a swing-out type, and told Mitchell: "I want you to get the back hatch area, too, because it's really dirty back there."

"Okay," Mitchell said as Joe flipped up the carpeted top of the rear area, exposing the third seat—and much more sand.

Mitchell climbed into the well and began scrubbing heavily. Again Joe started talking. "She's been screwing around on me. I found rubbers under the bed. She took off on me. She must've run away with her lover." He said he'd discovered the condoms while looking for one of his children's shoes and that he was certain they were not his brand.

Mitchell kept scrubbing away. The area was loaded with

sand, and the more he scrubbed, the more sand came to the surface. It was shooting out all over the place.

"How bad is it back there?" Joe inquired.

"Well, you know, there *is* a lot of sand."

"But it's not real messy or anything?" Joe asked, concerned that he'd left more than sand behind.

"No, just a lot of sand."

It was now about a quarter to one, and Joe walked back into the office to make some more calls. "How long does it take to get from here to New York?" he asked Lori Mitchell.

"About ninety minutes."

"I have to call my secretary," he said.

Actually, Joe first tried to reach Federico at home again. Still no luck. Then he tried the lawyer's office, where he spoke to a secretary. Next he called Sandy at home, leaving another brief message on her machine, explaining that he'd picked up the children and was returning to New York. Then he called Arnhold & S. Bleichroeder and told his employer he was running late.

Joe then turned to Lori and, as though not realizing he'd already told her his story, started talking again about the stock-market crash and how his wife had left him, how he'd found a condom, and how it wasn't his brand.

Claudia came into the office and said: "Daddy, we need air fresheners. The car smells." She picked out sixteen air fresheners and Joe paid for them with a fifty-dollar bill. He then headed back to the vacuum aisle.

A few minutes later, Lori entered the garage and told her husband: "The little boy just fell off the wall." Like most personal-service employees, the Mitchells' immediate fear was that the customer might sue, even though the wall was not very high. Then, too, as parents they were concerned that Blake might have hurt himself. Mitchell went into the front store area and looked out the big window. Joe was sitting on the wall, holding Blake in his lap. Mitchell felt sorry for the man, thinking to himself: "This guy's wife is having a good ol' time, you know, God knows where, and here's this poor guy trying to take care of two kids."

Mitchell didn't want to push the issue so he just watched from the window. Joe was rocking Blake on his knee. The kid wasn't crying and didn't appear to be hurt. Mitchell decided there was no need to file an accident report and went back to the Buick.

Joe came into the store area to try Federico's office one more time. It was now 1:17 P.M. "I *have* to meet him," he told whoever answered, "I'm leaving the country tonight."

Outside, Jim Mitchell completed the shampoo without ever touching the front section of the car—the driver's side or the passenger side. Joe was satisfied. There was nothing incriminating there.

Mitchell backed the car out of the garage and over to the vacuum aisle, where he told Moshinski to vacuum it out again.

As Joe walked back over, Mitchell noticed a light brown gun case, vinyl with a zipper, amid Joe's aisle of debris.

"What kind of gun you got there?" he asked.

"It's a 20-gauge shotgun."

"Can I look at it?"

"Sure." Joe took the weapon out of its case.

"Boy, that's nice," said Mitchell.

"Yeah, I bought it a couple of years ago. I bought it to shoot rats in my backyard. I only shot it twice, though. I'm worried for the children. I'm afraid one of them is going to get hurt with it. I had the gun in the house and it accidentally discharged and I almost shot myself in the foot. I blew a hole through the floor of the bedroom. If you're interested in it, I'll sell it to you."

"What do you want for it?"

"I'll tell you what, make me an offer."

Mitchell looked the gun over. He didn't want to give a price because he wanted to see what kind of money Joe was expecting first. "I don't know what it's worth. What do you want for it?"

"Give me twenty-five dollars."

In the back of his mind, Mitchell knew something wasn't right. Still, he figured, "Take it. Don't be stupid." He pulled out his wallet immediately, extracted twenty-five dollars, and got himself a hell of a deal. By the looks of it, the gun was probably worth at least $350.

"Daddy, don't sell the gun," said Claudia. "I want it. I want to hang it on my wall."

"No. I'll get you another gun when you're older. You're too young right now," Joe told his daughter.

"Oh, Daddy," said Claudia, disappointed.

Joe took the money, and Mitchell got the gun, no receipt.

Joe turned back to Mitchell. "You can't have the case. I gotta have the case."

Remington in hand, Jim Mitchell headed into the store area to show his wife Lori. "What did you buy now?"

"I bought a shotgun. But he sold it to me for twenty-five dollars," Mitchell said. Afraid the gun might be broken or stolen, he had Lori write down Joe's license plate on an envelope.

Mitchell took the gun into his office, then grabbed the envelope and walked over to the big plate-glass window to double-check the plate number. He wrote down Joe's explanation for selling the gun on the other side of the envelope, then put it aside for safekeeping.

Just then Rusch walked by. "Otto, look what I just bought."

"What'd ya pay for that?"

"The guy just sold it to me for twenty-five bucks."

"You're shitting me," said Rusch, taking the gun from Mitchell. Rusch removed the barrel and began looking it over. While cleaning the rest of the weapon, Mitchell noticed white scuff marks on the surface. It wasn't as if paint had spilled on the gun, but rather as if the gun had been pounded into a wall painted white. Mitchell rubbed and rubbed, but he couldn't get all the white off. He also noticed a hairline crack in the thinnest part of the stock, as if that, too, had been pounded against a hard surface. "This hit something," said Mitchell.

Just then, Mike Gordon brought the money in—thirty-five dollars for the shampoo and a ten-dollar tip for Jim Mitchell. There was another five for Lori and five for Davey Joe. Rusch saw the money and sent Gordon back out to ask Joe if he wanted an oil change. But Joe wasn't interested, explaining he'd get one next time he was in the area.

"You know, he was saying some really strange stuff," Lori said to the group as Joe drove off.

"He was telling me about how his wife was screwing around on him," said Mitchell.

"He probably offed his wife with the shotgun," added Rusch.

"Yeah. His wife and her lover," said Mitchell.

Everyone enjoyed a lusty snicker except Lori; she thought it was all disgusting.

When Joe pulled out of the Stewart Car Wash about 1:30, he'd been there an incredible two hours.

On the way out of town, he stopped at the Exxon station again. For some reason, he had failed to buy gas at the car wash. After filling up, he asked if he could use the pay phone. At 1:43 P.M., once again using a credit card, he called *Harper's*.

"Did Diane come in yet? It's not like her not to call in," Joe told the receptionist. The woman said Diane had still not appeared or telephoned. This time Joe spoke with Doug Ellis, the general manager and vice-president, telling him it was "unthinkable" that Diane had not called in.

Growing restless with the day's itinerary, Claudia and Blake began running around the station, playfully fighting with each other. In between calls, Joe told the kids to get back in the car, but they paid little mind to their father with the phone to his ear.

Meanwhile, the gas station attendants yelled at Joe several times to move his car, which he had abandoned in front of the pumps, but Joe didn't listen either. "In a minute, in a minute," he kept saying.

With Joe finally off the phone, the Pikul family—what was left of it—headed back to New York City.

Jim Mitchell and Otto Rusch took off for the back woods with the shotgun. Jim wanted to test it out with a little squirrel hunting. He fired the gun once to make sure it was all right, then pop—one shot, one dead squirrel.

Back at the station, Mike Gordon and Dave Bowman, two of the young wash-and-dry crew, came in to show Lori Mitchell their astonishing discovery; they'd found credit cards in the dumpster.

"Something is wrong here," said Lori, who previously had worked for two years in the credit-card department of a major New York City bank. "Number one, when you throw away credit cards, you tear them up." Anyone could go out and use these cards. "You better show Jimmy these when he comes back."

Then Bowman brought in a knife he found. "Get that thing away from me. Just get it out of here," Lori insisted.

When Mitchell and Rusch returned to the station about 3:45 P.M., they were met by a very upset cashier. Bowman apparently had no intention of showing the bosses the credit cards or the knife. "These kids are walking around with credit cards that are still good," said Lori, explaining that the bearded man with the missing tooth had apparently thrown away a big batch of his wife's plastic.

"Who's got 'em?" Mitchell asked.

"Mike and Dave," said Lori, adding that Mike had already put a couple of them in his wallet.

"Tell Mike to come here," Mitchell told his wife as she left to pick up their daughter at school.

Mike entered the office, his hands full of credit cards. "Look what I got," he said. It didn't work, but Mitchell wasn't very angry. His workers were basically okay boys and probably didn't have the nerve to try anything anyway. But he wasn't about to take a chance. "Give them to me," he said. Mike handed over several cards, including one for Saks and one for Bloomingdale's. They appeared to be current.

"Dave Bowman has some, too," said Mike Gordon.

"I want these credit cards. You tell Dave to give me whatever he's got," said Mitchell.

Bowman came in a few minutes later with his booty. "You should see all the stuff this guy threw away," said Gordon.

"Bring me what you got," said Mitchell. "I want to see what's out there." The two left and Gordon returned with a small hand vacuum cleaner, a wallet, and some costume jewelry.

"Dave Bowman's got a knife that this guy threw away," Gordon said.

"You tell Dave I want to see the knife," said Mitchell.

Bowman brought the knife in—a twelve-inch Italian import with a seven-inch blade; black handle, red trim. The tip of the blade had a stain on it, perhaps blood. It was also bent.

Mitchell looked over at Rusch. "Something's not right here."

"Maybe we should notify somebody," answered Rusch.

Mitchell agreed.

At that moment, Officer Greg Crisci of the Newburgh Police Department pulled up in his cruiser. The department had a contract with the car wash, so it wasn't that unusual for patrol cars to roll through.

Crisci and Mitchell knew each other well, having worked together several years back as ambulance emergency medical technicians. Lori and Crisci had gone to high school together. Mitchell spotted his buddy and went over. "You know, there was some guy here earlier this afternoon who got his car cleaned and he threw out a bunch of stuff. A lot of it is like current credit cards and stuff. We found a knife, too, and we figure we should notify somebody."

"Let me get the car washed. When I go through, I'll come back around and I'll talk to you," Crisci told him.

Crisci's unit went through the rollers and he pulled up to the front bays. Mitchell told him the story in more detail. It wasn't Crisci's patrol area, so he called headquarters. Officer Gary Cooper responded within minutes, and Officer Margaret Hansen followed shortly thereafter in a second unit.

Rusch, Mitchell, and Moshinski showed Cooper the credit cards and the knife. Mitchell failed to mention the shotgun, figuring that if nothing came of the episode, he could avoid any hassles in getting the gun back.

Officers Cooper and Hansen, along with Rusch and Mitchell, headed out back for the dumpster. Mitchell got the officers a giant green plastic bag, the ones used to collect recycled soda cans, and the officers started collecting the items.

There were several pairs of brand-new panty hose, the shrink wrap still in place. There was women's underwear: bras, panties, a bluish green teddy; a pair of jumbo-sized women's pumps.

"This guy's got a big wife," said Mitchell. The panty hose were queen size. He looked at a black bra and a pair of black, lacy bikini panties. They, too, were very large.

Everyone decided the underwear was "pretty gross" and declined to touch any of the garments. Cooper used his pen to gingerly lift them up one at a time.

Mitchell picked up one of the shoes. "These things are humongous," he said. He thought to himself: "This guy's wife must be one big heff."

Back at the station, Cooper began vouchering the recovered items. He marked his initials—GRC—on the inside or back.

Cooper logged in a Black & Decker car vacuum, a Ray-o-Vac flashlight, the fisherman's rubber gloves, and a twelve-inch Sanelli knife from Italy, seven-inch blade, black handle, red plastic trim.

In the ladies' underwear category, he recorded a white Felina bra, three Lady Marlene bras—in pink, white, and black—one pair of black Lady Marlene panties, six pairs of panty hose, and three pairs of light brown stockings. The seizure also included one Tripp tank top, gray-striped, a pair of gold socks, a pair of bright pink socks, and a pair of black pumps.

Diane's yellow Poco Loco gym bag was there, too, along with Joe's costume jewelry and an imitation gray fur rug.

Two Italian-made wallets belonging to Diane were also recovered: the brown leather one contained twenty dollars; the other—a ten-pouch, maroon credit-card holder—bore a gold inscription "handmade Bloomingdale's."

The pile of credit cards left a trail of clues to their owner's life-style: three from Bloomingdale's, an orange one for Mrs. Joseph J. Pikul, a yellow one for Miss Diane Whitmore, and a silver one for Mrs. Joseph J. Pikul. There were cards from B. Altman, Sears, Saks Fifth Avenue, and Macy's, a Chase Manhattan Visa, Chase Manhattan twenty-four-hour bank card, American Express, several telephone company cards, a check-cashing card for a Sixth Avenue market, an expired library card, and a Blue Cross–Blue Shield card from Arnhold & S. Bleichroeder Inc.

Some of the cards were made out to Diane Pikul. Others were issued to Diane Whitmore. Still more bore the names Diane Whitmore Pikul, Diane J. Pikul, Diane J. Whitmore, Joseph J. Pikul, and Mrs. Joseph Pikul. The Ellis First National Bank ID card from New Port Richey, Florida, was issued to Donald Whitmore or Diane J. Whitmore. Several of the items carried a New York City address.

At a minimum, Cooper and Hansen thought the circumstances to be unusual. They informed their desk sergeant, then Hansen called Sergeant Michael Clancy at home. Clancy in turn called Detective John Smith, and both men reported immediately to the station house.

CHAPTER • 11

Missing Person
No. 13150

BY LATE MONDAY AFTERNOON, THERE was still no sign of Diane Pikul in Manhattan or Amagansett. The *Harper's* people had continued to run through the Rolodex, calling everyone—even Diane's private eye Bo Dietl, an ex–New York City police detective. Friends were calling friends were calling friends. All of the calls were futile. One friend was certain Joe had killed Diane, another thought maybe she'd gone over the edge and got drunk.

But as the hours passed, everyone began to fear the worst and started kicking themselves for having allowed Diane to stay with her husband.

Joe, meanwhile, arrived back in the city about four o'clock. He took the kids upstairs, unpacked the car, and drove it over to the garage. As the kids began to unwind, he picked up the telephone. First he called Federico at his office, then at his home. At last, the two men connected. Federico agreed to fly down to Manhattan and meet with Joe that evening. Joe then called Christine Hamilton to verify that she had cleaned the house.

Then Carina Jacobson, one of the baby-sitters, called, having been alerted to Diane's disappearance by one of the *Harper's* people. Jacobson said she'd come over to help. Joe agreed and decided it was time for a rest.

But others were picking up their pace. Shortly before six, Donald Whitmore, Diane's father, placed a call to the police in East Hampton to express concern about his daughter's whereabouts. At about the same time, Ann

Stern redialed the number for the Sixth Precinct in Greenwich Village, where she was connected to Detective William Glynn.

In the New York City Police Department, cases are assigned to detectives in rotation, much like judges get assigned to cases. When a new case comes up, it goes to the detective at the top of the list. The process is known as "catching a case," and Bill Glynn—chain-smoker, brown hair, graying sideburns—was about to "catch" the Pikul case.

Stern identified herself as a co-worker of Diane Whitmore Pikul, who had failed to show up for work that morning. She said Diane was very dependable and had never been absent without calling in since she started working at the magazine seven months ago. "It's completely out of character," Stern told Glynn. "Diane is the type of person who would never leave the children without making some sort of arrangement for them."

Stern also explained that Diane was having trouble with her husband and that they were in the process of divorcing. She told Glynn that Diane had been depressed all week about the prospect of going out to Amagansett, but had told her "she was going out to make arrangements to clear up the estate. I'm very concerned for her safety." She then expressed a fear that Joe had locked Diane in the Amagansett basement, where she was "being held against her will."

Diane's husband had a violent temper, Stern explained. "I wouldn't put it past him to hurt her. I feel something is very wrong. I have a feeling she's out there, she needs help."

At about the same time that Stern and Glynn were talking, Randi Warner, another of Diane's co-workers, connected with Joe at the Sixth Avenue duplex. "Where's Diane?"

"We had a fight and she walked out. I don't know where she is," Joe answered. Warner doubted the truthfulness of that story and told Joe that several people at *Harper's* had been making calls all day, including queries to the cops in East Hampton and to the Sixth Precinct. She mentioned Detectives Ambrositis and Glynn by name. Diane wasn't in Florida either, said Warner, because they'd already checked with her father.

Joe exploded. "How dare you frighten an old man? I have this thing under control. It's strictly a family matter." Figuring he'd better find out what Don Whitmore was up to, he then dialed Florida. He told Whitmore that Diane was missing, which of course Whitmore already knew from the people at *Harper's*. In the course of the conversation, Whitmore mentioned that he'd already called the police in East Hampton and that they'd told him the house was empty.

It was 6:34 P.M. when Harry Field, a police radio dispatcher for the town of East Hampton, took Joe's next call.

"This is Joe Pikul. I live here with my wife." Field gave an "ah-huh" on the line. "I guess some people asked for the house to be looked after. Was that a call made to you, or what?"

"What's your name again?" asked Field.

"Joe Pikul. P-I-K-U-L. I mean, my caretaker, I guess— Amagansett doesn't have a police department." Stuttering, Joe sounded as if he wasn't sure where he wanted to go with the conversation.

"Right, that's us," said Field.

"Yeah, okay, what time did you make that call?" Joe asked, wanting to know when the Holmes security people came to look at the house.

"Umm, two o'clock," said Field.

"Oh, two, okay," said Joe. "Of course, everything was in order, I guess, right? I mean, she's not there."

"No, we haven't found anybody," said Field.

"Yeah," said Joe. "No, she left, you know. They got awful excited at the office. I was taking the day off, you know. I got back about three or four hours ago and so, um, we'll see, you know, check with her friends here and see what's happening, you know."

Field asked Joe if he was presently in the Hamptons. "No, no, no, I'm not home," said Joe. "No, I'm back in the city."

"Oh, you're in the city," said Field.

"Yeah, yeah, these guys get very excited. I don't know. You know, I wouldn't get that excited, but she's disappeared before, you know." Field gave another "ah-huh."

"And it never bothered me. But the only thing that's different this time is she didn't call the office," said Joe.

"Right," answered Field.

"She's done it differently. She leaves for days, you know, doesn't tell me where she is and, uh, so that doesn't bother me and, uh, I had the kids all weekend but I'll let you guys know, uh, and, uh—she wasn't there though, right?"

"No," said Field.

"Okay, uh," said Joe.

"Do you have any idea where she could be?"

Joe really started to stammer. "I—I—I—I don't, I don't—"

"She just takes off?" asked Field.

"She has a boyfriend, I think," offered Joe.

"Ah-huh."

"And I'm not sure; I know, I think I know who he is," Joe continued, going into a multiple-choice mode. "I think I know who he is. And I'm going to have to check that out, you know. And, um, I'm trying, you know, I'm trying to check it out from New York now and see what happens now, you know."

"Right," said Field.

"How long is it, you know, before you file a missing-persons thing anyways?" asked Joe.

"Umm, gosh, you could, you know, you do it within twenty-four hours. There's no really set time," said Field, sixty-five-plus hours after Diane's disappearance.

"You know, yeah, you see, I don't wanna, I don't wanna panic because I've known her. Tomorrow I would definitely do something, you know," explained Joe.

"Right," said Field.

"But I would give her twenty-four hours here, you know," said Joe.

"Right," said Field.

"So, um, what's your name, Officer?"

"Field."

"Field. So, um, my number, let me give you my number if you want to chat with me," said Joe. Field took down the number at the Sixth Avenue apartment. "Yeah, Joe Pikul. And I'll be here today and tomorrow. I'll—I'll probably stay here. If not, I'll be at the office, which is area code 212-943-9200. Or I might come out there, I don't know, you know."

"Okay," said Field.

"So anyways, Officer Field, I'll be in contact."

"Okay, thanks for your help," said Field.

"Right, thank you."

"Right, 'bye."

The call took just three minutes. Joe hung up and immediately dialed the Sixth Precinct, where he reached Glynn.

"The people at *Harper's* magazine gave me your name," Joe said. He explained that his wife's co-workers had told him he "had better talk" to Glynn because Diane had not shown up at work and they were concerned about her. He then began explaining that he'd driven out to his home in Amagansett with his children the previous Friday. His wife, Diane, had driven out on her own, arriving at approximately 1:30 A.M. Joe said he and his wife got into an argument and Diane then "walked out of the house and did not return." He said he had no idea where his wife was but expected her home shortly. "She's taken off before. I thought she would have been back by now."

Joe also told Glynn he'd found some used condoms while looking under the bed for his daughter's sneaker that Saturday morning. "They don't belong to me," he declared, adding that as a result he concluded that Diane had to have a boyfriend. Maybe she was with him.

At that point, Joe sought Glynn's advice. He said he didn't know whether to report Diane as a missing person or wait a day or so, anticipating her return.

A thorough officer, Glynn knew from experience that if you don't get the information written down immediately, it tends to get lost in the shuffle of the hundreds of cases that a busy precinct handles. He told Joe the best course of action was to file a missing-persons report promptly, and offered to come over to the apartment with one.

Glynn, thirty-nine at the time, had been around the block a few times. He joined the New York City Police Department in 1973 and was promoted to detective in 1981. He spent almost all of those formative years in the tough Brownsville section of Brooklyn. Here in the Village, as Glynn was apt to say, "You meet a different type of clientele." Unlike Brownsville, where missing persons are often juvenile runaways, police in the Village chase after students from New York University, which is in the Sixth Precinct, or bored housewives or sex-craved husbands who go off on a toot. "They're more the liberal yuppie type. They seem to be shocked at everything. I always say to myself, 'Shit, don't they know what the world is really like out there?' "

With a missing-persons profile about 40-percent female, Glynn had a lot of experience fielding calls from the parents of coeds from across the country claiming that their daughters "would never" run away. But, Glynn said, in almost every case, the missing person resurfaces unharmed.

Glynn thought back to a missing-persons case he had opened and closed just a couple of days before. A well-dressed man came into the precinct at about 8:30 in the morning, a young attorney who had been married only a short time. The guy explained that his wife had gone out for a business dinner the night before and had promised to come home as soon as she finished the deal. Well, said the distressed husband, she hadn't returned home yet. "This isn't my wife. She wouldn't do something like that," the man told Glynn. Adding to the concern was the fact that the woman had an important business meeting that morning; missing it would adversely affect her career.

Glynn checked the missing-persons files and then the morgue. Nothing. "Well, she could have met up with friends or what have you," the detective said. "More than likely she'll show up."

But the husband insisted something was amiss. "No, I'm telling you, she'd never do anything like this."

Sure enough, a couple of hours later, the lawyer called Glynn back. His wife had finally come home—disheveled but sexually satisfied. "She had an affair and she admitted it," said Glynn. "It's normal for us where legitimate people who have never done that before, have taken off and no one knows where they are, and lo and behold they come back—99.9 percent of the time they come back. They know exactly where they're at.

"It happens all the time. I get doctors missing, lawyers missing, cops missing—we had an FBI guy missing," said

Glynn. "It's one of two things: they're either with a girl-friend or a boyfriend, or they go on a toot and they land up wherever. The FBI guy landed up in the state of Washington. He got on a toot, left his car, left everything, jumped on a plane, and went to Washington. People do these things. I don't know why they do them, but they do them."

Glynn told Joe Pikul he would come over to the apartment and take down the information because experience had taught him a long time ago that you never know when the case you're working on is going to turn out to be the one that ends up bad. Glynn suggested seven o'clock, but Joe said he had just gotten home and wanted to bathe the kids, get them in their pajamas, feed them, and get them ready for bed. He also explained to Glynn that it had been a rough day. The two men agreed to meet a little after eight.

In upstate New York, Sergeant Clancy and Detective Smith arrived at Newburgh police headquarters at about 6:10 P.M. Cooper had laid out the credit cards and cheap-looking costume jewelry on a table in the booking room and placed the bag of clothing on the floor nearby. Smith and Clancy assumed the goods were the proceeds of a property crime, perhaps a burglary or a mugging. Maybe the clothing didn't have anything to do with the jewelry and the credit cards.

The bra collection was definitely strange. They ranged in size from 32 to 38, from cup A to cup D. The women's shoes drew extra scrutiny, too. Smith, who wears a size 11, measured his foot and came up short. Likewise for Clancy's 11 ½. Clancy and Smith started laughing. "This has got to be an ugly broad," said Smith, "or this guy might be some kind of weirdo." Smith was joking more than anything. But even if the guy had a fight with his wife and he threw her belongings away in anger, whose wife would have so many different-sized bras?

Clancy checked local records and determined that none of the items had been reported missing or stolen. But several of the cards bore an address: 446 Sixth Avenue, New York City. Clancy directed Smith to call directory assistance to get a number. Smith quickly came up with a match: 212-475-4560.

Smith dialed the number. "Hello," said the male voice on the other end.

"Hello," said Smith, neglecting to identify himself as a police detective. "Is this the Pikul residence?"

"Yes, it is."

"Are you Mr. Pikul?"

"Yes," said Joe.

Smith asked Joe if he'd lost some credit cards. The line was quiet for several seconds. Smith asked the question a second time, explaining that several cards had been found at a gas station in Newburgh. "Are they lost?"

"Yes," Joe replied, becoming very nervous. He asked Smith to hold on a minute, then put the call on hold. Smith, meanwhile, signaled to Clancy in the next room, telling him the guy on the phone had suddenly started stuttering, acting nervous, the whole bit. "Mike, there's something wrong here," said Smith.

Before Joe got back on the line, Clancy hooked up a tape recorder. "Hi," Smith said when the conversation resumed. The cop was going to say as little as possible, hoping to draw out the guy on the other end of the line.

"Yeah, uh, uh, yeah, I'd like to, uh, give you a reward. Or, or give me your name and phone number first," said Joe. Smith began with the area code, 914, and gave the number of a private line back in the detective's office.

"Uh, and your name?"

"My name is John," said Smith.

"Uh, uh, uh, John?" asked Joe.

Joe also wanted a last name, but Smith had a problem with that request. Name questions are always hard for a guy born John Smith. He frequently gives a phony name when he's involved in these kinds of situations because few people believe a guy who claims his name is John Smith. Worse, many suspect a "John Smith" to be a cop.

"Clancy," answered Smith, giving the name of his sergeant.

"Clancy," repeated Joe, letting it sink in. "Okay, and uh, uh, where are you located?"

"I'm in Newburgh," said Smith.

"Right, uh-huh."

"I'm on Route 17K, that's where I found them," said Smith.

"Route 17K?"

"Yeah, and I checked the directory, and I called the operator, and they gave me this phone number," said Smith, trying to explain the call.

Joe wanted to know how many cards "Mr. Clancy" had, and Smith explained he had about four of them.

"Uh, 17K? Uh, is that near anything?" asked Joe.

Smith told him that it was near the New York Thruway. "And there's one here for a Diane Whitmore," the detective continued.

"Oh. Uh, and the rest are for me?"

"Yeah."

"Uh, okay uh, oh terrific, uh, uh, so which ones did I lose?" asked Joe, on his guard and trying to feel out the situation.

"Well, there's a Chase one here, there's a Sears, I think MasterCard. There's something else here."

"Oh, okay, uh, and where did—"

This time Smith cut off the questioning to launch a query of his own: "You dropped your wallet?"

"Yeah," said Joe.

"I didn't see no wallet."

Joe didn't bite, didn't say anything about having ditched everything in the green dumpster. Instead, he continued to conduct his own investigation. "Where were they at?"

"They were just laying on the ground," said Smith, not giving an inch.

"Uh-huh, okay. Uh, why don't I—uh, why don't I send, uh,—can I send my driver up? Uh, where are you located? On Route 17?"

"Yeah, 17K," said Smith.

"Is that your address?"

"Yeah," said Smith.

"Uh, uh, well, where? Don't you have a street address?"

"No, this ain't New York City. This is upstate New York," chortled Smith. "We just have Route 17K."

"Uh, uh, that's what it would be? Uh, you know, uh, how, how would we find you?"

"Well, I could meet you," said Smith.

"Uh, where could you meet us?"

"Right where you dropped them, you know that gas station where you must have bought your gas?"

"Yeah," said Joe.

"The Texaco station?"

"Yeah," said Joe.

"Well, I could meet you there," said Smith.

"Oh, I see what you mean. I, uh, is it a Texaco station?"

"Yeah, right," said Smith.

"Yeah, I did go in there," said Joe.

"Right, well, that's where they are," said Smith.

Joe said he'd come up, but it was going to take him a little while to get there.

"Okay, well, take your time, see what time you'll be here, I'll wait for you," said Smith.

Joe started asking about the credit cards again. "Uh, uh, oh boy," he said. "It was a Sears?"

"Yup."

"Ah-huh. What else?"

"MasterCard and it says 'Chase twenty-four-hour bank' on one of them."

"Yeah," said Joe.

"And another one," said Smith.

"Right there?" asked Joe, no doubt trying to figure out how the hell those cards got from the bottom of the dumpster out onto the sidewalk.

"Right, laying on the ground," said Smith.

"B-b-b-by the station? B-by the gas station?"

"Well, there's a garbage can there, those big garbage cans," Smith explained.

"Yeah," said Joe.

"And it was just laying there, when I stopped in there to get my car washed," said Smith.

"Oh, I see. Uh, okay."

"I walked over there to throw some garbage in the thing, and there was this credit card laying on the ground, I said, 'What the hell is this?' " said Smith.

"Oh, my Lord. Oh, oh, oh, uh, well okay now. What if I send my driver up? Let me see if he's available first of all."

"All right," said Smith.

"Uh, I'll call, are you at home now?"

"Yeah, you want to call me at this number?" asked Smith.

"W-what number is this?"

"I gave it to you, 564—"

"Right."

"1878."

"Right."

"Area code 914," said Smith.

"And this is a gas station?" asked Joe, still trying to pin down the caller.

"No, this is my house," Smith lied.

"Okay, okay. Let me call you right back. You stay, you stay right there, okay?"

"Okay, sure," said Smith. He wasn't going anywhere. He was dying to know what this was all about.

The two men said good-bye. It was now twelve minutes to seven.

Joe quickly dialed his chauffeur, James Burns, owner of the American Dream Machine Limousine, the company on Joe's call. Burns was used to jumping for Joe the same way Malcolm Rattner had jumped years ago until Joe had come at him with a gun. Burns agreed to make the trip upstate, so Joe gave him the number for this Clancy fellow.

It was now 6:55 P.M. Events were moving at breakneck speed. Burns dialed the Newburgh detective's number, where "Clancy" answered. Burns identified himself as "Jim, Mr. Pikul's driver." He said he'd meet "Clancy" at the gas station–car wash about 9:00 P.M., where "Clancy" would receive a reward for returning the credit cards. Burns said he'd be driving a car bearing license plate QBW-903. "Clancy" gave Burns directions, described his appearance, said he lived near the car wash and would be waiting.

While Smith was busy posing as citizen John Clancy, the real Clancy was occupied trying to track down the car-wash employees for additional interviews. He reached David Moshinski, who related how he'd seen a white male and two small children in a blue station wagon at about noon, that the man was unusually eager to clean the inside of the car, and that he had placed some unusual items in the dumpster. Moshinski told Clancy the man appeared to be burying the items under other garbage.

After Smith and Clancy compared notes, Clancy called the main number for the New York City Police Department to determine which station house covered the Pikul apartment. Headquarters gave him the number for the Sixth Precinct in Greenwich Village, where Detective Christine Morgillo, one of Glynn's counterparts, answered the call.

Sergeant Michael Clancy, town of Newburgh police, upstate Orange County, said he was calling as part of a "recovered-property investigation." It seemed that some items, including a wallet, credit cards, and women's clothing, had been found in a dumpster at a car wash in Newburgh. Further, Clancy related to Morgillo, car-wash employees had seen a customer discarding the materials.

Clancy told Morgillo that the address on one of the cards indicated the person lived within the borders of the Sixth Precinct, and he wondered if the person or persons whose names were on the recovered items were either the victims of a crime or had reported any crimes. The names, Clancy told Morgillo, were Diane Whitmore, Diane Pikul, Mrs. Joseph Pikul, and Joseph Pikul. Morgillo said she'd check around, then put him on hold.

At that very moment, Glynn was on the other line with Joe, who had called back to postpone the detective's house call. He said he'd forgotten that his daughter had religious instruction, therefore everything was behind schedule. He also said he'd dispatched his driver to pick Claudia up, but he didn't want anyone coming over right away because he needed time to feed her and get her into bed. "The children had a very busy weekend and I don't want to upset them any further by having the police in the house." He then asked Glynn not to come before 9:30 P.M. The men agreed on about ten o'clock. "Geez, he's awful nervous," Glynn thought to himself.

Just then Morgillo walked back to the clipboard filled with the "60 Sheets," police jargon for the complaints filed in the precinct for the year, with the latest ones on top. As she was walking by, Morgillo asked the other members of her squad: "Anybody aware of a Pikul, stolen property? I got a call from Newburgh police."

"Pikul? I just got off the phone with Pikul," said Glynn, who quickly got on the line with Clancy.

Glynn gave Clancy Joe's story about Diane's disappearance. In return, Clancy provided Glynn with details of the car-wash episode.

Joe's actions upstate certainly were peculiar, but Glynn still didn't know what to think. "You gotta understand, in a thousand cases that come through here on a family dispute or something like that, it's not so unusual the husband gets pissed off, he takes the pocketbook, or he'll take her clothing and rip them up and throw them out. . . . From a layman's point of view, of course they're gonna say, 'Well, how could you say that?' But we see it every day. They wreck their own apartments, they break up their furniture." Still, Clancy's call had piqued Glynn's interest, and prompted him to wonder aloud: "What the hell's everything doing up in Newburgh, New York, when she was out in Amagansett, Long Island? We're talking about a wide gap here. Why are they up there?"

Maybe they'd know more in the next hour or so, Clancy said, detailing his plan to have Detective Smith meet undercover with Joe's driver at the car wash.

Joe hung up with Glynn and dialed Federico again. It was a little after 7:00 P.M., and the attorney wasn't in, but someone assured Joe that Federico was en route to New York.

By the time Claudia called to be picked up from Bible school, the baby-sitter Carina had arrived, so she went to retrieve her. Joe, meanwhile, called out for food. As they ate dinner, he mentioned that he'd broken a tooth, which Jacobson had noticed. "What happened?" she asked.

"I found half my tooth upstairs in a drawer. I don't know where the other half is," Joe explained. Not knowing what to say to that, Carina took the kids upstairs to read them a bedtime story.

A little after eight, Glynn contacted his boss, Detective Sergeant Kenneth M. Bowen, at home to fill him in on the quickly developing case. Bowen, who had been off that day, then contacted the state police. A simple missing-persons report was rapidly becoming complicated. The woman disappeared on Long Island, her belongings were found in upstate New York, and her husband was back in

Manhattan with the two kids. Bowen figured, and rightly so, if there was any physical evidence to be gathered, the work would probably be done out in Long Island, since that was where Diane had disappeared. That would be a state-police function.

When Glynn told Bowen that Pikul was sending his driver upstate, the two cops wondered if Joe might accompany the chauffeur, thus enabling the Newburgh police to obtain some additional information. But Bowen had a second concern. What was "John Clancy" going to do about the credit cards? Certainly he wasn't going to give them back, was he?

Like Glynn, Clancy had decided he'd better shoot this thing upstairs, so he called his chief, John Kulisek, who said he'd come to the station as soon as possible. No one was necessarily thinking murder at this point, but years of experience told the upstate cops that something was radically wrong. Maybe it was just a burglary, but no way all that stuff should have been buried in the dumpster like that.

Wearing a body microphone, Smith set off for the car wash at about 8:30, with Officer Cooper as backup. While Clancy waited for Chief Kulisek to arrive, the phone rang again; Sergeant Ken Bowen was calling from the Sixth Precinct, New York City.

Bowen told Clancy about Glynn's plan to visit Joe's apartment to take the missing-persons report, then requested that the rendezvous between Smith and Joe's driver be called off. That way Smith wouldn't have to explain what happened to the credit cards. Clancy agreed, and radioed word that Smith should back off, then headed to the car wash himself. Because of the possibility that Joe might recognize Smith's voice as "John Clancy," the real Clancy set up camp posing as a gas-station attendant.

At 8:40 a grayish blue Lincoln slowly approached the station. Burns, the driver, sat in his car for a few minutes, then approached the cashier's window. "Is there a guy named John Clancy around here?"

"Nobody by that name works here," said the real Clancy.

Burns explained that he was supposed to retrieve some

lost credit cards from a guy named John Clancy, who was to meet him in the parking lot around 9:00 P.M. Clancy told Burns that a man had been standing by the curb for about two hours, but that the guy walked east on Route 17K about ten minutes before the Lincoln pulled in. Burns shook his head in disgust, but said he was going to wait awhile to see if the guy reappeared.

A few minutes before nine, Burns returned to the cashier's window, asking if anyone had turned in a wallet that day. Clancy told him no one had, "but if you give me your name and address, if anyone turns it in, I'll give you a call." Burns gave Clancy his business card, got in his car, and drove east on 17K a few hundred yards to a Howard Johnson's.

Clancy radioed Chief Kulisek, who was now in position down the road with Smith in another car. Kulisek responded that he could see the guy reaching for a pay phone. As Burns placed a call, Smith received word over the radio that the telephone in the back room at headquarters was ringing and ringing.

Burns drove back to the car wash and parked near the exit to watch for "Clancy." At 9:10 the real Clancy decided to turn up the heat one more notch, so he walked over to inform Burns that the station was closing and that all the lights were going to be turned off. Burns, a stocky man with a mustache, explained that the credit cards were not his, that he'd just driven up on a rush job for his boss. Why, he even had reward money for the guy who'd found the cards.

"The boss must be extremely worried about the cards to have a hired driver come all the way from Queens at night to pick them up," said the real Clancy.

"My boss is a powerful man who pays well. So I jump when the boss calls," said Burns. "He's a big Wall Street guy. He's my exclusive customer."

Burns said he would wait a little while longer and had Clancy promise to call the following day if the guy with the credit cards showed up at the car wash. Burns also said he'd keep calling this Clancy fellow. Sure enough, the phone in the detective's room rang unanswered several more times that evening.

With the operation shut down, Clancy returned to his

headquarters to call Glynn and Bowen down in the Village with an update.

The doorbell rang about 8:30. Joe answered it, then told Carina: "I have to go out for a little while. I'll be back in about an hour." Joe took the phone off the hook and left.

Downstairs, Vincent Federico was waiting. The two men went to an East Side restaurant, where they discussed the case and Federico's fee. Joe would later explain that Federico wanted $15,000 on the spot, but he only gave him $5,000. Federico then called it a night at the Tudor Hotel on the east end of Forty-second Street. They made plans to meet again in the morning for breakfast. Joe liked to conduct business over food.

By the time Joe returned home about 9:45, Carina had tired of the mystery. She asked Joe flat out: "Do you know where Diane is?" He said he did.

"Well, where is she?"

"She's at a boyfriend's house out on Long Island."

"Well, do you know who he is?"

"Yes," Joe replied.

"We're all very worried about her. Why don't we call her and see that she's all right?"

"I don't want to do that. I'd make a fool of myself," he explained.

Carina went upstairs to check on the children, but Joe called her down to announce that someone else was going to watch the children for the rest of the night. He also told her the police were coming to take a report regarding Diane's disappearance. He then showed Carina the door. No doubt she had asked too many questions.

After getting the state police into the mix, Bowen headed for the Village, arriving at the precinct at about ten. Glynn briefed his sergeant for the trip over to the Pikul apartment. In the meantime, the two men awaited the arrival of Senior Investigator Donald P. Delaney of the New York State Police on Long Island.

In the interim, Glynn called Diane's father in Florida. "Something is very wrong here," Whitmore said. He said Diane was very predictable and reliable, and would never leave the children unattended in any way. With the string of baby-sitters parading through the Pikuls' life, that certainly made sense. Glynn assured Whitmore he was on the case.

Over in New Jersey, Marshall Weingarden, who had heard Joe's tale of woe on Saturday morning, dialed the Pikul apartment to check on Diane. He'd tried getting Joe in Amagansett on Sunday afternoon, but no one answered. Joe told his friend that Diane was still missing. "I can't talk for long," Joe said, explaining that he was about to rush off to the precinct house to report her disappearance.

Ten o'clock came and went without any visit from Detective Glynn. Now Joe was anxious to get the interview started. At about 10:45 he called the Sixth Precinct to ask if Glynn was still coming. "You know, you had an appointment for ten o'clock. How come you haven't arrived yet?"

"Well, I got involved in something else," said Glynn, stalling. "I'll be over shortly."

Finally Delaney arrived at the station house. Bowen filled him in: missing person last seen in Amagansett late Friday night, early Saturday morning, name Diane Pikul, worked for the publisher at *Harper's* magazine, some of Mrs. Pikul's property recovered from a dumpster upstate. It was a strange mix of circumstances to be sure.

At 11:05, Joe dialed Bayonet Point, Florida, again. He told Don Whitmore he was going to file a missing-persons report.

At about the same time, Chief Kulisek in Newburgh ordered up a final roust of Jim Burns. The chief wanted to officially know who his men were dealing with, business card and license plate notwithstanding. Officer Gary Cooper took a break from logging in all the items seized at the car wash and drove over to Route 17K with Officer Mark Merring.

Burns told Cooper his boss had sent him up from New York City to recover some property lost at the car wash earlier in the day. Burns said he was supposed to meet a guy but that he never showed.

A short time later, Kulisek and Detective Smith watched as Jim Burns left town. At about midnight, Clancy was notified by radio from a patrol car that the Lincoln was proceeding south on the New York Thruway, toward New York City.

But the Newburgh cops still weren't done for the night. Given that Joe had sent his driver up to get the credit cards *and* given that he decided to officially report his wife missing, the Newburgh team decided to secure the dumpster for safekeeping. A wrecker was summoned to flatbed the dumpster back to police headquarters, where Clancy and Smith fastened the cover with a chain and padlock. Cooper resumed taking inventory of the items seized at the car wash. The evidence bags were then put into the safe. From the Newburgh end, the investigation was now a waiting game.

Back in the city, Glynn, Bowen, and Delaney headed over to the Pikul apartment, where a handsome young man subsequently identified as Joe's assistant, Jean-Jacques, answered the door. Joe was lying down on the living-room couch. "I'm very tired," he explained. "It's been a long day, a lot of driving."

Glynn introduced himself, shook hands with Joe, who remained lying down, resting on an elbow. It wasn't until Glynn introduced Delaney and Bowen that Joe finally stood up.

"Why don't you sit down?" Joe motioned to the kitchen table. The group walked into the dinette area and grabbed some chairs. Jean-Jacques, or JJ as he was known, sat against the wall.

The detective looked Joe over. "I thought he was a little flaky, but I run into a lot of flaky people," Glynn said. Anyway, this was still just a missing-persons investigation. The cops needed Joe's cooperation. He was the guy filing the report. "I don't want to turn him off. I want to keep us on a good rapport," Glynn explained. "I mean I'm there 'cause his wife is missing. What am I gonna say, 'Do you jerk off?' 'Who do you go to bed with?' "

So the questioning began with a simple request: explain the circumstances when you last saw your wife. Delaney took notes while Glynn filled in his missing-persons report on a UF61 form. With Diane's disappearance now official Case No. 13150, Joe told the following story:

He and the kids arrived in Amagansett about 10:30 P.M.

that Friday, and Diane got there about one. In between, he'd called the parking garage and found out Diane had pulled out at nine. He and Diane argued until about 2:30 A.M. about why it took her so long, then he went to his bedroom and she went to hers, at opposite ends of the house. He woke up about seven and, while taking a shower, called out to his wife, but she didn't answer. When he went into Diane's bedroom, he determined that she was not there.

Joe told the cops he felt Diane had possibly gone off to meet a boyfriend, contending not only that she'd frequently disappeared, but that they had frequently argued about her having a boyfriend.

Delaney asked Joe if he knew who the boyfriend was; Joe replied that he had no idea. In response to another question, he acknowledged that Diane hadn't taken either car.

Almost in midstream, Joe, who was acting very hyper, began talking about a different argument, one that he and Diane had the previous July, at an Elks Club Fair in Southampton. It seemed Blake had received an award from Cub Scouts and Joe felt Diane had not been as appreciative as she should have been. Delaney interrupted to ask if the Cub Scout dispute had been part of the argument the night Diane disappeared.

Instead of answering the question, Joe began telling another version of the Friday-night sequence: he and Diane had not argued, and after she arrived, they just went to bed.

Almost as quickly, he switched again; they *had* argued. Delaney again asked for specifics. Again, Joe was evasive and unresponsive.

Under more prodding, he started to revise the whole story: Diane had left Manhattan about nine and arrived between 1:30 and two. Then Joe changed the time he last saw Diane from 2:30 to "closer to two o'clock." With each revision, Diane spent less and less time in the house.

In still another version, Joe said that when Diane walked into the house, he asked her why she was so late, but she went into the bedroom without answering him. She hung up her clothing and walked out of the house, all within several minutes of her arrival.

Joe's story was slipping and sliding all over the place; he insisted this latest version was the correct one, then switched to Saturday, explaining that at about 3:30 P.M. he and the children went to visit an old friend, Henry Sawoska, in upstate New Windsor. Joe said he stayed at the Sawoskas' house over the entire weekend with his children and that they all returned to the city Monday morning.

Delaney asked Joe several times what he had done Saturday morning before he and the kids left for New Windsor, but Joe said he wasn't sure—or didn't answer at all, hunched over at the table, his hands covering his eyes.

The detectives then asked for a photograph of Diane, and recorded some pedigree information: five-four; 117 pounds; medium complexion; brown eyes; last wearing a black skirt. Joe said he couldn't remember the other pieces of clothing.

Joe began looking for an appropriate picture, picking up packages of photos, going through them, putting them down, picking up another pack, unable to make a choice. At one point, he walked over to the table with several photos of Diane, then, as if he changed his mind, put them back in the folder and walked away. Three times Bowen asked Joe for a photo. Each time it was like talking to a wall.

Looking through yet another batch of pictures, Joe tentatively selected one, then put it down. "No, not that one," he said, walking back to the table.

Joe looked through hundreds of photos before finally making his selection: a terrible photo, in which Diane looked a mess.

Jean-Jacques, meanwhile, sat in his chair, taking in the entire proceeding, listening to every word but saying nothing.

Delaney wondered where Diane could have gone off to on foot. Joe didn't have an answer. "I didn't get up to look where she was going. She just walked out," he professed. He was stuttering, clearly agitated and swallowing hard. He said it was normal for Diane to walk out following an argument and couldn't understand why everyone was "getting so excited about a missing person." Diane had disappeared for days at a time in the past without warning and always reappeared. Joe said, "She'll probably show up tomorrow."

It was 1:15 now, and the detectives asked Joe to write out a brief permission slip so police out on the Island could look for Diane in and around the house on Windmill Lane. Glynn explained that since it was the last place Diane had been seen, investigators would want to start their legwork there. Also, Bowen said, state police wanted to utilize bloodhounds to canvass the area. Joe agreed, and with Glynn's help wrote out a brief approval statement on the back of a police complaint form.

Then Glynn asked Joe if he could provide a piece of Diane's clothing for the dogs. Joe went into the bedroom and started rummaging through Diane's belongings, the same way he had labored over the piles of photographs.

"Just a blouse, or anything that maybe they can pick some sort of scent up," said Glynn, seeking to move things along.

Joe finally appeared with a pair of panties. "She worked out in these. You should be able to get a good scent off of them."

"Call us if your wife comes home, all right?" asked Glynn, heading for the door with Diane's underwear.

Joe nodded.

Bowen, Glynn, and Delaney returned to the precinct house, uncertain of what to make of Joe. They didn't know if Diane Pikul was with her boyfriend, her father, off on a toot, being held captive, or worse. One thing was certain: the more Joe Pikul danced around, the more curious they got about him.

Bowen, Glynn, and Delaney sat down for a strategy session, joined by Sixth Precinct detectives Richard Composto and Ronald Finelli. There were more questions than answers. If Mrs. Pikul had a boyfriend, surely there must be some information available on him: a name, a telephone number, an address—something. They also needed to learn where she hung out.

Glynn went to the rear of the precinct to sleep. Delaney was ready to run the permission slip out to Long Island.

It was time for some new faces and a change of scenery.

The idea here, a standard police ploy, was to get Joe out of familiar surroundings and into a police setting.

Enter Composto and Finelli. Bowen instructed the two detectives to pay Mr. Pikul another visit. So shortly before 4:00 A.M. that Tuesday, they knocked on Joe's door, told JJ to wake Mr. Pikul, then "invited" him down to the station house for a couple of additional questions. "We'd like to clarify some matters," Composto told the Wall Street big shot clad in his fancy white bathrobe. As though he had a choice, Joe said: "Let me get dressed."

"Start from the beginning," Composto said as the interview began in a small office off the main detectives' squad room at the precinct house. "When is the last time you saw your wife? Start from there."

Joe explained that he and Diane had planned to go to their home in Amagansett after work the prior Friday to get the property ready to be shown to a real-estate broker. They had wanted to hire a baby-sitter for the kids in Manhattan, but at the last minute, they decided to take the children along.

"I drove out in the Mazda and took the kids with me. I left at about 8:00 P.M. and my wife was going to stay and clean up and leave in about twenty minutes in the station wagon." Before leaving the city, Joe explained, he stopped off with the kids at his other apartment, on Rector Place, to get some toys for the kids and some women's clothing that he had there. The last item made Composto perk up, but he let Joe keep talking.

Joe detailed his call to the parking garage next. At first he told the detectives he wanted to know what the hell was keeping Diane, but he subsequently claimed he made the call so the kids would be in bed when Diane arrived, and "she wouldn't throw a fit."

When Diane entered the house, according to Joe: "I said: 'Gee, Diane, that was a long trip.' She said: 'Are you questioning me?' I said: 'Not really. I was just wondering.' "

Joe said when he tried to pursue the issue, Diane screamed at him: "Shut the fuck up, you fag." Then, as she stormed off to her bedroom, he said she called out to him: "Fuck you. You're a fuckin' creep, you faggot."

In this version, Joe said he heard Diane leave the house

through the door near her bedroom, presumably to get more of her belongings out of the car, but still contended that he didn't see her for the remainder of the evening.

But a few seconds later, he amended that story, saying that Diane did come back into the kitchen and tried to discuss their schedule for the weekend, specifically what time he had an appointment with his masseuse on Sunday. Joe said he then went to bed and never saw Diane again.

He then turned the conversation to Saturday morning. "I awoke at about 7:00 A.M., and took my shower and then yelled into her room, 'Are you in there?' and there was no answer. I looked in and discovered that she was gone." After realizing Diane was missing, Joe said, he observed that "her garment bag and car were there. She has done this numerous times in the past and I was not too concerned."

At that point he told Composto and Finelli that when his daughter Claudia got up, he told her, "Mommy's taken off again," then fed her breakfast. He said he told Claudia to go into the other room and watch TV. "My masseuse called and I told her that my wife ran away again."

Then, Joe said, he called his dentist and left a message on the machine asking for an appointment for Sunday. He said that between 9:00 A.M. and 1:00 P.M., his dentist's receptionist called back to set up an appointment. "I also called the security people and had them change the code because I feel someone has been trespassing in my house."

Joe said he spent part of the day shopping at a hardware store, then played ball with the children in the backyard. In fact, he explained, that was how he got the scratches on his hand, reaching into a honeysuckle bush to retrieve an errant toss.

"Sometime Saturday my daughter told me she'd lost her shoe and can I help her find it. While looking for it I found two packages of condoms under my wife's bed. One of the packages was empty and one was full. I don't remember the brand name on them but they were not mine. After working in the garden, I called my friend Henry Sawoska, who resides on Gernsey Street in New Windsor, and told him things were getting worse between my wife and myself and asked: 'Can I come up and visit with you?' "

Joe told Composto that Sawoska said okay, and somewhere between three and 3:30 P.M., "we left and arrived at about 8:00 P.M. It is about 180 miles there. We stopped quite a few times, and because I was never there before, I had to ask Henry for directions. I had forgot to feed the kids, and when we got there my kids were starving and ate about six sandwiches. At about 9:30, I left New Windsor and came home to New York and arrived in the city between eleven and midnight. I parked the car in the street and went to bed. The kids had stayed in New Windsor. At about 11:00 A.M. I woke up—wait, backtrack—Saturday afternoon, after leaving New Windsor, I headed toward Boston. I went as far as Highway 128 in Massachusetts. I cruised around in Massachusetts, around Norwood, looking for my aunt's grave and to pay my respects. Then to Ware, Mass., and then to the Berkshires, and then to the Massachusetts Turnpike and to Lee, Mass." In this version, Joe returned to New York City at about 1:00 A.M. Sunday. He made no mention of his visit to Sandy.

It was now 8:00 A.M. Composto and Finelli had been sitting with Joe for four hours, sticking in a question here and there, but basically letting Joe go from version to version.

Seeking to make some sense of the hodgepodge, the two detectives now launched into a question-and-answer session. It would be improper to characterize the events as an interrogation because Joe was still "not a suspect."

Now Joe said he drove to Boston after leaving the Sawoskas, and figured he drove 800 miles all told. Figuring $1.25 a gallon, twelve miles to the gallon, Composto wondered how the eighty dollars' worth of gasoline had been purchased. Joe said he paid cash. "I don't use any credit cards," he claimed.

Asked to explain when Diane had run off previously, Joe cited two incidents: from his sister's house in Virginia about a year after he and Diane married and during a trip to California while Diane was pregnant with Blake. This was the trip where Diane claimed Joe threw her out of the car, but Joe didn't mention the car ride or their argument. "She wanted to get laid and I was tired. She took off and she was gone for three or four days." Joe also complained that Diane first hired a divorce lawyer after only one year of marriage.

Joe was bouncing around again. In between, he was being peppered with questions.

"Did you initiate any phone calls in an attempt to locate your wife?" asked Composto. Joe said he had not.

"Are you gay? Your wife called you a fag."

Joe explained that he sometimes wore women's clothing, "and my wife had encouraged me to do it and then used the pictures she took against me. I dumped all the women's clothing I had. The last time I dumped clothes was on Monday at about ten or twelve o'clock up in Windsor. There was also jewelry in the bag with the clothes."

Asked for more details about his Monday morning, Joe inaccurately said he bought gas at the Texaco station where he had his car washed and "dumped the bag" full of ladies' clothing, which he'd picked up Friday night at his other apartment. He said he took the women's clothing "because I feel insecure without my therapist," then admitted that he actually wore the clothing.

The detectives also wanted to know how Joe got Diane's credit cards. He said he'd taken the last batch that weekend, "Saturday in the morning, when she arrived and went to the bathroom." Joe said that he had previously removed other credit cards. "She was running up the bills," he explained.

Back to Saturday, Joe now admitted that he went to a hardware store and purchased "clotheslines, four or five pair of gloves, flashlight, batteries." Joe said he spent $325 and paid by American Express. At least now Joe was giving Composto and Finelli facts that could be verified. He also said he'd gotten a call from someone who claimed they found some of his credit cards upstate, but said he thought this "John Clancy" guy was a cop. "I knew it was a dick on the phone," said Joe. "That phone-book shit is bullshit."

Composto and Finelli were ready to close the operation down. Everyone was getting tired. But they wanted to know more about Joe's other apartment. Joe explained it was in Battery Park City. After taking their "complainant" out for some breakfast at a diner in the Village, the detectives asked if he'd mind giving them a tour of his bachelor's pad. Knowing full well that Diane would be nowhere around, Joe responded, "Not at all."

After taking a look around, the entourage headed over to the parking garage to check out the Pikul station wagon. That also appeared to be in order, so Composto and Finelli took Joe home, then headed back to the precinct.

It was now a little after ten, Tuesday morning. Diane had been missing more than eighty hours.

CHAPTER · 12

An Envelope
Marked "Divorce"

JIM MITCHELL CAME TO WORK a few minutes after seven that Tuesday morning. He hadn't slept well, despite his newly purchased weaponry. In fact, it was because of the shotgun he had bought from Joe that the night had been so restless. As he walked into the car-wash office, his boss Otto handed him the phone. Sergeant Clancy had a few more questions about the previous day's events.

It didn't take long for Mitchell to confess about the shotgun, explaining that he hadn't turned it in the night before "because I figured if there's nothing to this, I didn't see the sense of turning it in."

"Do you have the shotgun there?" Clancy asked.

"Yeah, I brought it in with me," said Mitchell.

"All right, I'll have somebody over there to pick it up."

No sooner had Mitchell hung up the phone than a police unit pulled into the car wash. Back using his real name, Detective John Smith was on the case.

Smith took the gun and gave Mitchell the canary yellow copy of the receipt. Mitchell also turned over a wallet that had somehow been left behind the day before, and a silver choker that one of the car-wash kids had thought about giving to his "sister." Smith also removed the debris from a wall vacuum unit and put it in an evidence bag. While he was at it, he removed the plastic bag from a garbage can positioned near the vacuum. Inside the bag, Smith found canceled and uncanceled checks from the account of Diane Pikul and a plethora of personal effects, including a photo of a gorgeous young blond boy and a couple of crayon drawings. Smith, with a seven-year-old blond son of his own, couldn't believe that someone had thrown away such a picture. He called Clancy to tell him that the gun had been cleaned the day before by the gas-station jockeys. Clancy told Smith to have Mitchell and Rusch come to the station to give more detailed statements.

At about nine, Sergeant Bowen in New York gave Clancy a call, revealing that his men were still talking to Joe, but that there was still no indication of foul play. Bowen offered, however, that Joe's story had bounced all over the place throughout the night, "like, off-the-wall. But he's no dummy." The sergeant said Joe was acting "crazy" and "nervous," yet appeared to be "pretty sharp. I think he's probably a paranoid schizophrenic.

"He don't tell you nothing. He just comes up with little tidbits, and then you have to drag the rest of it out of him," Bowen said. "He was telling us a couple of weird stories."

The two sergeants then discussed the virtues of contacting Henry Sawoska. Clancy offered to do it, explaining that the house was just a couple of miles away. "If you want, I can get myself and another guy, or I'll get a New Windsor detective."

But Bowen wondered if paying such a visit might be "a little premature. Our biggest problem at this point is he's very, very satisfied with just talking with us."

"Yeah," said Clancy.

"He hasn't asked for a lawyer and we wouldn't want him to reach out to anybody that might say, 'Hey, you need a lawyer,'" said Bowen, pointing out that they had no idea of the closeness of the relationship between Joe and the Sawoskas.

"Is the lawyer there with him?" asked Clancy, having misunderstood.

"No, we don't have a lawyer," said Bowen. "That's one of the things we don't want, somebody that would be sympathetic to him and say, 'Hey, you know, these fuckin' cops are asking me some heavy questions, you better get a lawyer.'" No, Bowen said, he was content to have Joe keep volunteering information, like how he'd gone to a hardware store and bought more than $300 worth of stuff, including five pairs of gloves and some rope. Bowen told Clancy that Pikul said he'd thrown the gloves away because he didn't like them, because they were too heavy, which made no sense at all.

Clancy asked if Joe had elaborated on why he sold the gun. "He says he has other guns at home," Bowen responded. Clancy then informed his counterpart that the shotgun had been cleaned the day before. And just at that point in the conversation, Smith reentered the squad room and informed Clancy that the gun had also been fired several times.

"Shit," said Bowen, explaining how he thought the worst when "this motherfucker," meaning Joe, had said he sold the gun. Now there'd be no way to check if Joe had recently fired it.

Bowen and Clancy played around with the idea of having Smith call Joe back as "John Clancy" and concoct a story about miscommunication or tell Joe "I just missed you," but it was starting to get too dicey, especially with Joe suspecting "John Clancy" was a cop.

"I don't know," said Bowen. "It's a weird one, you know, because, I don't know, she could be anyplace." Clancy promised to hold off on making another contact with Joe unless he heard from Bowen. "See, the only problem is that you're working on it and we're working on it and whoever ends up with this fuckin' body . . ." said Bowen, laughing heartily. This *was* becoming a jurisdictional nightmare.

Clancy pointed out that his department had this large stash of "found property," and that Diane Pikul had been "reported missing" in Manhattan. Bowen concurred, adding: "And she was last seen maybe 150 miles from here." He suggested that Clancy save the recovered items in case it turned out they had blood on them.

Bowen had to go, he had an appointment with Glynn to interview some of Diane's co-workers at *Harper's*. The two men agreed to trade notes again later in the day.

Glynn had gotten up from one of the six bunks in the sleeping area at the rear of the second-floor squad room about seven o'clock. He showered, shaved, had a cup of coffee, and got a brief rundown on the status of Joe's ongoing Composto-Finelli interview.

Joe was all over the lot: Diane had left immediately after the argument versus Joe had discovered her missing the following morning; they had argued versus they hadn't argued. The time of her arrival and the time of her supposed departure kept changing.

Disturbing as the long night of developments appeared, as far as Glynn and Bowen were concerned, this was still officially a missing-persons case, so they headed over to the *Harper's* office on lower Broadway. There, they went over the whole story with a half-dozen employees, hoping that one of them was a close enough friend of Diane's that she would have revealed any plans to cut out for a few days. But no one at the magazine had heard such a story. They searched and searched for a boyfriend, too, but none turned up, at least none that anyone was willing to admit to.

Glynn hadn't been briefed regarding Joe's claim about the large-sized women's clothing, so he inquired about Diane's size. "The question may sound crazy, but I gotta ask you: 'Is Diane a big woman?' " Glynn asked one of the *Harper's* workers.

"Oh, she's very small," the woman answered, describing Diane as five feet and a couple of inches. Glynn asked about approximate bra size, blouse size. Nothing matched.

"This is crazy," Glynn thought to himself. "Whose clothing are we talking about? It's not even her clothing. Here we think we got this woman that could be anywhere and it's not even her stuff."

In between interviews Bowen got a call about a possible solution to the Pikul investigation: a female torso, from the neck to just below the pelvic area, had been found floating in the Hudson River. The First Precinct was handling it. "Aw shit," said Glynn. "I wonder if this could be her?" It wasn't, of course. The body was that of a white female, but the victim was a redhead; the color of the body hair didn't match.

Before Glynn and Bowen left the magazine, they were handed two packages from Diane's desk. One envelope was marked "Confidential," the other said "Divorce."

Bowen and Glynn promised to keep in touch and headed back to the precinct, where Glynn immediately sat down to begin reading the material.

There were a half-dozen short stories written by Diane, as well as the two lengthy letters and several brief notes she'd written to Felder and his associates.

The letters made it clear why the women's clothes recovered at the car wash were so large. Glynn came across the following entry in one of the notes: "He has apparently resumed cross dressing and had two shopping bags in a closet in the basement of our house in Amagansett filled with women's lingerie, bathing suits, and falsies. When he began keeping a rental car secretly in the cemetery next to our house, parked next to an access gate to our backyard, the clothes disappeared from the basement, so I assume he is using the car to hide the clothes in the trunk." The case was starting to get kinky.

Glynn put the papers down and started calling telephone numbers provided by the people at *Harper's*. He determined first that no one had seen Diane on Long Island that weekend, and second that many of these people were very closemouthed. Since many were friends of Diane through Alcoholics Anonymous and had gone on to live successful, alcohol-free lives, they didn't want present spouses learning about their past. Others were afraid of Joe, and didn't want to be involved for that reason.

Yet behind the scenes these same people quickly began criticizing the investigation for its supposed slow pace. Most had no idea how law enforcement worked day-to-day. They were used to getting results on demand from those who served them and expected nothing less from the local police.

Informed of the car-wash developments and Joe's behavior during the all-night interview, police on Long Island also swung into action. Detective Kenneth Brown, eight years on the East Hampton police force, checked modes of public transportation in the area—the Long Island Railroad, the Hamptons Jitney to the airport and to Manhattan, the ferry to Connecticut, the feeder bus lines, and the taxis. He turned up nothing on Diane.

The weekend credit-card receipts from the hardware

store had already been transported to the store's main branch in the village of East Hampton, so Brown drove over there. Then, with the help of employees, he reconstructed Joe's shopping spree.

The key man, store manager Herbert John Kiembock, was not around, though; he had since left for vacation in Antigua. So after completing his interviews, Brown went back to headquarters to track Kiembock down.

Meanwhile, the state police cordoned off the Pikul property. An officer was posted round the clock. If this was a crime scene, no one was going inside. With the permission slip Joe had signed the night before, state police higher-ups gave the signal to enter the house. Senior Investigator Delaney, who accompanied Glynn and Bowen for the first interview with Joe, entered with Brown and another state-police investigator.

The main part of the single-story house was a fisherman's shack-type structure with weathered wooden shingles. Two modern wings were covered with gray siding. The old part of the house contained two rooms and a hallway. Down the hall, in the first of the ells, was the living room and kitchen, a bath, and a sliding glass door off to the deck and pool. Another hallway led down to a second ell, to another small bedroom, a bathroom, the laundry room, and finally the master bedroom, with another sliding glass door.

The policemen immediately sensed they were inside a crime scene. There wasn't an abundance of blood, but what appeared to be small bloodstains were found at several locations: on the doorframe to the master bedroom, on the wall near the sliding glass door that opens to the deck and pool, on the living-room floor near the sliding glass door, and on the deck boards, right outside the sliding glass door. There were also stains on the rug in the master bedroom that looked like blood.

Outside, Delaney noticed the wheels and tires of the Mazda were caked with mud. He ordered everyone out of the house. No use messing with anyone's constitutional rights; they were going to play this thing straight. It was time to get a search warrant.

It was also time for increased coordination. Troop L of the state police on Long Island was going to take over from the local East Hampton squad, and state-police Troop F upstate was going to take over for the town of Newburgh. A couple of troopers from Long Island were dispatched to Manhattan.

Investigator Kenneth T. Jones of the state police was sent to Clancy's office in Newburgh to pick up the items recovered from the car-wash dumpster. Jones also took custody of the dumpster, which was still under lock and key, and supervised its transport to a state-police garage for further processing.

That afternoon, Jones personally dug into the garbage-filled dumpster and uncovered the following additional evidence: a green and black leather change purse, containing $2.35 in coins and seven New York City subway tokens; a personal note signed by "Claudia"; two General Motors keys in a magnetic holder; two keys on a ring; prescription receipts for asthma medication; an uncashed *Harper's* magazine check for $9.73, dated October 14, 1987, issued to Diane Whitmore and bearing the written notation "Iron Maiden"; a bankbook, First Federal Savings and Loan of Rochester, New York, in the names of Diane Jackson Whitmore and Donald E. Whitmore, showing a balance on August 3, 1987, of $7,660.55; a business card with prices for some artwork; a New York State driver's license, bearing the name and photo of Diane J. Pikul; and two beach towels, one of them white, gray, and blue striped, the other white, gray, and yellow striped.

The personal note, scribbled on a small piece of yellow note paper, read: "Dear Mom you gave me a wonderful presenet. Mom, you realy desearve something. I really love you. You understand about my headace. You must have some nerve to clean up my throw up. Thanks again Claudia."

There were a few additional discoveries in the dumpster: a pair of pink panties, some more brown hose, a black sweatshirt, black Reebok sneakers, a few more towels, a pink nightie, a beige Lady Marlene bra, white lace panties, a pink lace bra, and a pair of multicolored lace panties.

Senior Investigator James O'Neill of the state police on Long Island was put in charge of preparing an application and affidavit for a search warrant. Police wanted to search the house on Windmill Lane, the 1984 Mazda in the driveway, and the 1986 Buick station wagon, then parked in a garage at 160 West Tenth Street in Manhattan.

In his affidavit, O'Neill summarized the events of the previous twenty-four hours. He also noted that Joe had given written permission for inspection of the interior of the house "to further the search for his wife." It was during that search, O'Neill explained, that Delaney discovered what appeared to be bloodstains on the doorways and floor and the mud on the Mazda tires. O'Neill wrote that all of those findings combined had given him "probable cause to believe that a crime has been committed and that evidence of said crime may be found in the above listed premises and automobiles." He specifically asked court sanction to seize "blood, hairs, fibers, and other serological and trace evidence." The papers were rushed over to a judge, who signed them immediately. O'Neill sent word back to Delaney in Amagansett, and a team of forensic and criminal investigators reentered the house in full force at about 7:00 P.M.

Upstate, Senior Investigator Joseph Tripodo, Sr., chief of the bureau of criminal investigation at the Newburgh state-police barracks, drove over to the Sawoska house, where he conducted a preliminary interview with Louise Sawoska. She recounted Joe's visit that weekend, how he'd left the children and disappeared for more than thirty hours. "He was very, very nervous. I tried to take his jacket and he wouldn't let me take it," Louise Sawoska explained of Joe's eventual reappearance. She said she tried repeatedly to get him to sit down and relax, but that he declined. Louise, who really didn't know Joe, said she had no idea what was up, but knew something was wrong.

Meanwhile, Louise's weekend charge, Claudia Pikul, called her mother's office at *Harper's* several times that day. "Where's Mommy?" she asked, sobbing. No one had an answer.

Her father, on the other hand, spent the rest of that Tuesday relaxing. By the time Joe had finished with Composto and Finelli, he'd missed his morning meeting with

Federico. He dialed the attorney's home in Weymouth, Massachusetts, and confirmed that he had left New York.

At 4:37 P.M., the social services system received its first "report of suspected child abuse or maltreatment" regarding the Pikul family. An anonymous caller, obviously one of Diane's friends, related that "father abuses drugs. Father uses cocaine, is incapable of caring for the children adequately due to his drug use. Father has history of violent behavior. When mother was present in the home, she protected children and took care of them. Mother, however, has been missing for seventy-two hours." The caller expressed concern for the children's safety now that they were alone with Joe, and she told the city Emergency Children's Service worker that the Sixth Precinct was "investigating a 'missing persons' on the mother" and that "police suspect 'foul play' involving the father and mother."

When the caseworker called the Sixth Precinct, Detective Morgillo opined that the children were "not in imminent risk." Glynn said detectives had physically seen the children just two hours earlier and they looked fine.

As Joe caught some sleep, Glynn worked the phones, not unlike a bored housewife trying to glean some neighborhood gossip. Baby-sitters Inga Davidson and Carina Jacobson, who'd been helped financially by Joe in starting a small business in the fashion industry, were among those contacted. "I'd really like to speak to the kids," Glynn told them. But no one could figure out how to arrange such an encounter without tipping Joe off. The women said they'd give it some thought.

Meanwhile, Glynn got a call from Michael Katzenstein, an attorney who had done the start-up paperwork for the baby-sitters' fashion enterprise. "I'm in a strange position. I'm Inga's and Carina's lawyer and also Joe Pikul's lawyer in their business matters. But I also know Diane. I'm very fond of her," Katzenstein said. "I'm concerned for Diane. If there's anything I can help you with, please call me and I'll do whatever I can from my end." Glynn filed the offer away for future reference.

Things finally started to click when Inga called Glynn late that afternoon with the news that Joe was planning to meet someone for dinner. She and Carina would be caring for Claudia and Blake.

The investigative minds at the Sixth Precinct began to spin. "Kids are your best pieces of evidence. They're naturally honest," Glynn later explained. "But at this particular point, we felt if there was any sort of foul play—not knowing if there was—but if there was any foul play, then possibly the father would tell the kids, 'You don't talk to the police.' "

Inga said she was willing to cooperate. So about 7:00 P.M. Glynn and Detective Christine Morgillo went over to Inga's apartment posing as married friends of Inga and her boyfriend psychologist.

Jim Burns, Joe's driver, picked up the Pikul children and drove them to Inga's downtown apartment, near Hudson and Chambers. The kids were told that friends were stopping over to share a couple of pizzas. On the ride over, Blake started screaming that his mother wasn't coming back, and had to be calmed down. Once inside Inga's apartment, though, both children ran around and played as if nothing were out of the ordinary.

Inga held off ordering the pizzas until her boyfriend arrived, so everyone sat around sipping Cokes while the two baby-sitters played games with the children. Blake had an especially good time, laughing and carrying on. It was impractical during the one-hour wait to ask any meaningful questions. With three young kids of his own, Glynn figured it was best to wait until the children sat down at the table before anyone tried to extract any information.

The last thing Glynn wanted was for Joe to know the cops had been interrogating his children. If he could get Claudia to volunteer, well and good. But at this point Glynn didn't know if she had witnessed a crime or if she knew where her mother was. The detective realized that he had to be careful not to pump. But from his own experience, he figured if he played it right, the child would jump at the chance to provide knowledge, to show how smart she was.

As he sat there drinking his soda, Glynn realized there were other concerns, too, most importantly the mental condition of the children if it turned out Mommy really had run away, or worse, if it turned out Daddy had done something to her.

Glynn had also learned over the years that kids tend to lie to protect their parents. "Even victims of child abuse, where parents have taken their hands and put them in a hot oven or what have you, and you as a cop come in— or you as a stranger come in—and question them about it, they'll lie about it. They'll actually lie about it to defend their parents. So I didn't want to have her feel uncomfortable."

Having seen the gap in Joe's mouth the night before, Glynn wondered if the tooth had been knocked out in a fight with Diane. As he started to bite into the pizza, he said to Claudia: "I have to be very careful because I bit into a piece of pizza once and I broke my tooth. Did you ever see somebody break their tooth?"

"Yes, I saw Daddy break it," the youngster replied. According to Claudia, her father had broken his tooth on a piece of hard candy.

Glynn also was curious to see if the kids could verify Joe's statements to Composto about driving upstate to see a college friend and getting lost. Again, he didn't want to arouse suspicion, so he simply stated in the midst of the conversation: "Did you ever get lost in a car? That can be scary, can't it?"

And Claudia responded: "Oh yeah, like this weekend."

"Oh," said Glynn. "It sounds like an exciting weekend. Tell me about it."

And she did. Claudia recalled going out to Amagansett on Friday, then leaving on Saturday to go upstate. She didn't know where they had gone, just upstate. "It was a long ride up," she said. "It was late at night. It was dark. It's scary up there. There's no lights and we were trying to find this guy's house." She then told Glynn that her father left after only staying for a little while. "He came back at the end of the weekend."

The dinner guests were made privy to other developments from Claudia's weekend: she remembered going shopping with her father, but didn't remember what store they'd gone to. She made no mention of the ice purchase either. But she did remember that "we had things we had to do Saturday morning."

Glynn was making a conscious effort not to bring up Mommy because the baby-sitters had told him both children had become quite upset when the subject was raised earlier. Still, he tried to delve gently. "Did your mommy go up with you when you went upstate?" Claudia told him that her mother had not joined the family in Amagansett for the weekend and had stayed in the city. If she was lying about not having seen her mother, she was good at it.

Under the circumstances, Glynn thought the children were in pretty good spirits. Claudia didn't appear to be traumatized. At one point during dinner, Blake started crying and had to leave the table. But otherwise, he, too, appeared to be in a relatively tranquil mood for a pre-schooler.

After about an hour of eating and chatting, Morgillo and Glynn left, convinced the children didn't know anything.

Back at the Sixth Precinct in Manhattan, Glynn called Diane's father in Florida to see if he had heard anything or had any other thoughts on where Diane might be. The call was especially important, Glynn felt, because Whitmore had told him Diane had a habit of calling him every Tuesday. Here it was Tuesday evening, and still no call from Diane. "Wherever she is, she would call," said Whitmore.

Whitmore also told Glynn that Diane and Joe frequently took walks in Amagansett and that there was a cemetery right next door to their house. Whitmore also mentioned that Joe had purchased a bunch of grave sites there and that he feared "Diane might be in one of them. I would have them look out there in those graves. If something's happened to her, I wouldn't be surprised if he put her out there."

Out in Amagansett, a neighbor also told police about Joe's graveyard investment and his frequently expressed desire to be buried there. A couple of men walked over to Oak Grove Cemetery to look for a fresh grave.

The cemetery is a tiny spit of land, as far as cemeteries

go. There's no perpetual care, and lawn care is performed by relatives or their gardeners.

The cops found one plot considerably sunken, but a check with the caretaker revealed the low spot had been there for quite a while, so they moved on—across the street, where they took a long look at a man-made pond before deciding not to dredge it. They also went out back to check the horse farm. Nothing doing there either.

Down the road in a large potato field, the cops found tire tracks along a stretch of brier bushes. The car's wheels had spun a crevice in the soil at the entrance to the farm as well. The forensic guys took a tire print but it wasn't a good one.

Several officers took the sniffing dog down to Indian Wells beach, on the ocean side, where the Pikuls belonged to the beach club. Perhaps Diane had been killed there. Situated at the end of a long row of beautiful old-money estates, Indian Wells is frequented year-round by teen-agers and by people just out for a walk. It would have been a crazy place to bury a body, but the investigators weren't prepared to rule anything out yet. Underneath the beach house, adjacent to the parking lot, the officers found a sand mound looser and cleaner than the rest, but it turned out to be nothing.

Inside the house on Windmill Lane, the forensic team spent four hours searching for clues. Investigators seized thirty-nine items of evidence, including a six-inch kitchen knife, two small vacuums, and a sample of what appeared to be a bloodstain from the jamb of the master-bedroom door. A piece of wood flooring that appeared to bear a bloodstain also was taken.

Part of a tooth was removed from inside a drawer in the master bedroom. The investigators also discovered thirty-eight condoms—four different brands and a variety of styles: nonslip, natural skin, lubricated, deluxe, X-tra. Left behind that night, they were secured by the end of the week in light of Joe's condom story.

Joe's Mazda was impounded and taken to the East Hampton Village highway barn. Detective Brown stayed with the vehicle until about 1:00 A.M., when the state-police forensic officials joined him. The investigators took several photos, vacuumed up some sand, and took a tire print. About three, they called it a night.

Back in the city, Glynn also called it a night and headed to his home on Long Island, to his three kids and wife Rosemary. The situation was beginning to look more bleak by the hour. There was no word of inquiry from Joe Pikul, the man who filed the missing-persons report. He seemed to remain confident that Diane would show up sooner or later.

Glynn brought copies of Diane's short stories with him to show his wife, an avid reader. The story where the female character killed the male especially caught their eye.

CHAPTER · 13

A Blockage in
the Ditch

WILLIAM HELLER, A LIGHT-EQUIPMENT operator, was riding shotgun in Doug Pfleger's truck along the shoulder on the northbound side of the Governor Thomas E. Dewey Thruway on Wednesday afternoon, October 28. Because it had rained heavily the night before, Heller was on the lookout for debris on the road between Mileposts 50 to 76 and in the drainage areas below the shoulder.

Just below a tiny turnoff at Milepost 56.5, about three miles from the Newburgh exit, Heller noticed something blocking the channel at the base of the culvert—a large green object covered with a tire and a couple of rocks.

Pfleger stopped the yellow Thruway Authority truck. Heller dismounted and descended the precipice. He took a quick peek at the package and instantly had an ugly suspicion of what he was looking at. He immediately recalled a grisly day a year and a half earlier when he was still working the Thruway division north of the Bronx. That day Heller had been driving the highway in West Nyack, about forty miles south of where he now stood, when he looked over the guardrail and spotted a sock protruding from a plastic bag. He thought someone had put the sock on a stick until he grabbed it and felt a foot.

Heller remembered the episode as if it happened yesterday. The badly beaten body had been wrapped in two plastic bags, one over the bottom, one over the top. The body was petite, accompanied by a pair of penny loafers. At first, Heller thought it was a child's body, a thought that almost made him vomit. It took police several days to identify the small-framed Chinese man as an unemployed cook from New York's Chinatown, and Heller later heard that the victim may have died in a "Karate Fight to the Death," where combatants battle it out for prize money and spectators bet on their favorite warrior.

With the horror of that day's work forever etched in his memory, Heller was none too happy to be peering down at a saturated tarp clinging to two legs like a pair of breasts at a wet-T-shirt contest. "Why me?" he thought to himself. Heller moved no closer. He instead walked back up the hill to extend an invitation to Pfleger.

"I think we got a body," he said. "Why don't you go down and make a positive ID."

Pfleger wanted no part of it, and the two men started arguing. "I've done this before. It's your turn to do it," Heller pleaded.

"No, no, no," said Pfleger.

Realizing that his partner wasn't going to budge, Heller took out his buck knife and headed back down the slope. As he cut open one end of the canvas, his suspicions were confirmed: he was now staring at a pair of woman's feet sheathed in black panty hose. Because of the towels and other paraphernalia stuffed into the tarp, Heller thought he had uncovered a bag lady—murdered, then discarded with all of her worldly possessions. He turned around and made his way up the slippery, leaf-covered hill. Back in the truck, Heller grabbed the radio and called his dispatcher.

That same morning, Joe took the children to school, and at First Presbyterian, he asked to see Marjorie Goldsmith, the director. Joe explained that Diane had been missing since the weekend and that he didn't know what to tell the kids, who were very upset.

Goldsmith heard his story and then some: Joe and Diane were having problems; he thought she was having an affair; he'd driven out to Amagansett that Friday with Claudia and Blake in the sports car, arriving about 10:30; he'd waited up for Diane, even called the garage back in the city.

Joe also revealed that he now stayed in the guest room

and that Diane used the master bedroom, that he'd looked under the master bed for Claudia's shoe and instead found condoms that were not his brand. "I must have been blind. I should have seen it sooner," he said, contending that Diane left the condoms lying around "to get a reaction" from him, that all of her friends were from AA, and that he believed Diane had been trying to get his goat.

He said that when Diane finally arrived, he asked what had taken her so long and the discussion quickly turned into a fight. "Then she went out in the yard for a walk," he said, explaining that both of them had been taking strolls to get away from each other in the heat of battle. Joe said he then went to sleep and never saw her again. "She's gone off on a toot," he said, explaining that he and Diane were recovering alcoholics. "She's done that before."

Goldsmith thought to herself: "Why is he telling me this?" Then she gave Joe some advice on how to help the children cope with their mother's disappearance.

Joe spent the rest of the day at Arnhold & S. Bleichroeder, trying to maintain his normal routine. He didn't get much work done, however. He spent a great deal of time on the telephone trying to reach Federico up in Massachusetts. He also chatted from time to time with Michael Katzenstein, his civil attorney in Manhattan.

Marshall Weingarden reached Joe in the early afternoon and was told that Diane was still missing. Weingarden suggested that Joe bring the children out to his house in New Jersey on Saturday. It would be Halloween, and there'd be a parade. The Weingardens had costumes for Claudia and Blake, and if Joe wanted, he could leave the children for a couple of nights. Joe said it sounded like a good idea.

About 3:30, Joe slipped out of the office to visit his dentist on Wall Street. While he was there he called Federico two more times to make certain the lawyer was coming back to New York.

Late in the afternoon, Joe headed uptown to Kronish Lieb Weiner and Hellman, 1345 Avenue of the Americas, to meet with Katzenstein again. While he was there he tried reaching Federico two more times to finalize plans for another meeting.

A Special Services for Children social worker called the Sixth Avenue apartment shortly after five o'clock, but no one answered. Claudia answered the next call at six. She told the worker her father was in the shower, and promised to tell him to return the call. Claudia said she and her brother were fine and added matter-of-factly that she did not know where her mother was.

A half hour later, an angry and upset Joe Pikul called the caseworker back. Adamant and abrupt, he demanded to know who had reported him, asked for a copy of the report and a "bill of particulars" before answering any questions. Joe said his lawyer would be calling in the morning.

In the meantime, Joe decided to keep a low profile, so he registered at the Warwick Hotel for the night under Katzenstein's name.

Tripodo Senior and Investigator Robert Venezia got the call shortly after three at a restaurant in New Windsor. A couple of maintenance men had found the body of a white female alongside the Thruway. Venezia rushed to the scene.

Investigator Kenneth T. Jones of the state police arrived about a half hour later to search for forensic evidence.

Directed to a stream bed below the road surface, Jones uncovered the tarp and saw the victim, dressed in a black corduroy skirt, black panty hose, black bra, red sheer panties, and a red, green, and yellow plaid flannel shirt. Her feet were bare. The collar of the flannel shirt had been ripped and tied in a knot. The clasp at the waistline of the skirt had been stretched and pulled, as if the body had been carried by the clothing. Several large towels, a striped, multicolored bathrobe, a pink throw rug, and a plastic sheet were packed around the corpse. Everything was wet, soiled, and sandy.

Both inside and around the tarp, the victim had been tied with a series of ropes—sash cord, telephone-wire-type line, and a pink plastic cord. There were three separate ropes tied outside, around her body and the tarp. From head to foot, a series of other ropes connected the cross ropes, forming a handlelike system, as if the package had been carried like a piece of luggage.

Inside the tarp, the victim's wrists were tied together with what appeared to be a dirty terrycloth belt. A pink plastic cord was wrapped tightly around her neck, then down around her wrists, and on to the feet, where it was loosely tied as well. A five-pound weight was threaded through the wire and attached to the overall package.

"Did you find any sand?" an investigator looking over the body was asked.

"Yeah, there's some in the mouth and in the ears," came the reply.

The clothing matched the description of Diane Pikul's, but that certainly wasn't enough. An investigator approached with a photo that had been rushed to the scene, but because the victim's face had either been bashed in or squished in during the hours or days since her demise, they had difficulty determining if the picture matched the body.

The investigator reached down, grabbed the corpse's nose, and tried to straighten it out. Then the cop looked from photo to body, body to photo. Finally certain, he proclaimed: "Yeah, that's her."

At Lehman College in the Bronx, Dr. Mark L. Taff, a forensic pathologist from Long Island, was chairing a meeting of the New York Society of Forensic Sciences, a group he had founded, when his beeper went off. As coroner's pathologist for three counties north of New York City, he was used to being summoned at all hours to perform autopsies. It was Orange County calling this time. The body of an apparent murder victim, a white female, had been found tied up in a ditch along the New York Thruway.

Taff said he'd drive up as soon as he could.

Farther south, in Greenwich Village, Detective Glynn set off in search of Joe Pikul, hoping to convince him to go upstate to take a look at the body. Glynn first stopped off at the duplex on Sixth Avenue. The door was answered by a Spanish-speaking woman, newly hired, who explained in broken English that Joe was not home. She said he was expected by nine, though, because she had to go home to take care of her own children.

Gazing over the baby-sitter's shoulder, Glynn spotted a thin blond girl at the top of the stairs. It was Claudia, staring in confusion at her pizza-party partner. "It was as if she was saying, 'Hey, you weren't a cop yesterday,' " Glynn said. The detective looked away, feeling bad for having tricked the child. He was almost certain the youngster's mother was dead upstate, and her father was a highly probable suspect. The night before Glynn had posed as her friend. Now he was at the front door as an enemy. The job did have its low moments.

Glynn left and went to Joe's place of business, then to his Battery Park apartment. Joe was nowhere to be found, but the doorman knew exactly who Glynn was looking for. "He's strange, but he's a good tipper," the detective was told.

Back at the precinct, Glynn returned a call he had missed from a William Schwartz, who identified himself as an attorney representing Joseph Pikul. He told Glynn that he understood the detective had been at Joe's residence and office looking for him. Glynn told Schwartz that he had indeed, explaining that a female body had been found in upstate New York fitting the description of Diane Pikul. Joe was needed to make an identification.

Schwartz said he expected to hear from Joe later and would pass along the request. "Do you intend to arrest him?"

"No," said Glynn honestly. If there was going to be an arrest, Glynn wasn't going to make it anyway; his missing-persons case was now a state-police homicide investigation.

At 9:32 P.M., Glynn filed the second suspected child-abuse complaint to the state hotline. He alerted officials to the discovery of Diane's body and the fact that she was a homicide victim. "Suspicion father is involved, father distraught and has guns in the home," the abuse report continued. Glynn said he believed the children were in "a potentially dangerous situation and should be removed." Glynn said he would await an update.

Tired of waiting for Schwartz, the detective dialed back.

Schwartz said he'd been in touch with Joe and had given him the message. However, the attorney added, his client was too distraught to make an ID. Glynn told Schwartz that Joe Pikul was the only relative available.

"She's got a father," said Schwartz. Glynn pointed out

that Don Whitmore lived in Florida, but Schwartz wouldn't budge. "Mr. Pikul is too distraught to come in to make any identification. He won't come in."

Schwartz's comments worried Glynn and then Bowen, for if the discovery of Diane's body sent Joe into a panic, he might turn on his children. After Bowen discussed the situation with the zone commander's office, the brass decided to remove Claudia and Blake.

Not knowing what to expect, Glynn headed over with a captain, a sergeant, two other detectives, a city social services worker, and several patrolmen. Just as the group arrived, Claudia and Blake were hurriedly exiting the apartment with their father's niece, Edleen Bergelt, and her husband. Bags in hand, the group was marched back up into the apartment.

Claudia told the social worker she'd last seen her mother the previous Friday and "that her father told her that he had a fight with her mother, and also told her that she was not going to see her mother anymore."

Mrs. Bergelt, who identified herself as a CIA employee explained that Joe had called to report that Diane had run away following an argument and that he was unavoidably detained. There was a baby-sitter watching the kids that evening, but she had to leave. "Now the kids are going to be there by themselves," Joe had told her. "Would you please go over to the apartment." Mrs. Bergelt asked if it would be all right to take the children back to their apartment, and Joe readily agreed.

Staring down at a dozen cops, the Bergelts wanted to know what was going on, especially since Uncle Joe had warned, "You're going to hear a lot of terrible things about me, but it's not true." One of the officers in charge suggested that it wasn't a good idea to discuss these matters in front of the children and invited everyone to come down to the station house.

Shortly after 11:30, Dr. Taff began carving up the corpse at St. Luke's Hospital in the city of Newburgh. A member of the Governor's Commission on Domestic Violence and a former member of the New York City Task Force on Acquired Immuno-Deficiency Syndrome, Dr. Taff knew his way around the autopsy table; he had performed some

1,700 autopsies and witnessed several thousand more. His curriculum vitae was impressive, an important issue if his work were ever challenged by a defense attorney at a trial.

Dr. Taff was joined in the autopsy room by one of the Orange County coroners, Mary Ellen Wright, and several members of the New York State Police. Briefed by the police officials, Dr. Taff unwrapped the white sheet that police had used to transport the body and began with an external examination—head to toe on the front, then head to toe on the rear—stripping away the corpse's clothing in the process. Because of the knot, the doctor had to cut away the top of the flannel shirt, which was covered with sand.

The body, 5 feet 3 ½ inches and between 115 and 120 pounds at time of death, was covered with leaves and dirt and sand. It was in the early stages of decomposition. There were no signs of external bleeding. There was a four-inch hole in the black panty hose over the left thigh area, and an absorbent pad over the victim's vaginal orifice.

A yellow ring was removed from the fourth finger of the victim's left hand, and Dr. Taff also removed a Swatch quartz Swiss watch from the victim's left wrist. The watch was still working when it was removed at 12:10 A.M., and state-police investigator Lawrence Shewark noted that the time on the watch read an hour later, 1:10. The time on the watch offered a potential key clue, given that the clocks had been turned back the previous Saturday.

Examining the corpse more closely, Dr. Taff found several pinpoint and large hemorrhages in the whites of the eyes. The eyeballs had burst and had been bleeding, a common trait with asphyxial death or strangulation. There were also pinpoint hemorrhages on the lung surfaces, another common indicator of asphyxia.

There were two small crescent-shaped marks over the right chin and neck, consistent with fingernail scratch marks produced by the strangler or by the victim trying to save herself.

A pink-coated cord was tied snugly around the victim's throat, with part of it rubbing into the skin. There was also an angled red mark running across the right rear portion of the neck, which matched up with the pink cord.

Before moving to his internal exam, Dr. Taff took a hair sample as well as nail clippings from each finger.

Internally, Dr. Taff examined every organ as well as the head, neck, chest, and abdomen. From his examination, he could tell that the corpse had been placed on its left side after death.

An incision was made into the scalp to facilitate an examination of the brain and skull. Peeling back the skin on the face and over the head, Dr. Taff discovered fresh multiple bruises that had not been visible externally. There were at least nine separate impacts of the same age distributed all around Diane's head: two wounds over the left eye, three wounds over the back of her head, two wounds over the right temple between the ear and the eyebrow, a wound on the left cheek between the nose and the ear, a wound above the left ear. There was a tenth blow, a two-inch-wide "blunt-force impact" to the back of the left elbow.

Both sides of the victim's neck showed recent hemorrhages as well, indicating manual strangulation, and evidence of hemorrhaging in the soft tissue of the muscle underneath the skin by the neck ligature mark. To Dr. Taff, this meant that the victim had been alive when the ligature was applied, as opposed to the ligature found on the victim's ankles. No signs of hemorrhaging were found around the wrists, indicating that the ropes there also had been applied after death.

This specific analysis might seem unimportant to the uninitiated, but these facts would serve to limit the range of a defendant's story in a trial.

The victim's hands and feet had a "washerwoman's appearance" from being exposed to the highway spring bed for an extended period of time. There was "skin slippage" on the left wrist as a result of the bindings, and superficial layers of skin had already started to fall off. Also, the hair on the back of the victim's head was matted with blood that had escaped from her left nostril during a postmortem process called purging.

Dr. Taff also detected hemorrhaging of the soft tissue on the left side of the rib cage between the eighth and eleventh ribs. The victim had been hit there with a blunt instrument, or her body had struck a fixed object. And a further examination of the middle neck uncovered a broken bone—the thyroid cartilage—and evidence of squeezing of the "vital blood vessels."

When he was through, Dr. Taff tentatively determined that the corpse before him had died of strangulation and a severe beating. If the victim hadn't been choked to death, she would have succumbed eventually from the assault. Diane Pikul, in other words, had been beaten senseless, then strangled.

Inside the second-floor detectives' room at the Sixth Precinct, Glynn gingerly approached Claudia Pikul. "How ya doing? You remember me?"

Claudia remembered, all right. "Daddy told me not to talk to the police." That was that.

It was after midnight now and the kids were obviously tired. Blake was already falling asleep. So they were taken to the bunks in the back room.

Glynn and the other detectives turned their attention to Edleen, who was eight months pregnant, and her husband. Glynn gave them a brief rundown on the previous three days, then broke the news: Diane had been found dead upstate.

When the social worker announced that the children were going to be taken into custody, Mrs. Bergelt became even more upset. Sensing the terror that the news had triggered, Glynn explained that he had three children about the same ages at home and offered to take Claudia and Blake with him. But Glynn's superiors pointed out the obvious conflict of interest. If Glynn took the children home, some defense attorney would almost surely allege that he'd mercilessly pumped Claudia and Blake for incriminating information. So in the middle of the night, the children were involuntarily drafted into the squalid homeless-welfare bureaucracy of the New York City Department of Social Services.

Glynn, thinking of his own kids, then Claudia and Blake, set out for Marylou's, a nearby bar on Ninth Street near University Place. He needed a stiff rye and ginger.

CHAPTER • 14

"Did She Have AIDS?"

THE STATE POLICE OFFICIALLY BEGAN looking for Joseph John Pikul at 1:00 A.M., Thursday, October 29. Not only had he refused to identify the body found upstate, but he was nowhere to be found. After receiving the preliminary autopsy results and reviewing the evidence, Senior Investigator Joseph Tripodo, Sr., and Lieutenant Jim O'Donnell, from the state-police criminal investigations regional headquarters in upstate Middletown, conferred with Alan Joseph, the chief assistant district attorney for Orange County. Joseph, who was still not certain who would end up with the jurisdiction to prosecute, told the police supervisors they had enough to make an arrest.

Two teams of investigators from Tripodo's Newburgh staff drove to Manhattan to join several state-police teams from Long Island. At daybreak some of them started conducting interviews with co-workers and friends of both Diane and Joe. Tripodo Senior also wanted someone to speak to the Pikul children. They may not have witnessed the murder, but it was hard to believe Claudia and Blake didn't know something important, especially given the events of that Friday night, their weekend upstate, and then the car wash. Maybe they heard part of the argument or saw their father putting something in the station wagon.

They were too late, however. By now the children were deeply entrenched in the New York City Human Resources Administration bureaucracy. In fact, when the Bergelts arrived at the city offices about 11:00 A.M., the social workers had no idea where the two children had been taken. It took another several hours before Claudia and Blake were located and reunited with the Bergelts. Caseworkers tried to interview Blake, but he was "too distracted." Claudia, on the other hand, kept "repeating that her father told her not to answer any questions from anybody."

With Edleen and Keith Bergelt's permission, the state child-abuse registry was checked to ascertain that neither was a known child abuser. A case worker then made an emergency visit to the Bergelts' apartment on the upper East Side. During the visit, Keith Bergelt played a taped message from Joe, telling them he was innocent of his wife's murder and that "someone was trying to frame him." A message had been left by Don Whitmore as well. Diane's father "delegated the paternal family to care for the children," according to an official report. Satisfied that all was in order, city officials released the children to Joe's niece.

One of the state-police teams, Investigators James G. Probst and Stephen J. Oates from Long Island, set up surveillance outside the Barbizon Hotel. They'd been informed by Jim Burns, Joe's driver, that he'd made an airport pickup for Joe and delivered his passenger—one Vincent Federico—to the midtown hotel. Operating on the theory that Joe was hiding out in the hotel under an assumed name, the investigators were justifiably interested in getting a look at a guest registered as "Joe Pike." But as the hours passed, Joe Pikul failed to appear.

Joe, of course, had spent the night at the Warwick Hotel, passing the time by making telephone calls. At 4:37 A.M. that Thursday, a call was placed from "Mr. Katzenstein's room" to one Sandra Jarvinen. Shortly after eight that morning, Joe called his sister in Virginia and told her, "Diane is missing. They're trying to pin it on me. I'm quite innocent." Joe then hung up without further conversation.

At the suggestion of her daughter Edleen, Joe's sister called Glynn to tell him about Joe's call. She told Glynn she was very concerned, given the fact that "Joe's always been a little strange."

Federico, of course, knew where to find Joe. At one

point he swiftly departed the Barbizon and jumped into a cab. The attorney was arduously pursued, but the state police lost him in a Manhattan gridlock.

According to Joe's subsequent recounting of events, when Federico arrived at the Warwick, he gave the attorney his additional $10,000—in two checks, because Federico wanted to cash part of the money immediately.

A short time later, Federico and Joe went over to the law offices of Gallop, Clayman and Dawson, on the corner of Forty-second Street and Madison Avenue, to meet with Charles Clayman and Katzenstein. It was then that Federico was told that his services were no longer required.

The game plan that Thursday called for Joe to sleep in a Manhattan hotel other than the Warwick, and under his own name.

With Joe AWOL, the police still needed someone to positively identify the body. Of all the women the detectives from the Sixth Precinct had interviewed, Glynn thought Inga was about the only one capable of handling the task. She agreed to go, but expressed concern about leaving a distraught Carina alone. Glynn told her not to call Carina after the viewing under any circumstances and to wait until she came back to Manhattan to give her any updates. Investigator Joseph Tripodo, Jr., a young trooper on loan to the Newburgh barracks for the Pikul case, was assigned by his father, the senior Newburgh investigator, to drive Inga up to the morgue, where she tearfully identified the corpse as Diane.

Despite Glynn's warning, Inga then called Carina, who became extremely upset. Sobbing herself, Inga called Glynn at the precinct. Told that Carina needed someone to lean on, Glynn thought of Katzenstein, the business attorney who had helped Carina and Inga. Glynn dialed and asked for Mr. Katzenstein. Instead, he got switched to a Mr. Schwartz's office.

The detective tried repeatedly to get Katzenstein, but each time his call was connected to Schwartz's office. Schwartz finally got on the line. It was William Schwartz, the same Mr. Schwartz who had called the night before on behalf of Joe Pikul.

Suspicious, Schwartz demanded to know why Glynn was

calling Katzenstein. Glynn, of course, had no idea that Katzenstein had been meeting with Joe, let alone allowing him to use his name on hotel registers. All he knew was that this Katzenstein had said he was a business attorney for Inga, Carina, and Joe, and was willing to help in any way he could. He explained about Katzenstein's previous offer, but Schwartz wasn't buying. He told Glynn to stop calling.

Back at the Barbizon, Probst and Oates kicked into gear with Vinnie Federico's reappearance at about 2:00 P.M. They watched as the attorney had a couple of drinks at the small bar off the lobby, then returned to his room.

The investigators followed a few minutes later and knocked on Federico's door. No, a disappointed and annoyed Federico said, he was not Joe Pikul's attorney; he'd been fired before he'd been hired.

Oates asked Federico to call the new attorneys to see if Joe was still there. Reluctantly Federico complied, and they learned that Joe was still there. Oates and Probst departed promptly for Forty-second and Madison.

At the same time Probst and Oates were bird-dogging Federico in New York, two police officers knocked on Sandy Jarvinen's front door up in Norwell, Massachusetts. Alerted by the car-wash employees that Joe had used his telephone credit card, authorities in New York had traced the calls to Federico and Sandy.

By now Federico's occupation—and therefore his connection—was known. But Sandy added a new wrinkle to the unfolding mystery. Who was she? Why would Joe, after just dumping his wife's body, call her? Mistress was the first logical guess. Perhaps this was a love triangle.

Sandy revealed to Massachusetts State Trooper William Gorman and Sergeant Don Bongarzone of the Norwell police that Joe Pikul was her former husband, but she lied about the rest. She conceded that she'd seen Joe in Manhattan the previous Thursday, but insisted that she had not heard from him since. Confronted with the phone records, she then claimed she had been contacted once by Joe, but that she had missed the call, it was nothing important, and she'd erased the message from her answering machine. Pressed to recall what Joe had said, Sandy characterized the call as your basic "How are you? I'll call you later."

Gorman and Bongarzone also asked Sandy about Federico. She told them he was a friend, and that he was supposed to be picking her up that evening to go to the theater. She explained his absence by claiming that it was not uncommon for him to fail to appear. Federico, of course, was in New York City at that very moment.

Under additional questioning, Sandy acknowledged that her attorney-friend had been at her house that Tuesday, the twenty-seventh—the day Federico had left New York after Joe missed their appointment—but she lied when asked if Federico had told her about his contacts with Joe.

After the police left, Sandy went to the theater alone.

Probst and Oates were standing waiting for an elevator in the lobby at Forty-second and Madison when they were met by none other than Joe Pikul, exiting with a large gym bag.

"Mr. Pikul, I'm Investigator Oates from the state police. You're under arrest for murder."

The man beside Joe, who identified himself as Michael Katzenstein, asked if everyone could go back upstairs to Clayman's office. Probst and Oates agreed, so the group took the elevator to Suite 1301.

Charles Clayman stepped from behind his desk as the two investigators identified themselves. "You're Joe Pikul's lawyer?" he was asked.

"Yes," said Clayman, in private practice with his own firm for the past ten years. Samuel Dawson, one of the firm's other partners, would later be identified as Joe's criminal attorney, but for this night Clayman was handling the show.

Oates explained that they were going to go to the state-police barracks in Newburgh and that Joe would later be arraigned on second-degree murder charges before a local judge in the Newburgh area. Oates gave Clayman the barracks phone number.

Clayman told Joe he would come up in the morning for the arraignment, then instructed the investigators not to speak to his client. "No problem, sir," Probst responded.

Borrowing a raincoat from Clayman—and conveniently

leaving his gym bag behind—Joe departed with Probst and Oates out into the hustle and bustle of Forty-second Street.

Back at the car, Oates radioed the other state-police units in Manhattan. Originally, Oates and Probst planned to hand off Joe to a couple of brother officers from upstate. That way the upstate investigators could take the suspect up to their home base while Oates and Probst headed back to Long Island. But the relief unit was way downtown, and rather than wait the half hour or more sitting in midtown during the height of rush hour, where who knows what could happen, Oates and Probst decided to keep rolling north.

Taking the wheel in the gridlocked evening traffic, Oates asked Probst if he knew the best way out of the city. Probst suggested they continue toward Central Park, where they could cut across town to the West Side Highway. Joe piped up that they'd be better off traveling a street east of the park, then cut across one of the transverse roadways through the park.

"I'm really parched," Joe continued, asking Oates to stop. "I really love apple juice."

Oates said he'd stop at the next deli. "Please get a big container, the largest you can get," Joe pleaded.

Over on the West Side, Oates pulled over, went into a deli, and bought a plastic half-gallon jug of apple juice and some cigarettes for himself.

Joe, who was not handcuffed, opened the container and took a few healthy swigs. He was warned not to spill any on the seat. "This is good apple juice," he said, chugging away.

Now on the highway, Probst started telling Oates about Sesame Place, an amusement park in eastern Pennsylvania where Big Bird, Oscar the Grouch, Bert and Ernie, and other characters from the Public Broadcasting System's "Sesame Street" show hold forth.

"How old's your son?" Probst asked Oates from the backseat.

"Four," said Oates.

Probst said he had taken his two kids, aged 3½ and six, and they'd really enjoyed it. "It's a great place. It's not your typical type of amusement park," he said, explaining the facility's hands-on approach.

Joe interrupted, asking how far the park was from New York City. He said it sounded like a great place to take his own children. "I always wanted to do things with the kids. Diane didn't want to. Diane never wanted to do anything with the kids."

He went on to explain how much he loved his children. "That's why I did it," he said, sniffling and whimpering. "She's such a bitch. I have two kids, four and eight years old. They are the best part of me."

As Joe lowered his head, Probst leaned over to hear better. "I was in Europe a couple of weeks ago, and when I got back, the kids told me they had a different baby-sitter every night. They didn't know where their mother was," he said. "She deserved it. I never did anything wrong before in my life. I can't change it now."

Joe asked if there would be bail. Probst told Joe it would be up to the judge to set bail, but based on Joe's background he guessed bail wouldn't be prohibitive. Joe seemed pleased about that. "I want to be able to see my kids."

Oates, who was exhausted, hadn't been paying much attention to the conversation, concentrating instead on the road. He did hear enough, though, to turn around at one point and comment: "You fucked up, pal."

Joe looked back at Oates. "Yeah, I know."

As the unmarked police car approached the Newburgh exit on the Thruway in a slight mist, Joe said he had to go to the bathroom. Oates pulled the car over and let him out. Suddenly Joe was rattled, perhaps because he was standing so close to where he had dumped Diane's body. "No, I can't do it here. I can't go on the side of the road." As he got back in the car, the investigators cuffed him. Procedure, especially on a big case.

At 8:30, the group was met at the barracks by Senior Investigator Joseph Tripodo, Sr., his son Investigator Joseph Tripodo, Jr., and a third Bureau of Criminal Investigations member, Robert Venezia.

"We've been expecting you," said Tripodo Senior. Joe instantly renewed his request to go to the bathroom. "Joey, take him to the bathroom," Tripodo Senior instructed his son. "Keep an eye on him."

"Did She Have AIDS?" 189

Cuffs removed, Joe stepped into the bathroom, but to his consternation, Tripodo Junior followed. "Gee, can I go in alone? I find it difficult with you standing there."

"He don't want me to stay there," Joey yelled to his father.

"No," said Tripodo Senior. "You leave the door open and you stay there and you keep an eye on him. That's too bad."

Tripodo Junior turned back to Joe and told him: "Well, I'll step outside here, but I'll leave the door open."

Meanwhile, Probst asked: "Where are the phones?" Tripodo Junior indicated down the hall. Probst left the group at the bathroom, sat at one of the desks, and jotted down a few notes on Joe's conversation during the car ride. Then he called his family; he was coming home.

A six-year veteran of the state police force, Joe Tripodo, Jr., had just completed two years of undercover work with the New York Drug Task Force in New York City, complete with beard and earrings. He also had participated in plenty of investigations during his prior years as a uniformed trooper. This was his first big case, however. He was among a group of six new criminal investigators who had started the week at an orientation program at the regional office just up the road from the Newburgh barracks. But when the Pikul case erupted, the rookie investigators were temporarily assigned to assist. Although his father was a career trooper—a solid, thorough investigator who pulled no punches and treated everyone fairly—it still didn't hurt young Joe to have family in the right places when it came to dishing out the assignments.

His father, noticing that Joe Junior and the suspect were hitting it off, figured, "Let's see what happens." Tripodo Senior had already consulted with the first assistant district attorney for Orange County, Alan Joseph, about how to handle the situation. "If he wants to talk, you can listen to him," the prosecutor instructed.

The two men walked to the Bureau of Criminal Investigations room and sat down on either side of a small desk. Joe Pikul starting jabbering away, explaining that he was "really uptight, nervous, and extremely anxious" over the fact that his attorney had not come up with him.

Everyone there knew Joe had a lawyer, but they also knew he wasn't a sophisticated criminal. As Tripodo Senior later remarked: "Thank God there's still a lot of people around who figure if you're silent, that's almost an admission of guilt."

Joe told Tripodo Junior that the evening's experience was "a traumatic thing to go through," and that he was at a loss to explain why his attorney had left him "basically stranded." He said he was "under extreme pressure," that the last several days had been very hard on him. He said he felt very alone.

Tripodo Junior shrugged his shoulders. "I'm sorry."

Joe, alluding to the tears streaming down his face, said, "Please excuse my state of mind."

"It's perfectly normal to be this upset," said Tripodo Junior. "Just, you know, take it easy."

Joe then asked Tripodo Junior: "What's your first name?"

"Joe," the investigator replied.

Joe Pikul appeared to relax and suggested they call each other Joe. "You're a lot more comforting to talk to than some of these guys from New York City. Where are you from?"

Tripodo Junior explained that he'd been living in Manhattan, in a condominium on Fifty-seventh Street. Joe said he knew the place, that he had occasionally visited an old girlfriend who lived there after she had gotten out of a psychiatric hospital. He immediately added that the woman really wasn't a girlfriend, "just a good friend." He then went on to compare this friend to Diane, contending the woman had given him "all kinds of support," but that Diane had never really supported him. "She was never happy with anything I ever did. Nothing that I did ever satisfied her."

"It's all right," said Tripodo Junior. "I understand how you feel."

Joe started talking about his job, again explaining that Diane was never happy with him. "You know, I'm not a young man anymore." He said he was thinking about quitting his job and spending more time with his children. "I love my kids dearly. My only dream is my kids." He said his wife was "so demanding, always wanting this and wanting that." As a result, he said, he couldn't afford to give up his job.

Joe was crying profusely now. He put his head down, leaned forward, and in a confiding whisper told Tripodo Junior: "Joe, she tried to kill me—not physically—but mentally. She tried to break me down. I just couldn't take it anymore. I hope the kids understand. I don't care if you guys give me ten or twenty years, I think everybody is better off without her."

With this off his chest Joe recovered his old aplomb. Sitting back in his chair, he winked. "I don't care what penalty I get, everybody is better off without her. She never did anything for the family or me, never gave me any support."

"I'm sorry that you had to live with such an ungrateful woman," Tripodo Junior said. "Anybody would feel the same way."

Tears flashed in Joe's eyes as he looked at the ceiling, shaking his head as if to say, "I can't believe this is happening."

Joe started talking about his family again, how he'd called his home from Zurich "and the kids were crying: 'Where's Mommy? Where's Mommy?' She stayed away. Things happened just like that. She had a baby-sitter for the kids."

His son, Blake, loved pancakes, Joe said, but "he was afraid to ask his mother to make pancakes for him because she'd probably say no." Diane "never did anything for them. Whatever the kids wanted, she never took care of them. If the kids wanted pancakes, I would have to make them."

Wiping the tears from his cheeks and clenching his fists, Joe offered yet another version of the condom story. "When I came home from Zurich, I found condoms under the bed." He said one of the condoms was used. "The condoms were not mine. Joe, how could I be so blind?"

At ten o'clock Tripodo Senior came over. "It's time that you go to be processed," he told Joe, who was then handed over to Investigator Robert Venezia, a twenty-three-year veteran of the state-police force. Immediately, Venezia turned Joe over to Trooper Louis Roman, who took him to be fingerprinted and photographed. When Roman was done, he walked the suspect back to Venezia's office for preparation of the General 5 arrest report, a simple form that contains a list of basic information required for processing an arrest.

Venezia read Joe his constitutional rights, the first time they were read to him that night. Joe said he understood, then advised Venezia he had an attorney and therefore could not discuss the case. As Venezia started taking the pedigree data, Joe interrupted to explain that he was disturbed that his lawyer had not come up to the barracks with him. He also complained about his $250,000 retainer and how the attorney was not going to get the money so easily from his bank overseas.

Then Joe started to complain about Diane again, and Venezia told him he knew how he felt, that his wife had divorced him and taken their son to England to live.

Having spotted a generous spread of lunch meats and salads on a nearby table, Joe mentioned that he was hungry. Venezia walked over to the buffet and made Joe a sandwich. "I'm thirsty, too. Can you get me a soda?" Venezia again obliged. This was one occasion in which a defense attorney was not going to score points with the jury by complaining the defendant was grilled for hours without food and drink. The barracks was flowing with food that evening because of a retirement banquet down the road, an annual affair for pensioned colleagues. The investigators working the Pikul case had bought tickets but, with Joe's arrest, could not attend.

Recognizing that his troops were being victimized by bad timing, Tripodo Senior had called over to the party. "Hey listen, we paid for the damn tickets over there. How about sending us some food?" So a big tray of cold cuts, bread, rolls, salads, pickles, and sodas was dispatched. As the night wore on, Joe went back to the trough at least three or four times. "He kept eating. He had a voracious appetite," said Tripodo Junior.

With a plate of food in hand, Joe asked Venezia what he was being charged with. Venezia told him the charge was "murder in the second degree." There is no murder in the first degree in New York State, a charge once reserved for the killing of police officers.

"My only hope is to beat this thing on a technicality," replied Joe.

Joe also asked where his wife's body was. He was told it had been taken to the morgue at St. Luke's Hospital in Newburgh.

"Did she have AIDS? Can she be checked for AIDS?" Joe asked.

"I don't know," responded Venezia to those most unusual questions.

"Did they do an autopsy?" the suspect wondered aloud.

"Yes," said Venezia.

Joe wanted to know if the autopsy revealed that Diane had had sex recently. Venezia told him that he didn't know of any recent sex.

Out of the blue, Joe launched into a monologue again, of which the salient points were: "I killed her for no particular reason. . . . She was divorcing me. . . . She was going through with the divorce. . . . You have to go back to last July to understand this," he said, referring to the summer of 1986, when Diane had hired Felder.

Sobbing once again, Joe told Venezia that Diane had been blackmailing him, that she'd hired a private investigator to follow him around, that she'd discovered he was a cross dresser and was telling everyone about it. "I wish someone would shoot me. My life is over. Then at least the children would be able to collect on my insurance."

Then Joe asked to see Diane. Informed of the request, Tripodo Senior said maybe Joe didn't believe they really had the body. He told Venezia it sounded like a good idea, for when a suspect is confronted with the body, their reactions can provide valuable evidence.

While Joe was having yet another sandwich, Tripodo Junior explained what to expect at the morgue. "It's a pretty traumatic thing," he said, making certain Joe wanted to go.

Joe responded by putting his coat on and saying: "Let's go see the stiff."

Joe mostly mumbled to himself during the twenty-minute drive to the hospital. When Tripodo Senior rolled the body out, Joe looked at it and stated matter-of-factly: "That's her."

On the ride back, he was talkative again: "Diane would

be very upset, if she was alive, over the fact that we let her be seen without any of her makeup on," he told Tripodo Junior in the backseat. "That's the kind of person she was, very egotistical. She was evil, a malicious person. She was always concerned about her looks. Everybody is better off without her. I don't care if you give me twenty years, fine. I don't care. It just doesn't matter anymore."

"Everything is going to be all right," said Tripodo Junior.

Back at the barracks, Joe requested yet another sandwich. Venezia obliged, bringing him another soda as well. It was now early morning, Friday, October 30.

"I'm very concerned about my children," Joe said as Venezia put the finishing touches on the General 5 form. "What will happen to me? What's going to happen to the children?" He began jumping around again. He wanted to know where he was, where he was going to be arraigned. Venezia turned him over to Senior Investigator Tripodo, the man in charge of the investigation.

There's an old story that cops like to tell about a pair of southern sheriff's deputies driving along with a murder suspect in a case where the body hadn't been found. Trying to tug at the suspect's emotions, one of the deputies says, "If only we knew where the body was. Then we could have a real Christian burial." With that, the suspect breaks down, the authorities find the body, and they get their man.

The policemen on this case had been busy conducting their own brand of psychological warfare on Joe: arresting officers who happened to have kids the same ages; chats about Sesame Place; chats about divorced wives taking the kids away; Tripodo Junior getting on a first-name basis, talking about condos and girlfriends. They had been chatting Joe up all night, and there was no reason to stop now.

Tripodo Senior had already alerted Town Justice Donald J. Suttlehan that they'd be bringing a murder suspect over for arraignment, but Tripodo Senior figured he had to make one try himself.

Briefed as to what Joe had told the others, he knew that incriminating comments aside, Joe really hadn't come clean. There were several key pieces missing to this puzzle, like exactly where and how the murder had taken place.

"Joe, just a few more questions," he said. "I want to clear up a few things." The two Joes, both born in the wake of the Great Depression, started out talking about Black Monday. "I went down good," said Joe the analyst. Asked how much, Joe replied, "I'm afraid to even think about it."

As before, Joe started complaining about his home life, how Diane didn't care about the kids, always had baby-sitters, and was too busy with her own activities. He said that when he called from overseas on business, the kids got on the phone and told him they were with a baby-sitter. Tripodo Senior didn't want to hear all that. "Joe, tell me, what really happened?"

Joe explained that the killing hadn't occurred inside the house. When Diane had arrived that night, they both started arguing. "What the hell took you so long? Where you been?" He said Diane yelled right back, calling him names. "She was really talking sharp to me. I can't believe how sharp she was talking to me. She never talked that sharp to me before."

Fearing they would wake the children, Joe said he and Diane had gone outside, got into the Mazda, and rode down to the beach—Alberts Landing, a small desolate clearing on the bay side—where the argument continued.

Tripodo Senior pressed for details that might help the forensic investigators uncover evidence. Joe described how the small parking lot ends and drops off into the sand, how he and Diane had walked off to the left. Joe said the confrontation did not take place near the water, but back in the dunes, quite a distance from the waterline.

Joe was describing what is locally referred to as Little Alberts Landing, and the sandy area to the left was the beach between Little Alberts Landing and Alberts Landing. The dunes between the two beaches had been the burial site several years ago of another murder victim whose body was found only after her lover confessed and provided the location to police.

Continuing with his story, Joe explained that as he and Diane walked, they argued some more, that she called him "a fag" and other names in a tone he'd never heard from her. Joe said they also argued about an incident two weeks prior, when he and the kids had gone to a show at Madison Square Garden's Felt Forum and Diane stayed out in the Hamptons, supposedly because she couldn't be bothered. In the course of the argument, according to Joe, Diane mentioned that "*we* had a good time on the weekend."

"She slipped," he told Tripodo, sure Diane had been with a boyfriend. "She didn't care about the kids. She always had baby-sitters."

Tripodo Senior moved the conversation back to the night in question. Joe said the argument eventually escalated. "We started fighting. The next thing, she was laying there, not moving," said Joe.

"Joe, tell me how you did it," Tripodo Senior asked.

"You know," said Joe.

The investigator repeated the question. "I want you to tell me."

Joe raised his two hands in front of him, turned his fingers inward around an imaginary neck, and shook in a back-and-forth, choking motion.

"Mr. Pikul, you choked her?"

Joe shook his head up and down, yes.

"Where was she when you choked her?"

"I really don't remember that much about it, but I believe she was down in the sand."

Joe said he left Diane partially buried and returned to the house. It was at that time, he now contended, that he found condoms under the bed in the master bedroom.

He told Tripodo Senior that he'd done some research on condom companies and was pretty familiar with the different brands. He knew the ones under the bed weren't his brand. As a result, he concluded, Diane had been using the condoms in the master bedroom with "some other person." The key to this version, however, was that Joe said he found the condoms *after* the fatal argument at the beach, not before.

Joe told Tripodo Senior that he'd washed the sheets and blanket on the master bed.

"Why, Joe?"

"Because she was in bed with some guy," Joe answered.

Tripodo Senior asked what he did the next day. Joe told him he went to a hardware store with the kids and then telephoned a friend in New Windsor, a Henry Sawoska.

Joe said he left the children in New Windsor, but couldn't remember everything that happened after that because he was "in a bad state" and had "blanked out for periods." He remembered going to Massachusetts, to a Route 128, down to Plymouth, then driving back to the Hamptons.

"Did you stop and see anybody?" Tripodo Senior asked.

"No," said Joe.

Joe said he had trouble remembering everything that had happened while he was driving around Sunday, but remembered sleeping here and there for an hour or two at a time.

Joe was apparently covering his tracks even as he confessed, however. In this version, he had not driven the kids to the Sawoskas with the body in the back. Apparently he had already realized how bad such a scenario would appear.

Instead, he said, he returned to the beach in Amagansett to retrieve Diane's body, then put it in the back of the station wagon and returned to Windmill Lane. He said he couldn't remember when he did all this, but was certain it was dark at the time. Upon his return to the house, he wrapped the body in a canvas that he used to cover lawn chairs, stuffed towels around the body, and tied it all up with rope from inside the house.

Again, not sure of the timing, Joe recalled driving back to New York City, sleeping in the Sixth Avenue apartment, and leaving Diane's body in the car.

The next morning, Joe said, he drove to the Newburgh area and believed he dropped the body on the Thruway. He said he picked up his children in New Windsor, but again couldn't remember the details.

Tripodo, a Korean War veteran with thirty years on the job, listened and analyzed. His gut feeling was that Joe was telling the truth. He'd just been arrested; he was upset and obviously under pressure. More convincing was the way Joe had been emphatic about certain details. Whenever Tripodo Senior would say something like "Okay, Joe, she's buried on the beach," Joe interrupted to correct that she was "partially buried." It sounded like the way it happened.

At 2:45 the judge called, asking for the defendant. As a standard security precaution, Tripodo Senior ordered a strip search. Over the years, especially with a murder suspect, he had learned to guard for surprises: weapons secreted in the crotch area, for one.

Joe had no desire to disrobe. "Jesus, come on," he said. "Look, I don't want to strip down in front of you guys. Let me go in the bathroom, take my clothes off, and I'll walk out naked."

"No, no," said Tripodo Senior, increasingly suspicious.

Sure enough, when the shirt and jeans were removed, the boys at the barracks got a look-see at Joe Pikul wearing a stretched-out size 33B Warner's bra, a pair of stained Diane Freis flower-print panties, and dark panty hose.

The women's underwear was a shock. Joe knew the police had been looking for him, and he'd been in his lawyer's office right before he was arrested. "My first thought was I knew something was wrong with him," said Tripodo Senior. "Me being a naive upstater, not used to the New York City action, I just thought he was a fag."

Embarrassed, Joe insisted he wasn't a homosexual, that he just enjoyed feeling women's clothing against his skin.

"Take them off, too," Tripodo Senior ordered. "Everything."

Just below the panty line, the investigators discovered a long scratch running around Joe's right side. It looked fairly fresh, and Tripodo Senior considered the possibility that the wound could have been connected with the fight on the beach he'd just heard about. "Where'd you get that from?" he asked.

"Playing with the kids," said Joe, without offering the detailed ball-playing story he'd given the cops in Manhattan.

Just in case, Tripodo Senior ordered official photos of the body wound as well as a couple of shots of the scratch on the back of Joe's right hand, a wound that already had a scab that was healing.

Six and a half hours after he had arrived for processing, the defendant was finally transported to the nearby courtroom.

———

The arraignment was brief and pro forma. Joe showed no emotion and was held without bail pending a hearing with his attorney. He said he had an attorney, but couldn't recall his last name.

Joe was then taken back to the barracks, where he was turned over to the uniformed patrol for the trip to the Orange County Jail. Just before he left, he told Venezia: "I want to thank you for not abusing me or mistreating me at the station."

The same degree of respect could not be counted on where Joe was headed, for word travels fast when the newest jailbird has had his bra and panties taken away.

Even behind bars, Joe was haunting Sandy. Knowing that the police knew she was lying, she called a criminal attorney, a former federal prosecutor by the name of A. Hugh Scott. He advised her to come clean and called the appropriate police authorities to set up a meeting for that Friday afternoon, the thirtieth, at his office in Boston.

But even before Sandy's change of heart, Tripodo Senior had decided it was time to pay her a visit. So he and Venezia traveled to Massachusetts to be part of the welcoming party.

Sandy wanted to cooperate, but, afraid she was in trouble, demanded immunity. She had several reasons to be worried: Joe's visit to her house after the murder, her meeting with him in Manhattan the day before the murder, and their discussions on Cape Cod back in August.

Scott told her she didn't need immunity, but she insisted. She wasn't going to give up one word without protection, so Scott drafted a letter to Massachusetts State Trooper William Gorman: "As I have informed you, my client, Sandra Jarvinen, has relevant information concerning Joseph Pikul and wishes to voluntarily provide this information to law enforcement agencies and cooperate fully with them. You informed me earlier today, after speaking with New York law enforcement authorities, that no charges will be brought against Ms. Jarvinen for any of the matters concerning Joseph Pikul about which she provides information. This is simply to confirm that this is correct." Under the heading "Agreed," Gorman signed one copy of the letter, while Tripodo and Venezia signed another.

Finally, Sandy began to talk. But even with immunity in hand, her story was vague. For example, she quoted Joe as saying, "I've got something to bury."

"Did you ask him what?" Tripodo wanted to know.

"No," Sandy replied, explaining that she'd suspected the worst but "just wanted to get rid of him." It was difficult to tell where she was coming from, but if she could stand up in court, she represented a hell of a prosecution weapon.

Based on Joe's confession to Tripodo Senior, state police in the Hamptons spent that Friday looking for clues at the beach. They also took soil samples near the house and in nearby woods.

The police found nothing useful, though it wasn't for lack of trying. They knew that the body of Tracy Herrlin had been dumped between Alberts Landing and Little Alberts Landing early the morning of New Year's Day, 1985. She had been murdered after leaving the Jag, an East Hampton nightclub. If the murderer hadn't told police where the body was, it might never have been found. Unable to find any evidence to corroborate Joe's story about having killed Diane at the beach, investigators wondered if he had used his knowledge of the highly publicized case to throw everyone off track.

At the old-age home in Ware, Bernice Pikul heard of her son's arrest from relatives. The news broke her heart.

"Oh, she looked so miserable," said Marie Legare, who found her neighbor sitting like a statue by the porch door. "She told me she had hardly slept and that if she slept she'd wake up and think she had a horrible dream. And then she realized it was true. And she would cry and say, 'Oh, I pray for Diane.' She kind of liked Diane. Of course, we kept telling her, 'Well, they're innocent until proven guilty.' But I think she knew in her heart; she knew her son. . . . He had a temper and she had that feeling that she knew he could have done it. She used to tell me, 'He always reached for the best. He had to be the head of everything, the best of everything.' Like I would tell some of my neighbors: 'No mother deserves to be hurt so badly.' She was a good woman."

Back in the city, the tabloid headlines blared away: "HUBBY CHARGED IN GRISLY SLAYING," "CRASH, DIVORCE JUST TOO MUCH FOR SUSPECT." Even the *New York Times* gave the murder good play under the headline "Securities Analyst Charged in Slaying of His Wife." Most of the stories mentioned Joe's suspicious visit to the car wash, but his trip to Sandy's house was kept under wraps. Joe was described as an eccentric workaholic who would call his dry cleaner's from Switzerland or Singapore to complain about too much starch. Every story prominently listed Diane's job as assistant to the publisher at *Harper's*, along with words like "prestigious" and "highbrow." Before the media blitz subsided, one story even referred to Diane as "a publishing executive."

The follow-up stories searched for answers. More headlines: "THE COUPLE WHO HAD IT ALL" and "LIVES ABOVE, AND BELOW, THE SURFACE." Everything became a matter of perspective; for example, one of Diane's Village friends described her as "a dropout of the sixties. She had a permanent tan."

Her writing instructor said the short story he liked most was about a very unhappy woman living in New York City who went to a makeup artist–hair dresser and had herself made over.

That Sunday, Diane's co-workers placed a sympathy notice in the *Times*. It read: "PIKUL—Diane Whitmore. The staff of Harper's Magazine mourns the loss of Diane and extends to her daughter Claudia, son Blake, father Donald and stepmother Gretchen, our deepest sympathies."

Later that day, with Edleen Bergelt making final preparations to deliver her baby, Keith Bergelt transported Claudia and Blake to Washington, D.C., to live with Joe Pikul's nephew, Edward Pawlowski, Jr., and his wife, Lauren—the other relatives mentioned in Joe and Diane's wills. The children were finally told about their mother's death. They became confused, upset, and started to have nightmares and hallucinations, especially Claudia, who thought her mother had grown wings, got out of a coffin and started to fly around the house. It was then that the family members, after consulting with the Grace Church School psychologist, decided it was best to take the children to Diane's funeral so they could face the reality of her death.

While preparations were under way for the funeral, Joe's lawyers moved in court to have bail set. Samuel Dawson, Clayman's partner, and the district attorney's office worked out a deal whereby Joe had to surrender his passport, report to the DA's office every Wednesday, and limit his travel to New York State unless given specific court approval. Orange County Judge Thomas J. Byrne set bail at the suggested $350,000. Joe immediately started calling his business associates for money: not surprisingly, he had great difficulty getting through to most of them.

Dawson, meanwhile, offered his impression of the case to reporters, contending that Diane's boyfriend was the key to the mystery. "After a very preliminary investigation, we have decided to put a great deal of investigative effort into locating the lover of the deceased. We believe that when the investigation is concluded, it will be determined that the boyfriend of the deceased had an integral role in the culmination of events that led to her death." A short time later, Dawson sent Joe, who had been seeing psychologists and psychiatrists off and on since the 1960s, for treatment to Dr. Daniel Schwartz, a noted New York psychiatrist who had gained notoriety in the Son of Sam case.

A few days later, Dawson took the opportunity of Joe's release to expand on the supposed connection between the murder and Diane's lover. Contending the boyfriend had played a key role in the death, Dawson told reporters: "We have a name. We're still drawing the picture in a finer detail. We know who's who now."

The attorney's claims were news to state-police investigators, so they set out in search of the mystery man. "We went out of our way, really did a lot of interviews, myself included," said Tripodo Senior. "We all went down to Long Island, New York City, all over. Talked to neighbors, anybody who we could possibly think of . . . And everyone we talked to said, 'No way, no how. She did not have a boyfriend.' We talked to so many people I just figure something would have come out somewheres along the line."

On Thursday, November 5, 1987, the body of Diane Whitmore Pikul was laid to rest next to her mother at Riverview Cemetery in South Bend, Indiana. Diane had not returned to her hometown since her mother's funeral in 1976. Joe's lawyers asked Donald Whitmore if their client could attend, but the request was denied. Few friends attended the services either; a memorial was held several days later in Greenwich Village.

Wearing a big black ribbon in her blond hair, Claudia walked up to the closed casket and just stood there weeping, alone, looking at the flowers and wreaths. Blake ran up to the casket, touched it, then walked over to his grandfather and sat down. "Mommy," he said softly. At the grave site, each child placed a single rose on their mother's casket.

PART · IV

THE
GOOD FATHER

CHAPTER • 15

Clearing the Conscience

ON THE VERY DAY OF Diane's funeral, another major case broke—the brutal beating of Lisa Steinberg. Incredibly, lawyer Joel Steinberg and his battered wife, Hedda Nussbaum, lived around the corner from the Pikul family in Greenwich Village. It was as if all the well-to-do crazies in the Village were breaking loose at the same time.

Virtually everyone in the Village was enraged about abuse: spousal abuse, child abuse. Diane Pikul, Lisa Steinberg, Hedda Nussbaum. The media jumped on the Steinberg story, and the Pikul case faded from the front page. Still, in the months to come, the issue of Joe Pikul's right to custody of his children would be widely publicized. Crowds would gather on courthouse steps to express their outrage at helpless children being placed within the grasp of an accused murderer. Against a hardheaded judge, lawyers and key players of the city's Human Resources Administration would battle for the safety of Claudia and Blake. An unprecedented chapter in child custody was about to be opened.

But Joe Pikul, who murdered his wife lest she take away his children, would stand firm against all comers.

After Diane's funeral service Claudia and Blake returned with the Pawlowskis to their home in Washington, D.C.

Joe, who gained his release from jail with the help of four friends and a substantial withdrawal from his Arnhold

& S. Bleichroeder pension fund, immediately insisted that the Pawlowskis ship his children back to New York for the weekend, which they did. Using the name of one of his private investigators, Joe then registered for the weekend at the Concord Hotel, a famous resort in the Catskill borscht belt, north of the city.

Wanting to make sure the proper authorities were aware of what was going on, one of Joe's relatives tipped off a New York City social services worker, who in turn notified the office of Manhattan District Attorney Robert Morgenthau. The DA's staff tried to reach Special Services for Children, the only city agency that can immediately remove children from unsafe circumstances, but it was nearly quitting time that Friday and no one answered.

The next logical step was to call the state child-abuse hotline and social service officials in Sullivan County, where the hotel is located.

At 7:45 P.M., Mary O'Donoghue, an assistant in Morgenthau's office, filed a hotline abuse report stating that Joe was "believed to have killed the mother and transported her body with the children in the car. Father is known to have AIDS and be a transvestite. In the past, father often blindfolded children and took them to 'strange locations' for unknown reasons." O'Donoghue said she felt the children might be in danger.

But the wheels of the bureaucracy were to move slowly that evening. As analyzed in one New York City official report, "Being that the (abuse) report was not too well substantiated, (social workers) consulted with lawyers, the district attorney and the state police in Sullivan County for a long period of time." The officials determined there was no legal basis to remove Claudia and Blake from their father.

Morgenthau's staff, which technically had no jurisdiction, kept the pressure on, however, insisting that the kids *were* in danger. Finally, at midnight, the state police and a social worker rousted Joe and demanded that he turn over the children. Joe called Paul Kurland, his new civil attorney, who just happened to be spending the night at a nearby hotel. Kurland in turn called a local family court judge, arguing that the children weren't in danger and that the criminal case had absolutely nothing to do with Joe's relationship with his children. He also asked that the children not be interviewed.

At 1:30, Sullivan County Family Court Judge Anthony Kane, over the telephone, ordered Joe to surrender custody. Claudia and Blake were taken into protective custody by the state police and placed in a temporary emergency foster-care facility.

But the entire exercise was for naught. The following Monday, Judge Kane agreed with the original caseworker's assessment. There was no evidence showing the children had been neglected or abused, so Claudia and Blake were returned to their father.

Back in Manhattan, social service officials contemplated taking action to prevent Joe from regaining custody of his children. But under a deal worked out with Joe's lawyers, Claudia and Blake would stay with the Pawlowskis in the District of Columbia during the week, then visit their father in New York on weekends under careful monitoring by a caseworker from the city government.

The plan seemed workable. From Joe's angle, he knew that the publicity was difficult on the children, and since he was constantly in meetings with his attorneys, he wasn't able to provide much child care anyway. From the city's point of view, two important points were gained: Joe would not have primary custody, and the weekend monitoring would ensure protection for the children.

The weekend visits began immediately and came off without a hitch, usually at the Vista Hotel in Manhattan, the city's recommendation. The caseworker, José Flete, spent considerable time with Joe and the children and filed regular reports. Joe denied ever using drugs and said allegations that he had AIDS were "a lie. I never felt better in my life." He said Diane had "probably started" the talk of AIDS.

Deprived of their mother's love, the children clung to Joe. What's more, their usually absent father was around now, and they thrived on the attention he gave them, including the purchase of a pet dog, Midnight.

Trouble was looming, however. The Pawlowskis informed New York authorities they could not keep the children past December 22, for they had other commit-

ments. Joe also had continued to harass them, first about
visits, then about getting the children back permanently.
As far as Joe was concerned, Claudia and Blake definitely
weren't going to spend Christmas vacation down in Florida
with their maternal grandfather as they'd done in previous
years; they were going to spend the joyous season with
him.

Unable or unwilling to refuse Joe's request, the Pawlowskis told New York City social service officials that
unless someone in authority told them otherwise, they
were going to return Claudia and Blake to Joe.

The social service bureaucracy in Manhattan had been
content to monitor the situation as long as Joe abided by
the agreement worked out between the attorneys, but
when Joe demanded sole custody, the situation changed
dramatically.

The thorny dilemma ended up in the lap of Robert Wayburn, the associate general counsel for the city's Human
Resources Administration. Wayburn supervised all abuse
and neglect litigation, from the tens of thousands of name-
less, faceless ones to the high-pressure, well-publicized
cases involving people like the Steinbergs.

Morgenthau had called Wayburn's boss to put pressure
on the system. Despite his lack of jurisdiction, the DA
was feeling heat from his constituents and couldn't understand why court action hadn't been filed to remove the
children from Joe.

Wayburn quickly realized that this wasn't going to be
an easy case. First of all, the social workers in the Catskills
had actually removed the children from Joe, only to see
them returned without a formal petition even being filed.
Wayburn didn't want to file an abuse and neglect petition
against Joe unless there were clear grounds, since the last
thing he wanted was for the children to be taken into
custody and returned to Joe again.

In the process of exploring a legal way out, Wayburn
received a call from Raoul Lionel Felder. The powerful
divorce attorney explained that he had represented Diane
before the murder and that her relatives were deeply concerned about Joe Pikul's custody. Felder demanded to

know what the city was going to do. "He's a maniac," said Felder, insisting that the children be removed.

Wayburn explained that only two people have protected parental rights to a child—the mother and the father—and those vested rights cannot be taken away unless the parent is found to be unfit, or unless a judge believes the situation constitutes "extraordinary circumstances," in which case a hearing is held to determine the "best interests" of the children—staying with their parent or being sent to live with other caretakers.

In order to be removed under the unfit-parent category, the children had to be in "imminent danger." A parent couldn't be cited for abuse or neglect solely on the fact that he or she had been accused of murder, even if the victim was the children's mother.

There wasn't any case law on the subject either, at least in New York State, because in most cases of spousal murder, the defendant stays in jail until his trial or doesn't care about his children. But Joe's case, with its $350,000 bail and expensive battery of lawyers, was a classic example of a rich man being able to wage a battle the poor could not. And with Diane out of the picture, Joe now had exclusive parental rights. As Wayburn saw it, the question was whether it was permissible for Joe to have gained the parental monopoly by eliminating the competition.

Wayburn suggested to Felder that Diane's relatives consider bringing a custody suit in their own right, in which they could argue that the case was worthy of consideration under the "extraordinary circumstances" doctrine, where parental primacy is suspended. However, Wayburn cautioned, this route would be an unusual and difficult one. It had been applied in cases involving long separations between parent and child—often because of prison time or abandonment by the parent. But the standard had apparently never been applied in New York where there was obvious parental contact and, more important, where the triggering event for the custody battle was the murder of the other parent, allegedly by the surviving parent.

Also, Wayburn told Felder, the children appeared to be bonded to Joe. Judging from the social worker's reports about their emotional and psychological states, they appeared happy to be with their father, didn't appear to fear him, and didn't appear to have any knowledge of the murder. The children, especially Claudia, were aware that their father had been accused of killing their mother, but Joe told them he didn't do it. Having lost one parent already, Joe was providing them with much-needed security. Joe would never be judged an unfit parent on that basis, Wayburn said.

In a custody petition, a lawyer could introduce evidence about Joe's pending murder case, any past violent behavior, and alleged drug use, Wayburn told Felder. The possibility could be raised that Claudia and Blake were material witnesses to the crime, and they could try to introduce testimony from Diane's concerned friends about Joe's bizarre behavior toward her and the children—for example, evidence that Joe had blindfolded the kids and taken them away from Diane for an unscheduled weekend. "Perhaps it's worth a shot," Wayburn concluded, offering his agency's help.

Felder agreed and said he would have Stephen Beiner, one of his assistants, look into the matter with Diane's relatives.

Beiner first called Diane's father in Florida, who said he would be willing to bring a custody petition but suggested two better possibilities: Diane's cousin Kathleen, forty-three, and her husband, William Michael O'Guin, of Yonkers, a suburb just north of New York City; or Peter Norman, forty-one, another cousin from Greenville, South Carolina, who had two children of his own. The O'Guins were Donald Whitmore's first choice. They were professionals and did not have children of their own.

Beiner immediately called Kathy O'Guin, who said she and her husband were willing to take physical and legal custody. At a quickly arranged meeting with Felder, the O'Guins agreed to have a custody petition brought in their names.

As he looked over their résumés, Felder thought the O'Guins were a perfect choice. They were renting a three-bedroom house in a quiet, suburban neighborhood in Yonkers. They used the second bedroom as an office and had two sleeper beds in the third that could be used by Claudia and Blake. It wasn't paradise, but it sounded like a warm, caring, loving home.

Eight months younger than Diane, Kathy was Diane's first cousin; her mother was Don Whitmore's sister. Kathy and Diane had grown up near each other in South Bend, until Kathy and her family moved to South Carolina when she was in elementary school. Although the two women had not been close, they had maintained their family ties throughout their adult lives, socializing occasionally with their husbands—usually at Manhattan restaurants. The O'Guins had even visited the Amagansett house for a weekend two years before.

Kathy had earned a bachelor's degree from Radford University, and in the next fifteen years worked as a teacher and then as a registered nurse in Charleston, South Carolina. In 1984, she earned a master's degree in developmental genetics at the University of South Carolina, which was where she met Mike O'Guin. After obtaining her master's, Kathy was hired as a molecular research technician at the Albert Einstein College of Medicine in the Bronx, researching Alzheimer's disease at the molecular level in the pathology department.

William Michael O'Guin, known as Mike, earned a B.A. in biology at the University of South Carolina. More than eleven years younger than his wife, he served as a graduate research and teaching assistant in the university's biology department from 1978 to 1984, and earned his Ph.D. in developmental biology/genetics there in 1984. Mike then moved to New York, where he was a postdoctoral fellow in cell biology at the New York University School of Medicine, dermatology department. In 1987 he became an associate research scientist, with a continuing focus on cell biology research, specifically how human tissue becomes cancerous.

Married in 1984, the O'Guins were active Episcopalians, belonging to St. John's Episcopal Church of Tuckahoe, New York. Both regularly served as ushers during services, among other church duties, and both were active in a church project in which volunteers provided a meal each month for the Sharing Community, a local food kitchen and shelter. Kathy earned about $21,000, Mike about $25,000.

It was clear to Felder that the contrast between the O'Guins and Joe Pikul would work favorably in court, but he knew he still had a heavy burden to overcome if he was going to prevent Joe from regaining custody.

In a motion submitted under court seal, Felder and the O'Guins made a host of demands: temporary custody pending outcome of an in-depth court hearing; sole custody; an order preventing Joe from having any contact with his children except in the presence of New York City social service caseworkers; $500 per week from Joe for maintenance and support; an order that the children be produced in court; appointment of an independent psychiatrist to examine all parties; and a complete investigation of the parties and relevant issues by the city's Human Resources Administration.

The O'Guins' papers said it was their understanding that Joe was going to be indicted for murder within the week; that he was wearing bra and panties when arrested; that based on information and photos given to Felder, he was "a transvestite, sexually deranged, and engaged in sexually deviant and violent behavior."

They noted that Joe had taken the children with him to buy rope at a hardware store, transported them in the car while Diane's body was in the trunk, and when they repeatedly asked for their mother, told them that "they need not be concerned, she was gone and they would never see her again."

"Joseph Pikul is not a fit parent and it is not within the best interests of the children to be placed in his custody," the O'Guins said. "We make this petition with heavy heart and wish to God that it wasn't necessary to do so. But because of the gravity of the situation and the potential harm that can come to Claudia Pikul and Blake Pikul, we are forced to step forward and seek to protect them."

Felder, who by this point had been accused by several of Diane's friends for not preventing her death and reproached for allegedly charging her $46,000 for what they saw as questionable advice, submitted his own affirmation in support of the custody motion. He told the court that Diane had told him and a member of his staff that Joe frequently displayed "violent outbursts, was bizarre, and was a sexually disturbed and perverted individual." Felder revealed that Diane had given him still photos and a videotape showing Joe "in grotesque, deranged sexual activities. The crazed intense expressions on his face, the bizarre attire, the gross nudity and perversion depicted shocked even this veteran divorce attorney with almost thirty years of legal experience."

"I thought that in the hundreds, perhaps thousands, of matrimonial clients I have represented, I had heard of every possible perversion and that nothing would shock me any longer; yet seeing the photographs and the videotape that Diane Whitmore Pikul gave me, horrified even this attorney, and made me fear for the safety of my client and her children," Felder wrote. "In fact, on a human level, I warned her of my personal concern for her safety. . . . She felt that she wanted to attempt to remain in the marital home with the respondent until the divorce was finalized so as not to cause the children any more displacement than was absolutely necessary. She did, however, indicate her continuing fear of the respondent."

Referring to the warning note Diane had sent along with the tape and photos, Felder added: "She apparently feared for her own life and mine as well, an indication of the irrationality of the respondent during the violent outbursts that she often witnessed."

In addition, to deflect accusations concerning the high fees he had already received, Felder told a newspaper gossip column that he'd been paid a retainer of less than $20,000 by Diane and that the remainder of her monies—the story didn't say how much—would be put in escrow for the children.

Perhaps acknowledging some of his guilt, Felder wrote in his custody petition that he was "shocked and horrified to learn of Diane's murder" and said he'd "spent many hours agonizing over what might have been done to avert this tragedy. . . . I think it is important for the court to know that I am seeking no fees for representing the O'Guin family in the instant matter, have received and expect no payment, have not received payment from the deceased or anyone else for the instant matter, nor am I applying any fees previously received to this matter."

Based on what he characterized as "incontrovertible evidence of [Joe's] sexually deviant and deranged activities, and based on the evidence of his uncontrolled criminal violence," Felder pleaded with the court to "protect the infant children from the respondent to avoid a potential further tragedy."

Five days before the December 22 deadline, state Supreme Court Justice Kristin Booth Glen scheduled an emergency hearing for the following afternoon.

While the legal issues were being sorted out, Diane's friends and former co-workers drew up a petition calling for laws that would protect children's rights over civil rights of parents. The grass roots petition was circulated in the Greenwich Village neighborhood and schools. Almost everyone who read it signed—nearly two hundred in all. For most, the canvassing effort represented a genuine attempt to pressure the system to take action against Joe. For a few, though, the petition also served to assuage guilt feelings for not having tried harder to help Diane.

"Friends had been warning Diane for years to get out of what they saw as a vicious, destructive relationship. Diane had filed for a divorce [she had not], and voiced her increasing fear of Joe to friends in the days before her death," the petition read.

"With the tragic death of Lisa Steinberg painfully in our minds, we the friends and neighbors of Diane Pikul are joined in public outcry. We believe that if these children remain in their father's custody, they will almost certainly suffer severe emotional damage. Their physical safety is also at risk. One member of this family is already dead.

"Child care policy in New York State must be changed. A child's best interests are more important than a parent's technical 'rights.' In custody rulings, the child's vulnerability should be of paramount importance. Diane's children deserve a safe, permanent home with a loving family. Willing relatives and friends abound. State and city child welfare agencies must act swiftly to reverse this outrage, before anyone else gets hurt."

The stage was set for an unprecedented legal battle.

CHAPTER · 16

In the Children's
Best Interest

THE CUSTODY HEARINGS BEGAN BEHIND closed doors on Friday, December 18, 1987, before Justice Kristin Booth Glen of the state Supreme Court, the trial-level court in New York State. Joe was there, of course, along with Paul Kurland, his civil attorney. They were joined by one of Kurland's old buddies, Ronald Jay Bekoff, an attorney from Long Island whose firm had replaced Dawson and Clayman as Joe's criminal attorneys. The O'Guins were present with Felder, while Bob Wayburn represented the city of New York. Judge Glen, a former matrimonial attorney, had garnered considerable publicity in the early 1970s while defending a woman arrested for nude sunbathing in Amagansett, of all places. "A nude body is not a lewd body," Glen had argued back then. As a member of the law firm of Rabinowitz, Boudin and Standard, this left-leaning feminist attorney also had presented "the people's side" of the Pentagon Papers case before the U.S. Supreme Court, clad in a drip-dry dress and a pair of sandals.

Given the fact that a murder indictment was believed imminent, Judge Glen barred the press and public to protect Joe's right to a fair trial. It was especially essential that the testimony of the first witness, Alan Joseph, chief assistant district attorney for Orange County, not get into the newspapers and therefore in front of potential jurors.

Joseph testified via telephone, outlining the case he was presenting to his grand jury: Joe's contradictions, his admissions, the bizarre episode at the car wash. When Joseph was asked about the children's knowledge, though, he indicated he had no evidence that they had witnessed the killing.

However, Joseph said, he had received conflicting information on that score and felt it important that someone speak to the children. As he understood it, Joseph said, the night Joe was arrested Claudia had told authorities that her father told her "he had a fight with her mother and also told her that she was not going to see her mother anymore." He said Claudia had indicated " 'Mommy and Daddy were arguing,' or 'Mommy came home late' or 'early Saturday morning.' Something of that nature. 'They were arguing. Mommy threw a fit. And Daddy said, 'Don't talk about it. . . .' So it's possible that the kids actually witnessed the homicide. It's possible the kids heard portions of what led up to the homicide, though they didn't witness the homicide."

Joseph suggested that Judge Glen interview the children and then let him know if they possessed information critical to his grand-jury presentation. That way he might be able to avoid additionally traumatizing the kids. All the parties agreed.

Under strict guidelines to protect Joe's rights, the attorneys then questioned Joseph, with Felder requesting the prosecutor furnish him with Diane's autopsy photographs. "I want to question Mr. Pikul. He is going to take the stand."

"Forget it," snapped Judge Glen. "This is not a side show."

Judge Glen then interviewed Claudia and Blake in her chambers, without any of the parties present. The children's message was clear: they loved their father, they wanted to stay with him, they were not afraid of him. The children didn't seem to know what had happened out in Amagansett, and although they might have been in the car with their mother's body, they apparently were unaware of that as well.

When the judge finished, the two youngsters were sent out to the courtroom, where they ran to their father and leaped into his arms. It was a dramatic, touching moment.

Next, caseworker José Flete and Wayburn privately reviewed the city's investigation for the judge.

The eighty-seven-page file was filled with interesting information, including the fact that criminal investigators and New York City social workers began hearing rumors about Joe and AIDS within days of Diane's disappearance. The file also detailed the city's efforts, sometimes hour by hour, to assess the health and safety of Claudia and Blake from the first call to the abuse hotline at the state capital, through the custody hearing process. A large portion of the material consisted of unsubstantiated, hearsay allegations by several of Diane's friends, given under demands of anonymity and with refusals to help document the claims or testify about them in court.

Some people said they were frightened of Joe Pikul but had never met him or had not witnessed any of his supposed transgressions against Diane. About a year ago, one woman said, Diane showed up with a black eye. When asked about it, Diane "became very uneasy and refused to give an explanation." That was supposed to mean Joe was responsible. Of course, in the eyes of the law, it did not.

The California incident where Joe made Diane leave the car after she said the word "fuck," had been embellished to the point where Joe had thrown her out of a moving car. The report about the witness's stories continued: "Just to antagonize Diane, Mr. Pikul used to sleep with Claudia. She does not think that anything happened in bed beyond that. Due to constant shouting in the apartment, Blake was not able to speak until he was three years old."

One former babysitter said she didn't think Joe was a danger to his kids but wasn't surprised when she heard Joe had been charged with murdering Diane. "The fighting had gotten so bad, I kind of expected it."

Another former longtime sitter said Joe and Diane "argued a lot, especially during the last year," but she'd never seen him hit or abuse the children in any way.

Dramatic allegations notwithstanding, nothing in the report provided a legitimate basis to bring abuse and neglect charges against Joe Pikul.

Back in the courtroom, Judge Glen observed that she'd heard nothing from the kids to make her believe they needed to be called before Joseph's grand jury. "I'm convinced that the children have no information concerning the circumstances of their mother's death."

As for the custody question, she said there was "no danger whatsoever" in allowing Claudia and Blake to stay with their natural father over the weekend. "If I were not absolutely convinced, as I am, that the children are not in danger, I would not do this. I would not risk it for a second."

Of the alleged litany of offenses Joe had inflicted on Diane, Judge Glen noted: "She was always concerned about her safety and she was never concerned about the children's safety. . . . I think it is in some ways a very convincing fact for me that in all of Mrs. Pikul's affairs which she alleged about herself, and even to Mr. Felder, and which she apparently conveyed to many other people as contained in the reports and investigation of the HRA, there was apparently no question in her mind, ever, that the children were in danger from this man, or that he was anything other than a loving and caring and totally competent parent to these children. In some ways, ironic as it may be, her voice from beyond, and her willingness to leave the children in that household for well over a year after retaining Mr. Felder and supplying him with the films and the pictures, whose contents I've been made fully aware of, indicates to me that these children are not in danger, they are not in any greater danger from this man than any child is, from any parent, in this city at this time."

Judge Glen ordered Wayburn's agency to monitor the situation and scheduled another hearing for the following Monday, four days before Christmas.

It was now past 8:00 P.M. Wayburn went to the parking garage and found it closed for the evening. It had not been a great day.

The hearing resumed on Monday with testimony from Sharon Space, an employee of a Manhattan alcoholic outpatient clinic who had sponsored Diane in Alcoholics Anonymous and knew Joe from the program as well.

Space testified that Diane had told her two years ago that she "had found Joe in Claudia's bed" and was "very worried that Joe was going to molest Claudia." She also quoted Diane as saying she'd caught Joe caressing Claudia's backside after a bath. Space said Diane quoted Joe as saying: "She has an ass on her like a woman."

The witness had other horror stories: she saw Joe lose his temper at an AA meeting and kick a chair "so hard it went into the wall and knocked a little hole in the plaster"; she heard Joe threaten to kill the husband of one of Diane's girlfriends because he had paid her a daytime visit; Joe told her he had once offered to fight a security officer where he worked after being asked for identification; he told her he had once sat in the living room of his apartment and shot holes in the ceiling; he also told her he'd thrown about six dozen eggs at the front door of the restaurant below the Sixth Avenue apartment because of the noise and smell.

"Did he ever discuss with you the use of any drugs, illegal drugs?" Felder inquired.

"Yes. Joe had said that prior to his entering AA, he was on cocaine," Space replied.

"It's a lie. It's a lie," Joe shouted back as Felder returned to his chair.

Space's testimony was generally hearsay, inadmissible in court, and Judge Glen took this factor into consideration. All the same, Space did know the parties quite well. For example, when news of Diane's death had first hit the papers, Space told Frances McMorris of the *New York Daily News*: "To Joe, love is possession. He loved her if she reflected him, if she was his perfect little possession. He would always say he couldn't survive without her." Space said she told Diane not to date Joe, but she wouldn't listen. She said Joe was attracted to Diane because "she was both beautiful and malleable. She really did not have a lot of self-esteem."

When Space left the stand, Felder submitted as evidence a copy of the final five-page letter Diane had written to him, "typed one week before she was killed." Felder said Diane had prepared the letter for an upcoming meeting. "She handed it to me. In fact, I went over it with her," he told the judge.

Kathy O'Guin also took the stand that day, explaining her background and desire to love and nurture Claudia and Blake. She said that although she and her husband were Episcopalians, they would raise Claudia and Blake as Roman Catholic. She told the court she would investigate the parochial schools in her neighborhood. Kathy O'Guin sounded like an excellent caretaker.

Then Joe took the stand, questioned first by Felder. Under advice of his attorneys, Joe took the Fifth Amendment to a wide range of questions, refusing to respond about Diane's death, his life with her, to questions about incidents mentioned in Diane's final letter to Felder—the melon incident, a threat to jump out of the hotel window in Zurich because of a lousy room, letting air out of the tires on Diane's car, removing parts from the car, losing $300,000 in Monte Carlo. Joe also took the Fifth when asked whether he'd ever threatened Sandy Jarvinen's life, whether he'd ever set up a tape recorder on the home phone, whether he had AIDS, whether he'd ever been tested for AIDS, and whether he'd ever told anyone he suffered from the disease.

Judge Glen later explained that she allowed Joe to take the Fifth on the AIDS questions because one possible theory in the murder case could have been that Diane "became aware of this disease or that the disease was in some way contracted as a result of (Joe Pikul's) sexual deviance. This arguably led to quarrels with the wife, which possibly led to her murder."

Felder pounded away at Joe's sexual practices, wondering how many times in the last month Joe had worn women's underwear. Bekoff objected on Fifth Amendment grounds.

"Are you wearing women's underwear today?"

Again Bekoff objected and again Judge Glen sustained.

"I noticed you laughed when I asked you that question," Felder noted.

"What do you want, a date?" Joe replied.

"Yes, I would like a date—the last time you wore women's underwear. Would you give me a date?"

Joe didn't answer, again on Fifth Amendment grounds.

As the grilling continued, Joe denied ever having taken drugs. "I don't know what cocaine is," he maintained. Not waiting for another question, Joe contended that Sharon Space had wanted him to be her lover when he first came to AA, "and I went out with Diane instead." Later in his testimony, Joe admitted having taken tranquilizers during his drinking days.

Describing himself as an expert on international financial matters, particularly Scandinavian securities, Joe admitted he'd been arrested about ten years ago after a fight, but linked it to his heavy drinking at the time. Asked if he had a shotgun in his trunk when arrested on that occasion, Joe said he didn't think so, but admitted that he'd owned several shotguns "over the years, starting when I was a young lad. I used to go squirrel shooting. I had a double-barrel shotgun, which I bought for something like two dollars."

"When did you own the last showgun that you had?" Felder asked.

"The last shotgun? Joe's last shotgun?"

"Did you just say, *'Joe's* last shotgun'? asked the startled attorney.

"Joe's," replied Joe Pikul.

"Who are you referring to?" asked Felder.

"Me."

"Oh, I didn't realize you were talking in the third person. *Your* last shotgun, yes," said Felder, who, absent knowledge of Chloe and Jasmine, was forced to move on.

Joe explained that he used his shotguns to hunt varmints, "rats and creatures that were on my property." He told of shooting a rat off the porch in Amagansett while the O'Guins were visiting. "I got that bugger. One shot," Joe told the judge before returning to issues of custody.

"I am a wonderful father. I am a wonderful caretaker," he said. "I don't have any doubt about my ability to take care of my children." He said he wanted to raise the children full-time while preparing his defense, "and hopefully in the spring, work part-time." He also said he was willing to give the children up during the murder trial with the proviso that he'd get them back when he was acquitted.

Joe said he wanted Claudia and Blake to have some stability in their lives in the wake of their mother's death, and he saw no reason not to keep custody until at least the end of the school year. "I think my daughter and my son at this point, after being moved around and the loss of their mother, are at a breaking point in terms of taking any more stress of new situations. I think my daughter is

at the point of rebellion. At the Pawlowskis, she was re-
bellious. Regarding the O'Guins, she said, 'It was bad
enough being separated from you, even though we knew
the Pawlowskis and the Bergelts very well.' She said,
'Going to a total stranger would be devastating to me.'
And when she saw Santa Claus over the weekend, this
was one of the things she asked him. I think it's a very
dangerous move for these children at this point. I think
we have a lot of healing to do together, and I think that
this custody question is something which should come up
after the school year. I am perfectly willing and I am perfectly flexible on that score. I think the next several months
are very critical to my children. I think I can offer them
the continuity of parenthood during this period and also
prepare them, perhaps, for a period when I am not able
to take care of them, to make the transition more gentle,
making them mentally aware of it and psychologically accept it. And preparing them for who it might be as well."

Joe said he was willing to keep the children in private
schools but desired to move out of the Sixth Avenue duplex, describing the Village area as "gross. It is an ugly
place. . . . The whole movement out there is one of drug
trafficking . . . mother-fucking language . . . noise and
confusion . . . and drug busts in front of my house."

Asked how he planned to pay for the private schools
and other expenses, Joe said he expected disability insurance to provide for him. Pressed to explain what kind of
disability he had, Joe first said he was "too busy" to work,
then said he couldn't travel internationally, and finally offered: "I have been psychologically given a blow that
would prevent me from working full time." The explanation made no sense and Judge Glen ruled that more
information was necessary.

In fact, Dr. Daniel Schwartz, the psychiatrist Joe had
been visiting twice a week at $200 per session since his
arrest, had requested the disability determination on a
diagnosis of "adjustment disorder with mixed emotional
features, and also atypical sexual paraphilia." Paraphilia
is defined as "aberrant sexual activity, expression of the
sexual instinct in practices which are socially prohibited or
unacceptable or biologically undesirable." The application, subsequently rejected by the insurance company, also

stated that Joe suffered from "anxiety and depression" related to his arrest.

At one point in the questioning about supposed disabilities, Bekoff, the criminal attorney, exercised Joe's Fifth Amendment rights because "it is not decided yet whether we have a psychiatric defense. If he's going to talk about what he's capable of doing and not capable of doing, it will come back to haunt us in a future date."

Joe was asked to describe what he had told the children about Diane's death. "It's pretty hard, because Blake is not verbal, and I have to be honest as I can be," said Joe. "I have told Claudia, as it seemed natural and appropriate, and without rocking the boat, that the police have been investigating this and are not sure what happened, and among other possibilities, they felt that it might be me. And we have our own people who are going to prove that it's not the case and that this is a continuing process."

Joe claimed that he'd been abused by his father as a youngster and admitted he was a recovering alcoholic. "I drank practically daily for twenty-five years." But, he contended, he hadn't touched a drop since May 1976, didn't use drugs, and had been in therapy for seven years. Asked to explain Space's testimony, Joe described the incident with the security guard as merely a verbal confrontation with an unpleasant employee who was subsequently terminated. He denied displaying extreme anger at AA meetings and denied in their entirety the allegations about egg throwing and shooting up his apartment ceiling.

As for his second apartment in Battery Park City, known as "the secret place" by Claudia and Blake, he explained that he took the rental after divorce became a serious possibility. He acknowledged taking the children there overnight and that they used sleeping bags. But, he explained, it would have been "bad faith" to have furnished the apartment while marriage counseling was ongoing.

Joe denied ever having taken the children there blindfolded, although he did admit that he asked them not to tell Diane where the apartment was located because he didn't want Diane's "detectives down there setting up a tape machine on my phone." He said both children knew the address and Claudia knew the phone number.

Joe said he had planned to eventually rent a larger apartment in the same building because he felt a divorce was inevitable. "I was fed up," Joe said. "She used to beat on the children. . . . She came out on weekends to the Hamptons and made life so miserable—"

Kurland interrupted to speak to Joe, warning him not to answer if there was a legal objection.

"When did you see her beat the children?" Felder asked.

"She—she beat on the children verbally."

"Verbally?" asked Felder.

"All summer," said Joe, explaining that he would "try to be quiet or leave the house" in the hopes of calming Diane down, "because there was no way of stopping her."

Felder wondered if Joe had ever tried to stop Diane from "verbally beating on the children."

"There is no way of stopping Diane," Joe said with certainty.

On the surface, just as Wayburn had feared, Joe sounded like an extremely responsible parent. In fact, the only issue that could possibly be raised as a question was his admission that he had spanked Claudia twice and Blake once in their lives. Usually, however, he and Diane had disciplined the kids by sending them to their rooms.

With the press and public still barred, forty-eight still photos, showing Joe in animated displays of erotic satisfaction and orgasm, were introduced into evidence. The courtroom was then darkened and everyone watched a twenty-six-minute video of Joe prancing around, dancing and masturbating while wearing a collection of panties, teddies, and lacy camisoles. The video had the casual home-movie touch to it. The camera never panned; it was stationed on a tripod. As the others watched, Joe read the *Wall Street Journal*.

At one point in the film, "Here Comes the Bride" could be heard in the background as Joe masturbated himself. At another point, Joe excited himself "with a dildo in his anus." Using the attic of the Sixth Avenue duplex as his stage, Joe performed with a playpen and TV set in the background.

When questioning resumed, Felder sought to contrast the film's contents with Joe's claim that he said prayers from the Bible every evening with his children.

"How about Deuteronomy? Do you read Deuteronomy? 'A man shall not put on a woman's garment or a woman a man's.' Did you ever read that?" Felder demanded.

Bekoff objected and the judge sustained.

Wayburn wondered if Claudia had ever "indicated a desire not to live" with Joe. "Quite the opposite," he replied. "Starting basically last year, the children kept telling the mother they wanted to live with me. They chose to live with me and not with her." (In fact, both children had told city workers that they preferred living with their father because their mother yelled at them so much. While Joe denied ever blindfolding the kids, he in fact had.)

The long day began to draw to a close. Joe denied ever fondling or touching Claudia or Blake for his own sexual gratification. Under prodding from Judge Glen, Joe explained that his father had been a drunk and "used to chase us out of the house at night." Joe said his father used to "slap me around" and throw his mother out of the house, "beat on her, physically and verbally." For Joe, the ugly episodes ended when he started attending college, he said.

Joe said he loved his two children "more than anything" and told the court the greatest thing that ever happened to him was "having the children."

Finding the sexual materials to be of "minimal relevance" since the children were apparently unaware, Judge Glen said her reading of the law continued to be that a "natural parent cannot be deprived of the custody of his or her children, particularly when that custody is by a non-parental figure. . . . I do not believe there is danger to these children at this time to require a removal." She ruled that Joe could keep the kids over the Christmas break, but directed that he send them to Florida to spend a few days with their grandfather. She said in the event a problem developed with Don Whitmore refusing to return the children, his actions would be covered under the Federal Parental Kidnapping Prevention Act.

With the agreement of all parties, Judge Glen also appointed Dr. Michael Kalogerakis, a noted psychiatrist who had appeared before her many times, to examine the O'Guins and the Pikuls over the holidays.

The Pikul case was adjourned until January 6.

Once outside the courtroom, Felder was livid. "It seems as if murderers have more rights than children," he grumbled.

Joe, meanwhile, walked over to Kathy and Mike O'Guin and shook their hands. He had won again.

Unbeknownst to Joe, the Pikul tragedy had claimed another victim. In Ware, Massachusetts, Joe's mother had succumbed that morning to a combination of a broken heart and old age. She had not been the same after hearing of her son's arrest. According to friends, she felt Joe's mind had gone on him.

Three days later, on Christmas Eve, Bernice Pikul was buried next to her husband in St. Ann's Cemetery in nearby Three Rivers. With the court's permission, Joe, Claudia, and Blake attended the funeral along with a babysitter.

The Christmas holidays were otherwise uneventful, except that all the parties were interviewed by the court-appointed psychiatrist and the children didn't go to Florida to see their grandfather. Joe and Don Whitmore couldn't get past arguing over who would pay for the plane tickets. Whitmore said he wouldn't pay until Joe reimbursed him for Diane's funeral.

Bob Wayburn was having a tough time, too. The public profile of the Human Resources Administration was not good. It looked like the agency had been neglectful in failing to file an abuse and neglect petition against Joe. With the O'Guins' custody petition failing in the short term, HRA Commissioner William Grinker and other top officials wondered if the neglect route was worth considering anew.

Wayburn knew that filing an abuse and neglect petition would make people happy from the political perspective. The courts would ultimately decide the validity of the petition and city fathers could defuse criticism by saying they'd tried their best. But the issue appeared to be unwinnable; Wayburn would have to prove Joe guilty of the crime or prove parental unfitness. Prosecutor Joseph wasn't going to hand over his case, which was circumstantial to begin with. And there still wasn't any credible evidence to prove Joe was an unfit parent. The custody route was still the only way to go.

When the hearings resumed Wednesday, January 6, 1988, some forty of Diane's acquaintances and children's rights advocates gathered on the courthouse steps in freezing, snowy weather to protest. They carried signs reading PROTECT THE CHILDREN, WIFE KILLERS MAKE BAD DADS. A banner was raised: INNOCENT TILL PROVED GUILTY THE AMERICAN WAY, BUT WHY SHOULD THE VICTIM'S CHILDREN PAY? Protection of Joe's constitutional rights was not the most important issue of concern.

A dozen supporters also wrote letters to Judge Glen, who later characterized several of them as threatening. "Have you taken leave of your senses?" one letter writer asked. "You would give custody of these two innocent children to that animal? . . . What kind of home did you come from? No wonder our criminal justice system is in such a shambles."

Many of the women were Diane's friends from AA. Some were divorced or, like Diane, had contemplated divorce for years. They tried to imagine themselves in Diane's position. At least several were being driven by a fear that this could happen to them. Many were scared, having even banned their children from playing with Claudia and Blake for fear Joe would kidnap them if he thought they might testify against him. Some admittedly felt guilty for having failed to help Diane, for having failed to convince her to leave—or worse, for having advised Diane aggressively on her divorce plans. It wasn't going to bring Diane back, but taking the children from Joe would make it feel better.

Joe walked by the screaming housewives sporting a large button on his lapel with a color photo of Diane and their two children. "This is my wife," Joe told Carol Jenkins of WNBC-TV. "She loved me very much. I'm doing this for her."

Inside the courtroom, the first order of business was a discussion about the possibility of opening the courtroom to the news media and protesters. Clearly, there was no legal reason for keeping all the testimony secret.

Judge Glen said she would open the doors, but ordered the attorneys not to discuss certain issues with the press and public in the courtroom: Prosecutor Joseph's testimony; any reference to admissions Joe had made to police; the sex videotapes and photos; and the investigative report prepared by the city of New York.

The judge also ordered the deletion of the names and addresses of all who requested confidentiality in the city report, usually Diane's friends. Furthermore, since she'd observed a pattern of hearsay, often contradicting other reports, regarding those interviews anyway, Judge Glen said the unsubstantiated allegations—for example, a claim by one of Diane's close friends that Joe had locked Blake in his room for two weeks after he failed to gain entrance to a private school—would have to be removed from the document as well.

Felder inquired why he was forbidden from referring to the videotape and photos. "It was publicly reported when he was arrested he was wearing women's underwear. I can't understand how that's going to introduce any element to hurt him in any possible way."

In what would become a regular occurrence between Judge Glen and Felder, she snapped back: "As I understand it, the press knows and has reported that Mr. Pikul was arrested wearing women's undergarments. The press does not know, as far as I understand it, that Mr. Pikul had made a half-hour videotape of himself engaged in masturbatory activity in women's clothing. And the press does not know, to the best of my knowledge, that that tape was in the possession of Mrs. Pikul and was turned over to her counsel in preparation for a divorce or separation. And the press does not know that she had photographs of him. So that the children do not know that their mother knew. The children do not know that this has been going on." Furthermore, the judge said, she felt public disclosure of those facts would be "damaging to the children."

Finally, the secrecy was ended. The reporters, along with a dwindling handful of Diane's supporters, streamed in. Judge Glen, known as a staunch supporter of the First Amendment, explained the need for secrecy under the domestic relations law to protect the parties and "best interests" of the children.

With that, Mike O'Guin took the stand, explaining, among other things, that he had seen Diane only four or five times since he and his wife had moved to New York in 1984.

O'Guin detailed his church activities, said he and Kathy lived in an adequate rented home, then outlined their prospective plans for the children. "Immediately they have to be put into an appropriate school. That's top priority, I would think, since they are on semester break. . . . We want to make sure that they have a stable, loving home environment, and we think that we can provide that."

Asked to explain why he and his wife wanted custody, O'Guin said: "It's obvious from what we have heard here, they are not necessarily in a good environment, and their continued association with their father is not necessarily guaranteed."

Under cross-examination, O'Guin acknowledged that aside from the custody hearing before Christmas, he had not seen Claudia and Blake during all of 1987 and that his most extensive contact with the children occurred back in 1984, when he and Kathy had spent a weekend at the house in Amagansett.

Judge Glen asked O'Guin if he had reason to believe the children were in danger with the father. "Well, I'm not a psychiatrist, but a lot of the information that I have seen would seem to indicate to me that they are not necessarily in a safe place. . . . I don't think any rational person is going to kill someone. Also, I have heard other things that make me feel that I wouldn't be comfortable if I had a child in that care."

Asked if he had any firsthand knowledge of abuse, O'Guin said he didn't. As for his observations of Joe and the children together, O'Guin acknowledged: "They got along just as well as any father and daughter and son."

The judge then told O'Guin that Dr. Kalogerakis, the court-appointed psychiatrist, had concluded: "There is no compelling reason to take the children from their father, although he has recommended that a long-term plan be made, given the possibility that Mr. Pikul will be convicted or will plead and will do time in jail. He also suggested that in terms of making that long-term plan, that there should be psychiatric guidance and so forth." Judge Glen wanted to know if O'Guin and his wife were willing to get to know the children "with a view toward ultimately becoming their caretaker in the event that Mr. Pikul is convicted."

O'Guin agreed, "provided their welfare is ensured."

"Obviously, to the best of everyone's ability, we'll do that," Judge Glen answered. "I understand that there are strong feelings here for everyone, and I can understand the dismay and anger that may exist on the part of Mrs. Pikul's family with regard to Mr. Pikul, given the indictment and the charges. Do you think you and your wife can put aside whatever feelings you may have—which may be justifiable or nonjustifiable, certainly understandable— in terms of dealing with the kids and dealing with him in what may be a transition period?"

Soft-spoken Mike O'Guin agreed to cooperate.

Because O'Guin had indicated he didn't think the children were safe with their father, Kurland wanted to know if he had ever complained to a public authority about Joe's treatment of his children. O'Guin said he had not, but had grown concerned because of the facts of the murder case and what he'd already heard in testimony at the custody hearing.

Felder then tried to expand the inquiry, asking O'Guin to reveal what he had learned about Joe from sources other than the indictment and court testimony.

"No, no, no," said Judge Glen.

"Judge, there is—"

"Mr. Felder, this is grandstanding for the press. I have told you that other than the particular issues that I ruled on, which have to do in my view with the best interests of the children, or with the integrity of the criminal prosecution in Orange County, you are free to disclose to the press anything in that transcript of who has already testified."

Felder said he didn't want O'Guin to reveal the still-secret courtroom testimony; he wanted the witness to discuss anything he had learned outside of the courtroom.

The judge took over, asking O'Guin if he had information other than "issues about Mrs. Pikul's death, and what may have been reported elsewhere, and what has been discussed here about Mr. Pikul's sexual proclivities" that would lead him to conclude the children were not safe with their father.

"Well, certainly we have heard evidence that he has a very violent temper and nature. Apparently he has threatened lots of other people—"

"Your Honor," Kurland complained.

Explaining that she wasn't taking the testimony for the truth of it, but just to ascertain why O'Guin felt the way he did, Judge Glen allowed the witness to continue.

"We also have, not necessarily in the courtroom—I'm not sure how I'm supposed to address this question with you—but we have heard stories of the children being blindfolded and driven around. We are also aware of information that Joe would take the children away without telling their mother where they were and keep them overnight, places that they couldn't tell where they were. Those kinds of things don't sound right."

Mike O'Guin was excused.

Later that day, Joe took the stand to explain his plans, with defense attorney Steve Worth, Bekoff's partner from Long Island, serving as Joe's Fifth Amendment protector against self-incrimination.

"This man has more lawyers than a dog has fleas," complained Felder. "If he wants to call him in, let him have Clarence Darrow with him, I don't care. But he has to make the objection, not the other fellow. And I don't have to argue against two lawyers."

Judge Glen agreed and told Worth to lodge his complaints through Kurland.

Joe said he wanted the children back in their Manhattan private schools. Headmaster Kingsley Ervin at Claudia's school and First Presbyterian headmistress Marjorie Goldsmith had both said they were willing to have the children return, as did the parents of the other students, he said.

Joe also explained that Bernetta Seegars, the baby-sitter who had walked out of the house in Amagansett in September, had agreed to come back. A student with morning classes, Seegars would be available full-time for the rest of the day.

As for the psychiatrist's long-term plan of having the O'Guins gradually get to know the children, Joe said he was "absolutely" in accord and promised to get to know the O'Guins better himself and to pay transportation costs so the children could see their grandfather. Joe was Mr. Agreeable.

He even went as far as to correct himself. Although he had testified at the closed-court sessions before Christmas that he had disciplined Claudia on two occasions by striking her with his hand, he now said Claudia had reminded him that he'd used a strap. "My recollection was, of course, with my hand, but I guess she was right. I'm not going to argue with her younger mind," said Joe.

Then Judge Glen posed a hypothetical question: "Let's just assume for a moment that the recommendation was that the kids be with you between now and June, that they in some way start to be incorporated in the lives of the O'Guins, that the O'Guins might have them on some weekends or might take them on some holidays, and that as the summer comes along, you might make arrangements for them to spend more time with the O'Guins, until it gets to be half and half, and then tapers off until the next school year, until when the trial is scheduled, and so forth. Are you prepared to accept that kind of situation, if that's what I order?"

Joe said he was.

"And would you cooperate with both the psychiatrist or psychologist who we might ask to supervise this and to do some aid in integrating the families in every possible way?"

"If the O'Guins are indeed the family," said Joe. "There is the issues of the Pawlowskis, who Diane really—"

Judge Glen cut Joe off as he sought to explain that Diane's will called for Joe's nephew, Edward Pawlowski, Jr., and Joe's niece, Edleen Pawlowski Bergelt, to act as co-guardians of the person and property of Claudia and Blake in the event of their mother's death and their father's death or unavailability.

"I understand that," she said. "But in this proceeding in front of me, there is you and the O'Guins. I have had no evidence from the Pawlowskis. I have had no evidence from the Bergelts. My understanding at this moment, based on this proceeding, that that's who there is. And Dr. Kalogerakis, he has found—as certainly I have observed—that the O'Guins would be certainly suitable, and they had indicated they would cooperate with you. I want to know if you will cooperate with them as well, notwithstanding their proceeding, which I am sure they have done because they are concerned about the best interest of the children."

Again, Joe said he would cooperate.

Now it was Felder's turn. He immediately focused on the spanking incident. He homed in on the contradiction between Joe's contention of hand spanking and now his switch to a belt. Try as he might—Felder even went as far as to ask Joe to demonstrate how hard he had hit his daughter—the attorney could not establish the fact that two spankings constituted a history of child abuse. On the contrary, only two incidents in Claudia's entire life showed considerable restraint.

Felder then moved on to another contradiction, one even weaker. He reminded Joe that he had testified about his desire to have the children resume their studies at the Grace Church School and First Presbyterian Church Nursery. "I'm not up on that, but those are Protestant schools?"

"Yes, they are, Mr. Felder."

Felder recalled that at one of the court sessions before Christmas Joe testified he was raising his children as Catholics. "Now, what happened?" Felder demanded. "Over Christmas you had a Protestant revelation of some sort?"

After some lawyerly sparring, however, Joe defused the issue with the observation: "The quality of the education in the Village is better than it is at the equivalent Catholic school."

When Wayburn, the city's lawyer, got his chance at Joe, he also focused on the belt-spanking incidents. Referring to a Christmas-time 1985 spanking, Wayburn asked Joe what kind of belt he had used.

Joe said it was probably like the one he was wearing. When Wayburn pointed out that the belt had a metal buckle at the tip, Joe contended he had struck Claudia in a way that the buckle did not touch her.

As for the second incident, which had occurred just

several months before Diane's death, Joe said Claudia cried "very little, if at all." He said he probably sent her to her bedroom for an hour.

Turning to Blake, Joe said he now recalled having spanked his son on one occasion, "when he didn't answer my calls, yes. When he, in fact, stayed watching television, instead of going to speech therapy."

Joe's comments prompted Wayburn to wonder how Joe's father had punished him as a child. "Well, he might punch me in the jaw, you know, when I was four or five, and knock me across the room, or kick me in the groin or chase me out of the house. He'd chase me and my family up the road, so we all had to hide in bushes, and stuff like that."

The contrast was not lost on anyone.

Pressing, Wayburn asked how old Blake had been when Joe spanked him. "About four years old." Did Joe think Blake understood? Joe said he did.

"In your opinion, if you were allowed to retain custody of the two children, would you obey a court order that you not inflict any corporal punishment whatever, of any form?"

"Yes," said Joe. "I don't need a court order." He insisted that he was in control on the occasions he spanked the children and contended that the fact he'd used a belt had "just slipped my mind" in the previous court appearance.

"You simply remembered that you did use a belt when the psychiatrist informed you during your evaluation that Claudia had mentioned it?" pressed Wayburn.

"Well, I asked Claudia. I wanted to know what she said. She said it was a belt. And then I agreed with her."

As the day's testimony ended, Wayburn made a motion seeking a temporary order of protection barring Joe from using any corporal punishment on the children. "I certainly don't find what was testified to was outside of ordinary disciplinary actions taken by parents against children," said Judge Glen. "But I think in the better interest of valor that it simply not happen at all. I'm ordering you not to even inflict any corporal punishment." Joe nodded in agreement.

When Judge Glen made it clear she was still of the mind-set to let Joe keep the children and send them back to their private schools, Felder angrily objected. "Judge, I want to make the record clear, as I have done on each of the other two occasions, that I am absolutely opposed to this man having temporary custody. My position is he's a murderer, he's a degenerate. That's my position. He's not entitled to have custody. My position is you are playing Russian roulette. He has been indicted for murder. There are things I can't say because of the ground rules. There is nothing to be gained by having him have the kids. I think, with all due respect, this so-called supervision is really a joke. They don't have the facilities. These people are fine people, but I don't think they have the facilities to really supervise."

Felder's remarks riled Wayburn. "The city has reported to this court that we conducted a child protection investigation, and we did not find a legal basis to establish a danger, nor to initiate a child protection proceeding, and to this point, we have not done so. We, of course, have concerns for the children. We have appeared in this court and have participated in this proceeding out of those concerns, and we have offered our services, subject to this court's custody proceeding, to facilitate whatever services or assistance we can give to the court."

As she had done following the previous two hearing sessions, Judge Glen delivered an interim decision. "The ultimate issue in this case is whether a nonparent should be permitted to take custody of children from a parent, and there is an extensive body of case law regarding this. We do not write on a tabula rasa here," the judge said. "That body of law affords the strongest constitutional provision to the rights of natural parents, barring danger to the children, or other extraordinary circumstances which impacts in a serious, negative way upon the children. I am second to no one in my concern for these children."

The allegations against Joe were heinous, she said. But proper procedures had to be followed. "Those procedures include indictment, notification of statements, notification of defenses, trial by jury, sentencing by another judge, and appeal. They do not provide for automatic revocation of custody of persons charged with crimes, no matter how heinous those crimes.

"I have interviewed these children extensively. I have appointed a psychiatrist, who came as highly recommended to me as anybody could possibly come, with credits that involve adult psychiatry, child psychiatry, and forensic psychiatry, who has served as as deputy commissioner of child services in this state.

"We have given him a panoply of access to anything that is necessary to aid me in my determination. He has given me a very full and fair report, which indicates that notwithstanding the problems arising from the indictment and the question that casts a pale over the continued relationship, it would not be in the best interest of the children to be removed from their father at this time; that the children want to be with their father; that the father wants to be with the children; that the children, to the extent possible, want to be returned to the life that they had prior to the unfortunate and untimely death of their mother. . . . Whatever Mr. Pikul did or did not do to his wife—and he is, of course, presumed innocent in the eyes of the law—he is not dangerous to these children at this time."

The sole issue, said the judge, was whether or not she should remove the children from their natural parent. "I feel that removing the children from their father, given the loss of their mother, and of all the changes in their life, removing them from the schools they have attended where they were happy, and which schools are, apparently, willing and anxious to resume their education, would not be in their best interests. So I am continuing custody with Mr. Pikul."

Outside the courtroom, reporters asked Joe for his reaction. He smiled like a crazy man, then lifted his tie to display a note reading: "Don't give up."

CHAPTER 17

No Danger to
the Children

As the demonstrations dwindled, then ceased, the custody hearing continued through a series of witnesses, but none changed Judge Glen's earlier decision. For Joe's cause, there were the positive findings of the court-appointed psychiatrist, Dr. Kalogerakis, and the Pikuls' baby-sitter, Bernetta Seegars, testifying that she had never seen Joe raise a hand to his children, but had witnessed Diane strike Claudia once with her hand. In reply, Felder and Wayburn called several expert witnesses and a friend of the Pikuls from AA, but none did Joe any harm. Joe was keeping his kids.

Along the way, though, there were important skirmishes.

Kurland sought, and received, a biting stipulation on the record from Felder stating that Diane had consulted the divorce attorney for more than a year prior to her death, but that he had never filed an application for an order of protection on behalf of Diane or the children "in any court."

Because the city's social services report indicated several people had said Joe had AIDS, Felder submitted a motion under court seal seeking to have Joe compelled to submit to an AIDS test. Felder argued that a person with AIDS has a minimal life expectancy, "which is certainly a consideration in the courts awarding temporary or permanent custody. The court will want to consider if a person facing a death-threatening illness is prone to take his own life and that of others." Surely, he hoped, the court would not allow the children to stay with an AIDS-infected, cross dresser accused of murdering their mother.

Kurland argued in a sealed six-page reply that the question of whether Joe had the AIDS virus was "totally irrelevant to the issues before this court." Also, he said, "I have been advised by Mr. Pikul that he is healthy, in good physical condition and has absolutely no symptoms of the disease AIDS."

The civil attorney said the request for the blood test was being driven by Felder's "morbid curiosity." He said Joe Pikul considered such a test to be "a serious invasion of privacy. . . . Drawing blood causes him great apprehension and physical pain."

With the press and public barred, Dr. Kalogerakis said that even if Joe was suffering from the disease, which by that point had claimed 25,000 lives, it wouldn't justify removing the children from their "long-term custodial care parent." The doctor also contended that Joe's knowledge of having the virus wouldn't represent a danger for himself or to his children. Judge Glen took the matter under advisement.

Then Dr. Kalogerakis discussed the psychiatric report he'd just filed with Judge Glen. The doctor wrote that following his eight hours of interviews with Joe, he had found him to be "a troubled man, who while successful in business, seems to have experienced continuing failure in his personal life." Joe described his first marriage to Sandy as a "business arrangement." He drank heavily from age seventeen until he was forty-one and had an eating disorder. He admitted to "transvestism, wearing women's underwear and stockings," for the past five years, placing the start of his double life to right around the time Blake was born. "Social relationships have been problematic, beginning with alienation from both parents and sister ('We were never close'), and continuing on through various other relationships. He seems not to have experienced great success with women before or between his marriages," Dr. Kalogerakis wrote in his seven-page report. "He was given to moments of rage, some of them explosive, and is described by some observers as having a short fuse. He tended to be reclusive and secretive, at least with

Diane on her wedding day in the garden at the Dreamwold Inn in Carmel, New York, 1978, and posing with Joe.

Young Joe Pikul with his parents, Bernice and Joseph. (Courtesy Sandy Jarvinen)

Diane with her parents, Jane and Don. Diane's mother died in September 1976.

Sandy Jarvinen on a fishing trip with Joe. (Courtesy Sandy Jarvinen)

Sandy and Joe on vacation, 1972, Lake Chapala, Mexico. (Courtesy Sandy Jarvinen)

Joe with a prize catch.

Joe Pikul with glass in hand.
(Courtesy Sandy Jarvinen)

Diane, May 1975, before joining
Alcoholics Anonymous.

Joe celebrates Fourth of July
wearing one of the robes he
later used to wrap Diane's
body.

Diane at a Greenwich Village
playground.

Claudia, Diane, and Joe returning from the hospital with Blake, born on December 28, 1982.

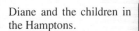

Diane and the children in the Hamptons.

Joe accompanying Claudia and Blake to school.

Claudia and Blake with the family pet.

The Pikul family in the backyard of their Amagansett home.

Blake and Claudia on vacation.

Diane feeding Blake while Claudia studies.

Diane opening a gift of lingerie.

Joe with Claudia the ballerina and Blake.

The Pikul family on their last family vacation in Colorado, 1986.

The driveway and front of the Amagansett home. The original house is at right. One of the two additions is at left.

The backyard of the Windmill Lane home, November 1987. Sliding-glass door on right leads to master bedroom, where Joe claimed the fatal confrontation took place.

Aerial view of the Windmill Lane area. Pikul property is in the middle, sandwiched between the pond and the horse farm below.

Aerial view of the pulloff on the northbound side of the New York Thruway. Diane Pikul's body was dumped in the culvert on left.

State trooper combs the foliage near where Diane Pikul's body was found in search of clues. (Leonard Greene / Middletown Times Herald-Record)

The Pikul family's 1986 Buick station wagon.

Diane's body after it was partially unwrapped by state police investigators. Rope is still tied around the neck.

The slash on Joe's right side. Joe testified that Diane had slashed him in the fatal dispute. Prosecution witness said he was certain the wound had not been caused by a knife.

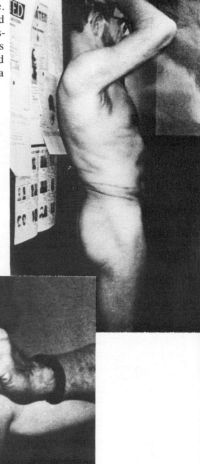

Joe's hand wound.

On the witness stand, Joe claims Diane attacked him with this kitchen knife and that he held her off with one hand and choked her with the other. (Dick Kraus/Newsday)

Raoul Lionel Felder, Diane's divorce attorney, who later represented the O'Guins in custody battle against Joe. (Keith Torrie/New York Daily News)

Robert Wayburn, Human Resources Administration attorney, who represented New York City government in fight to prevent Joe from keeping custody of Claudia and Blake. (Ed Molinari/New York Daily News)

First Assistant District Attorney Alan Joseph (on left) and defense attorneys Ron Bekoff (with pencil) and Steve Worth confer with Judge Thomas Byrne in Goshen, New York. (Jeff Goulding/Middletown Times Herald-Record)

Sandy Jarvinen points out key Massachusetts locations to members of the jury. (Jeff Goulding/Middletown Times Herald-Record)

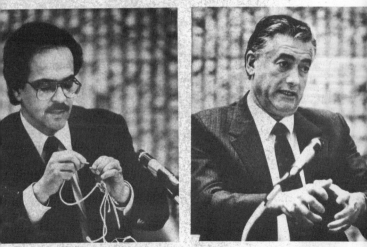

Below Left: Dr. Mark Taff, who performed the autopsy on Diane's body, shows circumference of ligature around the victim's neck. (Jeff Goulding/Middletown Times Herald-Record) *Below Right:* Investigator Joseph Tripodo, Sr., describes the choking motion that Joe Pikul made while confessing that he killed Diane at the beach. (Jeff Goulding/Middletown Times Herald-Record)

Joe Pikul led away by sheriff and his deputies. (Dan Cronin/New York Daily News)

Mary Bain Pikul faints as she exits Joe's funeral on June 6, 1989 at the Church of St. Joseph in Greenwich Village. Sukhreet Gabel, Mary's new friend, stands in the background. (Jack Smith/New York Daily News)

Kathleen and Mike O'Guin, guardians for Claudia and Blake, during a break in the custody hearing. (Alan Raia/Newsday) regard to some aspects of his life, describing alcohol as an 'amazing' substance which made him more successful socially.''

The single-spaced report noted that Joe was "obviously successful" in business, "but was described as highly competitive, almost obsessed (computers in three places), and clearly made work his number-one priority." Unable to discern any evidence of disturbed thought processes, Dr. Kalogerakis said Joe's emotional life nonetheless appeared to be "turbulent, labile and confused." It appeared, according to the report, that Joe was withholding information about his true emotions because he felt he might hurt his case. "He told me that Diane had essentially started him on the road to cross dressing by buying him women's stockings and tampons in the first year of their marriage. On repeated questioning, he could not, however, explain why she would do something like that nor why, even if she did give him such gifts, he would go on to make use of them. Here, his logic failed him, probably in his desire to portray her as emotionally disturbed, and he could not see how strange an act this would be in the average marriage."

In providing his life's history, Joe had displayed "considerable anger at Diane, presumably stimulated by her put-downs—'You're the lousiest lover I ever had!' 'You're a piece of shit!'—to which he would respond in kind—'You're a loser.' Arguments were frequent, especially after she began to talk of divorce, and both Mr. Pikul and the children described extensive cursing, predominantly by Mrs. Pikul. For many of these excesses, Mr. Pikul blamed the couple's joint alcoholic past."

Diagnostically, Dr. Kalogerakis tentatively found the following conditions: alcohol and substance dependence, in full remission; generalized anxiety disorder, with obsessive-compulsive features; and transvestic fetishism. "There is also evidence suggestive of an impulse disorder and at least one episode in his history involving a paranoid disturbance requiring treatment with anti-psychotic medication (chlorpromazine) on an out-patient basis. It is possible to entertain a diagnosis of mixed personality disorder, but additional supportive data would be necessary. Mr. Pikul made it clear that he felt very vulnerable to humiliation and his entire character structure is consistent with someone who could become enraged at denigration or even being opposed."

During his testimony, Dr. Kalogerakis said he found Joe to be "an alienated person," reclusive, someone who has problems with affective contact and someone capable of "moments of explosive rage."

Still, Dr. Kalogerakis said, "the overwhelming bulk of the evidence" indicated Joe's relationship with his children was "fundamentally good" and filled with warm and tender love. Joe had told the doctor he was even "willing to risk the criminal case" to keep the children, and the children made it clear that they wanted to remain with Joe too. "In all probability, the children represent the only real source of interpersonal satisfaction that exists, or has existed, in his life for some time."

Dr. Kalogerakis said there would always be "an open possibility" that Joe could harm his children, but felt greater harm could be inflicted by removing the children. He said homicide was often a "highly specific crime," and that the murder of one spouse by the other did not necessarily increase the danger to the children. What mattered was the relationship between parent and children.

"As far as the children are concerned, their father is innocent of any of the criminal charges. Secondly, as far as they are concerned, he is their daddy and they love him and he loves them," the doctor said. "There is no way in the world that any of us adults are going to be able to explain to those children that we are removing them from the custody of their father—who at the moment is not a convicted criminal—because we fear for their safety, when they have expressed no fear whatsoever, and have, indeed, demonstrated a feeling of total safety, in my observations, of the contact between the children and their father. . . . They have sustained a terrible loss. It's a question of whether the state wants to act in a way to impose yet a second important loss on them. Such a loss can have very serious consequences on personality, growth, and development." He said the adverse effects could include "a great deal of depression that would stem from their being left, essentially, without a parent, even if the replacements, the parent surrogates, are superior people."

Dr. Kalogerakis and Judge Glen then discussed a plan

for the children to spend the summer with Joe while getting to know the O'Guins. Claudia and Blake would move in with the O'Guins during their father's murder trial, with Joe having visitation rights.

Another witness, Robert Salisbury, the friend from AA, recounted how he'd erased one of Joe's business programs while showing Diane how to use the computer out in Amagansett, in 1985. An elderly investment banker with a Fifth Avenue address, Salisbury said Joe later angrily called him on the phone, threatening to kill him if he ever came near the house again.

But Felder's attempt to paint Joe as a lunatic quickly backfired. Although Salisbury claimed to be a completely recovered alcoholic who hadn't had a drink in ten years, Kurland was able to elicit an admission about an incident about six years ago where Salisbury was removed from Newark International Airport in New Jersey for creating a disturbance. Authorities had placed him in a straitjacket. Then while he was being transported to New York, either through the Lincoln Tunnel or Holland Tunnel, he tried to escape. Before he left the witness stand, Salisbury also admitted that he was hospitalized following the incident for "two or three weeks."

It was hard to believe that the pro-Diane forces couldn't find someone without their own damaging cross to bear. No wonder so many of Diane's friends didn't want to face cross-examination about their lives.

Before Seegars, the baby-sitter, testified, Judge Glen privately asked her several questions in her robing room. The judge wanted to know if Seegars feared reprisal "from the press or the community for testifying."

"I think probably from her friends, but I don't know who's out there exactly," said Seegars, then twenty-six.

"You mean Mrs. Pikul's friends?" asked Judge Glen.

"Yes," answered Seegars.

Asked if she was afraid of Joe, Seegars said she was not. "I told lots of people I'm not afraid. I was just upset with him that day I left, when I quit. I was more upset with him than frightened of him."

In court, Kurland asked Seegars, a steady baby-sitter in

Manhattan and the Hamptons since Claudia was two, if she'd ever seen Joe strike Diane. Never, Seegars responded. Had she ever seen Diane strike Joe? "She tried to, with her hands."

How about curse words? Kurland asked. "Not Mr. Pikul," said Seegars, "but Diane . . . when she got mad, or something didn't go her way."

The hearing then shifted back to the psychiatric testimony. Dr. Arthur Green, an expert in spousal abuse and its effects on children in the household, was basically called in support of Dr. Kalogerakis, who had very limited experience with young children. Ava L. Siegler, though, represented the radical fringe of the pro-Diane, child advocacy forces that had interjected themselves into the case.

A volunteer expert witness "found" through the auspices of the Manhattan district attorney's office, Siegler had previously been ordered to leave the courtroom because she was violating a standard rule of the court: witnesses cannot listen to other testimony. But Siegler didn't appear to be terribly impressed about those kind of rules, much in the same way the people clamoring for her to testify didn't seem concerned about matters of hearsay and uncorroborated allegations.

Siegler, a clinical professor of child psychology at New York University, also had appeared on TV to discuss the case, and in the process made it clear she'd made up her mind without benefit of a working knowledge of the evidence. Her position was unequivocal: anyone arrested for spousal murder should have their children taken away immediately.

Kurland questioned whether it had been appropriate for Siegler to appear on TV before talking to the judge or other parties. "You thought that was in the 'best interests' of the children to do that as an advocate?"

"It is definitely my custom where I feel that child advocacy is the issue to make the matters as public as possible so the people can be informed," Siegler said. "The rights of children are extremely paramount. Of course, part of what I am here to testify to, if the court permits me, is that I believe the rights of children are extremely crucial in a situation like this, and they should not be in anyway compromised. The physical-emotional states of the children should not be compromised even in a situation where the civil rights of an adult might be at stake. Yes, I believe that."

Judge Glen didn't like what she was hearing. Siegler admitted she hadn't examined Joe or the children and really didn't have solid knowledge of the case. Now that she was testifying, she was taking a biased advocate's position. "If I had wanted to appoint an advocate for the children, and if I thought that were necessary, I would have done so," said the judge. "I did not do so."

Emphasizing again that DA Morgenthau was "not a party here," Judge Glen protested: "I don't know what gives the district attorney's office the power to send someone to testify. This is highly irregular."

Siegler was asked if the child should be removed in spite of the natural parent's rights to his or her child in any instance where "the child's safety may conceivably be in danger."

"I would say yes," she answered.

"I thought that was what you are saying," said the judge with the conviction of a jury foreman reading a guilty verdict.

Before leaving the witness stand, Wayburn asked Siegler to assess the impact in a "hypothetical case" involving a nine-year-old girl whose father had been arrested for murder. Siegler said the girl would be "immediately placed in a situation of great emotional turmoil," and in a case where there has been no previous abuse, the emotional turmoil would be greater, because "there has been no understanding or comprehension or rehearsal or adaptation to repeated incidents of violence.

"I would say she was definitely in a situation of emotional conflict and struggle. Children love us for all kinds of ways that we have. We can be loved if we're cruel. We can be loved if we beat them. I have seen children who begged to be returned to psychotic mothers, children who have no trouble loving a father that whips them or whips their mother. So for a child to say 'I love my Daddy,' or 'I want to stay with my Daddy,' or 'I want to protect my Daddy,' or 'I don't believe that my Daddy did it,' is not something that we should take on face value," said Siegler. "Children operate on the premise 'what I don't know can't hurt me,' and in trauma, and I believe this would constitute a trauma, a child of nine years old would most likely begin to heavily rely upon defensive denial in order to continue to exist in the state that she was in. She might even cling much more poignantly to the remaining parent."

Siegler said placing a child in the custody of a remaining parent who is perceived by the child as the possible murderer of her mother would be catastrophic. "The mind has to struggle with two horrendous ideas at once," she said, contending that even therapy would not help in such a situation. "If we imagine the worst, and her father is guilty of this crime, then we have permitted her to live, and identify with, and absorb the emotional impact of a man who has turned out to be capable of homicide."

Putting aside the politics and behind-the-scenes shenanigans of getting Siegler into court, she had tackled tough issues. Especially to laymen, her testimony sounded right. It was testimony from the heart. Sexist and unconstitutional perhaps, but testimony that most mothers in America would agree with. Unfortunately, it was not the law, at least in New York State, so Joe Pikul was still in the driver's seat.

Two weeks after the hearings ended, Judge Glen summoned everyone back into her courtroom to discuss how to handle a potentially serious problem with Claudia, who was going to celebrate her ninth birthday in a couple of days. The youngster apparently was "beginning to act out in some way about her mother's death, and has been referring to her mother as if her mother were still alive," the judge said. Concerned school officials had contacted Dr. Kalogerakis.

Kurland said his client suggested the issue might be nothing more than a misunderstanding. "Claudia since the age of two or three has referred to Bernetta Seegars as 'Mamie' or 'Mammy,' which is a name that both Mr. and Mrs. Pikul approved of. In addition, in the recent month or so, I have been advised that Claudia has become very close with a playmate from Grace School named Jennifer Bain, and refers to her mother, Mrs. Mary Bain, as 'Mommy' or 'Mother.' It might be that Claudia was referring to the woman by using the same word." At Joe's suggestion,

Kurland requested that Claudia be seen by Dr. Kalogerakis to determine if there was a communications problem or if therapy was needed.

Bob Wayburn, the city attorney, then revealed another possibly troubling development: a city social worker visiting the Pikul home last week had observed a new set of scratches on Claudia. Claudia and Joe told the caseworker she scratched her arm while running to greet her father one day. The youngster said she had jumped up to hug her father, and while leaping forward brushed her arm against the wall. Although the caseworker had been a bit skeptical, Wayburn said, there was no reason to disbelieve the story.

Wayburn then asked the court's indulgence on an unrelated matter: the views of the HRA commissioner, William Grinker, as to what would constitute the "best interests" of the children. Noting that the judge had excluded those opinions from being considered as evidence, Wayburn said he wanted to deliver his boss's message for the record.

Wayburn said the city's top social service administrator felt that "notwithstanding the absence of any law which creates a presumption against the accused parent . . . the 'best interests' of these children would be served in any case—*in every case* where the facts are that the alleged murderer is the other parent, and the murder is brutal and vicious"—by not considering their father as an available resource.

Seeing that the judge was not going to cut him off on his political mission, Wayburn took a breath and continued. "The reasons for that position by the commissioner are, one, moral, in terms of a moral assessment; and two, a belief that the difficulty the children will have coping with the fact and the knowledge that they are residing with the alleged murdering parent, and dealing with the loss of the other parent, is a situation which cannot really be controlled or monitored, despite the best efforts and good intentions of all concerned."

Now Judge Glen did interrupt. "It has certainly come to my attention—as it has come to all of our attention, although it will not figure in my determination, because it's not part of the record—that there have been pickets and demonstrations outside this courthouse. The demands of those picketers, whose rights to demonstrate are certainly respected, are a call for a change in the law which would create a presumption" against the murder suspect. As a private citizen, Judge Glen added, she, too, might favor a change in the law. She wondered, then, if Grinker, "as the sort of senior statesperson of this area," would work to get the legislation enacted. "Or is he just going to come here and make the statement to the press in this case?"

Wayburn said he believed the commissioner was prepared to come out front on the issue. "But it's not as simple as that," he added. "Of course, whatever the policy and position of the city is reviewed by the mayor, and comes out of City Hall, and that's an involved process and not one that we could speak to. I do think this case gives rise to concerns as to what the law should be in this area."

Judge Glen agreed. "There is certainly no question that this case and the Steinberg-Nussbaum case, although it's a different case in many ways, crystallize this issue. There ought to be public and legislative concern about it." But, the judge continued, she was constrained to decide this case under the law "as it exists now."

Again losing on the legal front, Felder brought the discussion back to the original agenda: Claudia's problems dealing with her mother's death. "We predicted what would happen. It gives us no pleasure. I believe this child's ever-increasing upset and disturbance is caused by the fact she has been placed in the custody of a murderer and a degenerate and, worse yet, a murderer of this little girl's mother," Felder said. "It's going to get worse every day— every day she's in the custody of a man who killed her mother."

Felder also lashed out at the methodology employed for caseworker home visits. "I think you don't have to be Sherlock Holmes to figure out the way to do it; you just appear there one day and see what's going on. You're not going to accomplish much to tell anybody you will be there at three o'clock on Wednesday and everybody is going to be on good behavior."

A defeated man, Felder said he just wanted to have his say and expected "everybody to do what they want to do."

Judge Glen said she would ask Dr. Kalogerakis to interview Claudia and suggested that Joe consider having the psychiatrist talk to Seegars so the baby-sitter could better handle Claudia's "grieving and denial and the ways it may come out." She then adjourned court, the important problems supposedly addressed.

But there were no real solutions.

Recognizing that Judge Glen had raised several legitimate concerns, Commissioner Grinker instructed his assistants to propose new legislation. But that was easier said than done. First there was the internal squabbling in the department, for many were extremely disappointed in the way Bob Wayburn had handled the case. Then there were the unrelenting political pressures, including the petitions, pickets, and DA Morgenthau's stinging public criticisms that the city's Human Resources Administration had been too slow and indifferent in the Pikul case.

Even though he knew it was a losing proposition, Wayburn asked Judge Glen to "move the law forward"—to make new law—by judicially determining that the accused parent had the burden of proving that he or she should continue custody, and that the presumption against the surviving parent could only be rebutted with a strong showing that the children would suffer more if placed in any other custodial setting.

Citing Joe's history of "explosive and impulsive violent behavior," Wayburn implored Judge Glen to remove the Pikul children and asked her to reopen the hearings to take new evidence; his assistant, Doris McGarty, had tracked down Malcolm Rattner, the car-service driver Joe had attacked in 1973 at his Wall Street office.

McGarty, who would later marry Wayburn, had not only heard Rattner's tale of woe; he relayed stories that other drivers had told him about Joe. These allegations were subject to the same hearsay problems as the stories told by Diane's friends, but they shed new light on Joe's bizarre past. Rattner told McGarty that one of his colleagues once drove Joe and a woman to a remote location upstate where Joe made the woman dig a hole with a shovel, then warned her that the hole would be her grave if she ever "fucked" him again. On another occasion, Joe supposedly had someone drive him upstate to a remote spot where he shot holes in a photograph, then mailed the picture to its subject.

Wayburn knew the Rattner incident was fifteen years old, but at least Rattner could testify firsthand to Joe's violence. Then Judge Glen would see the real Joe Pikul, Wayburn hoped.

Judge Glen scheduled another hearing for March 2. Nervous and reluctant, Rattner had to be served with a subpoena to even come to court. He arrived with an off-duty police detective serving as bodyguard. It so happened that the detective had previously investigated the theft of Felder's Rolls-Royce. So the two acquaintances teamed up to get Rattner to take the stand.

But it didn't take long before Rattner's testimony backfired like the others trying to help the O'Guins. Rattner described his injuries as if they had approached the life-threatening stage, claiming that he'd been rushed to Beekman Downtown Hospital bleeding profusely from the arm and head. But the emergency-room report indicated only a bruise to the forearm and no bleeding in the arm, head, or forearm.

Rattner also produced a most unpleasant effect on the judge, standing to point and yell at Joe and almost leaving the witness stand to go after Kurland as he conducted an aggressive cross-examination. The man hardly seemed like a meek victim.

Later in the day, Joe took the stand, explaining away the Rattner incident as ancient history from his drinking days. "Ninety-nine percent of what Rattner said is false," he said. He claimed the gun he'd brandished had been a gift from a friend and contended he had intended to return it. Joe also professed to being unable to remember many of the details in view of his alcoholic condition at the time.

Although Judge Glen observed that Joe's version wasn't one of the most credible stories she'd ever heard, the Rattner testimony amounted to another disappointment for the O'Guins.

That should have been the end of the reopened hearing, except Kurland had an additional witness of his own— Mary Bain, the neighbor whom Claudia had been calling "Mommy."

Mrs. Bain told the court that she and her husband Stephen were willing to care for the Pikul children during Joe's legal difficulties and would even move with Jennifer, Claudia, and Blake to her parents' larger apartment in Brooklyn. She said that her daughter Jennifer and Claudia were classmates at Grace Church School and played together four or five times a week, often with Joe being the only supervising adult. Mrs. Bain said she didn't fear Joe Pikul, and in fact had faith in him.

The stylishly dressed witness, a chunky woman with a squeaky voice, said Claudia and Blake appeared to be in good physical and emotional condition and were benefiting from a very loving relationship with their father. Mrs. Bain also offered that she and her husband would adopt the Pikul children in the event Joe was convicted.

As a result of that testimony, Judge Glen ordered Mrs. Bain and her husband to undergo psychiatric and social service evaluations to determine if their home setting might be a better alternative than the O'Guins'. This, of course, served to delay Judge Glen's official decision even more.

Two days later Felder responded with a motion seeking a mistrial in the custody case, alleging that the court had made a serious error in designating Dr. Kalogerakis as its expert witness when, in fact, he was shown "to be no expert at all" because of his lack of experience treating children. Felder further accused Judge Glen of having interjected herself into cross-examination to "virtually rescue" her witness when the going got tough.

Kurland naturally opposed the mistrial motion, contending that Felder's real quarrel had to do with Dr. Kalogerakis's finding that Joe should be allowed to keep his children.

Judge Glen denied the mistrial motion and issued another related decision against Felder, under court seal.

The case, which concerned the subject of involuntary testing for AIDS, was entitled *Jane and John Doe* versus *Richard Roe* in a publication of court decisions. The Does were identified as maternal grandparents seeking custody of two minor children, but other details, including the involvement of Felder and Kurland, left an inescapable conclusion—one confirmed months later—that the secret decision involved Kathy and Mike O'Guin v. Joe Pikul.

In her ruling, Judge Glen held that involuntary testing for the Acquired Immune Deficiency Syndrome could only be ordered in civil litigation upon showing of compelling need, and "compelling need for such testing was not shown."

According to the decision, granting of the motion for the AIDS test would violate the Constitution's protection against improper search and seizure and state law prohibiting any laboratory from conducting such tests without a signed consent form. The judge also noted a relatively high inaccuracy rate for many AIDS blood tests, saying an erroneous positive test result could lead to the test subject being ostracized and suffering "psychic harm."

Judge Glen wrote that a court-appointed psychiatrist, a reference to Dr. Kalogerakis, had opined that even if the father had AIDS, and thus a shortened life span—perhaps less than two years—it "would not justify removing children from his long-term custody, especially where evidence suggested that the disease itself would create no danger to children or pose risk that father might harm himself or children."

Judge Glen made it clear she didn't believe Mr. Roe had AIDS, but noted that the man had offered to undergo a physical examination. "In the unlikely event that respondent actually does suffer from AIDS, this information will be necessary for him in terms of planning his own long-term care, as well as considering long-term arrangements for the children," the judge wrote. "The physical examination is both voluntary and nonintrusive and, to the extent that it would turn up evidence of AIDS itself, rather than simply seropositivity, is far more useful given the issues and facts in this case."

Joe had dodged another bullet. And the entire matter had been decided in secrecy.

While Judge Glen worked on her formal decision, Felder was quoted in a newspaper gossip column as saying that he was turned down for the part of a tough district attorney in Susan Seidelman's Lorimar film "Cookie" because he couldn't take directions on how to "shove around" actress Emily Lloyd or memorize the lines. Not to fear, Felder said, a TV pilot might be done on his career as a divorce attorney.

He also claimed to have held talks with representatives of another network on the possibility of playing himself in a TV movie about the Pikul case. "It would be in bad taste to do it until the matter is settled, so I'll wait," said Felder.

Joe conducted some public relations as well. Sitting in Kurland's office, he told Shirley E. Perlman of *Newsday*, a major Long Island daily: "I think I'm a nice person and I don't know why the media has picked up this other image." According to Joe, his kids are "only in danger of a loving, caring relationship."

"They want to be with me," he said. Unable to resist a swipe at his beaten and strangled wife, he added that Claudia and Blake had "always said they'd rather be with me. They said it right to her face, to Diane, that if there was a divorce, they wanted to live with me. . . . People who know me for a long time and my friends think that I'm a perfectly nice person and my kids certainly think that."

Later that month, Judge Glen issued a sixty-seven-page decision on the custody case. Continuing to keep certain facts secret in order to protect Joe's rights, the judge also wrote a longer sealed decision for the appeals courts. The extra five pages included details about the sex videotapes, evidence in the criminal case against Joe, and the psychiatric examinations of all parties.

As expected, Joe got to keep the children until the trial. Judge Glen said the only real issue was who would take care of Claudia and Blake during that proceeding. If Joe was acquitted, he would get his children back; if convicted, then someone would obviously be needed to assume the role of long-term caretaker.

In making her decision, Judge Glen said, she had assumed that Joe was guilty of murdering Diane, and that the O'Guins had the burden to show it would be in the children's "best interests" to override Joe's constitutionally protected right to raise his natural children.

Judge Glen felt it was equally important to state what was not at issue. "First, the case must be decided on the record before me, not on press speculations, out-of-court charges, or the like. Despite efforts to draw analogies between this case and the tragic death of Lisa Steinberg and the apparent abuse of Hedda Nussbaum, there is absolutely no evidence on this record either of abuse toward the children or of any abuse whatsoever toward Diane Whitmore Pikul prior to her murder."

Despite pickets calling for laws that would require removal of children from a parent charged with killing the other parent, "the court is bound by *current* law," which, the judge said, when combined with the hearing record, left her unable to find that the O'Guins had met the heavy burden required. "The lengthy, strong, and loving relationship between the respondent and his children, their strongly expressed desire to remain with him, the possibility of emotional trauma should they be removed, particularly at this vulnerable time after their mother's death, and the lack of evidence that remaining with the father at this time would be injurious or dangerous to them, compels the conclusion that custody should remain with the respondent father."

Judge Glen found Commissioner Grinker's position to be inconsistent with all case law, and she blasted the credibility of the nonexpert witnesses called on behalf of the O'Guins, characterizing their testimony as hostile, exaggerated, biased, based on hearsay from Diane, bizarre, convoluted, and at times "seriously controverted by physical evidence."

The judge did find the O'Guins to be "exceptionally bright, competent, and kind people who would undoubtedly be good caretakers for the children" and work with Joe to keep his relationship with the children functioning. But that was not the issue, she said, "notwithstanding the understandable pain and anger which all members of Diane Whitmore Pikul's family feel with regard to the charges against Joseph Pikul."

As for Joe, Judge Glen said she found him "somewhat combative" and sarcastic as a witness, prone to displays of anger or annoyance when questioned about prior alleged wrongdoings, a troubled individual, and "not always entirely credible." However, when Joe spoke of Claudia and Blake, he "appeared as an entirely different person. I credit that his love and concern for them is genuine and strong, and that his willingness to plan and to take whatever steps are necessary during this period is considered and real. His demeanor in speaking about the children was matched by my observation of him with the children, both when they were reunited on the first day of the hearing and as he interacted with them in my chambers. Whatever his other problems may be, my observation was that he is indeed a loving and caring parent who is totally devoted to his children and whose children return that devotion in a spontaneous, unqualified fashion."

Judge Glen said she felt Bernetta Seegars was "an extremely competent, solid, no-nonsense person, and I credited her testimony both as to the past and present relationship between Mr. Pikul and his children. She clearly is the person, among all the witnesses, who has had the best opportunity to observe this relationship over a long period of time, and her characterization and description of it was important to my decision."

So, too, was the last-minute testimony of Mrs. Mary Bain, said Judge Glen, finding the woman to be "a competent, accomplished, and convincing witness. Her parental feelings were strong, both toward her own child—and also toward a stepchild whom she shares with her present husband—and toward the Pikul children." Although Mrs. Bain had offered her family's home as an alternate resource, Judge Glen noted that "for reasons which have not been specified, that offer was withdrawn."

The decision noted that it had indeed been Mrs. Bain whom Claudia had taken to calling "Mommy" in the present tense. "Upon further examination by the psychiatrist and by the HRA caseworker, it became apparent . . . that Claudia was using the term of 'Mommy' for her best friend's mother, who had permitted and encouraged that terminology." Mrs. Bain was the only person besides Seegars who had the opportunity to observe Joe and the kids since he regained temporary custody, the judge said. "I credit her testimony about the relationship, and about the children's comfort with and affection for their father, as well as the clear lack of fear which they have exhibited to all who have seen them."

Judge Glen said she considered two other factors: Joe's alleged misconduct—the murder charges, a history of violence, and the cross dressing—and the wishes of the children.

"The law in this state is clear that amoral, immoral, or deviant behavior by a parent is grounds for denial or removal of custody *only* where that behavior has an impact on the children," said Judge Glen. "The law as to sexual deviance or sexual indiscretions is equally clear." As an example, Judge Glen cited a 1984 New York case where allegations of a mother's lesbian activities in front of her children were insufficient to justify removal of custody because no harm to the children was shown. "It is uncontroverted that the children had and have no knowledge of those practices and that respondent has never engaged in such practices in their presence or proximity."

Judge Glen said she also gave serious consideration to the wishes of Claudia and Blake. "Both children have expressed the strongest possible desire to remain with their father, and have similarly expressed strong reservations about going to live with the petitioners, with whom they have no relationship at all. Despite the heinousness of the crime with which he is charged, and despite isolated incidents of anger and even possible violence in his background, there is no evidence on this record that the respondent is physically dangerous to his children."

All that said, Judge Glen said she still had to deal with the children's care during the trial and in the event Joe was convicted. She said Joe's "willingness and flexibility" in dealing with a transition period demonstrated his love and concern for his children, and that his willingness to cooperate figured in her final determination.

Declaring that continued custody was premised on Joe's compliance with the plan, Judge Glen ruled that the children could remain with Joe and attend their old schools until the end of the school year. She ordered that the children be integrated into the O'Guins' lives immediately, with interaction gradually increased over the summer months.

Because the trial was expected to begin sometime in the fall, Judge Glen said it was incumbent that custody be transferred to the O'Guins that September so the children could settle into new schools. She noted that the O'Guins were the "only alternative caretakers and custodians" because Joe's relatives named in Diane's will had not come forward. She promised Joe liberal visitation, with access on weekends and school holidays, and emphasized that he would get his children back if acquitted.

"Given the children's enormous connection to their father, the need for stability following the death of their mother, and their lack of knowledge of, or connection to, the O'Guins, it is of the greatest importance that all parties cooperate to make the transition as easy and comfortable as possible for them," said Judge Glen. "This involves continued counseling of all parties."

The decision put the case back in the headlines. Kurland was ecstatic about the ruling. "The judge followed the law. Although there has been a great deal of public uproar from the beginning, I always thought that the law was very clear."

Felder was his usual quotable self. "We'll appeal and appeal and appeal until rights prevail and these kids are protected," he said. "I believe these children are in deep trouble and in deep danger. This case is precedent setting in the lack of common sense that it displays."

But Felder, who said he hoped the appeals courts would intervene "at the earliest possible time," never followed through with the appeal. Wayburn later claimed in a memo to a boss that Felder had "underlitigated the case and simply postures and gestures at the result."

Regardless of who, if anyone, was to blame, Joe had won again.

PART · V

LOVE SPRINGS ETERNAL

C H A P T E R • 18

M as in Maine

OCCASIONALLY, A MAJOR CRIMINAL CASE hinges on the outcome of pretrial hearings, proceedings in which a judge decides what evidence will be allowed to be introduced at trial and what will be excluded. Such hearings are like trials in and of themselves, with the conduct of the police and prosecutor invariably pitted against the constitutional rights of the defendant. It is the judge's job to protect against outrageous abuses of "law and order" by throwing out or restricting the use of improperly obtained evidence.

The overwhelming majority of evidence gathered during months of police work is almost always validated for use at trial. But on the rare occasion when a judge does prohibit the use of key evidence, an open-and-shut case can suddenly become very iffy.

The People of the State of New York v. *Joseph Pikul*, Indictment No. 87–488, was to be one of those cases.

Back at the turn of the year, 1988, in upstate Goshen, New York, the Orange County seat, a grand jury had indicted Joe for second-degree murder. The indictment had been only two paragraphs long and had not contained new details. However, a notice was attached explaining that the district attorney's office intended to introduce at trial "certain voluntary oral statements made by the defendant to Detective William Glynn, Detective Richard A. Composto, Detective Sergeant Kenneth M. Bowen, Senior Investigator Donald P. Delaney, Investigator Stephen Oates, Investigator James Probst, Investigator Joseph Tripodo, Jr., Investigator Robert Venezia, and Senior Investigator Joseph Tripodo, Sr."

At the time, the prosecutor's earlier request to subpoena Claudia and Blake to testify before the grand jury had been withdrawn. The matter had been a sticky one for Prosecutor Alan Joseph all along. Putting two youngsters on the stand to testify against their father—in the murder of their mother no less—was fraught with problems, including having to deal with the traumatic effect such an experience could have on the children.

As the weeks passed, Joseph, the chief assistant district attorney of Orange County, grew convinced that his case was solid enough without the children's testimony. He assumed Judge Glen's interview in Manhattan had been thorough, and that if Claudia and Blake knew something, it would have come out then.

While Prosecutor Joseph was satisfied that he had plenty of evidence to obtain a conviction, his case wasn't without pitfalls. For one, most of the bloodstains found inside the Windmill Lane house had turned out not to be human blood, according to the lab tests. And in one case where there was human blood, it couldn't be typed, so there was no way to tell if the blood belonged to Diane.

The negative lab tests made it much more difficult for police to determine where the murder had taken place. Also, there was no physical evidence to connect Joe with the knife or the shotgun or anything at the Thruway site where the body was found.

There were serious bureaucratic foul-ups with tests on Diane's blood, too. By now the authorities knew that Joe had told Sandy Jarvinen he was dying of AIDS. None of the investigators really believed the claim, but the curious remembered that on the night of his arrest, Joe had asked if Diane had been tested for AIDS.

The question of whether Diane had AIDS was not an insignificant one, with Joe's first defense attorney having promised that Diane's boyfriend would provide a surprise twist to the mystery. If Diane had the disease, then Joe could conceivably argue that she gave it to him. Having to prove who gave what to whom was one challenge the prosecutor didn't need.

What should have been very easy to determine was conveniently not. In reconstructing the "miscommunication," authorities determined that the battery of toxological tests being conducted by the main state-police laboratory did not include an AIDS test; a blood sample would have to be sent to the state Health Department. But the district attorney couldn't request the test; the medical examiner had to submit the paperwork.

Whether it was the original exposure of Diane's body to the weather, bad refrigeration, the passage of time before the AIDS test was actually requested, a lab or police mistake, a cover-up to protect the victim's reputation, or some other unfortunate but well-timed circumstance, the official explanation was that the AIDS test could not be done.

By the middle of March, defense attorney Ronald Bekoff filed papers seeking a wide range of relief for the upcoming murder trial. Bekoff requested that the indictment be dismissed outright, that he be allowed to see the grand jury minutes to prepare oral arguments for throwing the case out, that all evidence be produced, that he receive any information about grants of immunity to prosecution witnesses and any material that would be exculpatory to his client. Bekoff also wanted hearings held on the admissibility of the identifications made by the car-wash employees, on the legitimacy of the search warrant, the permission slip that Joe signed for the search at the Amagansett home, and on the statements Joe had made to the various police officers. Finally, Bekoff wanted a hearing held on whether the district attorney had any damaging information about Joe's past.

"The defendant may wish to testify in his own behalf," Bekoff wrote. In the event the prosecutor possessed information enabling him to cross-examine Joe about any prior "illegal, vicious, or immoral acts," Joe would be reluctant to testify, Bekoff contended, and would thereby "be deprived of the inherent benefit of defending himself properly in the event that any such acts are brought before the jury." The defense attorney also argued that any confessions were made involuntarily, after Joe was arrested without probable cause.

Bekoff gained a partial victory when Orange County

Judge Thomas J. Byrne ruled on the motions April 5, 1988. The judge looked at the grand jury minutes in private and decided the indictment was just fine. But Judge Byrne did order hearings on the admissibility of information about Joe's prior criminal history, the identifications made by the car-wash personnel, and the statements Joe gave to police in Manhattan, in the car on the way to the state-police barracks and during his interviews with the state investigators.

By the next month, Bekoff had not turned up Diane's mystery boyfriend, but he now had chosen his plan of attack: he would turn the hearing into an inquisition on how the police had mishandled Joe.

The pretrial was to be two proceedings in one, a Huntley hearing and a Wade hearing. The Huntley sessions would determine the admissibility of statements Joe made to various members of the New York State Police, the Newburgh police, and the New York City Police Department in the days leading up to and immediately following his arrest.

The hearing would serve as a dry run on the police testimony and could potentially make or break the case. More evidence would likely come out here than at the trial because Judge Byrne would hear the evidence eventually permitted as well as any testimony ultimately thrown out or limited.

As Bekoff saw it, the various interrogators had thought they had their suspect right from the start, a spurned eccentric/blackmail victim, so they simply plowed ahead, never pausing to protect the defendant's constitutional rights.

Bekoff had already notched one important concession: the statement Joe made to Tripodo Senior was clearly inadmissible and wouldn't even be part of the hearing. But the defense attorney lost another key battle: Judge Byrne refused to bar the press and public from the courtroom while Joe's various statements and their admissibility were discussed.

The second pretrial matter, called a Wade hearing, involved the admissibility of identification testimony made by three of the car-wash employees. If it could be established that police had improperly coached the workers, their identifications would be inadmissible.

If the defense could eliminate both the testimony about the car-wash episode and all of the contradictions and admissions Joe had given the police, there wouldn't be much of a case left.

So the stakes were high when Judge Byrne called the parties to order at noon, Tuesday, May 17, 1988.

Prosecutor Joseph started his case with Detective William Glynn of the Sixth Precinct in New York City, who recounted how Joe had first called him the Monday after the murder, but only after the *Harper's* staff had spoken to Joe and the police.

Guided by the prosecutor's questions, Glynn recapped the numerous versions of Joe's story on the telephone and during the initial missing-persons interview at the Sixth Avenue apartment: he and Diane fought, they didn't fight; Diane left right away, she stayed around for a while; she left before he went to bed, she must have left after he went to bed. Glynn also mentioned Joe's condom-boyfriend story, and how Joe had declined to identify Diane's body. The detective was only too glad to provide Joe's one-liner about Diane's panties: "Maybe you can get a good scent off of these."

Ronald Bekoff, a former assistant district attorney himself and an experienced trial veteran, rose to question the witness and in the process began his prosecution of the police and criminal justice system. Joe's crazy, ever-changing versions of the story actually worked against Glynn and the cops who would follow, for Bekoff used his client's illogical statements and contradictions to suggest the cops had gotten the story all wrong.

Bekoff focused on whether Glynn's testimony was rehearsed, on the detective's ability to remember certain facts now, six months later, that he had failed to note in his written reports at the time of the investigation, on his conversations with Joe about Diane's boyfriend, and on the issue of precisely when Joe became a suspect.

Glynn said he'd spoken to Prosecutor Joseph three times about his testimony, twice on the telephone and once in person in the company of Detective Richard Composto, his colleague from the Sixth Precinct. He said the new evidence he remembered while testifying had simply come back to him.

"Out of the blue?" asked Bekoff.

"Out of the blue," Glynn responded.

Richie Composto was next, and if ever there was a police official whose testimony could be compared to the old Abbott and Costello routine "Who's on First?" it was Composto's pretrial performance regarding the all-night interview he had conducted with Joe several hours after Glynn's initial house call.

Composto, who was planning to retire, had been preoccupied with the Lisa Steinberg case. Basically, he confessed that he couldn't keep Joe's versions straight. And he compounded that problem by being unable to testify accurately about his own written notes.

He thought Joe's other apartment was on Franklin Street, rather than Rector Place. Then he said Joe had told him he spent the weekend in question driving around Maine, rather than Massachusetts. "Did he tell you where in Maine he went?" Prosecutor Joseph asked, hoping the witness would catch his mistake.

"He said to his aunt's grave," said Composto.

Asked what towns Joe had mentioned "in that state," Composto said he could only remember Windsor, allowing in a masterful understatement that he was "not familiar with the state." The only Windsor in the case was New Windsor in New York State, residence of the Sawoska family and the community in which Diane's body had been found.

Realizing he had to make his examination of Composto an open-book test, Joseph asked: "Is there anything that would refresh your recollection?"

Bekoff jumped to his feet to object. "There's no testimony that his recollection is anything but fine."

"He said he did not remember exactly because he's not familiar with the state," said Joseph.

Judge Byrne overruled the objection, and Composto resumed. "I wrote in a report as he was telling me. One of the other places was Ware," he said.

As Composto continued to falter, Prosecutor Joseph moved rapidly. "Mark this three-page document as People Exhibit 1 for identification," he said to the court stenographer. Not missing a step, Joseph handed Composto the document. "I show you this three-page report, dated October 27, 1987, regarding conversation with Joseph Pikul. Showing you the second page, let me backtrack—"

"Objection to the form, judge," Bekoff interrupted. "The question was, 'What part of Maine did he drive in?' So the only refreshing of recollection could be, now looking at that document, can you tell from looking at that document—"

"Sustain the objection," barked Judge Byrne.

Joseph was not going to be able to spoon-feed Composto, but he was at least given the okay to give him the report, with a hint to look at page two, which was replete with references to Massachusetts, the Massachusetts Turnpike, Boston, Berkshires, and Ware, Massachusetts.

"Does that refresh your recollection?" Joseph asked.

"I didn't look at it, no," said Composto, apparently still not getting the point, or not caring to.

"Would you look at it to see if it refreshes your recollection?" Joseph pleaded. Composto finally read the document.

"Now," Joseph resumed. "Can you tell us *where* Mr. Pikul told you he went, which cities he went in after he dropped the kids off?"

"Objection," bellowed Bekoff. "The question is whether that refreshes his recollection as to what part of Maine did he go?"

"Sustained," said Judge Byrne, who didn't seem to be bothered by the cat fight.

Grudgingly, Joseph inquired: "Can you tell us what part of Maine he went to?"

"Norwood, Lee, New Windsor, and Berkshires," responded Composto, ticking off two towns and a region in Massachusetts and one community in New York.

Incredulous, Joseph tried one more time. "The Berkshires are in *Maine*?"

"I don't know, sir," Composto replied, oblivious.

As the tortuous testimony continued, Prosecutor Joseph breathed a sigh of relief when Composto finally announced the words "Massachusetts Turnpike" from his report. Feeling comfortable that the problem had been eliminated, Joseph proceeded to ask: "When did he tell you he was going to Massachusetts?"

"Excuse me, Maine," Composto corrected incorrectly,

proceeding to again contradict his own official report as to the order of events, times, and dates.

Even Joe hadn't mixed up the story that much.

By late morning of the second day of the hearings, Bekoff finally got his chance at Composto, and he immediately sought to challenge the official version that Joe was not a suspect and was free to leave at any time during the all-night interview.

Composto acknowledged that he'd been sent basically to find out two things from Joe: exactly what Diane had been wearing when he last saw her and any additional information available about his wife's alleged boyfriend. But under intensive questioning, Composto admitted that he made Joe tell his whole story again, that he never inquired about Diane's boyfriend, and that it took him until 8:00 A.M. to ask Joe about the clothing.

Instead, Composto was forced to acknowledge, Joe discussed incriminating things like his penchant for wearing women's clothing and Diane's blackmail use of the sex photos in the divorce.

Bekoff wanted to know what else had been on Composto's agenda. "Anything he could help us with."

But Composto denied asking Joe to come to the police precinct in order to break him down and get him to say something incriminating about Diane's disappearance. The detective said it was his policy to always ask people to come to the station house for interviews.

Like all witnesses held over through a lunch break or an overnight recess, Composto was told by the judge not to talk to anyone about his testimony. But when court recommenced, no one would have bet that Composto hadn't been given a crash course in New England geography. Everyone was mistaken.

"How long did Mr. Pikul tell you it took him to drive to Maine?" asked Bekoff.

"At what time?" Composto replied. That really threw Bekoff, so he asked Composto how many times Joe told him he drove to Maine. "He told me he drove to various parts at least three times." Incredibly, it appeared Composto hadn't gotten the message. "The first time he said he was heading for Boston, Massachusetts, and he got back in New York approximately one o'clock in the morning."

"Excuse me, detective. I'm asking about Maine," said Bekoff. "I asked how long he told you it took him to drive to Maine." No way Composto was getting off that easy. The detective said he couldn't remember, so Bekoff asked Composto where Joe said he went "when he came back from Maine."

"A couple of different places," said Composto, mentioning "New York" and to pick up the children in "Windsor."

Bekoff wanted to make sure Composto meant Manhattan when he said Joe had driven from Maine to New York. "No, he actually said he was in Connecticut," Composto now said.

"Did you ask him if there was any confusion?"

"If there was any confusion?" Composto asked back.

"Yes. You seem to be saying two different things."

"To me he said about four different things," said Composto, who was then forced to acknowledge that he never asked Joe which version was correct.

Bekoff wondered why the inconsistencies hadn't been deemed important. "I'm conducting a missing-persons," Composto insisted.

"And that question was not important to the investigation?"

Composto said he didn't think so.

Moving back to Composto's original report, Bekoff focused on Joe's claims about Diane having run away in the past. Composto had quoted Joe as saying a pregnant Diane had run off in California because "she wanted to get laid." But on the witness stand Composto linked Diane's supposed horniness to the time she ran away from Joe's sister's house in Virginia.

In his report, Composto wrote that Joe said he'd sent his driver upstate to recover the credit cards, but on the stand he said Joe didn't make the statement. Then Composto testified that he believed Joe said he'd paid cash at the hardware store in Amagansett, when his written report quoted Joe as saying he'd used his American Express card.

Composto was so mixed up that Bekoff even tried to get him to say that the all-night interview with Joe back in October might have lasted until 2:25 in the afternoon.

"Isn't it a fact that you wrote in your notes, Defendant's E, last page, '225, Rector Place, Apartment 20F'?" Bekoff asked, referring to the police visit to Joe's apartment in Battery Park City.

Prosecutor Joseph objected to the ploy, but Judge Byrne overruled, forcing Composto to fight his own battles.

"I don't recall, sir," said the witness.

Bekoff told Composto to look at the last page of his report. "Does it say that, sir?" asked Bekoff. Composto balked.

"Does it say 225, Rector Street?"

"Yeah, and—"

Bekoff cut him off. "I got a yes and a no. Does it say 225 Rector Street?"

"What does that have to do with two o'clock?" said Composto, for once in tune with his predicament.

Bekoff tried again, now directly suggesting that "225 Rector" meant they'd left "approximately 2:25 in the afternoon." But Composto insisted the number did not represent a time because Joe's address had been 225 Rector.

Bekoff had made great strides with Composto's help. When the detective wasn't remembering incorrectly, he wasn't remembering at all. Before the cross-examination ended, the detective responded "I don't recall" or "I don't remember" to more than 100 questions related to Joe's all-night interview.

Bekoff broadly touched on the constitutional issues again: no, Composto said, he had never told Joe he was free to leave; no, he had never told Joe he wasn't under any obligation to talk; no, he had never read Joe his Miranda rights; no, he had never asked Joe if he had a lawyer; and no, he had never told Joe he was not under arrest. "Did you ever mention to *him*, did you ever ask *him* if he had a lawyer?" Bekoff demanded.

"What for?" snapped Composto, showing utter contempt for this particular line of questioning.

"I take that to mean no?" asked Bekoff.

"No, *sir*."

His agony ended, Composto left the stand.

Back in his office, Prosecutor Joseph was not a happy camper. "What do you keep putting us in Maine for?" he asked Composto.

"I keep thinking Massachusetts, but I keep saying Maine," the embarrassed detective replied.

Composto's performance had made the police look bad, but the future of the Pikul prosecution rested on the next set of witnesses—the state-police investigators who had listened to Joe confess and make disparaging remarks about Diane after his arrest.

Bekoff's game plan was simple: paint the picture of a defendant denied his constitutional rights—distraught, no sleep, lawyer absent, tricked into talking, not knowing what he was saying.

Joseph A. Tripodo, Jr., assigned by his father to "keep an eye on" Joe the night of the arrest, went first.

With Glynn and Composto, Prosecutor Joseph had wanted to bring out Joe Pikul's state of mind before he was arrested: anxious, agitated, nervous. Joseph sought to use Tripodo Junior to introduce more of the same type of circumstantial evidence—for example, Joe's desire to be left alone in the barracks bathroom, presumably so he could get rid of the women's underwear beneath his shirt and jeans.

But the real pay dirt lay in getting Judge Byrne's approval to introduce Joe's incriminating comments, such as "I just couldn't take it anymore" and "I don't care whether they give me ten or twenty years, I think everybody is better off without her."

Joseph had a serious legal problem to overcome, though; he had to explain what this rookie investigator was doing "keeping an eye" on the suspect for ninety minutes. If Tripodo Junior hadn't been told to question Joe, what was he doing with him all that time?

Tripodo Junior said he hadn't asked Joe any questions, but merely listened. He maintained that his only assignment had been to watch Joe "until I was advised to do differently." He told Bekoff that it would have been impossible to have written down everything Joe told him. "Keep in mind that I talked to him for an hour and a half. I would have probably written an encyclopedia."

Bekoff zoomed in on the constitutional issues. No, Tripodo Junior said, he'd never read Joe his rights. Yes, he knew Joe had an attorney but talked to him anyway. Tripodo Junior said Joe lamented the fact that his lawyer had not accompanied him, and the investigator said he empathized with Joe. "I felt sorry for him," said the witness. When Bekoff wondered if the sympathy helped develop a better rapport with the suspect, Tripodo Junior said he wasn't sure.

The defense attorney also wondered if another investigator ever came over to complain: "What are you talking to this man for?"

No, Tripodo Junior said, no one had bothered him. "I don't know what else I was going to do. He talked to me."

But there was plenty to do, said Bekoff, like fill out the General 5 arrest form.

Bekoff was on a roll, making parts of the conversation sound like a con job, like when Tripodo Junior told Joe: "It's all right. I know. I understand how you feel," after Joe compared his "ungrateful wife" and his former girlfriend at the condo. Or when the investigator said he told Joe: "It's okay, Joe. A man can cry."

"Did you ever tell him that if you talked to fifty more Dianes in New York, you would find that she was fooling around right from the start of your marriage?" Bekoff asked.

Tripodo Junior denied that suggestion, but acknowledged under additional questioning that he might have told Joe "the boys in the barracks" were sympathetic and that "anybody would feel the same way" if they had such an ungrateful wife.

By the end of Tripodo Junior's testimony it was clear he'd done quite a bit more than just keep an eye on Joe—like even ask a question or two.

The stakes were greatly raised when Investigator James G. Probst, of the New York State Police out on Long Island, took the stand.

Probst confirmed that when he and his partner, Senior Investigator Stephen Oates, arrested Joe down in Manhattan, lawyer Charles Clayman had instructed them not to talk to his client.

But, Probst said, Joe started talking almost as soon as the two-hour trip to Newburgh commenced, first interrupting with the best directions out of the city, then asking for apple juice. The way Probst remembered the car ride, Joe "just joined in the conversation" about children and the Sesame Place amusement park, to proclaim: "That's why I did it. She's a son of a bitch. I have two kids, four and eight years old. I'd like to take my kids to this Sesame Place sometime."

And from there, according to Probst, Joe just kept going, complaining about the different baby-sitters and how Diane "deserved it. I never did anything wrong before in my life. I can't change it now."

Probst assured the prosecutor that Joe had made all those statements without benefit of prodding or coercion.

Under cross-examination, Bekoff broached the supposed coincidence of the similar ages of Claudia and Blake to Probst's and Oates's children. Probst said that Oates told him he had a son about four. "Oates told me, sir, at my question to Oates," said Probst.

Bekoff wondered why, since Probst knew Oates so well, he needed to ask the age of his son.

Probst contended he really didn't know Oates that well back in 1987. Yes, Probst went on to say, he had mentioned that he had two children of his own. "It was in the context of 'My kids are 3½ and six, and we took them to Sesame Place, they loved it.' " And yes, Probst also acknowledged, he knew at the time that Joe had two children approximately the same ages.

"Then you started talking about Sesame Place and children loving it, right?" Probst objected to the word "started." As he explained, "Investigator Oates and I had begun that conversation sometime prior that afternoon, and we just continued the conversation."

But if he and Oates had been talking about Big Bird and the rest of the Sesame Street gang earlier in the day, Bekoff wondered aloud, why did they need to mention their kids' ages during the car ride, in front of Joe, if they weren't trying to get him involved in the conversation?

Day four of the hearings commenced that Friday morning, May 20, 1988, with testimony from Investigator Robert Venezia, the man who had replaced Tripodo Junior on the barracks tag team.

Venezia's testimony differed from everyone else's in one

key respect: he had read Joe his rights. Venezia also acknowledged that as soon as he read the Miranda warnings, Joe announced that he in fact had an attorney and wasn't supposed to talk to anyone.

But just as those before him had claimed, Venezia protested that he hadn't asked Joe any questions; Joe just kept interrupting to volunteer or ask incriminating or bizarre questions, like volunteering: "My only hope is to beat this thing on a technicality" or asking if Diane had AIDS.

Venezia went on to deliver his litany of Joe's incriminating remarks: "He stated to me that he killed his wife for no particular reason, and he stated that at that point, he was being blackmailed in going through the divorce and his wife had hired a private investigator to follow him around. She had discovered the fact that he was a cross dresser and was telling everyone about him. He stated to me that he wished someone would shoot him, his life was over, and at least his children would be able to collect on his insurance."

Bekoff's questioning with Venezia took a familiar tact: Why had it taken so long to process Joe the night he was arrested? Why not just fingerprint him, take his picture, take the General 5 arrest form information and send him on his way to court?

"How long is the form, is it ten pages, twelve pages, twenty pages?"

"One-page form, sir."

"How long did it take to fill out this form with Mr. Pikul that night?"

"It took over an hour, sir."

"Over an hour?" Bekoff proclaimed in mock amazement.

The defense attorney then proceeded to go through the form line by line, asking Venezia how long it took to ask simple questions like name or address. "How long did it take to write 'One-inch fresh scratch on right wrist?' "

"One second," said Venezia.

"How long did it take to write 'United States citizen'?"

"Not very long." And so it went through the rest of the form, Social Security number, marital status, wife's maiden name, and so on.

The litany completed, Bekoff asked how long the process should be expected to take.

"Well"—Venezia squirmed—"under the right circumstances it could be done maybe in ten minutes."

"Isn't it a fact that you said to Joe Pikul right away, 'Joe, I understand. My wife took my kids, divorced me.' Did you ever say that to him?" Venezia admitted he may have made the statement somewhere during the conversation.

"Is it true that your wife divorced you and left with your children?" Bekoff inquired.

"That is correct, sir," said Venezia. So, in addition to two investigators who had kids the same age as Joe talking about Sesame Place, Joe had received empathy from an investigator victimized by divorce.

At the luncheon recess, Joe rose from the defense table and walked over to the witness stand. He reached into his suit pocket, removed his hankie, made a brushing motion in the air, and announced: "There's slime on the stand. Someone better wipe it off."

"I thought he was my friend," Joe said of Venezia. "He's a liar." Looking more like a rejected suitor, Joe paced in front of the jury box, explaining how he'd been sucked in by "the boys at the barracks," how he'd spoken to them only because they'd acted so friendly.

Bekoff walked by and pulled Joe away. He asked his client what he was going to do for lunch. "I'm gonna take a walk in the woods," said Joe, heading for the courthouse door.

The focus of the hearing next turned to the issue of the identifications of Joe by the car-wash employees. The admissibility of the identifications was important because conceivably anyone could have thrown all that stuff away—Diane's "boyfriend," for example. Solid IDs would go hand in hand with the other testimony about the man in the Buick station wagon telling the employees that his wife had left him and that he'd found condoms under the bed.

The testimony from the car-wash staffers was pretty straightforward. They had no problem identifying Joe Pikul as the man who'd visited the car wash the day in question.

More interesting than the testimony was Jim Mitchell's encounter with Investigator Kenneth T. Jones, one of the chief forensic men on the Pikul case, while they waited to be called.

Mitchell mentioned the shotgun he'd bought from Joe, asking when he'd be able to get it back. In the course of the chat, Mitchell also mentioned that before he had turned the weapon over to police, he noticed some paint etched into the butt. He said the gun also had a hairline crack.

Mitchell was surprised when Jones told him the information was news to him, especially given the fact that no one seemed to know exactly how Diane had been fatally beaten.

No forensic expert to be sure, but long on street sense, Mitchell wondered if the gun—surely a "blunt instrument"—had hit something a couple of times while missing Diane's head during the fatal argument. It certainly would explain why Joe sold the weapon.

Ron Bekoff opened his pretrial case by subpoenaing Detective Sergeant Kenneth M. Bowen of the New York City Police Department. The defense strategy of proving police misconduct remained unchanged.

Bowen fought off Bekoff's challenges as to when Joe became a suspect in Diane's disappearance. "He was the husband, who was the complainant in the missing-persons case."

Bowen said he wasn't initially concerned about Joe's different versions of what happened when Diane arrived in the Hamptons because nervous complainants often give mixed-up accounts. He said Detectives Composto and Finelli were sent to reinterview Joe because there were many unanswered questions, "questions we felt that only Mr. Pikul could answer."

The testimony heated up when Bekoff turned his attention to the telephone strategy session between Bowen and Sergeant Clancy from Newburgh, conducted while Composto had been winding up his all-night interview with Joe. Inexplicably, Clancy had turned on his tape recorder during the chat. When he realized the conversation about the credit cards between Joe and Detective John Smith (posing as "John Clancy") was on the same tape, Clancy knew he had to turn the recording over to Prosecutor Joseph, who in turn had no choice but to provide a copy to the defense. The secret taping of a brother officer, no matter how innocent the intent, had created an awkward situation.

At first Bowen said he couldn't remember using the words "this motherfucker" to describe Joe, but shown the transcript, he was left no alternative.

"Is that the way you normally refer to people whose wives are reported missing?" asked Bekoff. "Or is that just reserved for suspects?"

"No. It is not reserved for suspects," protested Bowen, nearly thirty years on the force. "It's police slang."

"Oh," said Bekoff, feigning to be taken aback. "You talk about judges and lawyers that way, too?"

"Objection," said Joseph, and Judge Byrne sustained.

When Bowen denied Bekoff's suggestion that the main reason police kept Joe in the precinct was to prevent him from talking to anyone who might suggest he get a lawyer, the defense attorney brought the transcript out again. "Do you remember this conversation with Sergeant Clancy? Sergeant Clancy: 'Is there a lawyer with him?' You: 'No. We don't have a lawyer. We don't want one.' Sergeant Clancy: 'Okay.'

"And you say, 'That's one of the things we don't want, someone who would be sympathetic and say, "Hey, you know those fucking cops are asking me some heavy questions, oh, you better get a lawyer." ' Do you remember that conversation?"

"I don't recall the latter part of it, sir," said Bowen. Bekoff handed the document over to Bowen, instructing that he read the red-lined portion.

"Isn't it a fact, sir, that you told Sergeant Clancy that you didn't want Joseph Pikul to talk to someone who might suggest that he get a lawyer because you, the police, were asking, in your own words, 'pretty hard fucking questions'?"

Bowen asked if he could read the transcript again. "Sure. Here," said Bekoff.

"Was one of your purposes to prevent Joseph Pikul from talking to someone who would tell him to get a lawyer?"

"No, sir," said Bowen.

"You said that to Sergeant Clancy, didn't you?"

"I said what is written here," said Bowen. "It wasn't our purpose to prevent him from getting a lawyer because he didn't need a lawyer at the time, counselor."

Bekoff pointed out that the Bowen-Glynn-Delaney interview had concluded at 1:00 A.M. and that Joe's second interview began at 4:00 A.M. "Is that standard police procedure?"

"I would say in the cases of missing persons under suspicious circumstances it would not be unusual," Bowen replied.

Bekoff asked if anything new had come up between 1:00 and 4:00 A.M.

"There was nothing new in regard to her disappearance, but there were many questions about her activities that we were interested in," said Bowen.

Asked for at least one question that the detectives thought of at 4:00 A.M. that they couldn't have thought of at midnight for the first interview, Bowen offered: "Was there any public transportation in that area?" Bowen wasn't going to win any prizes with that one as Bekoff pointed out that Investigator Delaney was present for the first interview with Joe and was stationed on Long Island. But, Bowen maintained, Delaney wasn't around when the question came up.

Bekoff was having a field day. "Let me ask you a question. Do you have a telephone in the Sixth Squad, Manhattan?"

"Yes, sir," said Bowen.

So, Bekoff continued, why not use the phone and say: " 'I'm a police officer. I am on an important investigation. I am a sergeant with the New York City Police Department. Do you have any public transportation in Amagansett?' "

Bowen conceded that he could have made such a call. Instead, Bekoff countered, "You brought him back, you saw fit to question him, Mr. Pikul, in the middle of the night?"

"I sent my detectives to his residence and he came to the station house. He was not ordered or dragged back to the station."

"You're avoiding the question," claimed Bekoff.

"I'm not," said Bowen, denying he had wanted to keep Joe awake all night to pressure him to talk. "Our interest was in trying to locate Mrs. Pikul."

"Did that make you think maybe he was a suspect?"

"No sir," answered Bowen.

With a dose of healthy skepticism, Bekoff wondered if Bowen thought the circumstances surrounding the credit cards found at the dumpster were sufficient probable cause to think Joe was a suspect. When Bowen responded in the negative, Bekoff abruptly ended his interrogation, extremely pleased.

Alan Joseph spent little time in his cross-examination of Bowen. He merely needed to make it clear that it was logical for police to ask Joe Pikul a lot of questions. "Isn't it a fact that to your knowledge, Mr. Pikul was the last person to see Diane Pikul, the missing person, before she disappeared?"

"That is correct," said Bowen.

"As such, isn't it a fact he would be in the best position to give you assistance in locating her?"

"That," said Bowen, "plus the fact he probably knew her the best."

With that, Bekoff called Sergeant Clancy, the other end of Bowen's recorded telephone call. A fourteen-year veteran of law enforcement, Clancy meant no harm by recording the conversation. Events had been unfolding rapidly that night, and he explained that he turned his machine on because he wanted to make sure he got the conversation right. Bekoff, of course, wasn't interested in any of that. "At any time did Detective Sergeant Bowen say to you that 'Mr. Pikul had some asshole lawyer'?"

"I made a remark that was on the tape and thought that I was repeating his words. I reviewed the tape later on and it appears I misunderstood what he said," answered Clancy.

"You thought he said that but he did not say that?"

Clancy agreed. "Apparently he said 'ask for' and I thought he said 'asshole,' " said Clancy. Absolutely nothing in this case was simple.

Bekoff then tried to get Clancy to interpret Bowen's comments on the tape, suggesting that Bowen was suspicious of Joe. But Clancy disagreed. As far as he was concerned, Bowen was simply trying to obtain more information about Diane.

Shown the transcript, however, Clancy, too, was forced to admit that Bowen had said they didn't need a lawyer to get involved and stop the interview sessions.

Like everyone else, Clancy was asked if he thought Joe was a suspect. "It sounded like maybe something was wrong, but we didn't know what it was," he said, acknowledging that the potpourri of items found at the car wash "certainly aroused natural suspicion."

That was all Bekoff could get from Clancy, though.

Outside the courtroom, Bekoff was ebullient, contending the testimony proved police considered Joe a suspect early on because they had interrogated him through the night rather than arrest him and read him his rights.

The testimony of Bekoff's final witness, attorney Charles Clayman, didn't take long, but it played an important part in the defense strategy. Bekoff wanted the statements Joe had made in the car ride ruled inadmissible because Probst and Oates knew Joe had legal representation and Clayman had warned them not to talk to Joe. If those statements were inadmissible, it was likely all of Joe's statements at the barracks would be thrown out, too.

But that strategy rested on a narrow reading of the famous Supreme Court decision, *Miranda* v. *Arizona*, which applies to "custodial interrogation" as opposed to statements volunteered or given spontaneously. Although the arresting officers were not allowed to interrogate Joe, they could listen, just as Probst said they had.

Clayman, a former assistant U.S. attorney in Brooklyn, not only insisted that he told Probst and Oates not to talk to Joe, he claimed they arrested Joe only after he refused to cooperate. Clayman then implied that he missed Joe's arraignment because Probst, Oates, and Prosecutor Joseph, on the telephone, misled him about the exact time of the court appearance.

Stung, Alan Joseph asked Clayman if he'd made any notes of the conversations in question. Clayman said he had not.

"Isn't it a fact that I advised you that he would be arraigned initially in front of a judge, one of our local magistrates, and then there would be a new date set for appearance with an attorney?" Joseph asked. Clayman said he couldn't recall.

"Isn't it a fact that you told me that day you would not come up for the arraignment?" Again, Clayman said he couldn't recall.

His credibility and honor intact, the county's chief assistant district attorney sat down.

The hearings were completed pending written briefs.

Testimony had lasted seven days, spread out over three weeks.

Investigator Oates never testified.

When he filed a thirty-three-page memorandum of law several weeks later, Bekoff included a plethora of legal argument, including his usual dose of Miranda.

He conceded that the telephone call Joe made to Detective Glynn and the statement Joe gave to Glynn, Bowen, and Delaney were both admissible. But Bekoff wanted everything else thrown out.

The all-night interview needed to be thrown out because the detectives knew Joe had to take care of his children, but dragged him to the station house in the middle of the night despite the lack of new developments, according to Bekoff. "It is thus clear that the sole purpose for the time and place of this next 'interview' was to remove the defendant from his familiar surroundings, disorient him, and intimidate him, in the hopes of obtaining some sort of inculpatory statement."

Bekoff contended the key issue was determining when police came to consider Joe a suspect in Diane's disappearance. Given the eyewitness accounts of Joe's actions at the car wash and his "conflicting and inconsistent statements" to Glynn, Bekoff argued that his client was "the prime and indeed the only suspect" by the time of the Composto conversation, and as such was entitled to have his Miranda rights read to him.

Further, the defense attorney offered, there was Bowen calling Joe "a motherfucker" at the same time the supposedly innocent interview was taking place.

The inadmissibility of the statements Joe made to Investigator Probst was even more clear-cut, Bekoff said.

Under New York law, statements taken from a defendant when police know the suspect has an attorney must be suppressed, even if the attorney has been hired on an unrelated but pending criminal matter. The only exception to the rule allows for the use of so-called "spontaneous statements." But in such cases, the prosecutor has the burden of establishing the spontaneity and the absence of any inducement or encouragement by police.

Bekoff maintained that the statements Joe made were "the product of careful and designed police questioning . . . in blatant disregard of the defendant's right to counsel." He sneered at the "coincidence" that Probst and Oates both "happened to have small children approximately the same age as the defendant's children," and then they just "happened to initiate discussions about their children with the defendant." Even after the amusement-park discussions prompted Joe's first set of incriminating comments, the investigators still failed to read Joe his rights, Bekoff asserted, and instead encouraged him to keep talking.

Turning to Tripodo Junior, Bekoff said the young investigator had displayed "a shocking disregard" for Joe's rights. He pointed out that Tripodo Junior conceded on the witness stand that Joe's comments were made in response to questions. Therefore, Bekoff argued, the statements could not have been spontaneous.

Bekoff fired his largest cannon at Venezia, pointing out that the investigator actually read Joe his rights and stated that his job was simply to take pedigree information. "Officer Venezia would have this court believe that it took over one hour for him to elicit from the defendant responses to seven pro forma questions." The attorney then cited a specific New York State case, *People* v. *Rodriguez*, where the courts found that if police questioning was designed to "uncover facts of criminal activity or to establish criminal responsibility, it should not be permitted under the guise of pedigree."

"There can be no credible argument made as to the spontaneity of these statements," said Bekoff. "This defendant was questioned in the absence of his attorney and in total disregard for his right to counsel for the sole purpose of eliciting statements that it is now incredulously argued are spontaneous. This would easily make *The Guinness Book of World Records* for 'the longest spontaneous statement ever made,' bettering the former mark by fifty-nine minutes and thirty seconds."

It was indisputable, Bekoff argued, that the "undeviating intent" of all the officers involved was to extract a confession: waking Joe in the middle of the night, questioning him for hours without a break, accosting him at his lawyer's office with a choice of an "interview" or arrest, questioning him despite being told by an attorney not to, failing to read Joe his rights, continuing to question him *after* his rights were read to him, confronting him with his wife's body after having been in police custody for hours, and then delaying the arraignment until approximately 4:00 A.M.

"The defendant, in the face of such relentless conduct, and having seen how apparently ineffectual his attorney's instructions to the police were, could only reasonably assume that he was totally at the mercy of the police and that he must provide a statement to every officer who demanded one. Under the circumstances," concluded Bekoff, "it is respectfully submitted that the only conclusion which this court can reach is that every statement from the Finelli-Composto statement forward, was the product of police coercion, and must be suppressed for all purposes."

Alan Joseph responded in late June, listing a slew of reasons why police had probable cause to arrest Joe, including the facts that he was the last one known to have seen Diane alive, that he admitted arguing with her and gave conflicting stories about the argument. There were other troubling factors, Joseph contended, like Joe taking the children to his old college buddy despite the fact that his wife had supposedly walked out on him, his conflicting stories about whether he stayed the weekend, his failure to treat Diane's disappearance as an important event, and the fact that he was not the first person to report her missing.

Then there was the car-wash scene, Joe's tossing away the credit cards, driver's license, savings-account passbook, the personal note from Claudia; his concern about sand removal; his claim that Diane had taken pictures of him dressed in women's clothing and planned to use them against him; the body of the victim being clad in clothing fitting the description that Joe had provided when he reported Diane missing; the body being found close to the home of Joe's college buddy; and Joe's initial refusal to view or identify the body.

That was quite a laundry list, Joseph argued, and it added up to plenty of probable cause.

As for the statements made to police, Joseph maintained that they all should be admissible. The prosecutor argued that Composto didn't think Joe was a suspect because at that point there was no body and no proof that a crime had been committed. He suggested Joe voluntarily went to the station house because he didn't want his children to overhear the conversation. Most important, Joseph argued, Joe eventually left the station house and returned to his own home, proof that he was not under arrest and not involved in a custodial interrogation.

Joseph maintained Joe's statements to Probst were acceptable because they were spontaneously blurted out. He contended that none of the state-police investigators intended to question Joe after the arrest, and that any conversations were prompted by Joe's interruptions. Since the conversation about Sesame Place did not directly involve Joe, "it is difficult to imagine how such a conversation could constitute interrogation, much less have been reasonably anticipated to evoke any response from the defendant."

The assistant district attorney used the same rationale for Tripodo Junior's testimony, asserting that Junior wasn't in a position to interrogate Joe because he had little knowledge of the case, was an inexperienced investigator, and had been assigned basically to transport people and keep assignment records for the Diane Pikul investigation. "No court has yet held that a police officer must take affirmative steps, by gag or otherwise, to prevent a talkative person in custody from making an incriminatory statement within his hearing." Investigator Venezia's testimony should be admissible, too, said Joseph, because he didn't question Joe about the crime; he was "only attempting to complete the pedigree information as required by policy," a process made difficult by Joe's constant interruptions.

As part of his submittal to Judge Byrne, Joseph included summaries of each of Joe's statements to police. Since the hearings were conducted in public, the only news was contained in the inadmissible confession Joe gave to Tripodo Senior.

The New York City newspapers didn't cover the filing of the prosecutor's briefs, but jurors were going to be selected from among the populace of Orange County—not Manhattan or the Hamptons. Not surprisingly, Joseph's disclosure found its way into the next morning's *Middletown Times Herald-Record*, ensuring that thousands of potential jurors read how and where Joe said he had killed his wife.

The story, by Fred J. Aun, was accompanied by several excerpts, enlarged in richly inked letters: "He indicated he killed Diane at Alberts Landing and left her partially buried on the beach. . . . He indicated that he choked Diane with both hands, then said that he went back to the house, and at that time he saw the condoms in her bedroom and believed that she had been using them with some other person."

With one subtle maneuver, Alan Joseph showed that he, too, could play the game of courts.

Another Mrs. Pikul

BACK IN NEW YORK CITY, Human Resources Administration lawyer Bob Wayburn had been delegated to draft a bill to remove the parental rights of a mother or father accused of murdering their spouse.

It had been a long spring. The internal squabbling, some of it precipitated by Wayburn's public posturing, continued unabated. Wayburn wrote a memo to Commissioner Grinker observing that he was not a yes-man and hoped that his approach to the case would not be viewed as "anything other than sincere." But he didn't stop there; Wayburn then complained about his thankless, low-paying job and said he hoped the commissioner would support him in his upcoming application for a judgeship. Wayburn also attached a lengthy article about the Pikul case from *New York* magazine, which included a photo of Wayburn, to show "that our position is responsible and well reasoned. . . . I hope that I have done your position justice."

Grinker was far from pleased with the story and Wayburn's note. "I frankly think that despite your best intentions, you continue to misinterpret my position in public discussion of this case," Grinker wrote back. "Therefore, if future opportunities arise outside of the courtroom, I would appreciate your referring any questions as to my position to me for direct response."

As he worked on the draft legislation, Wayburn continued to be stymied by the same roadblock: his superiors wanted a provision allowing a judge to find "neglect" by a parent simply as a result of someone being indicted for murdering their spouse. Such legislation was unnecessary, said Wayburn, arguing for a law stating that an indictment for such a murder would qualify as the "extraordinary circumstance" required to trigger a custody hearing without having to first prove parental unfitness. In such a case, there would be a presumption against the parent suspected of murder being able to keep custody.

Grinker, who suggested Wayburn was suffering from a bruised ego, essentially agreed with Wayburn's suggestion on the need for new legislation, even if he didn't think it was necessary in the Pikul case. Grinker believed Judge Glen could have taken the children from Joe without a new law. "The judge simply saw the facts differently as far as I can tell. My position in this case in no way obviates the need for legislation because obviously the judge needed a different burden of going forward or proof or whatever to come out as I would have."

Wayburn and the social service bureaucrats weren't the only ones squabbling over the Pikul case. Judge Glen had seen to it that the behavior of one Raoul Lionel Felder was extensively investigated by the lawyers' disciplinary committee in Manhattan, which has the power to disbar attorneys. The main complaint concerned Felder's alleged leaks to *New York* magazine of sealed testimony from the custody case. Prompted by Felder, the state Commission on Judicial Conduct pursued allegations of misconduct against Judge Glen, too.

In time, both investigations were dropped, but the animosity between Felder and Judge Glen continued to escalate.

Felder filed a motion seeking to vacate Judge Glen's custody decision and asked that the children be turned over to the O'Guins immediately. He demanded that his motion be referred to another court because of Judge Glen's "clear animus expressed about me and indeed even about the district attorney. This decision is wrong, improper, and represents a clear danger to the Pikul children," wrote Felder. "As a piece of paper burning at the edges, the fabric of the life mandated by the court to these children is crumbling and disintegrating."

In his motion, Felder contended that immediately after
the custody ruling, Joe threatened Don Whitmore in Florida that he would never speak to his grandchildren again.
Then Claudia had come to school dirty and with cuts.
When asked by the nurse to explain, the girl supposedly
responded in "a paranoic manner," said Felder, adding
that Claudia's writing, previously described as "brilliant,"
was now characterized as "incoherent."

Felder took the opportunity to list some of the most
incriminating revelations to come out of the pretrial hearings. He also noted that Joe was more than $18,000 behind
in his rent on the Sixth Avenue apartment. "It is time the
court realized that it has made a dreadful mistake. Nobody
likes to be wrong and nobody likes to admit they are
wrong. But here the welfare and indeed perhaps the lives
of two children are at stake. The appellate process may,
because of the time involved, be too late to help these
children. Unless one believes there is a massive conspiracy
of everyone involved, Pikul is indeed a brutal, callous,
obscene, unrepentant murderer of these children's
mother."

As usual, there were explanations: a pet cat was blamed
for Claudia's scratch marks, her unkempt appearance and
withdrawn behavior were attributed to grieving over her
mother's death.

Judge Glen rejected Felder's complaints and his request
that she resign from the case. She instead signed an order,
submitted by Joe's civil attorney, formalizing her April
decision. She gave custody to Joe, provided he keep the
children in their present schools, provided he take them
to qualified child therapists under the general supervision
of Dr. Kalogerakis, and provided he turn them over to
the O'Guins on September 1 so he could prepare for his
murder trial. The formal order also called for three single-
day visits between the O'Guins, Joe, and the children as
a start for the summer transition period. Judge Glen op-
timistically said that additional visits would be worked out
by mutual consent of the parties.

Joe had won again.

Several weeks later, on Friday night, June 10, 1988, the
telephone rang in the O'Guins' Yonkers residence. It was

Joe calling about the children's first visit, set for that Sunday. Kathy and Mike had grown more and more frustrated in the weeks since Judge Glen's original decision. They failed to comprehend why it had taken so long for the formal order to be issued. Weeks were passing by, and they hadn't begun to get acquainted with the children. They feared that before they knew it, September would arrive, along with two young strangers.

Kathy answered the phone expecting Joe to provide a time schedule. Instead he began haranguing her about how much her cousin Diane had hated her. He said that if she and Mike wanted to see the children, they would have to travel to some backwoods area three hours from the New York City area where "they" were camping.

The O'Guins took the "they" to include Mary Bain—the friendly neighbor who testified on Joe's behalf at the custody hearing and had offered to care for the children during Joe's murder trial with her husband Steve. Joe and Mary had been seen a lot together lately. There were even whispers of a romance.

Kathy O'Guin was terrified at the prospect of traveling three hours to a remote location to rendezvous with Joe. She couldn't even find the place on a map. The conversation ended.

The next evening Mary Bain called the O'Guins' home, and Mike took the call. Mary wanted to know if Mike could offer a compromise location. But when he suggested the Bronx Zoo or the Westchester County Fair, Joe got on the line and began berating him in the same belligerent tone he'd used the day before with Kathy. As far as Joe was concerned, the only option worthy of consideration was for the O'Guins to get in their car and make the long trip north. And there was one other stipulation, he said, both he and Mary had to be present during any visit with the children.

Establishing a rapport and visitation schedule with the O'Guins wasn't Joe's only problem. The landlord of the Sixth Avenue duplex filed a civil court suit for back rent. The matter was adjourned twice, then a court-imposed June 15 deadline came and went; Joe simply moved out.

Out in the Hamptons, the Amagansett Beach Association wrestled with the delicate problem of whether to send its most infamous member a renewal form for the summer of '88. A supporter of the association's "hurricane fund," Joe had contributed to the campaigns of several local politicians. The beach-club board finally decided to send the form "for the children." Everyone breathed easy when Joe didn't return the paperwork.

Although he was seen on Long Island that summer, Joe kept a low profile. The mortgage on the Windmill Lane property was in serious arrears, and Joe also took several secondary mortgages as collateral for various debts, including legal fees.

As the summer progressed, the O'Guins continued their efforts to get along with Joe, knowing that the more they got to know Claudia and Blake, the better the children would take to them come September. But as weeks passed—and Joe continued to obstruct, make excuses, and act obnoxious—the O'Guins reached their limit.

On July 27, they met with Felder at his Madison Avenue office and told him the situation was intolerable. In the eight weekends since the beginning of June, they had seen the children only three times, for closely scrutinized lunches.

Also, Joe's relationship with Mary Bain was far more serious than first suspected. The O'Guins told Felder the children were deeply attached to Mary and, in fact, were calling her "Mommy." Kathy also told Felder that she had been unable to enroll the children in any school in Yonkers because she and Mike did not have legal guardianship.

The O'Guins also informed Felder that Joe told them he had "the case in his pocket," and that when his legal troubles were over, he was going to "get" Felder and ruin his reputation. To back up his threats, Joe claimed he had tapes of telephone conversations between Diane and the attorney, in which Felder was mean to Diane.

Angry and upset, Kathy and Mike were at their wits' end. Our lives can't go on like this, they said. They seemed to have no alternative but to withdraw from the custody arrangement. As hard as it is to say, they continued, perhaps things will work out better for the children this way.

Felder was disappointed, but he understood. Doing battle against a maniac wasn't easy. He drafted a letter to

Judge Glen, Bob Wayburn, and Paul Kurland explaining that the O'Guins would not be taking temporary custody of Claudia and Blake in September. "I have this evening met with the O'Guins and they have come to a serious and painful decision, a decision which they feel is the only responsible one," Felder began.

After detailing the summer of broken promises, he wrote that the O'Guins now felt "it would be absolutely cruel and irresponsible to wrest these children away from yet another maternal figure whom they call 'Mommy' and to whom they are bonded. Therefore the O'Guins do not wish to press further in the custody situation, and at this juncture step out of the children's lives. To say that this decision has been made with regret and sadness is an understatement. Literally their hearts have been broken. But impelled by that same original concern that they had for the children, they feel that they can take no other course. They told me it is a final and absolute decision."

Felder also stated he was under the impression that Mary Bain was living with Joe and suggested that they might marry before the murder trial.

At age thirty-four, Mary was twenty years younger than Joe. A design graduate of the Fashion Institute of Technology with a chunky build but striking blue eyes, she was employed at Royal Silk Inc. in Clifton, New Jersey, as a fashion designer. She traveled throughout the Middle East and India purchasing materials, earning "not quite $80,000" a year.

Felder and the O'Guins were on the mark with their suspicions about Joe and Mary. After thirteen years of marriage, Mary had suddenly obtained a divorce in late May from Steve Bain, the man she had told Judge Glen weeks earlier would co-adopt the Pikul children if need be. Under terms of the divorce agreement, temporary custody of their daughter Jennifer went to her father.

Now a childless mother, Mary had rented a summer place in upstate Lanesville, near Hunter Mountain, closer to the site of Joe's murder trial. The eerie thing about the apartment, the top floor of a two-story chalet, was that it overlooked a small stream, not as large as the Ware River in Massachusetts, certainly, but similar in setting to make it worthy of comparison. On July 2, nearly a month before the O'Guins decided to withdraw their claim to custody, Mary Bain had become Mrs. Joe Pikul No. 3 in the tiny upstate community of Cobleskill.

Claudia brought wildflowers from Mary's backyard and Blake served as ring bearer. The honeymoon consisted of a barbecue in the backyard and watching fireworks that evening in nearby Kingston. Claudia and Blake were asked to keep news of the wedding "our little secret."

It wasn't until five and a half weeks after the marriage that Kurland sent Judge Glen and Bob Wayburn "a wedding announcement," in the form of a motion requesting that Joe and Mary be given temporary custody of Claudia and Blake until at least the end of the criminal trial.

In an accompanying four-page affidavit Mary Bain said she and Joe had been living together as husband and wife since the wedding. "Since the early part of 1988, I have become very much involved with the lives of Claudia Pikul and Blake Pikul and have helped to take care of them. We have 'bonded' together as a parent and children. . . . It is my intention to seek to adopt Claudia and Blake Pikul irrespective of the outcome of the criminal trial."

Repeating the offer she had made in March with her first husband, Mary said she had received permission from her parents, Rudolph and Elizabeth Eik, to move into their home in Brooklyn in September. The house would be available because Mary's folks lived most of the year in Florida and only used the New York residence in July and August. Joe and the children would move in with her, and both Pikul children would attend Grace Church School, the exclusive Village facility Claudia had previously attended. "They will be attending school with my daughter Jennifer, who will spend part of the week with me and part of the week with my former husband, Steven Bain," Mary wrote in the affidavit, explaining that Jennifer was a close friend of Claudia's and a classmate since prekindergarten. Mary said she believed it was important for the children to attend Grace Church School, where they were "known."

Noting the O'Guins' announced intention to withdraw, Mary stated that she felt it in "the best interest of the children" that they have "continuity in their lives and continue to live with me and their father."

In closing, Kurland asked that his letter and motion papers "remain sealed and the contents not be revealed to anyone except for Mr. Wayburn and the court." Kurland said he was worried about the effect renewed publicity might have on the Pikul children and pointed out that the court papers revealed where Claudia and Blake were going to live during their father's trial.

The same day Kurland delivered his motion, Judge Glen received a letter from Raoul Felder detailing a telephone conversation Claudia and Joe had had with Don Whitmore the night before.

First, Claudia demanded to know why her grandfather had "stolen" her education money. Then Joe got on the line and accused the eighty-year-old man and Felder of stealing $240,000 of his money. Cursing and screaming, Joe threatened both men. Before he hung up, he told Whitmore that he would "never be permitted to speak to the children again."

The very next day, August 11, 1988, Judge Byrne issued a shocking fifteen-page decision on the pretrial hearings.

Finding that police had violated Joe's constitutional rights, the judge said he was suppressing all statements Joe had made after he was brought into the state-police barracks the night of his arrest.

"It is clear to the court that the defendant was placed in the custody of Investigator Tripodo Junior and Investigator Venezia for the specific purpose of eliciting statements from him, or to inspire the defendant to incriminate himself. . . . The need of the defendant to talk to the police was created by their actions in holding him from 8:30 P.M. until 2:30 A.M. for arraignment. It is telling that when asked why he delayed in questioning defendant regarding his pedigree, Investigator Venezia replied, in effect, that he was waiting for Investigator Tripodo Junior to finish talking to the defendant."

On the other hand, Judge Byrne noted that although Detective Composto had never inquired about Diane's possible boyfriends and took about four hours to ask Joe anything about the clothes his wife had been wearing when he last saw her, any statements made by the defendant until the time he was arrested, including statements made during Composto's all-night session, were admissible.

Since Glynn and Composto's testimony was less than conclusive, that left Probst and Oates as the key players.

Judge Byrne ruled that Joe's statements during the car ride were not the result of custodial interrogation, "nor were they obtained by trickery or device," despite the fact the investigators had been told not to talk to Joe. Therefore, the statements were spontaneous and admissible.

The decision to bar the statements at the barracks was a crushing blow to the prosecution, but Alan Joseph could take some solace. Although the statements could not be used to establish the People's case, Judge Byrne ruled they could be used to impugn Joe's credibility if he decided to take the stand in his own behalf. Not only that, but Probst's testimony from the car ride was solid evidence, though not as juicy as Joe's comments at the barracks. In addition, all testimony from the car-wash employees was admissible.

Even without the barracks boys, the defense still had an uphill fight.

Back in New York City, Bob Wayburn informed Felder of Kurland's new custody motion, which quickly sent the divorce lawyer back on the rampage. Angry about not being notified, he suggested in a letter to Kurland that the O'Guins' plans to withdraw could very well have been "based on deliberate misconception and misinformation. . . . I specifically asked you if there were any plans for Mr. Pikul to marry. You told me you did not know."

Felder also pointed out that while the O'Guins had announced plans to withdraw, it would take a court order to remove them. He noted that the only outstanding order of the court called for the O'Guins to take custody "in a matter of weeks."

Felder, Wayburn, numerous child-rights activists, and Diane's friends lobbied the O'Guins to get back in the fight. "We can't let this happen," the O'Guins were told repeatedly by supporters. Of course, the "we" weren't going to have to wage this painful battle day in and day out.

By month's end, Felder and Kurland were trading barbs in yet another round of affidavits. Felder pointed out that the O'Guins had requested permission to withdraw based on what they perceived were the best interests of the children. In fact, though, Mary Bain had "deliberately misled the court as to her relationship" with Joe in her original testimony, and Joe "deliberately misled the court and everybody else as to his relationship with Mrs. Bain," Felder said. "The 'monitoring' apparatus set up by the court was absolutely inadequate to determine even the simple fact that Mr. Pikul had been married. It is literally inconceivable that a psychiatrist who was supposed to be policing this situation did not know this."

Given the circumstances, the O'Guins had "rethought their position," Felder said, and would accept custody, under five conditions: they be given legal guardianship immediately; the relationship between them and the children "be permanent and stable"; any visits between the children and their father be arranged and carried out by a third party, such as the New York City Human Resources Administration; there be a court order prohibiting Joe from coming to the O'Guin home; and a trust fund be established providing for both the physical and educational requirements of the children.

"I might point out an obvious additional fact," Felder wrote the court. "What happens if Mr. Pikul is convicted and sent away and in those lonely years Ms. Bain decides to change her mind, or comes to her senses?"

Craig E. Penn, of Kurland's office, volleyed right back. He characterized Felder's pique over not being notified about the marriage as a spurious argument that should be dismissed out of hand as "arrant nonsense." Mary Bain had been great for the kids, according to Penn—"far from posing a negative or destabilizing influence." He said the home environment for Claudia and Blake was much more stable now than it had been during the custody hearings. "Mary Bain Pikul was clear in her affidavit that she now functions as mother to Claudia and Blake Pikul. . . . She has sworn that she intends to seek their adoption regardless of the outcome of Joseph Pikul's criminal trial. Indeed, Mary Bain Pikul is ready, willing, and able to adopt Claudia and Blake immediately and unconditionally."

Mary's unconditional commitment "stands in stark contrast to the five conditions (including the establishment of a 'trust fund') that petitioners have imposed," said Penn, contending that the O'Guins originally pulled out because they recognized the close bonding of Mary and the kids and knew that it would be "absolutely cruel and irresponsible" to wrest the children away from their new mommy.

Obviously, there were legal issues that needed to be resolved, so Judge Glen scheduled a hearing for September 14. As is apt to happen in the game of courts, word of the Bain-Pikul marriage eventually leaked.

"PIKUL IS WED TO A WITNESS" read the *New York Daily News* headline. The story detailed how Mary had been described by Judge Glen as "the mother of Claudia's best friend" and a "competent . . . convincing witness" for Joe Pikul. Felder, always available for a good quote or TV sound bite, accused Bain of misrepresenting herself during the first custody hearing. "She came under false pretenses as a happily married woman." Lamented Don Whitmore down in Florida: "I've been suspicious all along that this would happen. She will get custody of the kids. I assume that's his scheme.

"It's a lousy situation all around. I lost a daughter, the kids lost their mother, and now this."

The new hearing convened in the same fourth-floor courtroom at 60 Centre Street that had served as the site of the first confrontation between Joe and the O'Guins.

Dr. Kalogerakis and two psychiatrists called by Kurland testified they thought Joe and Mary had a warm and loving relationship and should be allowed to keep the children. A stable family unit would probably produce a settling effect on the children's lives, said Dr. Kalogerakis. José Flete, the city caseworker, reported everything had been fine during a visit to the new Pikul home.

In fact, Flete wrote in a report on his upstate trip that Claudia said she liked her new surroundings, especially because of school sports. Blake appeared happy as well because "he can ride his bike and skateboard on the street and not be afraid of traffic." Joe and Mary spent a great deal of the visit calling each other "love, dear, and honey." Mary cooked, Joe watched a football game on TV, then did the dishes. Claudia told Flete she was "very glad" that

Mary and Joe had married and said she loved both of them very much.

Flete's report concluded with the observation that since the Pikuls had spent the summer upstate he doubted the psychiatric oversight had been as thorough as planned. He also wrote that because of the pending murder charges, he believed Joe was an inadequate caretaker for the children. "The O'Guins have always been a preferable alternative."

Then Mary took the stand and began a convincing tale of domestic tranquillity. She explained that Claudia and Blake loved her "deeply and unconditionally" and that she reminded the youngsters constantly about "their real Mommy."

"You were here in March to testify, Mrs. Bain?"

"That's right, Mr. Kurland," answered Mary in a singsong voice.

"At the time that you testified, was your testimony honest and truthful?" Joe's civil attorney continued.

"Absolutely, Mr. Kurland," replied Mary.

Kurland walked Mary through the origins of her relationship with Joe, paying close attention to the status of their romance in March, when she had first appeared in court and testified under oath. Back then, Mary explained, she was merely a friend of Joe's "because I was acquainted with him through his children."

Asked when the friendship became romantic, Mary said, "I would say that as problems with my husband increased, Joe became more of a confidant, whereas by—I would guess—May, we were seriously considering marriage."

Under gentle questioning Mary said she had divorced her own husband on May 28, and that sometime after that she received a copy of the divorce decree. As for custody of their daughter, Jennifer—Claudia's supposed best friend—Mary explained, "We have joint custody of my daughter and it states in my agreement since I travel overseas, if I am going to be physically away from the home, it will be physical custody with my husband. However, once I cease working overseas and find a job in which I'm working domestically, then we will rearrange that."

This raised an interesting question: while Mary was overseas, how was she going to care for Claudia and Blake?

For every disturbing question, though, Mary chirped a happy answer. "Have you seen your daughter on a regular basis?"

"Yes, I have. She has been away for summer camp . . . for ten weeks. But I saw her before that and I just came back this past weekend when school had just started and I saw her this weekend."

"Did you make any attempts to conceal the marriage?"

Of course not, said Mary. "Why would we?" She and Joe had applied for the marriage license in New York City and then went way up yonder to Cobleskill to marry.

Kurland next had Mary provide more details of her relationship with Claudia and Blake. "I am their stepmother. I am a very loving parent. They love me deeply and unconditionally. They love their deceased mother, of course, and I never let them forget about their mother. We go to church every Sunday, where we always light a candle and say prayers for the 'real Mommy,' as we call Diane Whitmore Pikul. There are pictures of Diane Pikul with the children in the house. I certainly don't try to conceal any of that. When they want to talk about it, when Blake said on one occasion, which I did discuss with Dr. Kalogerakis, when he brought up the murder of his mother, I clearly discussed it with Blake. I let him open up his feelings. We had a very good rapport."

She said both children were back in school—public school—Claudia in the fourth grade and Blake in pre-kindergarten. According to Mary, the decision to send the children to public school had been made in consultation with Diane's father down in Florida. "I had told Mr. Whitmore he must help me make that decision whether to continue with the Grace Church School or to enroll them in their present environment. That was the first place we had lived together as a family." The obvious inference to be drawn was if Claudia and Blake were going to go to private schools that fall, Whitmore would have to pay.

Mary said she'd spoken to Whitmore four or five times "this past week alone," in anticipation of bringing the children down to Florida for a visit. "I had reservations on Sunday and you must also remember, Mr. Kurland, the summer is very hot in Florida and I did invite Mr. Whitmore and his friend to come up and spend time with us in our home in our extra room. He said he wasn't able to, as his friend, his roommate, was undergoing chemotherapy. He said that we were invited to go down to visit them. I did make reservations to go down this past weekend until Joe informed me we were having a house visit from HRA. I did tell Mr. Whitmore we would probably come down this following weekend." Sadly, no one objected to Mary's mischaracterization of Whitmore's wife as "his roommate."

Mary said her intention to adopt the Pikul children was unconditional and permanent. While noting that Joe was broke and the house in Amagansett had been repossessed by the bank, she said she could support herself, her unemployed husband, and the two Pikul children through her job. She promised to do so even if Joe were convicted.

"You have to remember I have done this before. Back in May of 1982, I was separated from my former husband for three and a half years. I was only working part-time then. I didn't receive any support whatsoever from my former husband. And I worked full-time and supported myself and my daughter and was able to send her to private school. I was able to have household help and keep an apartment in the city. So I am certainly capable. Again, Mr. Kurland, if I can stress it, I have been consistent with the Pikuls since January. I have not had, if I may say something, as Mr. Whitmore said to me—and I quote— 'The O'Guins have had hot and cold feet all along.' I have not, Mr. Kurland. I have been consistent."

"No other questions, Your Honor," said Kurland.

Given his turn, Felder swooped in like a hawk.
"Are you happily married now?" Felder asked.
"Happily married?" Mary asked, using what would emerge as a familiar ploy, either repeating or failing to hear an unpleasant question.
"Yes," said Felder, confirming she'd heard right.
"Most times I am happily married," answered Mary.
"Has he been a good husband to you?"
"Excuse me?"
Content to wait her out, Felder asked: "He's been a good husband to you, Mr. Pikul?"
"Yes. He's okay," said Mary.

"He treats you well?"

"Well, I think there is always a period of adjustment in a marriage," she said.

Under a barrage of questions, Mary denied having fled to New Jersey or to the Bain family apartment on Second Avenue because Joe beat her up. "Mr. Pikul has never been brutal toward you?" Felder asked, and Mary replied: "No, he hasn't."

"He never lost his temper?"

"He has lost his temper. We have had verbal arguments," she said. Felder asked Mary to explain what Joe usually did when he lost his temper. "Usually he will take the keys to the car, go out for a while, and come back a couple of hours later."

"Not abuse you, curse you, threaten you?" asked Felder.

"No. He may get loud."

Switching tacks, Felder bored in on Mary's testimony in March, when she had said she was happily married, wanted to take in the Pikul children, and was going to move everyone to her parents' large apartment in Brooklyn. Felder pointed out that he had inquired how Mary's husband Steven felt about this proposed custody and she had testified he was in favor of it. Yet somehow two months later she was in divorce court.

"Subsequent to your appearing in court, you changed your mind, right?" asked Felder.

"*I* changed my mind?" Mary repeated. "No, I didn't change my mind. My husband changed his mind." Felder asked when all this occurred. "It was within the next few weeks. After my court appearance, and when it appeared in the paper, he became distressed. His former wife, so he tells me, said, 'If you are going to have extra children in the household, I am going to take back custody of our mutual son.' Obviously this distressed him greatly. Also, while we were offered the larger apartment, which would have given us an extra 500 square feet of living space, he chose not to take it because he did not want to give up our river view."

So how did the divorce come about? "I had inquired with a lawyer about the divorce the end of March, beginning of April," said Mary.

"The same month you were in court, then?" asked Felder.

"Excuse me," said Mary.

"You were in court in March, the same month you were in court?"

"That's right," said Mary. "I was in court the beginning of March."

"By the end of March, you were seeking a lawyer about a divorce, all in a month?"

"I was discussing it. That's right, Mr. Felder. As I just explained—"

"Try to answer my question, please," said Felder, cutting her off. "In one month you presented yourself to this court being happily married, moving to bigger quarters, wanting custody of the children, and the same month, *the same month*, you were going to a lawyer to divorce that man?"

"That's right, Mr. Felder," Mary said matter-of-factly.

Under additional questioning, Mary conceded that she and Joe hadn't told the O'Guins about the marriage when they saw them, but claimed there was no special reason for the omission.

"You are telling us it was just a coincidence that you waited until after the O'Guins withdrew for you to inform everybody that you got married?" asked Felder.

"No, it wasn't just a coincidence."

"What was the reason it took you a month to speak to a lawyer to find out what to do?" Felder pressed.

"We had been talking to Mr. Kurland all along."

"Did Mr. Kurland advise that you not tell anybody until—"

Kurland had heard enough. He rose to object, cutting Felder off in the process.

"Sustained," said Judge Glen on the grounds of lawyer–client privilege.

"Again, I will ask you what was the reason for waiting over a month before informing the court, before making this motion and informing the court you got married?" asked Felder.

"It's extremely complicated, Mr. Felder," Mary said, contending the matter was connected to Joe's criminal case.

Felder reminded Mary that she'd promised in her affidavit to move everyone to Brooklyn "on or about September 1." Felder wondered if Mary had changed her mind in the past couple of weeks, given the fact it was now mid-September and everyone was living upstate.

"As explained to the court, it was not only myself making this decision. I had Mr. Whitmore also making this decision with me," she said.

"Mr. Whitmore told you to move to upstate New York?"

"No, of course not. Regarding whether the children should continue with Grace Church School, as I am now the sole support of the family and tuition is upwards of $20,000 per year, where if the children were to continue with the continuity they have had since the early part of the summer where we have lived together as a family, have rapport with friends and neighbors in the neighborhood."

"Did you hear me read anything about schools yet? I just read that you said it's your intention to move the children to Brooklyn on or about September 1, 1988. Did I say anything about school?"

"Fine, Mr. Felder."

Mary's mixture of nonanswers, repeated questions, and revised testimony continued unabated. First she blamed the kids for asking in July to stay upstate for the new school year. Then she said she started thinking seriously about staying as far back as May, when she signed the lease. "I fell in love with the area right away. So I guess in the back of my mind I had always thought about it," she said.

"Yes," said Felder. "You always had that thought and yet here you are on August 4 telling the court and swearing to the court about your plans, which I quote, 'Our intention to move with the children to the Brooklyn home owned by my parents on or about September 1, 1988, and for the children to attend the Grace Church School for September '88 term.' " He looked Mary straight in the eye. "So they are not going to attend the Grace Church, are they?"

"No. They're enrolled in Hunter School. As I said, I made this with Mr. Whitmore's consent, the children's grandparent," said Mary.

At that point, Joe started groaning. Felder, taken aback

by this outburst, snapped, "I don't understand what the noise is about."

After a few seconds Joe quieted down, and Felder inquired as to when Claudia and Blake had enrolled in their upstate school. Last week, Mary answered. And would they be attending the same school as Jennifer, as promised in the affidavit? "No," Mary said. "As it turns out, they are not going to be."

"Is it your testimony today that Jennifer is going to be living with you now?"

"No," said Mary. "Pending the outcome of the trial and pending the fact that I travel overseas, she will physically be living with my husband as it states in our divorce papers."

Taking a breather from his verbal assault, Felder asked for, and received, what was purported to be a copy of the divorce papers. He then requested two minutes to look the document over.

In the meantime, the phone rang on the clerk's desk in the courtroom. It was important—for Bob Wayburn. Judge Glen ordered a five-minute break so he could take the call.

What Wayburn heard was to turn Mary Bain's testimony—and the unprecedented custody battle—upside down.

CHAPTER • 20

"A Period of Adjustment"

WAYBURN PICKED UP THE EXTENSION behind the judge's robing room. It was Barbara Ditman, the child protective manager in his office, with news of a confidential report about the Pikul case.

"What does it say?" asked Wayburn. Ditman began to tell an incredible story. A newlywed named Mary Eik had visited a local mental health center in upstate New York at least five times, most recently in the past week, to complain that her husband had been abusing and assaulting her. The worst incident had occurred two weeks before, on the Friday before Labor Day, when the husband attacked his new bride with a hunting knife, cut her dress—*while it was on her*—held the knife to her throat, then chased her out of the house with a gun and a flashlight. This Mary Eik had told one of the social workers that her new husband was currently out on bail awaiting trial for killing his previous wife. And according to the information from up north, the murder suspect's two children had been in the house during the attack on their stepmother. The key here, said Ditman, was the name Eik, Mary Bain Pikul's maiden name.

"She's on the stand right now telling us what a wonderful relationship she and Joe are having," said Wayburn.

Returning to the courtroom, Wayburn approached Judge Glen. "I have to tell you something, but I'm going to tell it only to you." The judge waved the other attorneys away, an uncommon action in a court proceeding, since nothing is supposed to occur between one side and the judge without the other side being privy. In this instance Judge Glen didn't have the usual restrictions, though, because Wayburn was representing the city as an amicus curiae, a friend of the court.

The color drained from the judge's face as Bob Wayburn whispered the story. The judge turned and looked at Mary Eik Bain Pikul, and as Wayburn later put it, "She saw for the first time what a lunatic she was dealing with."

Wayburn returned to his table trying to act as if nothing had happened, but a bench conference between the judge and just one attorney is so rare that everyone knew something was up.

Their voices almost begging, Kathy and Mike O'Guin asked if the development was a good one.

"Very good," Wayburn replied.

Felder leaned over so he could be filled in. "I can't tell you," said Wayburn. This was going to be Wayburn's moment.

Judge Glen reconvened court and Felder resumed his cross-examination in the dark. The interrogation was a strong warm-up for what was to follow. Now his questions concerned love and marriage. "Were you disturbed about marrying a man indicted for murdering his former wife?" asked Felder.

Mary said "of course" it disturbed her. "I certainly never planned on falling in love with Mr. Pikul. Sometimes these things happen, Mr. Felder, whereas I feel that love is sometimes just a once-in-a-lifetime opportunity. And if you see something so real, you just can't walk away from it. It was an agonizing decision that I had to make."

"And did falling in love just happen in a month, like that?" Felder asked. "You fell in love and got rid of a husband and married Mr. Pikul within a month?"

"Absolutely," said Mary. "I thought it was very peculiar also, but Joe did explain to me this is what had happened to his former wife and him. They were married within just a couple of months. In other words, these things do happen, Mr. Felder."

"I know," said Felder. "I see they happen. Did it disturb you marrying a transvestite?"

"I don't think that has ever been proven that he is a

transvestite," said Mary. "I do know he did tell me about some of the sexual practices with himself and his wife—his consenting wife—in the privacy of their bedroom."

"Whoa," said Judge Glen. "I don't want any discussion about this on the record."

Felder turned to another subject. "If Mr. Pikul goes away for twenty-five years to life, or whatever, are you going to take care of these kids as your own kids even though he is off in jail?"

"Absolutely, Mr. Felder," said Mary. "I have been consistent in my commitment to these children."

"And this love you developed for Mr. Pikul—as you call it, the once-in-a-lifetime situation—that took place sometime from May until now, is profound enough and deep enough to keep you going maybe twenty-five years in the future?"

"Absolutely. I am committed to the children. I have been in their life since January on almost a one-to-one daily basis."

"What about your own kid?" Felder snapped. "Your own kid is not living with you. Aren't you committed to her?"

"Of course, Mr. Felder. I have been away from my daughter, Mr. Felder, for sometimes six weeks at a time," she said, as if that answered the question. "It was my overseas travel. She was in good care. There is nothing wrong with my former husband as a caretaker."

That wasn't the point, Felder said, pointing out that Mary had testified in March, then changed her statements. "You swore to an affidavit in August; there were changes from you. How is this judge sitting here going to know if she makes you custodian and Mr. Pikul goes away, you are not going to change your mind again?"

"Because Mr. Felder, I have been consistent with my care and my love for these children. . . . These children have lost their mother and they face losing their father. I don't think they should face losing another mother image."

"How did they lose their mother?" Felder demanded, drawing an objection from Kurland. Lost in the shuffle was the question of whether Jennifer de facto had lost her mother.

Felder turned to Joe's health, with the hope that he

could somehow work in the issue of AIDS. "Did Mr. Pikul ever discuss his health with you?"

"Yes, he did," said Mary.

"Did he tell you about any serious medical condition?"

Kurland objected, and when Judge Glen questioned the relevance, Felder sat down. The topic was going to remain taboo.

Soon thereafter, Judge Glen ordered the courtroom cleared; it was time for the real fireworks to begin.

Bob Wayburn, on the cusp of the biggest cross-examination of his life, decided to take his time, careful not to make a misstep. The idea was to relax Mary and draw the story out of her.

He started off with a couple of questions about her involvement with the Pikul children stretching back to January.

Mary launched into a long reply about the first time Claudia had come over to their house, how the play date had stretched into dinner and making cupcakes. When she had called Joe to apologize, he had been perfectly charming and said that was fine. Soon Claudia and Blake were invited to spend the night, and Joe came over twice, to say good night. Loosening up, Mary explained how the relationship had evolved from there, until Claudia was calling every night and both children were spending more and more time at her house.

At that point Wayburn asked: "Did there come a time when you started going over to Mr. Pikul's residence?"

"Yes," Mary said. "I believe the first time was January 31, as Claudia's birthday was February 1. And we had Claudia again overnight. It was a Sunday night. She slept over Saturday and it was Sunday now. And the tradition in school was to bake cupcakes and bring them in. Claudia, Jennifer, and myself had baked cupcakes. I went over that night to deliver them to the Pikul home so that Joseph Pikul could bring them to school the next day, and I also brought all the birthday presents that I had purchased for Claudia with wrapping paper so I could wrap them in the home," said Mary.

Asked if the situation developed to the point where she saw Claudia and Blake every day, Mary said: "I wouldn't say almost every school day, but I would definitely say three or four times a week."

"When did that start?"

"In May—" said Mary before quickly reconsidering. "I think it was when I stopped working on a full-time basis, which was toward the middle of February, because I was more active in school since then. . . . Also, I had volunteered my services to Mr. Pikul as far as taking the children to the doctors or whatever."

A picture of fairly close contact was emerging. Certainly the relationship with the children had developed considerably by the time Kurland had put her on the stand at the first custody hearing. Mary had snookered everyone.

Wayburn inquired about the withdrawal of Mary's original offer to take custody with Steven Bain. "My husband was cooperating with me less and less. We had had a home visit by HRA in our house. Mr. Flete came over for approximately three hours, at which time Claudia's former teacher was also present because she was spending the night at our house. My husband knew it was important that he be there. And I kept getting phone calls, let's say every maybe hour or so, from my husband saying, 'Well, I am busy. I can't come home yet,' 'I am coming home soon. By the way, is Mr. Flete still there?' So he was definitely expressing reluctance."

Wayburn struck a chord when he asked if Steven Bain ever objected to the Pikul children coming into the household. After Mary responded that he had, the city attorney inquired as to the time frame for this dispute.

"I believe it was the second week of March. It might have been around my birthday, which was approximately March 15," she said. "Mr. Pikul wanted to reciprocate for the fact that I and my husband would have him and the children over for dinner and the children over for weekends, et cetera, and he invited all of us out to see a Broadway play called *Cats*. My husband declined the offer as he said he had seen the show, but I should go with Jennifer and Douglas because he hadn't seen the show. My stepson then said simply, 'I want to be with my friends on the weekend.' So nobody went except Jennifer and myself with Mr. Pikul and his children. I think I'm getting off the course a little bit. Could you repeat the question again?"

Wayburn repeated the question. "Yes, it was around that time, after the tickets, the issue of the tickets where he didn't go to the show and then he threw it up in my face that I went and he didn't go. But it was his decision not to go," said Mary.

"Did there come a time that your own daughter, Jennifer, expressed any concern as to the attention that was being spent by you on the Pikul children?" asked Wayburn.

First Mary said no, then amended with a comment that really upset Wayburn: "She did say to me, 'Mommy, I know you love me more and I know we have to be nice to Claudia.' But I also explained to Jennifer that I did love Claudia also."

Wayburn sought to determine if Mary knew Claudia as well as she projected. "I hadn't seen her very often. I went over my photo albums in the house. I did have lots of pictures of her since her junior kindergarten days. But I didn't spend a lot of time with her. You have to understand most of the times I was traveling overseas and my husband arranged most play dates," said Mary. "She was present at things like birthday parties and school plays and functions like that."

So Mary didn't really know Claudia that well. At the minimum, this "best friend" thing with her daughter sounded overblown. Furthermore, Mary hadn't even spent that much time raising her own child because she was busy traveling.

Mary explained in response to Wayburn's persistent questioning that her husband Steven eventually became adamant that her involvement with the Pikul family cease. He was fearful that he would lose custody of his son Douglas.

"Did you make a choice as to whether it was better for you to stay in that marriage or leave that family and stay involved with the Pikul children and Mr. Pikul?" asked Wayburn.

"Well, it wasn't so much that it was deciding between the two of them. I was deciding about the reason for going on with my present marriage. My former husband had a volatile personality. The situation was becoming increasingly more difficult. Obviously it was not an easy choice for me to make to leave my home."

Wayburn was curious about Steven Bain's purported volatility. "Well, I think the perfect example is the fact that in front of the entire third grade of Grace Church School he expressed his willingness to help out. He even offered to move into the Pikul home to help out, et cetera, et cetera. He had agreed to this larger apartment and then changed his mind, saying it's more important to have a river view. He would become nasty at times, belligerent at times."

Reviewing details of her relationship with Joe, Mary said she moved in with him at the end of June but was in fact celibate until "a little bit" after the July 2 wedding. She said her primary interest initially in becoming involved with her current household was the children, although she did admit to having fallen in love. "We became confidants, and I was explaining the situation and the heartache I was going through in my home, and he was very supportive of me and he truly was a very good, caring friend, and I think I became more and more attached to him."

Finally getting to the matter at hand, Wayburn asked if she'd ever been afraid of Joe. "Not afraid in the sense that I think he would do anything to me. I have been angry at him."

"Why have you been angry at him?" asked Wayburn.

"I have been angry at him because I guess I expected our marriage to go a little more smoother than it had."

Asked to explain, Mary said Joe was sometimes impatient with her, especially if she didn't do things quick enough. "He felt my travels away from home were too long. He wanted me to go on a diet. He felt I wasn't losing weight quick enough. Things like I didn't have dinner ready quick enough."

Kurland and Joe were now deeply in conversation, but Wayburn didn't stop. "Has he ever raised his voice to you?"

"Yes, he has," said Mary, estimating some four times since the wedding. No, he hadn't threatened her physical safety.

"Do you realize you are testifying under oath?" asked Wayburn.

Kurland rose from his chair. "Your Honor, may I approach the bench?"

"No," said Judge Glen firmly. "There is a witness on cross-examination right now."

"I have an application to the court, Your Honor," Kurland pleaded.

When Wayburn said he didn't mind "as long as it is away from the witness," Judge Glen relented. "We will go into my chambers," she said, and all the lawyers headed for the back room.

Kurland requested permission to withdraw as Joe's attorney. Judge Glen agreed that there appeared to be a conflict. At the very least, she said, it appeared Kurland could not represent Mary Bain in the custody petition. Kurland agreed. "I am not letting you out of representing him. He has to be represented here. I am not stopping this cross-examination right now."

"I am not asking you to stop it, but I am asking to withdraw as his counsel and her counsel," said Kurland. "I intended to do that at the end of the session, but I intend to do that now with respect to her certainly."

"I want to find out what the situation is here right now," said Judge Glen. "And I don't want an evening to go by where if there is some danger to this woman, we don't have the ability to do something about it."

Everyone marched back into the courtroom, where Judge Glen advised Mary she was no longer represented by Kurland in view of possible conflicts but that the attorney would continue to represent Joe until the end of the session. The judge also told Mary that as a witness she was not technically a party to the proceeding, and as such, was not especially entitled to counsel any more than any other witness.

Mary wanted to know what all that meant. "Does that mean I should continue to answer questions?"

"Yes, absolutely," said the judge. "And you are under oath. If there is a question which you think in any way might incriminate you in any criminal activity, you may take the Fifth Amendment. . . . I am talking about your criminal activity, not anyone else's."

Wayburn then resumed where he'd left off: with Mary's

honesty. He asked Mary if she was aware that if she violated the oath she could be prosecuted for perjury, adding for emphasis, "With possible imprisonment."

"No, I wasn't aware of that," said Mary.

Having warned Mary, Wayburn then wondered if Joe had done anything other than raise his voice four times, anything that threatened Mary's physical safety.

"Well, I think it depends on how you construe it," said Mary, trying desperately to find safe haven.

"Did he do anything else that put you in any fear for your physical well-being?" When Mary didn't say a word, Wayburn continued: "I don't want to quibble."

"No. I know what you are saying," said Mary. "There was an incident, and I don't know if you can consider it to be a threat to my well-being."

Judge Glen stepped in. "What is the incident?"

Silence.

Wayburn asked it next: "What is the incident?"

Judge Glen said firmly: "Tell us."

"I viewed it as a domestic altercation," said Mary, still searching for euphemisms. "We were arguing and I tried to pacify him and he didn't let me pacify him. He kind of just stood there. And he pushed me."

"When did this occur?" Wayburn asked.

"After I had come back from my trip. It was sometime after August 23."

Wayburn then inquired if she had spoken to any outside parties concerning her relationship with Joe at their upstate home. When Mary replied in the affirmative, Wayburn demanded details. Her perkiness gone, Mary said that she'd gone to the Ulster County Medical Center to speak to someone in the county mental health service.

Wayburn asked what name Mary had used.

"My maiden name."

It was like pulling teeth. "What is that?"

"Eik, E-I-K."

Wayburn wondered if there was any particular reason Mary hadn't used her married name. "Oh, absolutely. I wanted to be basically anonymous. I was going through a period of adjustment with my marriage and I didn't want— we couldn't afford marriage counseling. And I was trying to get Joe to come to marriage counseling. And I basically didn't want anybody to know who I was married to."

As Mary told the story, she first spoke to the mental health official in late August and related several "incidents." Wayburn pressed, but Mary said she wanted the incidents to remain confidential. Wayburn then suggested that the incidents might have a bearing on the matter before the court.

"No, not at all," she replied, characterizing the "incidents" as domestic altercations between husband and wife. "I had always stressed what a wonderful and loving father he's been."

Mary's voice was strong again, but Wayburn wasn't about to let go. "You don't feel that these so-called domestic altercations are important to bring to the attention of the court so that the court, in making its assessment as to what actually is in the best interests of these two children, can make a proper and fit appropriate assessment?"

"If I might point out, during these domestic altercations, as I called them, the children have not been present. Joe and I do not fight in front of the children," Mary protested.

But Wayburn knew that wasn't true. The information from upstate indicated the children had been present.

"At one time they were in their bedroom," Mary allowed.

"And that's not present in the household?" Wayburn barked.

"They were not present in hearing distance."

"Isn't it a matter of fact on that very incident that they were present in the household that the children told you that their father was looking for you?" asked Wayburn.

"Yes," said Mary. "That he was angry at me."

Exasperated, Wayburn retorted, "Are you going to tell us the truth about these altercations or do I?"

"Can I think for a moment?" asked Mary.

"Yes, certainly," said Wayburn. "I remind you, you are under oath."

Mary turned to Judge Glen. "May I ask you a question, Your Honor? What sort of criminal implications would there be if I were to take the Fifth?"

"No," said Judge Glen, shaking her head. "You may only take the Fifth if you have committed a crime or you can be reasonably suspected of committing a crime by giving an answer. Not someone else's crime."

Wayburn plowed ahead, demanding details on the incident where the children were at home.

"I had been out grocery shopping and I had picked up a neighbor walking along the road. I was driving back from grocery shopping and I dropped the neighbor off at the house that he requested to be dropped off at, his brother's home. And I drove home and I went upstairs to the house and the children were in bed. And they came out to me and said, 'You were gone over an hour. Daddy is looking for you. And he is angry at you.' And they ran back into their bedroom and closed the door. . . . Joe came in and he was angry at me, questioning me. And we had a fight."

"Can you describe the fight that you had?" Wayburn pressed.

"He tore my dress," said Mary.

"How did he tear your dress?" asked Wayburn. "Tell me exactly what he did."

"I was wearing a two-piece dress. It was a blouse and a skirt. And he tore it."

"How did he tear it? Did he use his hands?"

"No."

"Did he use a hunting knife?"

"Yes," said Mary.

Wayburn asked her to describe the knife. "It was—I think it was Claudia's Girl Scout knife."

"How big was it? How long was it?" Wayburn asked rapid-fire.

"Maybe two inches. Two-and-a-half inches. It was something that children take on a hunting trip."

Paul Kurland stood to address the judge. Wayburn objected to the interruption, but Kurland was undeterred. "May I approach the bench?"

"Is it very important?" Judge Glen asked.

"Yes," Kurland replied as everyone approached.

"*On* the record," said the judge, motioning the court stenographer to join in.

Kurland explained that Joe wanted to withdraw his application to continue custody, thus conceding custody of the children to the O'Guins during the murder trial.

"I think we should take that concession, but I also think

we must establish what happened in the household while the children were there," said Wayburn.

Kurland contended that if Joe withdrew his application, there'd be no reason to continue the hearing. "Then I object to the withdrawal," said Wayburn.

Judge Glen knew she couldn't force Joe to continue if he wanted to withdraw, but she wanted desperately to get to the bottom of Mary's story. "I certainly want to know because I want to make sure whatever happens tonight, these kids and this woman are safe. I am not going to know that if you withdraw the proceeding and everybody walks out of here. So if you want to make some arrangement right now where he stays in your apartment tonight or she goes back up there and gets the kids and gives them to the O'Guins, that is one thing, but otherwise I'm not going to take any chances here. . . . If, indeed, I hear there are serious threats of violence in this case, I do not want him to be with these children tonight. I want to make sure they are removed, and I want to make sure she is safe and that she has a right to safety and I will issue her an order of protection barring him from that house. I have an absolute right to do that, and I will do that."

Quickly thinking through what was unfolding, Wayburn raised an important technical issue in the hopes of salvaging the rapidly eroding situation. He asked Judge Glen to convert the proceedings into a child protective hearing under the Family Court Act on the basis that the children were in "imminent danger." Under Family Court rules, Judge Glen could suspend privileges protecting a husband or wife from testifying against their spouse.

Judge Glen pondered that proposal, then ruled that the hearing would continue jointly as a custody petition and a child protective proceeding under Family Court law, "based on the good-faith representation by Mr. Wayburn that there is evidence here which will show imminent danger to the family unit—if not to the children, to Mrs. Pikul."

"Excuse me, Your Honor," Mary interjected. "May I ask you a question? I am not quite sure what all of this means. I am not afraid of my husband. I love my husband. My husband has never demonstrated he is anything but a loving and caring father. I plan on going home tonight to my husband and to my children."

"*My* children?" Wayburn thought to himself. What about Jennifer?

"You are free to do whatever you want," said Judge Glen. "I want to elicit this testimony and determine for myself whether I believe that the children are in some danger or whether my order should be changed. Your husband has just—based on what I assume he imagines your testimony is going to be—withdrawn his application for temporary custody of the children."

"But I am not withdrawing mine," said Mary.

"But you are not an interested party to this action. I know you wrote an affidavit, but technically it's not your affidavit."

"Am I guilty?" asked Mary.

"You may make a separate application if you wish through separate counsel, tomorrow or at any time in the future, but right now you don't have an application before me. I will consider you as a possible caretaker or temporary caretaker, but I do not have an application here at the moment. You are his wife and not a separate party to the proceeding."

Wayburn resumed the questioning. Infuriated by Mary's use of the term "my children," he couldn't resist asking: "I believe they are your *stepchildren* by virtue of your marriage?"

"Yes. Of course, that's what I mean," said Mary. "But the children view me as their mother. We have a very close bond."

Sucking in his rage, Wayburn moved on. There was more important business at hand. "How did he *tear* your dress?"

"He cut it," said Mary.

"With the knife?"

"Yes, Mr. Wayburn, with the knife," said Mary with a tone of resignation.

"Where did he cut it?"

In two places, Mary said, "on the bodice and on the skirt," each cut being approximately six to eight inches.

"Were you moving when he cut the dress?" Wayburn asked. Mary said she was sitting on the couch.

Wayburn next wanted to know if Joe had held the knife to Mary's throat, but Mary now denied that part of her story. "What I said was he had this knife, this hunting knife, and it was toward the bodice, the upper part of the garment, and he slashed it."

"That evening when Mr. Pikul cut your skirt and bodice, did you leave the household?" asked Wayburn.

"Yes, I did," said Mary. "I was angry. I was upset. I was very disillusioned. We had been married for just a short time." Mary said she ran down the steps of their second-floor apartment and toward a neighbor's house. "There are about seven steps, there is a landing, then another approximately seven steps."

"When you ran down the stairs, did you see Mr. Pikul?" Wayburn asked.

Mary said she didn't see him because she didn't take the time to look behind her. "But," she added, "I knew he was there."

As she ran to the neighbors in the dark she still didn't see Joe, but knew he was there because of "a flashlight behind me."

Armed with the information from the upstate authorities, Wayburn asked Mary if she had seen Joe carrying a gun along with the flashlight as she ran from the house.

"Absolutely not," Mary insisted.

"Do you recall telling anyone that that's what you saw?"

"Absolutely not," said Mary. "I did say that I know he talks about hunting, so I have the thought in my mind, but absolutely not. It was dark. I did not have a flashlight. Mr. Pikul had the flashlight." Nobody asked her if she had the flashlight. Wayburn had asked her if Joe had a gun.

Wayburn asked Mary if she had been scared while Joe was chasing her. "I might have been a little afraid, but mostly angry and irate and very humiliated," she said.

As Wayburn asked what happened next, Joe gave Mary an ugly stare. All during this time he had been sweating profusely and groaning.

"The neighbors weren't there, so I stayed in their garden until they came home," Mary said.

Wayburn asked her if she'd fallen, and Mary said she had. Yes, she had gotten wet in the fall. It had been raining. "Did there come a time after you fell and got wet that you noticed a neighbor's car?"

"Yes," said Mary.

"What happened when that occurred?" Wayburn asked.

"The neighbors pulled up and I ran over to their car and they were surprised to see me on their property. They said, 'What's wrong?' And I said, 'I had a fight with Joe. And he is very angry at me. And I don't want to go back there tonight.'"

Asked to explain what else occurred that night, Mary said she told the neighbors she wasn't going to return home, so they then drove her to a friend's house.

"Did you tell those neighbors who were driving that car that you had to get out of there quick and please just drive you away, close the car door and drive you away? Did you tell them that?"

Mary said she didn't want to involve them in her "domestic problems" and didn't want Joe to know she was talking to them, so she had the neighbors drive her down the road, where she spent the night at another friend's house. The next morning, Mary explained, her neighbor intervened with Joe and subsequently told Mary that Joe wasn't mad at her anymore.

But Mary had skipped a little there, too. Under further questioning, she confessed that she actually had tried to return on her own when she woke up at seven, but Joe had declined to let her in, even to get a change of clothing.

Asked if Joe had a gun, Mary said he did, a hunting rifle. Had she called the police? "Not concerning that incident, no."

Wayburn knew the answer was not true, so he tried again. "Did you call the police on the night we just discussed or on the morning you returned back to the house?"

"No, I didn't," said Mary. "I called the police that afternoon."

"Oh, thank you," said Wayburn, dripping with sarcasm. He was disgusted with the interrogation, and couldn't help thinking back to Mary's beguiling testimony in March. He'd given her a free pass. Mary's misleading testimony had helped Joe keep his children.

"Just tell the truth," Wayburn said. "When you called the police in the afternoon, what did you say?"

"I told them I had a domestic altercation and I want to get my car and leave," Mary said, acknowledging that she had asked the police to go to the house to retrieve her pocketbook and the car keys inside the bag.

"Did you say anything else to the police?" Wayburn inquired.

"Originally, no, I didn't say anything else," said Mary. "And they explained to me that they had no jurisdiction, as this was a domestic dispute, a family dispute, and they would be trespassing on the property and they didn't have a search warrant and they could not accompany me to the house."

"And you called the police in the afternoon because when you went back to the house in the morning, Joseph wouldn't let you in to get a change of clothing, is that why?"

"Yes," Mary said. "That, and he wouldn't let me in the house. He was kind of forceful regarding that." When Wayburn asked how forceful Joe had been, she said, "He pushed me away from the door."

Turning away from the fight, Wayburn next inquired about Mary's original contacts with the upstate mental health center before the knife attack. "I had gotten back from overseas, from Hong Kong, and within a couple of days Joe and I were fighting. And I was just so tired of always being told I didn't make enough money, that what I made in a day Joe was able to make in a minute. And it was just this constant kind of verbal abuse. I wasn't thin enough. I wasn't as pretty as Diane. And et cetera, et cetera. It was just this constant tirade of abuse. And I knew we couldn't afford marriage counseling as we had so many bills and I wanted to see what I was able to accomplish with trying to get some inexpensive counseling to help with this marriage, as I was committed to the marriage. I loved Joe and the children and I had no intention of walking away from it."

Mary said she called the center from the upstairs bedroom, believing Joe was on the porch. But he actually listened in, then angrily came over to hang up the phone, Mary said. And each time she tried to call back, Joe hung up the phone again and again.

Wayburn wanted to know if Mary had told the mental

health people on the phone that she "needed to get away, that your husband had been indicted for murder and you needed to get away to talk."

Mary admitted she had made those comments, but insisted she had not been afraid. "Mr. Wayburn, if I was afraid for my own physical welfare and well-being, I would have gotten an order of protection from Joe. I would not have kept coming back to Joe. There is, I think, a period of adjustment in new marriages. There is a considerable age difference between us. We have some different points of views. But we love each other and we are trying to make our marriage work."

As Mary and Wayburn then sparred over her failure to tell the children's therapists or the New York City caseworker about any of the upstate incidents, a court officer approached the bench.

"Wait a minute," Judge Glen interrupted. Increasingly concerned about Joe's behavior, the judge ordered some extra security. Joe had been squirming in his chair like a wild animal preparing to break out.

The supplemental security took up positions around Joe as Mary chattered on about her and Joe being "loving, caring parents" and how "the children have never been disciplined physically." Wayburn's case had been made, though. He dismissed the witness and sat down to await Judge Glen's next move.

First the judge allowed the newspaper reporters back into the courtroom, but she warned them "not to sit particularly close to Mr. Pikul." Then, declaring that "a knife is a knife," Judge Glen said Joe's attack on Mary had convinced her "that at this moment, the kids are safer with the O'Guins."

She pulled out a blank Form No. 4, subtitled "Nonfamily Offense Temporary Order of Protection," and began handwriting numerous orders of protection. She ordered Joe to stay away from the home, school, business, and place of employment of Kathleen and Michael O'Guin; to "refrain from harassing, intimidating, threatening or otherwise interfering with Kathleen and Michael O'Guin, Raoul Felder, Esq., Paul Kurland, Esq., Robert Wayburn, Esq., and José Flete," the HRA caseworker. Under the category "Any Other Condition," the judge also ordered

Joe to "stay away from the children, Claudia and Blake, until otherwise ordered by the court, and any school in which they may be enrolled." Even though Mary didn't want one, Judge Glen issued a protective order on her behalf, too.

The O'Guins were granted legal custody so they could enroll the children in school and authorize medical treatment, and told that Joe's only contact with his children was to be a telephone call, daily at 8:30 P.M.

Finally, Flete was directed to accompany Mary and the O'Guins to get Claudia and Blake from the upstate babysitter. Joe assured the judge he would spend the night in Manhattan.

Mary then left the witness stand and walked over to Joe, who by now was surrounded by six beefy court officers. She extended her arms to give him a hug. Joe sat unmoved for several seconds, frozen with anger, before he finally embraced his bride.

CHAPTER • 21

"You Can't Kill Them All"

AS MARY LEFT THE COURTROOM, Joe told her, "Drive carefully." He said it several times, *"Drive care-ful-ly,"* to make certain Mary got the hint.

Joe wasn't sly enough for Bob Wayburn, though. After a fruitless visit to 1 Police Plaza, headquarters for the New York City Police Department, he visited the precinct near his home, where he got a desk sergeant to place a call to authorities upstate.

Sure enough, despite assurances that he would stay put, Joe set off for the home of Richard Roberti in rural Lanesville, where his daughters were baby-sitting the Pikul children.

The Roberti family had gotten to know the "Baine family" over the summer when Joe stopped by to purchase eggs. Claudia and Blake, who usually accompanied their father, loved to play with the animals around the property, located about one mile from the Pikuls. Over the summer, Mary had asked several times if the Roberti girls, Nicole and Michele, would like to baby-sit, but they'd never connected until that morning, when Joe gave Nicole a note instructing school officials to release the children to her after classes.

Joe had said he'd be back before dinnertime, but here it was after six, so the Robertis fed Claudia and Blake. As the evening wore on, Nicole mentioned that she had keys to the Pikul house and suggested she take the children back to put them to sleep. Her father agreed. Figuring that Joe and Mary would arrive shortly, Richard Roberti told his daughters to give him a call if they needed a ride home.

Around ten o'clock a call finally came, but it was from local police. Telling Roberti to go pick up his girls, the police officer explained the new custody order. Though he assured the Robertis that Nicole and Michele were not in any danger, Roberti was thoroughly alarmed when he learned that his soft-spoken, bookish-looking neighbor "Joe Baine" was actually accused wife murderer Joe Pikul.

Mrs. Roberti started the car as her husband ran to a second house to get his pistol. As he was dashing across, Richard Roberti noticed Joe standing at the front door and a reddish-colored car parked down the road by the firehouse. Roberti didn't know what to say.

Just then his wife pulled the car around out front and honked the horn. "Hurry up. We have to get over to the house to pick up the kids," she yelled through the car window.

That was the last thing Roberti wanted Joe to hear, so he tried to cover it up. "Gee, it's about time you made it up here. It's ten o'clock," said Roberti. "What did you get into, an accident?"

"No. The traffic was bad. How come my kids aren't here?"

Roberti explained that his daughters had decided to take the kids back and "tuck them in." He said he was just on his way over to check on his girls because it was getting late and they had to go to school in the morning.

With that, Roberti sped off to retrieve all of the children. He had no intention of taking them to the Hunter police barracks, as the police on the phone had requested. He had five other children to tend to, and figured everyone, including Claudia and Blake, would be safest back at his place.

Shortly after the Roberti entourage returned home, they were met by the state police, who removed Claudia and Blake. Once again the bureaucracy took over, and the Pikul children were put into the foster-care system. Driving 35 m.p.h. on the interstate, Mary, with the O'Guins following in their car, didn't arrive on the scene until well past midnight. The two children weren't given to the O'Guins until 3 A.M.

Joe, meanwhile, seeing a police car speeding by with sirens blasting, thought the police might be looking for him. He drove off in the other direction.

Claudia and Blake didn't hear from their father again for two days, until that Friday night, when under the provisions of Judge Glen's order, he called the O'Guins' home in Yonkers.

Mike O'Guin listened in on the children's end of the conversation, and judging from their responses, Claudia and Blake were being quizzed about who was in the house—they mentioned that a bodyguard had been hired.

"What do you mean you're coming?" asked Blake at one point. "Is that okay with the court?"

Blake listened for a few seconds, then began jumping up and down with excitement. "Shall we tell?" The little boy, not quite six at that point, listened again carefully, then told his father: "We'll just make this our little secret." He was learning his part well.

Later that night, when Mike O'Guin pressed Blake for more details, the youngster told him that the call had been confidential.

In the morning, the O'Guins abandoned their home, taking Claudia and Blake into hiding.

Mary Bain started calling the O'Guins' house about 9:00 A.M. that Saturday, but no one answered. Joe had been doing the wash for the past day and she wanted to deliver the laundry and a package of toys. As the day wore on, though, it became obvious that the O'Guins had disappeared. Distraught and disappointed, Joe got in his car and took off for a ride.

A mile away at the Roberti household, everyone was just starting to calm down when they heard a loud crash in the road. Richard Roberti, who was outside working, feared that one of his children had run out into the road, or that his horse, grazing in a field across the highway, might have broken loose.

Running around the corner of a building, Roberti noticed a small red car had crashed. The driver kept trying to get the car to move, but the bumper was pushed on top of the tire, which was flat.

Approaching the scene, Roberti recognized the driver as Joe Pikul, a very drunk Joe Pikul. "What are you looking for, trouble? If you want trouble, I will give you trouble. You have no business over here. Get the fuck out of here," Joe warned.

Roberti said he'd heard the crash and observed that it looked like Joe could use some help. "I don't care what you did. What you did is your business and it has nothing to do with me," said Roberti. "But I'm here to help you, if you want help."

"Well, I do," said Joe. "Change the fucking tire. I want you to take the tire out of my trunk and change it. I'm on a mission."

Richard Stokes, who lived with the Roberti family, arrived on the scene, having first walked up the road to make sure the horse was all right. Stokes opened the trunk and immediately noticed a 12-gauge pump shotgun. He also noticed an automatic pistol, some clothing, and a video camera.

Roberti pushed Joe out of the way, grabbed the spare tire, tossed it to his buddy Stokes, then slammed the trunk down. He didn't know if Joe had intentions of using one of the guns, but he wasn't going to wait around to find out.

As Stokes changed the tire and pulled the damaged bumper back, Joe squawked that he hadn't expected the Roberti family to set him up. "I wanted to take my kids and go to the border. I was on my way to Canada. Do you think I had time?"

Trying to think of anything to say, Roberti assured Joe he could have escaped with the children if he had tried. "When you came to my house to get the kids, I made up all kinds of excuses," Roberti explained. "But I really didn't know what was going on at that point."

The subject of baby-sitting fees then came up, since Nicole Roberti hadn't been paid for the other night. When Joe started looking in the car's interior for his wallet, Roberti got concerned he might be looking for another gun. "Listen, we'll worry about the money later."

When the car was fixed, Joe asked the two men to follow

him to his house to get the money. Roberti and Stokes agreed, but Roberti went back inside his house to get his .45-caliber pistol, which he stuffed into the front of his pants.

Back at the Pikul house, Joe gave Roberti thirty dollars for his daughter. In the process the three men started talking. Joe explained that he hadn't wanted to hurt Roberti's wife and kids over what had transpired that Wednesday night, but felt he'd been set up when his children were turned over to police. "I'm on a mission. I have nothing to live for," he said several times. "I'm a dead man. I'll never get anything back. I'm dead."

Joe's mood swung back and forth. In between downing heavy swigs of rum, he laughed and showed the two men photos of Claudia and Blake. Then he drank some more and cried. Pacing back and forth, he said he loved his children and claimed he hadn't killed his wife. "I wouldn't hurt anybody," Joe said. Then he just sat there in silence, spaced out.

"Well, if you didn't do anything wrong, what are you driving drunk for, with weapons in your car, looking for trouble?" Roberti asked. "You hurt your family enough. Why don't you just sleep this off?"

"I'm on a mission," Joe answered, again assuring Roberti he could prove he didn't kill Diane. "My first wife was bad. She testified against me, as good as I treated her; my second wife can't testify against me because she's dead, and I don't believe my third wife will testify against me. We love each other very much." Joe gave a robust chuckle, then continued: "Well, you can't kill them all."

A few minutes later, Joe announced: "I'm gonna go to the border."

"What border?" asked Roberti.

"Mexico or Canada," replied Joe. "Now that I don't have the kids, there's nothing keeping me here except my dog and two cats." First, though, Joe announced, he was going to relieve his frustrations at a "tough-guy bar" down the road. Roberti warned Joe about getting into a fight, but Joe boasted: "I'm not going in there to fight. I'm going to take my shotgun."

———

The next night, Claudia asked the O'Guins if she could call her father from their hiding place. This time Mike O'Guin listened in on the extension as Joe enlisted the assistance of his children in his latest effort to get them back.

Joe wanted to know if the bodyguard had left yet. Told the man had departed, Joe said he was glad and told the children that they were all going to be together again soon. But, he warned, they had better not tell the O'Guins about this.

Convinced that they were no longer living at the O'Guins' house in Yonkers, Joe started quizzing his offspring about the names of nearby streets. He asked if they knew how far away they had moved and when they'd be returning to the O'Guins' house. "This is going to take some real planning because the O'Guins are a complication," he said. He suggested they get the phone number of where they were staying, but not by asking the O'Guins. "Tomorrow I want you to look up the street name and get the house number," he told Claudia. "This is very important. Don't ask anybody; just find out."

Joe instructed the kids to call him the next day with the information, and again insisted that they tell the O'Guins nothing.

Joe then embarked on another of his tirades, telling Claudia and Blake that the O'Guins were "assholes" and "jerks." He said their mother hated Kathy O'Guin and never wanted them to be with her. Kathy was also mean to cats, Joe said, launching into a story about how Diane had accused Kathy of murdering her cat when it died while Kathy was taking care of it.

Joe's comments during the phone calls appeared to constitute violation of Judge Glen's order against harassing the O'Guins. Further, his action the evening after the court hearing in Manhattan, as well as his subsequent behavior, appeared to be violations of the order of protection, and possibly the custody order.

That Monday morning, the O'Guins updated Felder, who immediately drew up an order seeking to have Joe held in contempt of court. In his court papers, Felder blasted Joe as "a homicidal lunatic" whose "intention seems clear. His history for violence and erratic behavior is also clear. Something has to be done to take him off the streets immediately."

Wayburn submitted his own motion papers, attaching a copy of a statement that investigator John N. Knight of the Orange County District Attorney's Office had obtained from Roberti. Wayburn wanted criminal contempt charges brought, not just civil.

That evening, as Judge Glen departed from teaching a class at New York Law School, she signed an order setting a hearing for later in the week. She suspended Joe's phone privileges with his children pending the hearing.

Meanwhile up in Orange County, Prosecutor Alan Joseph petitioned Wayburn's office and the Ulster County Mental Health Agency for records pertaining to Joe's attacks on Mary. He then launched his own court action to get Joe's $350,000 bail revoked based on the Roberti incident and Mary's testimony before Judge Glen about the dress slashing.

Joseph told Judge Byrne that Joe had been seen drunk the previous Saturday, heavily armed, and talking of fleeing to Canada. But Steve Worth, one of Joe's criminal attorneys, demanded that Knight, the DA's investigator, be put on the stand to be cross-examined. Worth characterized the allegations as unsubstantiated and said they were part of "a relentless attack from all different quarters on this man to deny him his liberty."

Judge Byrne refused to act immediately, instead scheduling a hearing for the following Monday. He instructed Prosecutor Joseph to bring witnesses to support his position.

The postponement meant Judge Glen got first crack at Joe. When she convened court, things immediately started going Joe's way. The criminal contempt charges were withdrawn, leaving less serious civil contempt allegations.

Mike O'Guin testified first, relating the overheard telephone call and explaining that he and Kathy had gone into hiding "because we were afraid the kids were going to be snatched." Mike also contended that although Joe was constantly trying to turn the children against him and

Kathy, the children regularly asked them "to sit in the bedroom with them until they fall asleep."

Wayburn then called Joe to the stand. With Kurland having resigned the previous week, Bekoff and Worth nowhere to be found, and Joe claiming to be destitute, Judge Glen appointed attorney Heriberto Cabrera at taxpayers' expense.

Cabrera, who told the judge he had never represented anyone in a civil contempt proceeding, tried to advise Joe that he had the right to assert the Fifth Amendment to all of Wayburn's questions. But Judge Glen promptly informed him that his opinion was incorrect. "Clearly he can't take the Fifth to everything in the world, but anything which might tend to incriminate him in a crime." The only crime Judge Glen said she could think of that Joe might possibly be charged with as a result of his behavior was custodial interference in the second or third degree.

Wayburn started off by getting Joe, who wrung his hands continually, to acknowledge that he'd received copies of the judge's orders removing the children from his custody and directing him to stay away. Joe explained that he tried to stay with friends in Manhattan, but they weren't in town. He had no money, so he couldn't stay in a hotel. "So I had a friend who is a cabdriver and he took me up."

Joe proceeded to tell a preposterous story about a Yellow Cab driver named Peter Peterson. The story was immediately at odds with Roberti's observation that the car he saw that night was reddish in color. Asked to explain where he had gone once he got to Lanesville, Joe contended he didn't go directly to his home because he thought his children might be there. This contradicted the fact that Joe had arranged that morning to pick up the children at the Roberti home.

"I wasn't sure when you guys were coming up, and I went to where the kids had been, the baby-sitter's house, to clear up the location of the children," Joe said. "I didn't want to interfere with the process of the kids being taken away."

Joe claimed that when he told the children on the phone that they would soon be reunited, he was trying to cheer them up, not rile them, especially Claudia. "I just tried to soothe her, because it was hurting. And doing whatever a concerned parent would do under those circumstances. I let her listen to her cats. I told her we still had the cats and dog and the dog had barked. And I couldn't get the rabbit, but nonetheless I just tried to make her feel at ease."

Under questioning, Joe admitted asking who was in the house, maintaining he became concerned about the body-guard because Claudia "was scared about this gun. She doesn't see guns around the house." That, of course, was another lie.

Joe conceded that he had asked Claudia what floor they were living on, but only to allay his safety concerns. "These are new parents and caretakers, and I don't want Blakey falling out of the third floor if there are not window guards on there."

"Did you tell Claudia that you were coming for her?" asked Wayburn.

"I said, 'Someday I will come for you.' "

"Did you tell Claudia not to tell the O'Guins that you were coming for her?" Joe said he didn't want to disturb the O'Guins.

Joe admitted asking Claudia for the address of their hideout in the second call, but again claimed his motives were innocent. "I wanted to send her some cards and stuff. She said she thought she would be there awhile."

Wayburn wanted to know if Joe told Claudia that he was coming for her and Blake. "You know," said Joe, "these children were hurt so bad, I wanted to let them know we were going to be back together as a family someday."

Joe then admitted he and Claudia had talked about Kathy O'Guin, but contended it had been Claudia who spoke negatively, having been force-fed unfavorable comments over the years by Diane. "Claudia has been afraid of the O'Guins. Understand that. She has been afraid of them." Asked why, Joe replied: "Because of the stories that her mama told her."

One of the stories, Joe said, pertained to how Diane had become allergic to her two cats while pregnant with Claudia. "The doctor forced her to send the cats away," said Joe. "Her father wouldn't take them, but Kathy did. And she was single then. And shortly after the cats got to wherever she was, one of them died, her favorite cat died. And Diane was hysterical and had an autopsy done. . . . I don't think that Diane ever forgave her for that. And it was an important part of Diane's feelings about why the O'Guins were not considered as caretakers in our wills, and Claudia knew that story and said something about it to me."

Following a recess, Wayburn inquired if Joe recalled testifying about Claudia's concern over the bodyguard's gun because she "doesn't see guns around the house."

"No," said Joe. "She never saw a *handgun* in my house."

"Did she see other types of guns in your house?"

"I had a rifle," said Joe. "I have a 30.06—"

"Objection, Your Honor," said Cabrera. Judge Glen sustained but the lunacy of the testimony was readily apparent—Claudia was supposedly not afraid of the rifle but terrified of the bodyguard's holstered handgun.

Felder went on the attack, and Joe's fabricated story became more and more muddled. He couldn't remember cabbie Pete Peterson's telephone number but somehow he had remembered just the week before; he claimed he put the $300 cab fare "on the cuff"; he denied having told Mary to drive slowly so he could "get there ahead of you and take the kids away." He also disputed having told Claudia that Diane hated Kathy and Mike O'Guin. "I don't think their mother disliked them, I think she found them hopelessly boring," Joe told Felder at one point. "Diane can't stand boring people. You know that."

Felder also inquired about Joe's demand that Claudia and Blake keep his rescue plans secret. "I didn't want to disturb the O'Guins' peace of mind and their new job by reminding them that I'm coming after them again at some point. I have told them face-to-face during our few meetings in the summer that I will spend $2 million to get these kids back, when this thing is cleared up, that I'll just keep on coming and coming. I'm going to keep coming after them. I don't care if it's two million or what. Because the kids mean more to me than anything in the world."

"And you're going to keep coming?" asked Felder.

"I think it's nice for a father and children to have a little secrecy," Joe answered back.

Felder asked why Joe felt it necessary to get the names of nearby streets if all he wanted to do was send Claudia a card.

"Well, I figured if she wasn't able to figure out the address, I could send it to a cross street or something," said Joe.

"Now wait a second," said Felder. "You are under oath, Mr. Pikul."

"I am under oath."

"Do you seriously expect us to believe what you are saying?"

"I'm not sure I said that, but it would only be—I have a mess of cards. We are a family of sending cards. We send loads and loads of cards," Joe offered.

"What did you think, in case the postman gets lost, if you find out nearby streets, he will be able to locate them?" Felder mocked.

"I imagine Yonkers is a small town," said Joe, referring to one of New York State's largest cities. "I think the postman knows where a house is if you give him a relative idea."

As the court day drew to a close, it became clear that the hearing would not be completed, so Judge Glen had to make another interim decision. She said the question wasn't whether Joe *wanted* to steal his children or interfere with their custody, but whether he in fact did so, in violation of her court order.

"That is the law," said the judge. "I am sure many people here would like it to be otherwise, and we would like to put Mr. Pikul on trial. He may or may not have done something quite terrible here, but that is not the issue in this case. . . . The order of contempt is a violation of a lawful order of the court, not doing something bad in the world at large."

Judge Glen issued a new order barring Joe from entering the Yonkers city limits and from talking or writing to his children. But once again Joe was allowed to walk free.

More of the same occurred when court resumed the next day: Joe told incredible stories and Judge Glen said none of it proved he'd violated her orders. Sometimes it was difficult to decide which was more amazing—the fact that

Joe had the audacity to tell his wild stories under oath or the fact that he somehow always seemed to get away with it.

When Felder asked Joe if he was still certain he'd gone upstate in Peterson's Yellow Cab, Joe proceeded to change his story. Claiming he'd been confused, Joe said he mixed up the trip with one Peterson had taken him on three years ago to Long Island. "What I did the night of the fourteenth is I took a cab from the street and went up that way."

"And so you suddenly remembered old Pete Peterson was really something that happened three years ago?" asked Felder. Yes, Joe insisted.

Having established that a total stranger had supposedly driven Joe, Felder wanted to know how the cabbie had been paid, since Joe had previously claimed he was penniless. "There was money, some money in my wallet, and I had some money up there."

"Wait a minute," said Felder. "Yesterday you said you had no money with you."

"As I said, I had the story confused at that time."

With his court-appointed lawyer, Joe also attempted to put a better spin on his first call to the O'Guins' house. "Claudia said, 'I miss you very much. And Blakey misses you. And Blakey and I cry a lot. And we don't want to be here. And we want to be with you forever. We miss Mommy. We miss our cats and dogs and rabbits.' And I had the animals talk to them, you know, in their way. I assured them that the animals were still there in good shape. And that someday we would be back together again."

Joe said the children cried a lot on the phone, and Claudia told him that Blakey had been crying just before the call. Joe said he cried a bit, too. "I always had the capability of crying with my children in good times and bad times."

Cabrera asked Joe to explain his actions during Claudia's call that Sunday from the hiding place. Joe recounted that Claudia told him, "Blake and I miss you so much. . . . We would like to leave here and come back to you and live with you forever." Joe said he told Claudia: " 'You have to excuse me,' and I went to the other room and cried for about three minutes until I could compose myself and come back."

Joe explained that the only reason he wanted to know where the O'Guins had moved his children to was so he could talk to them. As for his questions to Claudia about cross streets, Joe again insisted his intentions were pure. "We are a card-sending family. I wanted to send cards, plus I bought them some hats and stuff for them. I have always been a present giver. I love to give presents and the kids sort of appreciate them. Perhaps I spoiled them on presents. But I thought if they got an assortment of presents from Mary and me, it would make them feel better."

Showing much more familiarity with Yonkers than he had the day before, Joe said he was "very concerned about the neighborhood" because he'd been to Yonkers once or twice when he was growing up. "When I was a teenager in Massachusetts, I came down to the racetrack—otherwise the only other time I was in Yonkers was when we brought Mary's child to go to camp—and Yonkers has always been a town that turned me off tremendously, a place that I wouldn't want to live in or for that matter have my children live there. And so I wanted to know whether they were in a nice section of Yonkers or in a less-than-nice section."

When Cabrera finished, Judge Glen asked Joe if he was aware that Mike O'Guin had eavesdropped during the call from the secret location. "You know, I kind of believe in people, you know. And I had been through a lot of trouble over the years and I believe that people wouldn't do things that I wouldn't do," said the man who had compiled hundreds of hours of secretly made tapes of his wife's calls.

Wayburn wondered if Joe wanted to change more of his testimony about his cab ride, suggesting that Joe had driven himself that night. No, Joe insisted, it was a cab.

What did it look like? asked Wayburn.

"It was an off-the-street Yellow Cab."

"And when you hailed this off-the-street Yellow Cab, you made an arrangement with that cabdriver to take you up there?"

"Well, there are two," answered Joe. "I hailed one, who got a flat tire on his spare. So, somewhere in the

Village he was changing it. He said 'I can't take you up there because my spare is flat.' And then another cab came along and said 'I will take you up there.' And that's the one I went up with."

So Pete Peterson was gone from the picture. The Yellow Cab was now an *off-the-street* Yellow Cab—and not even the first one but the second one because the first one had a flat.

Still seeking to explain why he'd gone upstate, Joe said he simply wanted to be with his "animals and my familiar circumstances and music and stuff so that I could mourn in a familiar circumstance. . . . I have a very beautiful country setting with streams behind me, wonderful mountains in front. And places I can take long walks, you know. I have had a lot of trouble with living in the city, and I thought I could get peace quicker up there. I didn't want to be alone in the city necessarily. I was, you know, hurting a lot. I was distraught and I thought if I could be in my familiar circumstances, it would be better for my grieving."

That all sounded so nice, but what about the guns Roberti had seen in the car trunk? Wayburn wondered. Joe admitted having a 30.06 rifle in his trunk but said it was unloaded and that he had planned to use it at a turkey shoot down at the gun club.

When Judge Glen told Wayburn it was irrelevant whether Joe had any weapons in his trunk, the city attorney contended that a child snatching, certainly an armed child snatching, constituted contempt in his book. But Judge Glen disagreed along the same lines she had the day before. "An intent—no matter how strongly Mr. Pikul may have held it, no matter how many acts he may have taken to further that intent, if it did not result in a violation of the order—is, in my view—unless I am shown otherwise— not a violation of the order."

The hearing was going nowhere.

That afternoon, as Felder again hammered away at Joe's supposed cab ride out of New York City, the judge grew impatient. Summoning Assistant District Attorney Mary O'Donoghue, who had observed the day's testimony, Judge Glen said: "If a crime was committed, whether it was the crime of concerted interference, attempted kidnapping, or any other crime, there is a determination to be made by the district attorney's office, whether Mr. Morgenthau in your county or any other district attorneys in any other counties which may have jurisdiction."

Judge Glen told O'Donoghue that since she'd heard the testimony—and could further question Roberti or the various attorneys—she was in the best possible position to determine if Joe had broken any laws. She said she was sure Judge Bryne and Prosecutor Joseph upstate and Morgenthau's office in Manhattan would take any appropriate action. "The law cannot be bent out of shape to reach a result which people may otherwise desire. At this moment this contempt proceeding is not the appropriate place to jail Mr. Pikul. If there is some other appropriate place, I am sure that that will occur."

Judge Glen said that she was willing to resume the hearing the following Monday, but Joe had to be upstate for his bail revocation hearing. She then dropped one final hint.

"Obviously, if Mr. Pikul has his bail revoked, that would be the end of that, or the necessity for this hearing. Obviously if Mr. Morgenthau chooses after reviewing the evidence and what he believes to be the situation here, if a crime has been committed, then he certainly need not wait on the outcome of this hearing to make that determination because if he believes a crime has been committed, I am sure he will act appropriately."

As court adjourned, detectives from the Manhattan DA's office surrounded Joe and placed him under arrest. The scene was the stuff of melodrama. First Mary embraced Joe. Then, as the cuffs were placed on him, Mary fainted, hitting the floor with a rather loud *whomp*. A court officer and one of the detectives had to drag her over to a chair.

A few minutes later Joe was taken away, to be held overnight pending arraignment on charges of custodial interference in the second degree, a misdemeanor punishable by a year in jail and a $1,000 fine. Morgenthau finally had his hooks in the Pikul case.

The next morning, Criminal Court Judge Daniel P. Fitzgerald of Manhattan got to handle the latest courtroom chapter in the Joe Pikul saga—an arraignment request from Morgenthau's office for $25,000 bail on the custodial interference charge.

Steve Worth appeared on Joe's behalf, telling Judge Fitzgerald how Judge Byrne had refused to revoke $350,000 bail on the same issues without a full hearing and how Judge Glen had let Joe go after two days of hearings because she hadn't heard any evidence that her order of protection had been violated. "If you look at the complaint, which reads like a cheap novel rather than a complaint, at best you have an attempt at custodial interference—assuming any of this is true—which makes it a B misdemeanor," said Worth. "But the district attorney doesn't like that. They want to say the enticement makes it a completed act."

Worth said the Manhattan DA's office had no business with Joe Pikul. Jurisdictional questions, he argued, rested with Judge Glen or Judge Byrne. "It's important to know at this juncture this is not Miss O'Donoghue's, of the district attorney's office, first attempt with Mr. Pikul. Months ago, while he had the children and was at the Concord Hotel, Miss O'Donoghue sought in the middle of the night to take the children away. That went before a judge, too, and the result of that one [was that] custody was returned to Mr. Pikul and things went along up until the point of the hearing that you heard so much about. This is not the first time."

Judge Fitzgerald agreed that Judge Byrne and Judge Glen had both had ample opportunity to take action if they so chose. "Judge Byrne clearly has the serious case in front of him and has been working on it quite some time. . . . Judge Glen has another serious aspect on the civil side and she's been working on that quite some time." The judge said the case before him appeared to be a simple misdemeanor. "It appears you are asking me to be an appellate court on the actions of both Judge Byrne and Judge Glen because they haven't put him in jail yet," he said, denying the district attorney's motion for a high bail amount.

Worth interrupted to inform the judge that Joe was so destitute he would be unable to post any kind of bail. "Routinely on a B misdemeanor a person could be released on his own recognizance," said Worth. "We have a hearing to do Monday before Judge Byrne and have to appear there. I ask Your Honor in due fairness to all of the defendants that appear with a B misdemeanor and with his criminal record, or lack thereof and lack of convictions, that you release him. If he flees, he'll lose $350,000. . . . He's made literally twenty to thirty court appearances over the last nine months and shown his ability to return to court. He wants to fight the murder case and is pleading not guilty, and he's still presumed innocent. I ask Your Honor to release him." Judge Fitzgerald agreed.

That evening, Joe and Mary returned upstate to what they described as their "lovely country setting" to prepare for the bail revocation hearing.

The criminal justice system didn't fare much better when the bail hearing reconvened upstate. It seemed that the cops took down virtually every word of Joe's incriminating statements, but had neglected to mention in their reports that Joe had claimed to Roberti's neighbor, Richard Stokes, that he could prove he hadn't killed Diane. "You told police that he said that, and the police picked out what they wanted?" asked Worth.

"I imagine that that's the way it looks," Stokes answered.

Alan Joseph tried to introduce a transcript of Mary Bain's New York testimony about the dress-slashing incident, but Judge Byrne said he wanted to hear the story firsthand.

When the hearings resumed later in the week, they were a virtual repeat of the New York City proceedings. Prosecutor Joseph presented evidence, Judge Byrne listened, and Joe walked out a free man. It didn't matter that Joe had been evicted from his Sixth Avenue apartment, that his Amagansett house was being repossessed, that he'd lost custody of his children after Mary testified about the dress slashing, or that she had sought help from upstate mental health officials.

Mary sought to downplay the slashing incident, describing it as a "domestic altercation" and claiming she fled the house because she was "very angry and humiliated," not because she was in fear. Mary pointed out that she had not filed a criminal complaint against her husband.

"You've heard testimony as to the defendant's erratic behavior and erratic mental condition," said Prosecutor Joseph, pleading that Joe be jailed. "This is not the same Joseph Pikul who appeared before this court in November 1987." The prosecutor even claimed that most of the bail money didn't belong to Joe—a point that Worth protested with such vigor he left the impression he had a stake in it, which it turned out he and Bekoff did.

Worth contended Joe had earnings potential of $500,000 to $1 million a year. "That's pretty substantial financial incentive," said Worth. "He intends to go to trial in this matter."

Judge Byrne agreed. "I do not feel that Mr. Pikul literally meant what he said," the judge said in reference to Joe's statements about fleeing the country with his children. He also observed that Joe had always appeared in court when scheduled. Joe was ordered to turn over all of his weapons to the DA's office. But otherwise, he was free to go.

Rising from his chair, Joe wiped away his tears. Mary rubbed her husband's back and hugged him. They walked out of the courthouse hand in hand.

The following day, September 30, was Bob Wayburn's last day as associate general counsel for Family and Children's Services at the New York City Human Resources Administration.

His job-performance evaluation reports had been less than sparkling. The political in-fighting had taken its toll. Wayburn wasn't going to get the judgeship he wanted either; that was going to a superior with whom he'd been at loggerheads over the Pikul case.

The draft legislation was dead in the water, too. Researchers and lawmakers had raised an interesting wrinkle—one that none of the feminists or child advocates had focused on during their demands for the removal of parental rights in family murder cases. It turned out that many such cases involve a battered wife claiming self-defense in the killing of her husband or boyfriend, or involved mothers killing one child but wanting to retain custody of the rest of her offspring. If this blanket legislation was enacted, those mothers would automatically lose their custody. The bill was going nowhere.

In view of the imposing wall of legalese Wayburn kept encountering, it also seemed pointless to continue the civil contempt against Joe. So in a final letter to Judge Glen, Wayburn asked her to dismiss the complaint, which she subsequently did.

Wayburn dropped a note to Felder, giving him his home number "if you ever need to reach me." He finished cleaning out his desk and, after eight years in the Office of Legal Affairs, departed his office for the last time.

Joe's murder trial had been scheduled to begin in October, but a rape case before Judge Byrne was taking much longer than expected. "It's like being a fighter," defense lawyer Ron Bekoff said one day. "You get psyched to go in there and fight. You wind up thinking about it all the time. Then they call it off."

On the advice of the children's therapists, Joe started seeing the kids again during the delay, under an informal agreement with the O'Guins in which he—and Mary—could see Claudia and Blake several times a month in the presence of Mike, Kathy, and a bodyguard.

By this point, Joe and Mary had moved from Lanesville to another rural community upstate called Cuddebackville. Joe spent a great deal of his free time getting drunk and getting arrested. On October 6, he was charged with driving while intoxicated after state troopers spotted him driving erratically in Hunter. Joe also was cited for driving on a suspended license and failure to keep to the right. This time he spent the night in the Greene County Jail, unable to post $750 bail.

Freed the next day, Joe proceeded to get into another "domestic altercation" with Mary, who called state police, then declined to press charges.

Several weeks later, Joe was arrested again, this time for doing forty-five in a thirty-five-mph zone in Middletown, also upstate. He was issued a ticket for speeding as well as for driving on a suspended license. The police computer showed Joe had three active suspensions from different courts throughout the state. On this occasion, though, Joe avoided another night in jail; he had the $100 bail money. Joe subsequently pleaded guilty and was fined $230, plus court costs. He was free again.

Desperate for cash, Joe and Mary applied for jobs as door-to-door Census Bureau enumerators at $5.50 per hour. They took the test, and on his application Joe answered no to questions asking if he had ever been arrested or if he was under investigation for a crime. Nonetheless, Joe and Mary did not get hired.

Joe also tried to sell 3,500 shares he and Diane owned in Securitron Magnalock Corp. of California for $2.60 each. He claimed he'd lost the stock certificate and applied for a new one. It wasn't a lot of money, but in Joe's financial condition, $9,100 seemed like a million.

Sometime in mid-October, Joe received a check in Cuddebackville "c/o Mrs. Bain." With the signatures of Joseph J. Pikul and Diane J. Pikul and the notation "for deposit only" written in on the back, the check was taken to a local bank, where an employee subsequently recognized the name and knew that Diane Pikul couldn't possibly have endorsed the check. The prospective stock buyer's check was returned, with the endorsement protested.

Juan R. Cabezas, Securitron's controller, immediately wrote Joe a letter, informing him that Diane's signatures on the affidavit and the check could not have been valid since she "died some time ago." Cabezas told Joe that if he was still interested in selling his stock, he should contact him so the proper documentation could be compiled.

Undeterred, Joe filed a new set of professionally prepared documents, naming himself as survivor of the joint tenantship of Joe and Diane Pikul. Joe claimed the "right of survivorship," even enclosing a copy of Diane's death certificate—which mentioned homicide as the cause of death, but not that he was a suspect. Meanwhile, the prospective buyer—an attorney—determined that under California law Joe wasn't guaranteed rights of survivorship.

Cabezas wrote Joe another letter. "It has come to our attention that you have been charged in the beating death of your wife, Diane J. Pikul, and a judgment has not yet been rendered in your murder trial." Cabezas told Joe there appeared to be only two ways that he could sell the stock: be acquitted of murder, or obtain an unqualified opinion from a New York attorney, "satisfactory to any potential purchaser," that he could convey good title on the shares.

Joe abandoned the stock sale scheme, and it was never determined who forged Diane's notarized signature or who helped Joe prepare the phony documents.

C H A P T E R • 22

Behind Closed Doors

THE LEGAL FOREPLAY IN *PEOPLE* v. *Joseph Pikul* reached an advanced stage on January 9, 1989, with the commencement of jury selection. As always with sensational cases, the process wasn't going to be an easy one, for it was tough finding people who hadn't made up their minds.

As the questioning of potential jurors dragged on, the lawyers met privately with Judge Byrne. As had been the case with much of the preceding civil and criminal matters involving Joe, what occurred behind closed doors was more interesting and more important than any of the public developments. As with the pretrial hearings, decisions made during these meetings would affect the direction, and very possibly the outcome, of the murder trial itself.

The parties still had to resolve the admissibility of testimony about Joe's cross dressing and incidents of violence in his past, issues that Prosecutor Joseph maintained pointed directly to Joe's motive. These matters had to be decided before the jury was selected because defense attorneys Bekoff and Worth needed to know whether they had to ask potential jurors about possible prejudices involving quirks like transvestism.

In one important session, Worth outlined six areas of concern: the cross-dressing issue in general; the photos and videotape of Joe dancing around and masturbating that had been introduced at the custody hearing; the letter that authorized Felder to turn the material over to police if Diane died under suspicious circumstances; Joe's comments to Investigator Composto about Diane having encouraged the cross dressing only to blackmail him with the photos; Sandy Jarvinen's intention to testify that Joe told her that Diane was trying to blackmail him; and the fact that Joe was wearing bra and panties when arrested.

Worth wanted all that information kept from the jury, even if Joe took the stand, declaring it all to be irrelevant. Even though Composto's testimony had been approved for use at trial, Worth argued that Joe's claim that Diane knew about the cross dressing and was "trying to hold it against him," was prejudicial, inflammatory, and did not clearly show a motive.

On the contrary, Joseph said Joe's statements to Composto about cross dressing "clearly indicate a motive . . . and should be admitted in that respect." The prosecutor said that although he was not required to prove motive, "We have the opportunity and are entitled to prove motive at any time that we deem appropriate. Motive is an important piece of evidence." Joe's statements to Sandy Jarvinen also pointed to motive, said Joseph. "The statements to the first wife indicated basically that the victim was blackmailing him, that whatever she had on him would have destroyed and humiliated him. . . . I think his statements to Detective Composto also allow that inference based on the fact that he did in fact say, 'my wife had pictures of me and she was using them against me.' I don't think that any of that testimony should be precluded on the People's direct case."

In view of the fact that all of the testimony at the state-police barracks had been thrown out, Prosecutor Joseph said he had no plans to introduce information about what Joe was wearing the night he was apprehended. As for the videotape and photos, Joseph said that based on Joe's numerous statements and the testimony at the custody hearings, "It's clear he was aware of the existence of both the video and the Polaroid pictures. Based on the statements that he made to Detective Composto, it's clear he was aware of the Polaroid pictures." Diane's accompanying note, which provided that the materials could be returned to Joe unless she died under suspicious circumstances, was further proof of motive, said Joseph, especially given the fact that Joe tried to steal the pictures from a bank box.

Judge Byrne moved swiftly through the items. He said he'd already passed judgment on Detective Composto's testimony and all of it was admissible. He also approved testimony from Sandy that Diane "had something on" Joe and was trying to blackmail him. There was no need to rule on any mention of Joe's attire the night he was arrested, since those investigators weren't going to be able to testify on the state's direct case.

That left the sex-related material. Generally, Judge Byrne ruled he was going to allow mention of cross dressing as it applied to motive. But, he continued, he was disallowing introduction of the photos, the videotape, Joe's attempts to retrieve the material, and the letter from Diane to Felder. "The inflammatory nature outweighs the probative value."

If Joe took the stand and denied cross dressing, however, the materials could be used to impeach his testimony, the judge ruled. From Joseph's perspective, Joe was locked in on that part of his private life; introduction of the filmed proof would be a lot worse.

Then Worth opened an entirely new line of inquiry, demanding to know what the prosecution intended to introduce on cross-examination in the event Joe took the stand in his own defense. Specifically, Worth was curious about Joe's 1973 assault arrest, his 1974 drug arrest, the recent driving arrests, any incriminating information that came out at the custody hearing, the civil contempt arrest after the second custody hearing, the alleged assaults on Mary Bain, any lies he told on the census application, the incident where Joe allegedly pushed Diane out of the car while pregnant, and the taping of Diane's telephone calls.

It was quite a list, but before anyone could comment on it, Alan Joseph added another item: "And dragging her around the house by the hair while she was nursing Blake."

Worth, of course, didn't want any of it brought in. Never quite certain of what the defense strategy was going to be, and realizing the difficulty in getting such prejudicial evidence admitted, Prosecutor Joseph said if Joe did take the stand, he wouldn't bring up the two-decade-old arrests, any evidence involving Mary Bain, the custody case, or anything that occurred after Joe's arrest for murder unless Joe said something on the stand to open the door to those areas.

Joseph said he did intend, however, to introduce Joe's "tapping the phone, pushing her out of the car, and dragging her by the hair." But Judge Byrne ruled that those three items also were too prejudicial and could not be introduced unless Joe took the stand and offered contradictory testimony.

Judge Byrne seemed to be bending over backward to make certain that everything not directly related to the murder be kept out.

A week later, as the laborious process of picking a jury continued, the lawyers met again with Judge Byrne. The main subject of discussion for this session was the possible testimony from the Sawoskas that might relate to motive. The defense team had requested that Joseph reveal precisely what the testimony would be. But the prosecutor balked, contending he was under no obligation to give away his case.

Under prodding from the judge, however, Joseph divulged that Joe had told Henry Sawoska he had "bad news from the doctor and was unable to tell his wife."

"He didn't get into what it was?" asked Judge Byrne.

"I don't think so. There are other people that Mr. Pikul has indicated he had AIDS," said Joseph matter-of-factly.

"*AIDS?*" asked a startled Judge Byrne.

Joseph said several witnesses, including Sandra Jarvinen, had been told by Joe that he had AIDS or had only five-to-seven years to live. Joe hadn't mentioned AIDS to his old college roommate, just that he "had a bad report from the doctor," said Joseph.

Bekoff knew if AIDS was mentioned before the jury, his client was sunk. The denizens of Orange County don't have the liberal bent of those in Manhattan or the Hamptons. Though not all of the jury candidates were showing up in blue jeans and flannel, they certainly weren't the type of people to cotton to a rich Wall Street cross dresser accused of fatally beating and strangling his wife.

"Judge, if there's going to be any testimony to AIDS, if Mr. Joseph plans to bring that out, I have a vehement objection to that and I think that the prejudice of that is just so overwhelming that I would move to preclude any statement that Mr. Pikul allegedly made to anyone that he had AIDS," said Bekoff.

"I'm going to object to that," said Joseph. "If the defendant told somebody that he had AIDS or was dying of an illness, I think that's material. It goes toward his motive as well.

"As I indicated on a number of occasions, one of the issues, or one of the theories the People contend, is that part of the motive for this homicide was the fact that he did not want Diane Pikul, the deceased, to obtain custody of his children and, as such, faced with the fact that she had pictures of him and a tape of his cross dressing, the fact that he was aware of this information and she was using it against him in order to ensure that she would retain custody during the course of the divorce situation and not the defendant, that the defendant's statement that he had AIDS indicates, again, that he has nothing more to lose. He did not want Diane Pikul to get custody of his children and I think after the court hears some of the testimony as it comes out from certain witnesses, it becomes even clearer.

"The defendant made extensive efforts to ensure that the victim would not get custody of his children and I think the AIDS issue—you can get AIDS from anything—could be a bad blood transfusion, any number of things," said Joseph. "The fact remains these are statements that the defendant made, he made to several witnesses, and I don't think that this is something that should be precluded."

Judge Byrne said he would think about it, but said his initial reaction was that if AIDS got mentioned—and it wasn't made clear that Joe got it from something like a blood transfusion, which no one was saying he did—then the inference would be left that the AIDS was related to Joe's cross dressing and sexual practices. If the witness simply testified that Joe told him he had "bad news from the doctor—cancer, kidney failure, or any other major illness that doesn't have the stigma attached to it—it would be an entirely different situation."

Joseph pleaded with Judge Byrne that if he was going to forbid mention of AIDS and prevent the witnesses from mentioning it, that he at least allow as a compromise all the testimony about Joe telling people he had five-to-seven years to live. "There's no prejudice with respect to that," said Joseph. "Again, it is important. If the defendant is dying and if his intention is to ensure that Diane Pikul does not get custody of the two children, then the motive for the homicide becomes clearer."

Preventing him from proposing a potential motive to the jury would be unfair, Joseph argued, especially in light of the fact that Joe's incriminating statements to the state-police investigators had already been thrown out. "You're dissecting the People's case to an extent where you're not letting me prove motive," said Joseph.

At least, Joseph reasoned once again, let him mention "that the defendant has stated that he got bad news from the doctor, which is one statement that he made to somebody, or that he didn't have long to live, which is another statement, or that he was dying from an illness. Again, he did make these statements."

"Judge, my response is simple," Bekoff fired back. "AIDS is such an explosive situation. If we're going to convict this man of murder based on the fact he cross-dressed, based on the fact he told people he had AIDS, I have to look at what country I'm in."

Prosecutor Joseph quickly interjected: "We're trying to convict him because he murdered a woman and he's admitted he murdered a woman. Let's put things right on the table."

Judge Byrne said he was concerned the AIDS would be "locked in with" the cross dressing and would therefore unfairly be prejudicial to Joe. "He runs the possibility of being convicted because of cross dressing, AIDS, and other things that are not looked upon with the greatest favor by a large cross section of the general population. If you're going to prove him guilty beyond a reasonable doubt of murder, let's prove him on the basis of murder, not on the basis of something that's highly prejudicial."

The prosecutor then reverted to the subject of at least introducing Joe's statements about having five-to-seven years to live, contending a doctor could tell someone that for a wide range of terminal illnesses.

Judge Byrne continued to balk, so against his better

wishes, Joseph was forced to unveil a key element of his case as it related to motive. "The defendant met with his ex-wife, Sandra Jarvinen, prior to the homicide. He gave her a will. He wanted her to take custody of the kids. He did not want Diane Pikul to have the kids. When his ex-wife told him, 'You've got to be nuts, I can't be guardian, Diane Pikul is your wife if you die,' this is when he told her he had AIDS—one of many people. She said, 'If you die, she's the natural guardian,' and he said, 'Well, then she's going to have to have an accident.' He did not want her to have custody of those children under any circumstances. The fact that he was dying and the fact that he did not want her to have custody under any circumstances—he tells the Sawoskas he's dying, he tells a number of other people he has a terminal illness, again—is another factor that I contend, the People contend, entered into his intention to murder Diane Pikul."

The reason he had not brought the issue up before, Joseph said, was his concern for Sandy's safety. If anything happened to Sandy before she testified, he was going to hold Joe responsible "because this man has attempted to kill her on a number of occasions when they were married. . . . He has beat her up, he has put her in a hospital, she is deathly afraid of this man.

"I cannot put armed guards around this woman until we start the trial in this case. There's just no way I can do that. That's why I was hesitant beforehand to bring this forth. But you're now dissecting my case piece by piece and taking away—"

"Wait a minute," Judge Byrne huffed back. "I'm not dissecting it. You have a responsibility and the burden of proof is with the People, and if the man is going to be convicted, I have a responsibility to see that he's convicted on what the charge is, and not on something that comes in that is so inflammatory that it would lead the jury to that conclusion based on the inflammatory nature of these side issues."

Bekoff asked for a hearing on possible testimony involving Joe's illness and said he also wanted to see the will Joe had shown Sandy. Joseph said he didn't intend to introduce the will, just testimony that Joe showed the will to Sandy. "That's why he wanted to meet her and that's the discussion, 'I don't want Diane Pikul to get custody of the children.' It goes to his motive." However, Joseph continued, if Joe took the stand and tried to impeach Sandy's story about their meeting to discuss the will and custody of the children, he then would produce the document. "There's no other way she could have gotten a will in Pikul's name."

There would be no hearing. Judge Byrne ruled that Joseph could introduce testimony about Joe having shown Sandy the will, but only as it pertained to Joe's not wanting Diane to have custody of the children, his asking Sandy to be their guardian, and his saying Diane would have to have an accident after Sandy explained that she couldn't be guardian. For now the will itself would not be introduced. Even though the prosecutor again was being restricted, Joseph had at least gained the threat of being able to bring in the additional evidence. If Joe did take the stand, he wouldn't be able to deny the meeting with Sandy, or the new will would be brought in.

Joseph seemed to lose so many of these points. But in a way, the prosecutor was winning. Every ruling left Joe less room to maneuver. If he and his lawyers failed to safely wiggle through the mine field of incriminating evidence, the more damaging information would be brought in from the sidelines.

The battle lines had finally been drawn.

PART · VI

THE TRIAL

CHAPTER • 23

Back-Room Bargaining

"HELLO, DON," SAID THE BEARDED, bespectacled man walking through the lobby of the Orange County Government Center. Feeling a hand on his shoulder, Don Whitmore turned around. It was his son-in-law, grinning broadly, as if he didn't have a care in the world.

"Hi, Joe," Whitmore replied coolly.

"He always tries to stop and talk to me," the easygoing gent later explained. "Thinking that I'm not going to have to put up with him much longer, I say hello. I hate his guts, but what can I do? I've had thoughts about how I could take care of him, but I'm figuring the courts will."

The trial of *People* v. *Joseph Pikul* was finally underway.

Jury selection had taken three weeks, but the drudgery ended with a panel of eleven men and one woman selected under a defense strategy calling for as few females as possible. The process had been an arduous one, so boring that on one particularly tedious day, Joe wished aloud for a bed next to the defense table. Bekoff had planned to ask that the trial be moved to another county on the grounds that excess publicity made it impossible to pick an impartial jury. But when Joe looked the final panel over, he liked what he saw. "They'll be fair," he told Bekoff.

There were fifty-five names on Alan Joseph's prospective witness list; Claudia, now an officer of her fifth-grade class and a staffer on the school newspaper, and Blake, in kindergarten, were not among them. That was good news since the children were already going through a grilling from their classmates following a Pikul update on the Fox Network's "A Current Affair" program. Several had recognized the Pikul children in the film clip and the next day confronted Claudia and Blake with statements like: "Hey, I hear your father murdered your mother." The classmates didn't mean any harm, kids being kids. But they made a terrible time worse for the two innocent children.

Alan Lloyd Joseph, a dark-haired man in his early thirties, stood up and outlined his case for the jury.

"The defendant, Joseph Pikul, and his wife, Diane Pikul, were on the verge of a divorce. They left New York City for Long Island for their summer home in Amagansett in separate cars on Friday, October 23, 1987. They left the city in separate cars, separate times. The defendant, Joseph Pikul, arrived earlier in Amagansett with their two children. He had driven his 1984 Mazda. Diane Pikul left later that evening and she left in their 1986 Buick station wagon. You will hear from witnesses that the defendant claims that Diane Pikul arrived at the Long Island summer home in Amagansett at approximately 1:00 to 1:30 in the morning on Saturday, October 24, 1987. You'll also hear that they had a slight verbal argument and that was the last time that anyone saw her alive."

Joseph proceeded to lead the jury through the events that culminated with the discovery of Diane Pikul's body in a drainage ditch off the New York Thruway: the visit to the hardware store, the drive to the Sawoskas, Joe's trip to Sandy Jarvinen and what he told her, his meandering through New England that weekend, the final dumping of the body, and Joe's bizarre actions at the car wash. Last but not least, they learned of the determination from the autopsy and the incriminating statements Joe volunteered to police officers.

"Now," Joseph concluded, "the outline which was drawn for you in this opening will be filled in by various witnesses and they'll paint a picture for you which will leave no reasonable doubt in your minds as to the guilt of Joseph Pikul for the crime of murder in the second degree. Thank you."

Joseph, with only four murder trials to verdict under his belt, was relatively brief and had supplied a bonus to boot.

The existence of Sandra Jarvinen had been kept a secret throughout months of high-profile publicity.

Warning the jurors that opening statements are not part of the evidence, Ron Bekoff responded to Joseph's comments by saying that his reaction, "as yours should be, is: 'prove it.' " He asked the jury to put the case "under a microscope, to look for a reasonable doubt. . . . It's presumptuous for me now to get up and say there's going to be a reasonable doubt. Just as perhaps as presumptuous for someone to get up here to say there isn't a reasonable doubt, because you haven't heard anything yet. So what I'm asking you to do is to be fair. What I'm asking you to do is to pay attention and give us the good honest shot, the feeling that this is America and we can get a fair trial, irregardless of cameras in the courtroom, irregardless of watching what you might have heard or seen in the newspapers, and I think you can do it, each and every one of you, because that's why you're on the jury.

"I particularly want you to keep an eye on the tenor and the focus of the police investigation. Were they trying to find out what really happened? Was it a search for the truth? Or were they looking for an arrest, an easy arrest of an eccentric individual?"

Before Joseph's first witness, Sandy Jarvinen, was called to the stand, Bekoff requested another private meeting with the judge. Once again, what wasn't being said in open court was more important than what was.

In Judge Byrne's chambers, Bekoff observed that Sandy had repeatedly volunteered in her grand jury testimony and statements to police that over the years Joe "had injured her, had hurt her."

"Furthermore, in reading these materials, every other line it's posed that she would volunteer to say that she was afraid of Joe Pikul—she had looked at the clock because she was afraid of Joe Pikul, looked out her window because she was afraid of Joe Pikul. It goes on and on like that. . . . I'm asking the Court to instruct Mr. Joseph, since he's responsible for the witness, to curtail that. It's not admissible and to warn his witness, a highly educated woman who's a professional, not to indulge in this type of behavior while she's testifying on the stand."

Alan Joseph interjected that it was he who had originally raised the issue and had tried to keep such statements out of the grand jury. He promised to try to keep them out of the trial. But, Joseph continued, some testimony about Joe's violence to Sandy would be necessary to explain her motive for having originally lied to the police about Joe's visit to her house after the murder.

The prosecutor said he could live with Sandy simply stating that she lied because she was afraid of Joe, provided the defense attorneys didn't open the door more. "This is an individual who was a battered spouse for the better part of fifteen or nineteen years of marriage to the defendant," Joseph said. "Based on my observation and discussions with her she was genuinely afraid of him, she is afraid of him to this day, and therefore I don't think it would be proper to prohibit her from basically indicating the reasons for her actions."

Judge Byrne said that Sandy could say "she was in fear of him, period." He said additional statements would be allowed depending on what she was asked on cross-examination. Further, the judge said, Sandy was to be instructed "not to respond in such a way that she comes out with, 'I was afraid, I was afraid, I was afraid' so as to overemphasize this aspect of the matter. If we get into that, we're going to have some problems."

Bekoff was not swayed. "The court and Mr. Joseph is telling me, 'We'll hold some of it out on direct, but if you go in there and ask what you have to ask on cross-examination about any inconsistency or anything that she didn't do with the police, then I'm opening a door to having abuse come in. . . .' If we can bring in testimony that he battered his former wife some fifteen, seventeen, eighteen years ago, it's devastating. We're charged here with a violent murder. We can't be in a vacuum. We know the Joel Steinberg jury is out. There isn't a person on the East Coast that doesn't know about Hedda Nussbaum. How can we take that chance?"

"I'm not saying we're taking that chance," said Judge Byrne. "I'm not going to make a determination until we get there."

Back in the courtroom, it didn't take long for Alan Joseph to plant the seeds of a guilty verdict in the minds of the jurors. Sandy Jarvinen was going to be a crucial witness, one who could set the tone and pace for the entire trial.

Joe's first wife explained that she was self-employed, doing secretarial work, accounting, managing money, and "real-estate deals." Because of the numerous rulings, the jury heard a great deal about Sandy's life with Joe, but nothing about the dark side of the relationship—the beatings, the mysterious car accident, Joe's attack with a statue.

Sandy was asked to relate the series of calls between her and Joe in August and September 1987, during which Joe had said he was unhappy, that Diane was never around and was sleeping with someone else. "He claimed that she wasn't taking proper care of the children and he didn't know who was with them when he was out of town, that she was blackmailing him. He was just generally very upset." One night in particular, Sandy said, Joe called her crying, "and he said that he was dying."

Without discussing the illness any further, Sandy said their meeting on Cape Cod was convened in part so that Joe could discuss his estate with her, especially the custody of his children.

Being careful, Joseph prompted Sandy with a handful of narrowly focused questions, starting with why Joe didn't want Diane to have custody of Claudia and Blake. "He didn't feel that his wife would take good care of the children," Sandy said. "He had asked if I would be their guardian and trustee, and I explained to him that I could not be their guardian, that his wife was the guardian of the children if he passed away. And he made the statement that she'd have to have an accident."

"What was your response?" Joseph asked.

"I just said, 'Don't be ridiculous.' "

Sandy explained how Joe continued to call her after that meeting, sometimes from Europe. "There was no conversation. I would pick up the phone and he would speak: 'She's out again. I don't know where the children are. She's been out five nights now, different baby-sitters every night,' and then hang up the phone."

Then, Sandy explained, she came to New York City on Thursday, October 22, 1987, to discuss settlement of her civil suit for back alimony. Although she acknowledged the lawsuit never got discussed, she neglected to say what they did talk about. With all the restrictions, some of her testimony sounded very incomplete, which, of course, it was.

When it came to the calls and the visit the day after the murder, Sandy was equally incomplete, even though Joseph had no restrictions on that portion of her testimony. This time it was Sandy who was guarded; and understandably so after years of being battered. Deep down inside, Sandy knew that she could have been Joe's victim. (In fact, when the story of Diane's murder broke, a man from New York had called Prosecutor Joseph to say he had lived next door to the Pikuls and that Sandy had frequently sought refuge in his apartment when Joe attacked her. The man hadn't read the stories carefully enough to realize that Sandy was not the dead Mrs. Pikul.) With Joe still on the loose, Sandy could not be sure she would not still be a victim.

Afraid to look directly at her ex-husband, Sandy swore she had no idea what Joe wanted to hide while talking to him on the phone, but assumed it was just an asset, like the kind he'd hidden from her during their bitter divorce. Then she dropped her bombshell, telling the jury that Joe had told her: "I had to eliminate her."

Sandy also repeated her line about having a "high water table," which drew a chuckle from spectators. She went on to relate that she had lied to police when they first knocked on her door because she was afraid of what Joe might do to her. But again because of the restrictions, that was all she could say.

When Bekoff got his chance the next day, he almost immediately sought to attack Sandy on her alimony suit. Bekoff focused on her motive for conning Joe into sending her the $500 check so the statute of limitations was removed. Sandy claimed she only found out after the fact that the timing of the $500 check enabled her to file her lawsuit.

"You realized, did you not, by getting Joe to pay that $500, that stopped the statute of limitations and let you sue, did you not?" Bekoff asked.

"That was a moot point," said Sandy. "It could or it couldn't. That was for the courts to decide."

"Well, it wasn't a moot point, because you went and hired an attorney shortly thereafter," said Bekoff.

Joseph objected to Bekoff's argumentative tone and Judge Byrne sustained.

"Isn't it a fact, ma'am, that after he paid you that $500, shortly thereafter you went and hired a New York attorney and sued him?" asked Bekoff.

"I already answered that question and I told you, yes, I did," said Sandy.

"And isn't it true you were aware of the statute-of-limitations problem before that occurred?"

"I don't recall being aware of it before speaking with the attorney," Sandy said.

As Bekoff pressed ahead, Sandy was forced to admit that she'd won a $28,000 settlement, plus interest. But, she added, the case wasn't settled in her mind because she hadn't received her money.

"You're annoyed at Joe for not paying you that money, aren't you?" asked Bekoff. Sandy insisted she was not.

Bekoff let it drop. He had raised a legitimate ethical point about Sandy, but Sandy wasn't on trial. All she did was run an end-around on a legal technicality to get money that was due her anyway. Would the jury really care?

After focusing on the calls from Joe during the summer of 1987, Bekoff zeroed in on the Cape Cod meeting. "And he told you, did he not, that he was considering changing his will?" asked Bekoff.

"He said he *was* changing his will," replied Sandy.

"And that he was going to—"

"Excuse me, Your Honor," said Joseph, cutting off Bekoff. "May we approach?"

The prosecutor was livid. His hands had been tied concerning the will, and here was Bekoff mentioning the will for his own purposes.

The lawyers approached for a conference out of the jury's earshot. "Your Honor, I'm objecting to this line of questioning," whispered Joseph. "We had extensive conversations both in chambers during the course of the jury selection as well as the other day and prior to Miss Jarvinen's testimony. And defense counsel objected to anything regarding the will coming in, anything regarding the spending of money or the way money was set out. The only substance of conversation that it was decided I was entitled to bring out about that conversation between defendant and Miss Jarvinen at Cape Cod, Hyannis Airport, had to do with the issue of custody of the children. At this point in time, what I feel is that I'm being sandbagged by defense."

Bekoff tried to explain. "The only thing I'm trying to bring out—and I'm not going over any documents or anything like that—is he brought out that Joe was trying to make Sandy the guardian of the children, thereby excluding Diane. I think I have a right to just say, 'Didn't he also ask her to set up a trust, a third for Diane, a third for each child?', to negate that. . . . If he's allowed to go on with the guardian to show the exclusion of Diane, I'm allowed to show there's a trust for Diane, that he meant to include it."

Judge Byrne said he recalled there being an agreement that everyone was going to stay away from the will, other than "the guardianship aspect of it." If Bekoff was allowed to bring in what he wanted to about the will, it would look like Joseph had withheld certain information, so Judge Byrne said he would sustain the prosecutor's objection.

But Bekoff still wanted to say the new will provided for a one-third trust for Diane. "Then there's no sandbagging."

"No," answered Joseph. "Because they're still going to get the impression that I was keeping it from them. Again, if you're going to start getting into any of that, then we're going to get into the entire conversation."

"That's where you come in with AIDS," said Judge Byrne.

"You come in with AIDS, with everything," Joseph warned.

Judge Byrne said he'd restricted Joseph enough and was not going to budge further. Joe's asking Sandy to be the guardian for Claudia and Blake would be allowed, but AIDS would remain out and the will would be out.

When the search for the truth resumed in public, Bekoff got Sandy to admit that she really didn't believe Joe when he said Diane would have to have an accident. But she did believe Joe when he said he called home five nights in a row from Europe and talked to a different baby-sitter every night.

She admitted giving Joe a $750 bill in New York the day before the murder, and that the bill included her purchase of a $300 dress from a shop in Boston. "I didn't have that many clothes," Sandy explained. But she denied knowledge of her lawyer-friend Federico supposedly getting $15,000 from Joe.

Bekoff also challenged Sandy about Joe's visit to her home the day after the murder. Sandy had testified earlier that Joe called saying he had "something to hide." Bekoff pointed out that when she testified before the grand jury less than two months after Diane's death, she said: "I received a phone call in the early evening and he said he had something to *bury* and he asked if he could bury it at my place."

Sandy protested that her grand jury testimony had been incorrect, "because he did not use the word 'bury,' he said 'hide,' on recollection in the past year."

"Was your recollection of that phone call better now than it was two months after it happened?" asked Bekoff. Sandy said it was not. "But yet you thought it was 'bury' then and you think it's 'hide' now?"

"Yes," said Sandy, explaining that she realized the error after reading her grand jury testimony.

Moving on, Bekoff pressed hard on Sandy's explanation for having erased her answering machine tapes. "I never keep my tapes. They're always erased at the end of the day when I get all my business messages that come in on them. . . . Why would I keep them?"

"Why?" Bekoff asked back. "You say your ex-husband came up, you say he said words to the effect to you that 'he eliminated her,' you say you talked about hiding a body, and then he calls you and talks about not hiding a body in a spot because it's not a good site and you have it on tape and you want to know why?"

Joseph objected and the judge sustained. But Bekoff—having extracted a reason for the erasures other than Sandy's fear of Joe—couldn't resist continuing. "You erased the tape yourself, ma'am?"

"I do every day," said Sandy.

"Before you spoke to the police?"

"Yes," said Sandy.

"Do you get calls every day about people burying bodies or packages?" Bekoff demanded.

"No, sir," said Sandy, glancing over Bekoff's shoulder for help from Joseph.

"There was nothing special about the tape? Look at me, not him, please."

"Obviously there was, but I can't put myself back there," said Sandy. "I erased it."

The grilling so unnerved Sandy that at one point, Judge Byrne had to declare a recess. "Let her calm down, think things out."

"I'm sorry, Your Honor. I'm so confused," Sandy apologized. She later told the judge she suffered from tachycardia, an abnormally fast heartbeat.

It was an ugly moment, but a typical daily scene in courtrooms across the land—witness against lawyer, justice regardless of truth, anything to make the jury disbelieve Joe had said "I had to eliminate her."

For the next two weeks, the trial featured a parade of the expected corps of witnesses: dental receptionist Patricia Sarlo, the deli man where Joe bought the ice, the cops in East Hampton, the car-wash contingent, the Exxon gas-station attendant, the Newburgh cops. The jurors listened to all of that evidence in the context of Sandy's introductory testimony.

As each witness filled in their little piece of the circumstantial puzzle, Joe alternated between attentiveness and indifference. Some days he would listen to every word. Other times he appeared ashen, slumped over, elbows on table, leaning against his right hand. Whenever testimony was particularly damaging to his cause, he pulled out color photos of Claudia and Blake from his breast pocket. He would stare longingly at them, sometimes for twenty minutes at a stretch, as if to explain, "This is why I did it."

One court officer stood watch to the left of Joe, another sat directly behind the witness stand, across the room.

Joseph had Barbara Weingarden of New Jersey and the Hamptons testify about her phone conversation with Diane at her office on the night she died, and to identify three beach towels that she recognized from the times she and her daughter had gone swimming at the Pikul home on Windmill Lane. More pieces of Joseph's circumstantial puzzle, the towels appeared to be from a set—gray and white stripes on each towel with a single, different-colored third stripe—red, yellow, or blue.

Marshall Weingarden also testified, relating his phone conversation with Joe the morning after the murder. In the course of recounting Joe's tale of woe, the witness worked in the fact that Joe had interjected: "And I had a bad report from a doctor." Under cross-examination, Bekoff got Mr. Weingarden to acknowledge that Joe told him Diane had grown angry because she knew he had been checking up on her, plus the fact that he'd found condoms and that he suspected she had a boyfriend.

The hardware-store manager testified about Joe's spending spree, and Prosecutor Joseph took the opportunity to introduce several shopping bags of evidence, including the rope, the gloves, and the flashlight.

Appearing in black dress and white pearls, Ann Stern from *Harper's* told the jury how she'd arrived at work the Monday after Diane disappeared and, when told that Diane had not arrived, grabbed her colleague's Rolodex. Under cross-examination, Stern acknowledged that she had never met or spoken to Joe Pikul and never saw any injuries on Diane. Asked to describe her social relationship with her slain colleague, Stern said Diane had taken her to lunch once. "That was the extent of outside the office socializing." Asked what Diane was wearing when she left her office that Friday night, Stern provided an elaborate description of Diane's "Kenzo outfit." Turning her head up, and to the jury box, Stern explained: "Kenzo is a Japanese designer."

Louise Sawoska was subpoenaed to testify, but her only new tidbit was a claim that the Pikuls had stopped coming to football games with them "because Diane didn't like football."

Then the attorneys adjourned for yet another closed-door meeting to squabble about the next witness, Louise's husband Henry.

In reviewing Sawoska's grand jury testimony, Bekoff had come across Joe's call to Henry in August 1987 to tell him he had a terminal illness. Bekoff noted that he didn't see much difference between testimony about AIDS and testimony about terminal illness. "At one point he says to Henry Sawoska, 'I have bad news, the doctor said it's five months to five years,' " said Bekoff. "I'd ask that that part be excluded because that's clearly the symptoms of AIDS. If you can't say that he's suffering from AIDS, why allow him to give the symptoms of AIDS?"

"Why don't you leave it terminal illness?" Judge Byrne suggested. Everyone marched back to their places, and Henry Sawoska took the stand.

After providing background on his long relationship with Joe Pikul, Sawoska answered several narrowly focused questions about Joe's call in August of 1987.

"During the course of that conversation did he tell you that he was dying of a terminal illness?" asked Joseph.

"Yes, he did tell me that."

"Did he tell you that he couldn't tell his wife?"

"That's correct, he told me that," said Sawoska. Then the subject was dropped. Once again the most damaging testimony would not be heard.

When it came to the discussion Joe and Henry had had in the basement of the Sawoskas' New Windsor home, the jurors got to hear a bit more. The two men talked about three subjects, according to Henry: the Black Monday stock-market crash, Joe's terminal illness, and Diane's supposed abrupt departure the night before. "Basically he said she had left and also that he had found a condom under the bed, that he realized she had a boyfriend and also that she had left him several times before."

As he had done with Sandy Jarvinen, Bekoff made sure on cross-examination that he pinned Sawoska down on the fact he couldn't swear that there was a body in the trunk. For some reason the defense felt it important to argue that the children and Diane's body were never together, and that Joe had not spent the entire weekend carting the corpse around.

Sawoska was willing to concede only partially about the body. He acknowledged that he had not seen a green tarp sticking out while unloading the station wagon, but added that "it was dark back there."

With a recess in testimony, reporters questioned the parties about Joe's supposed illness, but got nowhere.

Worth said he couldn't discuss the matter, and Joseph said he had no idea of the status of Joe's health. It sounded bogus anyway—like Joe telling Sandy, who wanted her alimony money, that he was dying.

Regardless of the side skirmishes, Joseph continued to assemble his case piece by piece, as circumstantial cases always are.

Carina Jacobson, who had baby-sat for the Pikuls several nights a week and some weekends for six years, testified that she'd run into Joe at a party about two weeks before the murder and he told her, "Diane wanted a divorce and he was afraid of losing the children." She also recounted how Joe had told her Diane was with a boyfriend on Long Island when she went to the Sixth Avenue apartment the Monday after the murder. Starting to cry, Carina identified several beach towels and said the tarpaulin looked like a green cloth Joe used as a car cover for the Mazda.

Under cross-examination, Carina admitted she was closer to Diane than Joe and that she and her partner Inga Davidson had not repaid Joe any profits from his investment in their business. But, she contended, that was because of insufficient profits. Bekoff also pointed out that Joe had asked for his investment back since the arrest, but that Carina had refused. Seeking to defuse any supposed intent to murder on Joe's part, Bekoff also got Carina to acknowledge that Joe had called her the day before Diane's death to ask her to baby-sit out in the Hamptons that weekend. Carina said it was true that she had declined because of other plans.

Marjorie Goldsmith, the director of Blake's nursery school, testified about her chat with Joe and Diane several days before the murder, relating how they discussed the impending divorce and the consequences it would have on the children. She also related that when she met with Joe after Diane's disappearance, he had talked about Diane's friends being from AA, his belief she had a boyfriend, how Diane "went out in the yard for a walk" after the fight and never returned, and how Diane had said she was afraid of ending up fifty, alone and broke.

A teary-eyed Inga Davidson recounted identifying Diane's body at the morgue. Pressed to admit that Detective

Glynn was not really a "social friend" when he came by for pizza in the midst of the police investigation, Inga said she "wouldn't call it a lie." Treading very softly, but still trying to sound indignant, Bekoff made his point. But again it was hard to imagine the jurors getting enraged about such a police tactic.

Then Joe got a taste of his own medicine as the jurors heard his nervous, stammering voice on the tapes secretly recorded by East Hampton police dispatcher Harry Field and "John Clancy" up in Newburgh.

Step by step, the case was being built.

C H A P T E R · 24

A Rummage Sale of Evidence

JOE SEEMED TO BE HOLDING up fairly well to the rigors of the criminal trial. He arrived on Ash Wednesday with his forehead blessed, waited for court to convene by eating Peanut M&Ms and reading the *New York Post*.

He always sat at the left end of the defense table, the farthest position from the jury. He came to court every day wearing a suit and sometimes the smell of alcohol as well. Mary Bain Pikul, who attended frequently, was likewise stylishly attired, often with bright red lipstick and a smirk. She sat in the left-hand corner of the first row, directly behind her husband.

Joe had another supporter in the court nearly every day, a garish-looking woman who alternately claimed to be Blaze Starr, the famous New Orleans stripper, and a psychic from Egypt named Samira Starr. Joe and Mary both regularly confided in "Blaze," and on days when Mary couldn't attend, "Blaze" moved up from the rear of the courtroom to Mary's spot in the front row.

Behind the scenes, Joe's lawyers kept up their fight to prevent incriminating evidence from being brought before the jury. Joseph wanted to introduce the Securitron stock scheme, contending Joe had committed a forgery. Worth objected strenuously, contending the incident should be kept from the jury "as a matter of fundamental fairness . . . where the forgery concerns the supposed signature of his deceased wife, Diane Pikul, the very woman he's accused of murdering." Judge Byrne disallowed the evidence.

The trial entered a decisive stage as Joseph called forth the state police on Long Island, the cops from the Village, the forensic experts, and the identification investigators.

As they had at the pretrial hearing, Bekoff and Worth tried to put the police witnesses on trial. And as before, they pressed on the topic of *when* Joe had become a suspect. Although this tactic hadn't worked with Judge Byrne at the hearing, the strategy was worth another shot with the jury. In addition, there was always the possibility that even more evidence of police misconduct would be uncovered. The tactic was not without risk in the conservative, law-and-order region, though. So the best the defense lawyers felt they could hope for was to soften up the jury for the rest of their strategy.

The testimony of Senior Investigator Donald P. Delaney of the New York State Police was a case in point. Bekoff asked Delaney what he thought about Joe after he, Glynn, and Bowen had chatted with the defendant. "I considered him a suspect," Delaney said matter-of-factly. But it didn't sound as though a shocking constitutional sin had been committed. Instead, Delaney came across as having concluded what any reasonably intelligent person would have after listening to Joe ramble back and forth that night. How could Joe not have been a suspect?

This time around, Detective Composto, who had since retired, studied his lines excellently. He knew what state he was in and knew precisely which states Joe Pikul had visited. Composto explained he'd read his notes before coming to court and assured Bekoff that he'd been mistaken last time when he mentioned Maine. What Composto didn't tell the jury was that his colleague Glynn and half the Orange County DA's office had good-naturedly given him a hard time about his pretrial foul-up.

Forensic testimony provided an insightful view of how tiny details can help tie up loose ends in a circumstantial case.

Much attention was given to the discovery and eventual seizure of the condoms at the Windmill Lane house by state-police Inspector Roger Chillemi of the state-police

ID section. Most of the condoms were Ramses Extra Reservoir, but Worth seemed most interested in the ones bearing the brand name Gold Tex.

As the testimony unfolded, the defense team brought up the name Gold Tex with virtually every law enforcement official who knew about Joe's condom story. Each time the question was asked, the witness replied that Joe had never mentioned the brand name. As an aside, Chillemi also explained that the search of the house had failed to turn up any sign of the dozen bags of ice.

Investigator Kenneth T. Jones testified about the materials recovered at the car wash. As item after item was introduced into evidence, many in brown paper bags, the courtroom well began to take on the appearance of a bazaar. "It's a rummage sale," Worth joked at one point.

During his two days on the stand, Jones also testified at length about his work at the Thruway site where Diane's body had been found. Sounding and looking like a polished college professor, Jones captivated the jury members with his firm and professional testimony about the condition of the body, the items found with it, and the series of ropes found inside and out of the tarpaulin. It was pretty strong stuff, and even though Jones would eventually acknowledge that he found nothing to connect Joe to the scene, Joe's visit to the nearby car wash and his leaving the children so close at the Sawoskas had pointed a finger strongly his way.

Sporting a red power tie and a fashionable gray suit, Jones didn't guess at his facts; he asked if he could refer to his carefully prepared notes—eight pages, marked Exhibit 117. Through Jones, Prosecutor Joseph introduced a series of photos of the Thruway scene—surface views, aerial views, and several close-ups of Diane's body.

As Jones discussed the ligatures and photos, Joe sat with his hands folded in front of him, as if praying, then he dropped eight of his fingers, pressing the two index fingers to his bearded chin. Like everyone else in the courtroom, Joe was mesmerized by the details. Unlike so much of the trial testimony, Joe also was learning of this for the first time.

Of the three towels identified by Barbara Weingarden, Jones had recovered two of them from the car-wash dumpster. He said he got the third from inside the tarp that held Diane's body. They all bore the same brand name—C.O.L.O.R.S.—and carried a tag that said "100% cotton, made in Brazil."

Also, analysis of fibers from the terrycloth belt used to tie up Diane were consistent with those contained in the peach Hotel Ritz robe recovered from Windmill Lane.

A fingerprint expert as well, Jones sought to explain why the police had not recovered any fingerprints on the towels, tarp, plastic sheet, knife handle, ligatures, or shotgun: most of the materials had been quite wet and heavily soiled. In several instances, tests to recover trace evidence for hair, fibers, and secretion, which can be destroyed by a fingerprint test, were deemed to be potentially more important, Jones said.

Under questioning, however, Jones admitted that only two items had been submitted to the lab to check for latent fingerprints—the station wagon and shotgun.

As the evidence became more graphic, several members of the jury started to squirm. When one of them gagged, the judge offered a cup of water and apologized: "That's the best I can do right now." Joe, too, began moving around in his chair, drawing the attention of the court officer stationed nearby.

Joseph's assistant brought in two more boxes of cord, rope, and clothing. Exhibit 127 was a portion of the coated cord that had been tied directly around Diane's neck sometime before she had been placed in the tarp. It contained tiny filaments inside the outer coating, while the cord attached to the car tarp appeared to be telephone wire and contained four distinct colored strands. Jones said the ligature had been removed during the autopsy.

Jones also testified about fingernail clippings removed from Diane's body during the autopsy, one from each finger, and stated that a hair sample also had been taken. For good measure, Jones produced a photo of the Swatch watch removed from Diane's wrist, and stated that it had been working at the time.

Joseph called two more forensic analysts to bolster the scientific aspects of his presentation.

Investigator Edward Pilus, a fingerprint expert, testified

that the blade of the knife recovered at the car wash was clean and that the surface texture of the knife handle was not ideally suited for a fingerprint test. He admitted on cross-examination that a field investigator had requested that the knife handle be tested for latent prints, but Pilus contended that following a visual inspection of the handle's textured surface, he decided not to bother. "It's my discretion," Pilus explained. "In this case it would have been a waste of time."

Worth disagreed. He contended, and Pilus eventually conceded, that the handle was a composite material, implying it was smooth enough to have been chemically tested. To help make his point, Worth passed the knife around to the jurors for examination.

Pilus didn't give much more. He said the "somewhat textured surface was totally unreceptive to fingerprints" and maintained that a surface's susceptibility to a print test depended on the type of composition.

Worth wanted to know if it would have been impossible to get a print off the knife. "Highly improbable," said Pilus.

"So improbable that it wasn't even worth dusting that knife to see if it was there?" Worth asked.

"Correct," said Pilus, adding in response to an additional question that he was willing to state "absolutely and unequivocally" that there were no partial prints anywhere on the knife.

Forensic scientist David Innella then testified that he found a human hair, red cotton fibers, white cotton fibers, gray synthetic fibers, light blue synthetic fibers, animal hair, and vegetation on the left glove recovered at the car wash. He said the root of the hair was intact and could have fallen out naturally.

More to the point, he said tests indicated that the hair on the glove, the four human hairs found in the car-vac debris, and the hair found on the terrycloth belt used to wrap Diane's wrists could have come from the same head as the hair sample taken from Diane's body at the autopsy.

Innella, a balding elderly man, also said he'd found "grains of sandlike material" in the hair sample from the autopsy.

The fibers from the terrycloth belt found tied around

Diane's wrist were similar in color and nap size—four millimeters—to the fibers contained in the peach bathrobe confiscated at the Pikul home in the Hamptons, Innella said. The knife found in the car-wash garbage can appeared to be from the same set as the knife seized by police from the Pikul kitchen in Amagansett.

Innella said his tests detected glitter in the contents of a vacuum from the Windmill Lane house and in the pink rug recovered with Diane's body; he also found glitter— along with sand and vegetation—in the rug sample taken from the recessed well area of the back of the station wagon.

The prosecutor and Innella also focused on lab samples and items that were taken to be tested for blood. Innella explained the procedure. The initial test is to see if the stain is blood. If that is positive and there is a sufficient sample size, a test is conducted to determine if the blood is human. If that test is positive and there is a sufficient sample to conduct the next level of analysis, a test is conducted to determine blood type.

There was no blood on Diane's clothing, the tarp, or the towels, according to Innella. He also said there was no blood on the broken tooth or on the knife with the nicked tip. The substance recovered from the door jamb at the Amagansett home was blood—human blood for that matter, he said. But the sample size was insufficient to determine blood type.

A stain on one of Diane's ligatures also was human blood. But Innella continued that it couldn't be tested for blood type because the cord was embedded in the neck tissues of the victim.

The material scraped from one of the ten fingernail clippings taken at the autopsy—the left pinkie—also tested positive for blood. But Innella said a test could not be performed to determine if it was human blood because of insufficient sample size. The witness noted that the fingernail clippings did positively contain sand, however, another indication Diane's body had come in direct contact with the beach.

The testimony had been impressive, but what did it mean? The crucial questions remained unanswered: Was it Joe's blood under Diane's fingernails? Whose blood was on the door jamb? How long had it been there? With Diane having the most common Type O, test results wouldn't have been that conclusive anyway.

The failure of these tests led to the inescapable conclusion that the prosecution was going to try to convict Joe Pikul of murder without stating precisely where the murder took place.

It was possible that Joe's confession about the beach scenario had been actually inspired by the previous murder there. Perhaps Joe had been trying to throw everyone off with his confession.

But as always, the real question was whether the jury cared. As Innella proceeded through the test results, five of the six jurors in the front row spent more time staring long and hard at Joe, trying to detect his reaction.

Equally impressive as a witness was Dr. Mark Taff, the forensic pathologist who had performed the autopsy on Diane's body.

Dr. Taff started by providing his impressive credentials and explaining that he'd previously appeared as an expert witness in four of the five New York City boroughs, four other counties in New York State, New Jersey, Connecticut, and in Detroit, Michigan.

Easing into his testimony, Dr. Taff said that he had started Diane's autopsy with an external exam. As the witness began explaining about Diane's burst eyeballs—and how this was common in strangulation—Joe removed his glasses and stroked the bridge of his nose with his left thumb and index finger.

The jury members, meanwhile, were fixated on every intimate and gory detail, especially the testimony describing the blunt-force impacts to Diane's head. To assist the jurors in their task, Dr. Taff brought along some visual aids: a skull model and color-coded drawings of the throat area, complete with the appropriate five-syllable medical terms.

During his second day on the stand, Dr. Taff noted each of the head wounds in red marker on the model. He wanted the jurors to see, and understand in layman's terms, how Diane had been brutally beaten and choked to death.

Along the way, the pathologist added helpful details: he

found no drugs in Diane's body other than trace amounts of a breakdown product of Valium; Diane showed signs of being asthmatic, but the condition didn't contribute to her death; and she had eaten a full meal two to six hours before her death. The latter detail again raised the possibility that Diane had met with someone before leaving the city or out in the Hamptons. But unless there was going to be evidence that she'd met with a boyfriend, the whole issue seemed spurious.

Dr. Taff also provided more information about Diane's internal injuries: the bruises to the head were indicative of more serious injuries to the brain, consistent with a hand or fist striking the victim; some of the bruises could have resulted from the victim being slammed against a fixed object; there was superficial hemorrhaging on the brain; blood vessels were broken in her tongue, another indication of asphyxiation. Hemorrhages in Diane's scalp varied in diameter from one to four inches, according to Dr. Taff, who said he could not detect the sequence in which the blunt-force wounds had been administered.

Of the neck injuries, Dr. Taff testified that the vital blood vessels "were all squeezed, front to back," with "severe force," preventing oxygenated blood from getting to the brain. Diane's voice box was fractured, with the greatest force being applied to the left side of her neck. There was hemorrhaging on the rear of the esophagus. He said there was "a clear break" in the thyroid cartilage.

Asked how Diane had died, Dr. Taff explained: "It is my opinion that Diane Pikul sustained traumatic hemorrhages of the brain as the result of multiple—at least ten—blunt-force impacts to her head. Simply said, she sustained a beating to the head area."

"Did you find any other causes of death?" asked Joseph.

"In addition to the blunt-force impacts to her head, there was evidence that Diane Pikul also sustained neck injuries from being manually strangled, causing the injuries in her neck, and in her eyes as well as the lungs. The presence of a ligature mark on the right rear of her neck, with hemorrhaging in the underlying skin, and the presence of other ligatures wrapped around her neck at the time of discovery—those findings indicated to me that she was also a victim of a strangulation, both manual and from ligature."

"Would either of those causes of death which you just described, independently, in and of themselves, cause her death?"

"Yes," said Dr. Taff.

Joseph wanted to know if Dr. Taff could tell "based on a reasonable degree of expert medical certainty" whether Diane was strangled or beaten to death first.

"Blunt-force impacts are types of injuries that do not cause a rapid death. Instead, injuries from neck depressions can cause a more rapid death, with death occurring anywhere between thirty seconds up to two minutes if there is a sustained or even an intermittent force applied to an individual's neck."

Dr. Taff said that in his opinion the head injuries were administered before Diane was choked and strangled. But he added that he was convinced if Diane hadn't been strangled, she would have died from the beating. "The fact that there were hemorrhages on both sides of the neck speaks more for a manual strangulation from a grip across the neck, squeezing the tissues on the right and left side of the neck. The squeezing of the neck pressured and caused the fracture of the superior horn of the thyroid cartilage, which makes up the voice box."

Steve Worth had a difficult task ahead of him, trying to discredit Dr. Taff's compelling testimony. Nevertheless, the nattily attired attorney zeroed in doggedly on a wide range of medical findings during his sometimes heated interrogation. He started off by noting the fact that as a central-nervous-system depressant Valium can reduce the flow of oxygen to the brain, and that the Valium in Diane's body had contributed, however minimally, to the lack of oxygen going to her brain during the strangulation.

When Worth inquired if Diane's chronic asthma could have also contributed to her death, Dr. Taff conceded that Diane's heavily congested lungs weighed more than expected. But, Dr. Taff defensively snapped back: "I know she didn't die from asthma. . . . I wouldn't be weighing her; she'd be alive."

Worth focused most of his effort on the supposed multiple causes of death. He first made Dr. Taff acknowledge that he had mistakenly mentioned only two causes on the death certificate—the beating and the ligature strangulation, neglecting to list the manual strangulation. Considerable time also was spent getting Dr. Taff to concede that the blunt-force head injuries, as well as the red mark on the rear of Diane's neck, conceivably could have been administered *immediately* after death, while Diane's body was being carried by the cord. But, Dr. Taff added, if that were the case, he couldn't understand why the mark wasn't around a larger portion of the neck.

Dr. Taff repeatedly defended his findings, insisting the beating had been inflicted prior to any of the choking, and insisting that the ligature mark had been made on Diane's neck while she was still alive, pointing to the internal hemorrhaging beneath the neck mark.

Many of Worth's questions appeared to be designed to establish a specific scenario. For example, he asked if the fracture in Diane's neck had been consistent with her having moved forward rapidly into someone who straight-armed her at the neck.

"That's absolutely inconsistent," said Dr. Taff, "categorically" denying that any of the neck injuries could have been caused by the blunt-force impacts. The only way that scenario could have conceivably occurred was if the victim had been inflicted with multiple blows to the neck area, a scenario not supported by the other evidence, Dr. Taff said.

Worth wanted to know if Diane, with the assistance of a hard object in her hand, could have knocked Joe's tooth out. Dr. Taff conceded the possibility, but said other facial injuries could be expected about the mouth. Dr. Taff said he couldn't rule out the possibility that the voice-box injuries were caused by a straight-arm, followed by a struggle, during which time Diane had been strangled. But, the doctor continued, such a prospect was remote.

Could someone appear to be dead, even release their bowels, but be unconscious, barely alive? Worth asked. Dr. Taff not only agreed to such a possibility, he said he was unable to estimate how long someone could survive in that state.

Worth then solicited Dr. Taff's reaction to the following

hypothesis: pressure is applied on someone's neck, resulting in a fracture of the superior horn; the victim appears to be dead; assuming the victim is dead, the person who applied the pressure moves the body quickly without any particular care, picking it up by the feet; the body is moved over a metal track of a sliding glass door; the body is moved down several wooden steps and placed in a station wagon with metal edges.

Dr. Taff conceded that if the person was still alive and unconscious at the time the body was moved, and the body was really manhandled and banged around, he couldn't rule out such a scenario as the cause of the hemorrhages in the tissue. However, he questioned how the "internal injuries of the brain" could be sustained. Instead, Dr. Taff contended, the pattern of injuries were "consistent with a beating." Also, he said, one would expect to have found injuries or drag marks on the rear of the head, rear of the shoulder blades, the back, and possibly the buttocks—none of which had been present.

The doctor's testimony that Diane died from being strangled by the pink cord was far less convincing, especially after Dr. Taff was forced to admit he had failed to mention the important neck hemorrhage in his autopsy report. Matters got even more murky when Dr. Taff said he believed manual strangulation was the primary component of the asphyxial cause of death, despite his failure to mention it on the death certificate. That made more sense, given the full picture. But why hadn't it been listed?

The rest of Dr. Taff's scenario appeared to hold up through the cross-examination, though, especially the morbid details of the internal injuries caused by a beating. There appeared little doubt that Diane had been brutally bashed about the head with some type of blunt instrument, perhaps a gun butt or baseball bat, and then choked for the minimum thirty or forty seconds.

Still, the hypothesis left some room to wiggle. Worth was after something, just as he had been with the condoms and the state police's failure to perform a fingerprint test on the knife handle.

When Dr. Taff left the stand, another behind-the-scenes fracas broke out between the attorneys, prompted by Bekoff's request for any police reports filed by Stephen Oates, the state-police investigator who had driven Joe up to the Newburgh barracks. Since Joseph had told the defense he wasn't going to call Oates, Bekoff wanted the material to cross-examine Investigator Probst, whom the prosecutor planned to call as his final witness.

Since the defense team was now expressing interest in Oates, Joseph announced that he planned to summon the investigator to testify. This development was especially interesting in view of the fact that Oates had not testified at the pretrial hearing.

With everyone once again behind closed doors, the reason for the new battleground quickly became apparent. Oates would testify that he had heard only parts of Joe's conversation with Probst in the backseat. He'd heard the part about "she deserved it," but didn't hear the part about "that's why I did it." In addition to having missed the crucial parts of the conversation, Oates had also neglected to write down in his report any statements he now claimed to have heard Joe make.

On the surface, this put Oates and Probst at odds. Bekoff demanded that a hearing be conducted before he cross-examined Probst so that Oates could testify outside the presence of the jury as to what he did and didn't hear.

Judge Byrne disagreed: "I mean, everybody would like to know what all the witnesses are going to say before they testify, but again, that's not the way it works." Recognizing that the defense should have been notified about the additional statement, Judge Byrne ordered Oates produced for a defense interview before court resumed in the morning.

Bekoff was enraged, for his witness Oates—a police witness at that—had been stolen from underneath him.

The following morning, Joseph called Oates to the stand first. The investigator tried his best to explain why he and Probst just happened to start talking about Sesame Place during the ride up to the barracks with Joe. But given the context of the testimony—coming after weeks of convincing circumstantial evidence—it was hard to imagine anyone getting riled up about Joe's constitutional rights anymore.

Oates said he remembered Joe saying, "She was a bitch" and "she deserved it." The witness also quoted Joe as saying that Diane had never wanted to go to amusement parks like Sesame Place; "she never wanted to do anything."

But that was all Oates testified to on direct. He made no mention of the "you fucked up, pal" line; Judge Byrne had thought it over and ruled it inadmissible.

Bekoff rose to request a delay in Oates's cross-examination until after Probst's testimony, "in view of the fact that this is my witness." Judge Byrne summoned everyone to yet another bench conference, where it was decided Oates's cross-examination would be postponed until everyone was done with Probst.

Dressed in a blue suit and tan sweater, Probst provided the jury with the full treatment: "That's why I did it," "She was such a bitch," "She deserved it. I never did anything wrong before in my life. I can't change it now," etc.

Stalking back and forth in front of the jury box, Bekoff grilled Probst about the fact that he and Oates had just happened to mention the ages of their kids during the car ride, in view of the fact they knew each other's family and had been talking about vacation spots earlier in the day. But as before, it sounded like the two had merely primed the pump. Joe's confessions thereafter had been entirely voluntary.

Next came Oates's cross-examination, during which time Bekoff zeroed in on what the investigator didn't hear. "I was in and out," said Oates at one point.

"Well, you weren't in and out. You were still in the car, right?" asked Bekoff to the chuckles of the jurors.

"I meant in and out of the conversation," Oates explained.

Reading from his notes of his court-sanctioned interview with Oates, Bekoff asked the witness if Joe had told him: "I always wanted to do things with the kids; Diane didn't want to. Diane never wanted to do anything with the kids. We have a nice house out in Amagansett. She didn't like to go and spend weekends. She was a bitch. I always wanted to do things with the kids; she didn't. She deserved it."

"Isn't that what was said?" Bekoff asked.

"Correct," said Oates.

"Did you ever hear Joe Pikul say, 'That's why I did it'?" the defense attorney pressed.

"No sir," answered Oates.

In a question perhaps designed more for a possible appeal, Bekoff inquired: "Were you ever asked specifically by a district attorney if Joe Pikul ever said that to you?"

"Of course."

"And you said, 'No, I'm not going to, right?' "

"No," said Oates.

"You told him you never heard him say that, right?"

"I told him that I could not swear to that," Oates answered.

Bekoff then produced Oates's lead sheet report, the only document he had filed on the car ride, and offered it into evidence. "No mention of any admissions?" Bekoff asked.

"No," Oates replied.

"Thank you very much," said Bekoff, striding back to his table. "No further questions."

Judge Byrne asked what was next on the agenda, and Alan Joseph announced: "The People rest, Your Honor."

The People's case had been sort of a sandwich: with Joe's incriminating statements to Sandy Jarvinen and to Investigator Probst serving as the top and bottom to the thick circumstantial middle.

The method hadn't been precisely determined, but ample evidence indicated a severe beating and a prolonged choking. What still remained unclear was where Diane had been for part of that Friday night and precisely where the murder had occurred.

CHAPTER • 25

Unable to Let Go

STILL STICKING TO THE STRATEGY of putting the police on trial, Bekoff called defense lawyer Charles Clayman and Sergeant Bowen from the Sixth Precinct in Manhattan as his first two witnesses. The testimony was a virtual repeat of the pretrial hearing: Clayman told the jury that he had warned Probst and Oates not to talk to Joe, and Bowen left the impression that early on he had distrusted Joe's version of events.

Outside of court, reporters and TV crews flocked to Bekoff that Monday, February 27, inquiring about his next move. He would only say: "Just be here at two o'clock. We might have some fun."

The defense contingent seemed tense when court was set to resume. The attorneys milled around in the hallway; Joe's psychic friend "Blaze" took his left hand and kissed it. Mary Bain—attired in a blue blazer and gray skirt, complemented by a two-tone gray scarf and tan cashmere sweater—ran from Joe to the telephone to the water fountain to the bathroom to the telephone.

Joe also appeared to be more nervous than usual. Several times he took a long sip from the fountain, letting the water run down his brownish beard for long moments. Then he withdrew the photos of Claudia and Blake from his suit coat and stared at them eternally.

"He's not gonna testify, is he?" one of the court buffs who'd attended the trial from the beginning asked Bekoff as he returned to the courtroom.

"You wanna make a bet?" Bekoff replied.

Judge Byrne welcomed the jurors back from lunch, then turned toward the defense table. "Mr. Bekoff, Mr. Worth?"

Steve Worth stood up. "Your Honor, at this time the defendant will testify in his own behalf."

For the defense, Joe's appearance on the witness stand was vital, though fraught with danger. On the one hand, by giving his version of events, he would have the opportunity to deny or explain the horde of incriminating statements attributed to him. On the other, the prosecution would be able to bring in both Tripodos and Investigator Venezia as rebuttal witnesses.

Joe ambled from the defense table to the witness stand, smartly dressed in a dark blue suit, light blue shirt, and reddish paisley tie. Joe had given little thought to trying for a reduced verdict of manslaughter or criminally negligent homicide. For him this was winner take all; he was going to tell his story.

Word spread instantly throughout the government building, and within five minutes the back rows were jammed with spectators.

"Joe, take your time, speak nice and loud and slowly so that everybody can hear you, okay?" said Worth.

"Yes," Joe answered softly.

"Joe, did you cause the death of Diane Pikul?"

"Yes," Joe said, sending a gasp through the courtroom.

"Are you guilty of murdering Diane Pikul?"

"No."

Joseph rose to object. "That's a leading question." But Judge Byrne allowed it.

In the front row to the left, Mary removed her oversized glasses to wipe away tears.

"Let's go back, Joe," said Worth. He and Joe then began a lengthy walk down memory lane, told from Joe's perspective. Joe reviewed his youth, his years with Sandy, his alcoholism, his divorce, his jobs, his meeting Diane at AA, their stormy life together.

Joe admitted what he couldn't deny, such as the calls he had made with his telephone credit card. He lied when he had to, and tried to wiggle wherever the physical evidence and direct testimony left him room.

With a phrase here and a sentence there, Joe admitted to facts that Alan Joseph and his witnesses had spent weeks fighting to establish. He even abandoned much of Bekoff's insinuation of police misconduct, claiming for the most part that he'd been treated courteously and hadn't been pressured into talking.

Joe even acknowledged that Diane had only given Felder $20,000 of the $46,000, saying he had no idea what she did with the rest.

But the one thing Joe wouldn't do was admit to murder.

He acknowledged having met with Sandy on Cape Cod to discuss what would happen in the event of his death or the mutual deaths of himself and Diane. He said it was possible he told Sandy, "Diane will have to meet with an accident," but contended that he wasn't serious and that Sandy had laughed afterward.

Whenever possible, Joe tried to get across his tormented view of life with Diane, giving the backdrop for their final argument. Providing testimony he knew could not be directly challenged, he asserted that Diane "would use very minor incidents to blow up and then spend the evening by herself. . . . Her behavior was very erratic. There were consistent senseless arguments, called pretext arguments." He said Diane had left many warning signs that she had a boyfriend—she had cosmetic eye surgery, kept an entire wardrobe of disco clothes in Manhattan, used different baby-sitters every night during one of his business trips, and frequently was not where she claimed she'd been. Still, Joe claimed, he and Diane continued to have sex until three months before her death.

Mumbling softly in a tone subsequently attributed to tranquilizers, Joe gave his version of the fight the night before the murder, when Diane had chased him into the street. Joe said the argument had been prompted by his sending the baby-sitter home early. "I preferred to put the children to sleep myself. I enjoyed that. Diane didn't enjoy that," he said. "I enjoyed reading stories to them and playing with them and putting them to sleep and so I always let the baby-sitters go. I pay them for the full evening and let them go."

When Diane arrived later that evening from some un-disclosed event, she was very angry and became "abusive and aggressive," Joe contended. He said the two of them argued, and that Diane had called him " 'faggot and motherfucker, creep. . . .' Then she attempted to do something she did a lot, which was to scratch my face, so I'd be embarrassed at my firm."

Joe said he ran out of the house as Diane chased him. Pointing out that Joe was nearly six feet tall and Diane but 5-3½, Worth had Joe explain that he ran not because he was physically afraid but because he didn't want to get scratched and didn't want the children to hear their mother's foul language. Joe said he spent the night at his other apartment.

The stage was set for The Story—what had happened the weekend after Black Monday.

After giving so many conflicting versions, Joe proceeded to give a brand-new one. He started with a completely different time for his discovery of the condoms, claiming that after he and the children had arrived at the house and Claudia watched some TV, she told him she'd lost one of her shoes. This was late Friday night *before* Claudia went to sleep, *before* Diane arrived. It was then, Joe now swore, that he found the condoms underneath his side of the queen-size bed in the master bedroom. He said the brand name was Gold Tex, a name he did not recognize.

Joe claimed he was familiar with condoms because he'd come up with an idea, approved by his employer, "to look at the condom market as an investment opportunity in view of the AIDS scare." After all the closed-door legal battling, here was Joe mentioning AIDS in front of the jury.

As a result of his investment idea, Joe told the jury, he personally conducted considerable market research on the numerous firms that make condoms and how many each company sold. Arnhold & S. Bleichroeder, his employer, eventually sponsored the largest condom company in the world, a firm from England, Joe added. Worth asked if with all that research, whether Joe had ever heard of Gold Tex. Joe said he had not.

Joe said he didn't mention his discovery to Claudia, instead read her a story and put her to bed about eleven. "I was devastated," he said. "I realized that, you know, not only was Diane having affairs, but she was also bringing them in, back to my bedroom, which is right next to my children's room, and I was just terribly hurt." He said he then watched TV in the baby-sitter's room, on the opposite end of the house, while waiting for Diane to arrive.

When Diane finally appeared, according to this version, Joe asked her what had taken her so long, and she replied simply that she was tired. Joe said he followed as Diane walked into the master bedroom. They were discussing their schedules for the weekend—the kids' recreation, the massage appointments.

"I couldn't hold it back any longer. I confronted her with the condoms, I waved them at her and I said, 'Who do these belong to? What does this mean?' "

Worth wondered what Diane's response had been. "She says, 'None of your business' and became abusive and angry."

"I said, 'You know this means I'm going to fight you in this divorce. This is not going to be an amicable divorce. I'm going to get these children under my control. They'll live with me.' And I said, 'I'm going to leave you broke.' "

"Were you angry when you said that?" Worth asked.

"Yes, I was angry," said Joe. "I was very hurt."

According to Joe, Diane "called me a faggot and a creep, and then she left the bedroom in kind of a rush and went to the kitchen area."

There was nothing else to say, Joe said, so he got ready for bed. He said he was taking his shirt off when "she came back in the master bedroom. I felt a pain in my back and my side toward the back. And I turned and I saw that I had been cut and that she was coming at me with a knife."

"How was she coming at you with a knife?" Worth asked.

"She had a knife up like this and—" Joe made a downward thrust with an imaginary knife. Worth interrupted to ask what Joe had done when he saw Diane advancing. "I moved to stop her, I put my hands out—one of my hands— I put my hand out and I grabbed her by the neck to push her away, to get some distance, and I struggled to get the knife away from her."

Worth retrieved the kitchen knife recovered at the car wash.

"Yes, this is the knife," Joe said immediately. "The

knife Diane was holding, was about to stab me with."
There was no doubt in his mind, Joe said.

"Now, Joe, when you put out your arm, what part of
her did you grab?"

"I grabbed her throat and I started to squeeze her throat
as I struggled for the knife," Joe claimed.

"What did your other hand do?"

"The other hand was trying to get the knife."

"What happened during that struggle?"

"Well, she brought the knife down," said Joe. "I deflected it and the handle hit me in my mouth and knocked
out a tooth."

"What tooth, Joe?"

Making no mention of peanut brittle, Joe pointed to the
right front of his mouth, where the tooth had fallen out.

"When you say you deflected the knife, did you get cut?"

"Yes, I got a cut on my hand here," said Joe, attempting
to color in another portion of his canvas.

"From the knife or from the struggle? Either if you
know," Worth asked.

"I don't know," said Joe, backing off, leaving room to
maneuver. "I think—I don't know."

"How long did you struggle for?"

"It seemed like seconds."

"During the time of this struggle, did she still have the
knife?"

"Yes."

"Did you still have your hand on her throat?"

"Yes, I did."

"Were you squeezing?" asked Worth.

"As hard as I could."

"Why, Joe?"

"Because I was going to be killed."

Joe said that Diane's body went limp "very quickly,"
that the knife dropped. He said he immediately stopped
squeezing Diane's neck. "Her bowels let go and she vomited." Joe said he was sure that Diane was dead. "She was
on the floor and I lifted her body onto the bed, put a pillow
under her head."

During the entire struggle, Joe insisted, he had never
punched Diane, never hit her head on the wall or on the

floor. He also said he never used any rope or cord on Diane during the struggle.

"When you put her on the bed, what did you do, how did you feel?" Worth asked.

"I just couldn't believe this was happening and I was scared. I also realized I was bleeding, so I went into the bathroom to get a towel to wipe my wound. . . . Then I panicked. I thought that I should get the body out of the house as quickly as possible so that if my children heard anything and came in to see us, which they would, they wouldn't see Diane dead and me bleeding."

Joe said he went quickly out to the Mazda for the tarp, brought it back inside the house, and wrapped up Diane's body at the foot of the bed.

"Joe, you've seen in this case a number of other items—towels, bathrobe, the belt, did you put all those items there?"

"Yes, I did."

"Nobody else did it, did they?" Worth continued.

"No," said Joe. As the questioning progressed, Joe also admitted that he had put all the ligatures on Diane's body and the tarp. But he claimed the pink cord, the crucial cord used to tie the ligature directly on Diane's neck, had been attached to the tarp before that evening and that he always used it to tie the canvas to the Mazda.

The immediate availability of the pink cord was critical to Joe's story if he was to put himself into the very limited window of opportunity created by Dr. Taff's professional refusal to say the word "impossible." The neck ligature would have had to have been placed on Diane's neck almost instantaneously after death.

Joe said he was in shock and couldn't remember specifically how he had tied the body up, but remembered getting additional rope and cord from the utility closet. He also recalled that he accomplished the job quickly, "to get the body out of the possible vision of the children. . . . I pulled her by her legs down the hallway" in the tarpaulin. Again, Joe said he believed Diane was already dead, though he claimed he never checked her pulse or breathing after she went limp.

Joe said he dragged Diane through the sliding glass side

door by the kitchen. "Does it have a metal track that holds the door in place?" asked Worth.

"Yes."

From there, Joe said, he went down the deck stairs, negotiated a second flight of steps, made of railroad ties, and put the body in the station wagon. "I came back in the house and took some cleaning material from the utility closet and cleaned up blood that had got on the rug."

Joe said he then picked up the knife.

"You touched it with your hands, right?"

"Yes," Joe replied.

"And Diane also touched it with her hands, right?" asked Worth, his voice growing stronger.

"Yes."

"And if anybody had ever bothered to check that knife for fingerprints, maybe they'd be there, wouldn't they, Joe?" asked Worth, shouting.

"Objection," Joseph shouted back. Judge Byrne sustained.

Continuing with his story, Joe said he had written Claudia a note explaining he was going out for a while, and left her "the panic button," an alarm device linked to the security service. Joe said he didn't press the button himself because he was "afraid that the police would come and that they'd wake up the kids and they'd, you know, see all this disaster. . . . They would see their mother dead and me bleeding."

It was at this point, Joe claimed, that he drove to the bay side of the Hamptons, to a place called Little Alberts Landing. "I had a raft in the car that would be used and I took the raft to the water's edge and I took Diane's body to the water's edge," said Joe, adding that he also took a barbell weight because he "had an idea of leaving her in the water and to weigh it down."

"Did you put Diane's body in the water?" Worth asked.

"No."

"Why not, Joe?"

"I couldn't let go of Diane."

He said the beach was desolate; no one was there to disturb him. Still, Joe said, he dragged Diane's body back to the station wagon and returned to Windmill Lane. Joe said he parked the car along the path on the side of the house by the cemetery, cleaned the raft, and went into the house. He said he didn't sleep a wink that night.

In essence, that was Joe's story, a neat package intended to explain many of the vital points. But he was far from done. Joe provided additional key claims for the critical Friday night–Saturday morning period:

—The blood on the doorway was his, not Diane's. Diane was nowhere near that door during the struggle.

—He didn't know about the law of self-defense or whether he was responsible for what had occurred.

—The next morning he told the kids their mother "had gone out to see one of her friends."

—He went to the town dump to discard "the regular household garbage" along with "a variety of things I thought would be incriminating," including the pillow that Diane's head had rested on.

—He purchased all those items at the hardware store because he still had the body and didn't know what he was going to do with it.

—He bought the twelve bags of ice to keep Diane's body cool.

Joe said that at about 2:00 P.M. that Saturday he left the children in the house watching videotapes—"children's tapes"—and returned to Little Alberts Landing. "I took Diane's body out of the car up to an area which was remote and with my hands put sand on top of the tarp to cover it," he explained, pinpointing the area that had been used in the previous homicide.

Joe said he didn't dig a hole or use a shovel to bury Diane, although he could have if he wanted since the beach was again empty. "I couldn't let Diane go, I felt that was the breakup of the family, and I just couldn't let her go." He said he left Diane's body at the beach and drove back to the house, where that afternoon someone from the hardware store came over to put a new lock on the basement door. "Somehow the lock in the cellar had disappeared and I became paranoid about Diane's boyfriend maybe having access to the house with the alarm codes and I wanted to prevent him coming in."

When it came to his chat in Henry Sawoska's basement, Joe acknowledged he had told his former roommate that he was dying. "As you sit here today, do you think you have a terminal illness?" asked Worth.

"No," said Joe. "I feel terrific physically, my weight is up at a nice level, and I don't have any symptoms." Worth traveled no further down that road. Denied access to the closed-door conferences, the reporters covering the trial as well as the regular court buffs kept wondering why there weren't more questions about this terminal illness. What was it? Why wasn't anyone talking about it? Was Joe sick or wasn't he?

Instead, Worth switched to why Joe had failed to tell his friend Sawoska the truth about what had happened with Diane. "I didn't want to get the Sawoskas, Hank and Louise, involved with this," Joe explained. When asked why he had lied to the Weingardens about the condoms, Joe said he "didn't consider the Weingardens close enough friends to share that with."

Joe next confirmed most of Sandy Jarvinen's testimony, the parts that really didn't matter. But he denied having waved her away from the car, insisting that Diane's body was not with him for the trip throughout Massachusetts.

The testimony made no sense, though. Why did Joe drive around the Berkshires looking for a place to bury a body if it was buried on a beach several hundred miles away in the Hamptons?

According to Joe, he also told a sympathetic Sandy that he'd killed Diane, but insisted he'd told her he did it in self-defense. "I told her I had to kill Diane, she was trying to kill me," said Joe.

"Joe, you heard in this trial Sandra Jarvinen testify that what you said was, 'I had to eliminate her,' " said Worth. "Did you say to Sandy Jarvinen that Sunday morning, 'I had to eliminate her'?" Joe swore he never used the word.

Seeking to discredit Sandy more, Joe said his ex-wife advised him not to do anything without first talking to a lawyer, then gave him the name of her friend, Vincent Federico. Joe said he told Sandy he was thinking of shooting himself with the pump shotgun, but that Sandy insisted that he speak to Vinnie first.

Although discrepancies existed between Joe's story and what the witnesses had testified—especially Sandy—Joe's itinerary for the fateful weekend was basically in sync with the other versions given at the trial, except for his travels that Sunday.

The prosecution's basic outline of the weekend's events had presumed that Joe had spent most of the day riding around Massachusetts before driving back to the apartment on Sixth Avenue in Manhattan. But in his trial version, Joe said he definitely drove from Massachusetts to the Hamptons, dug up Diane's body, then returned to the city. The significant difference in the two versions was the location of Diane's body during most of the weekend.

In the less favorable version, Joe carted the children around with their mother's corpse in the rear well, then meandered from locale to locale in search of a perfect dumping ground. The more favorable version made Joe appear distraught, panic-stricken, but certainly not one to heartlessly transport Diane's corpse around in the same car as the children.

Despite a wealth of documentation that helped pin down other key times and events, Prosecutor Joseph had failed to find anything to prove or disprove Joe's whereabouts during that Sunday afternoon and evening. Joe's telephone credit-card receipts were no help, for the toll records were blank from Saturday night until Monday morning. Sandy confirmed that Joe had called her several times that Sunday, but Joe said he used cash. Also, not a single witness claimed to have seen Joe during that time period.

Joe said he left the Lee, Massachusetts, area in early afternoon and returned to the Hamptons in late afternoon. Details of this trip were sketchy, but all the same, Joe would have had to set a record pace. "I went home first to see that the house was okay and to have a bite to eat," he said. "Then I went to Little Alberts Landing to the beach."

By now it was about six or 6:30, said Joe. The beach was empty.

"Had Diane's body been disturbed at all?" asked Worth. Joe said it had not. "I took the body and uncovered it, took the body to the car." He said if he had wanted, he could have buried the body there or put it in the water. Offering no reason, he said he instead put the body back in the wagon. Returning to the house, he said he placed the bags of ice on Diane's body, the ones he had purchased thirty hours before.

Joe said he then departed for the apartment in Manhattan, arriving about 1:00 A.M. He said he left the car out front overnight, at a meter on Sixth Avenue, and inside the apartment "had a snack—some watermelon," then went to bed on the couch.

Worth eventually worked his way to the pull-off just before the Newburgh exit on the Thruway. Joe said he stopped there because it appeared to be "the last spot I could leave Diane's body."

"I would be at the Sawoskas' house in ten or fifteen minutes," he said. "I didn't want Diane's body to be in the car when I picked up the children. The work week was beginning, the school week was beginning, I had decided to live. I wanted to take care of my children. I love them so much and that was it."

Joe said the photos introduced at the trial accurately depicted where he had placed the body. He said he placed the tire on top "as camouflage."

"You were trying to prevent it from being found by the police?" asked Worth. Joe said he was.

At that point the judge declared a recess for the day, and Mary rushed to her husband's side. Outside of court, Bekoff looked satisfied. "All the pieces were there," he said. "If the police wanted to, they could have put this together real easy." The defense attorney went on to say that at the completion of the prosecution case he had told his client: "We got a shot. I like the way the jury's reacting." But, Bekoff said, Joe replied: "No good. I gotta tell them the whole thing."

Getting a big hug and smooch from Mrs. Pikul No. 3, Joe began his second day on the stand by explaining that a great deal of his actions after Diane's death were designed to cover his tracks. He said he made the telephone calls to *Harper's* to cover his tracks. Ditto for the calls to Donald Whitmore in Florida and to the East Hampton police and NYPD. He didn't quite explain away why he had called Sandy after he disposed of Diane's body, but said he used the code words "the package is down" to cover his tracks. Joe said he was covering his tracks when he went to the car wash, when he hid out from police in the New York City hotel under one of his attorney's names, and when he told everyone he'd found the condoms on Saturday instead of Friday, before the murder. He said he lied about when he found the condoms because he feared police would think a discovery before Diane's death would have angered him and given him cause to hurt Diane.

Joe said he wasn't trying to cover his tracks when he sold his expensive shotgun for twenty-five dollars, though. "I had decided to live. . . . I had no reason for the shotgun anymore. It was also a dangerous instrument to have in my house. The children were getting older, I just felt safer without it."

Joe's strategy was to mix 'em and match 'em as to when he had been telling the truth or covering his tracks. Moreover, he tried to cast doubt as to when the police were telling the truth or covering *their* tracks. For example, the story about Joe finding the condoms was supposedly true, but untrue as to when he supposedly made the discovery. The jury had to decide if Joe had actually said what the cops testified he said, then whether Joe meant it when he said it. For example, Joe admitted that he'd told Composto he scratched his hand going after a soccer ball in the honeysuckle bush. But, he now said, that was not a truthful statement.

Worth asked Joe how he did get the scratch. "In the struggle with Diane."

How? Worth pressed. "I don't know. I think her fingers." The day before he'd said he deflected the knife, then backed away.

Accepting Joe's version that he used only one hand to hold Diane off by the neck, his right hand would have been on the left side of her neck, as supported by the medical testimony. Then, according to Joe's story, he would have been trying to ward off the knife with his left hand.

Diane supposedly brought the knife down in her right hand, Joe deflected it with his hand—it would have had to have been his left hand—then the handle knocked his tooth out and somehow his hand got cut. But the cut was on his right hand, the one supposedly holding Diane by the neck, not the hand warding off the knife.

In order for Diane's fingers to have inflicted the wound, it would have been her left hand doing the scratching, not her right, since her right hand supposedly held the knife. That would have meant Diane's left hand went after Joe's right, which was supposedly holding Diane off at the neck. Nothing in this scenario explained how the knife knocked out the tooth.

Moving on, Worth sought to clarify some of the testimony regarding Joe's conversation with Investigator Probst. "You heard testimony that you referred to Diane as 'a bitch.' Is that true?"

"Probably true," said Joe.

"Testimony that you said that 'she deserved it.' Possible you said that?" Worth asked. Joe replied in the affirmative.

"Joe, you heard testimony here that you said to them, 'That's why I did it.' Is that true?"

"That is not true," said Joe.

Practicing the theory that it is best to explain impending bad news in the best possible light, Worth asked Joe if he was aware that by taking the stand, Prosecutor Joseph now had the right to call the three investigators he'd spoken to at the barracks the night of his arrest. Joe said he'd been fully briefed, then sought to decredit the testimony that was almost certain to follow on Joseph's rebuttal case.

Joe said the fellows at the state-police barracks had sucked him into thinking they were his buddies. He said Tripodo Junior was especially friendly. "He said, 'Call me Joe, I'll call you Joe. The boys in the barracks are behind you. They know what you went through. I investigated this case in New York. I know what a bitch your wife is.' "

Joe said he felt "stranded and isolated" without his attorney. "Somebody said, 'Where is your attorney? He should be up here with you.' " He claimed Tripodo Junior told him his investigation had disclosed Diane "was cheating on me right from the beginning."

"Joe, at some point did you say to Investigator Tripodo Junior that 'she,' meaning Diane, 'tried to kill me'?"

"Yes, I did," said Joe. "I had felt pretty good about, you know, the way he had treated me and I wanted to be honest with him."

"And what did he do when you said that?" Worth asked.

"I looked up and he was motioning to somebody else

to come over. I could see that he was not my friend but a policeman and I probably shouldn't be talking to him," said Joe.

"So did you say anything more about the truth of what had happened?"

"No," said Joe, explaining that at that point he simply added to his statement, "not physically but psychologically."

"Why did you say that, Joe?"

"Because I felt he wasn't my friend," Joe replied.

Joe then tried to explain some of his other incriminating remarks. He admitted telling Tripodo Junior, "Everyone is better off without her" because when he had found the condoms he had realized, "It was going to be very difficult in a divorce with Diane, wanting my children, I didn't want them with her. And also she had tried to kill me." Suffering from "despair and frustration," Joe said, he told Tripodo Junior he wanted him to shoot him.

Joe said he also remembered Investigator Venezia treating him like a good friend, recounting how Venezia claimed he "identified with me because he had been divorced and his wife went back to England and took his child with her. . . . He said, 'You don't need these fancy lawyers, all they're going to do is charge you a lot of money.' He said, 'Cooperate with us and you'll do better.' " Of course, this testimony meant that even after Joe realized Tripodo Junior had been deceptive, he fell for it a second time with Venezia.

As for the most damaging statement made to Venezia—"My only hope is to beat this on a technicality"—Joe said he was only being sarcastic.

"Why did you want to be sarcastic?" Worth asked.

"Because I realized, I realized they weren't my friends and that they were trying to get me to say—"

He hesitated, so Worth stepped in: "That he wasn't your buddy?"

"He was not my buddy," Joe readily agreed.

Joseph rose quickly from his chair. "Objection, Your Honor. Let the witness answer the question."

Trying to anticipate another likely topic, Joe said he'd told Venezia that Diane had been blackmailing him. "I said she had pictures of me in women's clothes."

Worth wondered if that was true. "Yes," Joe said, explaining that the photos, along with a tape, had been taken over the course of "the previous two or three years," putting the time frame back to 1985 or so.

Seeking to eliminate a possible motive, Joe said he knew that killing Diane would not have enabled him to get the incriminating sex tape and photos back. According to Joe, he knew that from August 1986—when Felder was hired—until the fatal weekend, the tapes were "at Diane's attorney's office."

This was an out-and-out lie, given the fact that Felder hadn't received the goods until January 1987. But Judge Byrne had disallowed the dated letter Diane had written when she gave Felder the materials and had disallowed testimony about Joe trying to gain access to Diane's safe-deposit box. So once again Joe was free to wiggle.

"What did you mean then by saying she was blackmailing you? In what sense was she blackmailing you?" Worth asked. Joe said that Diane had promised to make the sex tape "an integral part of any divorce proceeding" and that their contents would be cited in the divorce papers.

"Did Diane say to you they would be released?"

"She said they could be released," said Joe, a reference to Diane's discussions of the Joan Collins divorce case with her associates at *Harper's*.

Moving on, Worth asked Joe why he'd asked to see Diane's body. In a sad, halting voice, Joe said: "I had a sense that she wasn't dead. I couldn't believe she was dead."

"Joe, she had died after your struggle with her, isn't that right?" Worth asked, seeking to straighten out Joe's remark.

"Yes."

"You still asked to see her?"

"Yes."

"You knew she was dead at this point, didn't you?"

"Yes," said Joe. "But I didn't understand it on another level." It wasn't until after he saw the body, Joe said, that he "realized that my family was over with."

Turning to Tripodo Senior, Joe said the investigator had brought up the beach scenario, not him. Quoting Tripodo

Senior, Joe testified: " 'We're not sure how it happened. When you went to the beach with Diane, did you do this?' and he motions hitting her head on a rock or something." He said Tripodo Senior also made the two-handed throttling motion, not him.

"He said, 'It was at the beach, wasn't it?' " said Joe.

And Joe said he answered yes, but only because he was tired.

"Was that the truth?" Worth asked.

"No," said Joe.

"Where had it happened, Joe?"

"It happened in our master bedroom."

Joe said he didn't really use two hands as he had agreed he had, and he also said he inaccurately agreed when Tripodo Senior asked him if he had partially buried Diane *before* he put the tarp on. Actually, Joe insisted, the tarp was already on. He said he was so worn out he would have told Tripodo Senior anything he wanted.

He said he might have told Tripodo Senior "she deserved it," but contended he meant the remark in the context of "anybody who tried to kill somebody deserved to be hurt. And also she broke up the family and had humiliated me with bringing men back to my house sleeping in my bed next to my children."

An intriguing aspect of the Tripodo Senior version was that Joe had claimed he returned from Plymouth, Massachusetts, to the Hamptons, but in doing so obviously lied about other places he visited that Sunday morning and afternoon, like his visit to Sandy and to their old weekend homes.

Joe's story to Tripodo Senior, and his new story to the jury, had both been more of the same stew—part fact, part fiction, part mystery.

Virtually everyone in the courtroom, especially three of the jurors, had been lulled into boredom by the time Worth inquired about photos taken by the state police the night of the arrest.

"That's me," said Joe as Worth handed him a color photo of his naked right side.

"Is that picture a fair and accurate description of the way you looked that night?" asked Worth.

"Yes," said Joe. Worth offered the photo as evidence. Prosecutor Joseph said he had no objection, provided all three of the relevant photographs were offered. Worth agreed, but insisted he would perform the task one at a time.

Suddenly everyone was paying close attention. "Joe, what does that picture show?" Worth asked, still referring to the first photo.

"It shows a cut along my side to my back."

"Joe, did the state police take that picture?"

"Yes."

"Your idea or their idea?"

"Their idea," said Joe.

"After that picture, did anybody ask you *one single question* about how that mark got there?" Worth raised his voice for the three key words.

"No," said Joe.

The photo was carried over to the jury box, where each member of the panel looked at it intently.

Worth picked up the second photo. "This is a close-up of the cut," said Joe.

"A close-up of that same shot, right?" Worth asked.

"Yes, it is."

"Guess they thought it was important, huh?" said Worth, raising his voice.

Joseph objected and the judge sustained.

"After they took the close-up, Joe, did anybody ask you *one single question* about how it got there?" Joe told Worth no one had.

Worth offered the close-up into evidence, then moved to the third photo. Joe said he recognized it as a photo of the scratch on his right hand.

"Where did you get that scratch?" Worth asked.

"In my struggle with Diane."

"Is that where she scratched you?"

"Yes," said Joe, no longer uncertain as to the origin of the wound.

"When they took that picture, did anybody ask you *one single question* about that?" Worth asked. Again, Joe replied in the negative.

Returning to the body cut, Worth asked: "Joe, did the

two pictures of your side show the mark where Diane slashed you?"

"Yes."

"Does the picture of your hand show the evidence of the struggle?"

"Yes."

Worth showed the other two photos to the jury, then told Judge Byrne he was finished questioning his client.

Rather than start cross-examination, Judge Byrne declared a ninety-minute recess for lunch. The reporters rushed to the well of the courtroom to get a look-see. Sure enough, there was Joe Pikul buck-ass naked with this big slash on his right side. The mark on his hand looked like a roundish scab. It didn't look like something a knife or fingernails could do. But to the untrained eye the photo of Joe's right side was quite a startling development.

Out in the hallway, Bekoff was asked why Joe had kept his story a secret all these months. "We felt that the jury should hear it from Joe himself. He was the one who lived it and he's the one who should tell it to them," Bekoff said. "He's been wanting to say this for a long time. Now is the appropriate time. He's looked forward to this day for many months. And he did what he said." Bekoff contended "an obvious assumption" could be made that the police had coerced Joe into making incriminating statements because they'd commiserated with him. "I think that flows freely from the evidence. They tried to manipulate him. They broke him down. The statements themselves are not admissible. . . . We let them come in because Joe had to tell the story."

The testimony had so impressed one TV reporter that she asked Bekoff to explain his defense. "Justification, self-defense," said Bekoff. "You are entitled to use physical force to protect your own life, including deadly physical force, if necessary."

"Are you gonna cop a plea here?" the reporter continued.

"No," said Bekoff. "It hasn't even been discussed."

"So you're hoping the jury will see that he was acting in self-defense?" the reporter continued in disbelief.

"Yeah. I think they can evaluate his testimony," said Bekoff. "If you line it up with all the other physical evidence in the case, you'll see it makes sense."

The news photographers spent their lunch hour taking pictures of the pictures.

CHAPTER • 26

Yes, No, Maybe So

ALAN JOSEPH ALSO LIKED THE direct approach, so he began his cross-examination of Joe on the same point Steve Worth had, only he wasn't as nice about it. "Mr. Pikul, is it your testimony that you admit causing the death of Diane Pikul?"

"Yes," said Joe.

"There's no question about that, is there?"

"No."

"There's no question that you were aware of that on Saturday, October 24, 1987, is there?"

"Yes."

"Yes, there is a question?"

"No," said Joe.

"No, there is no question, is that what you're telling me?"

"Yes," said Joe.

The grilling had begun.

Joseph veered from the central issue, just as Worth had, and started to peck around the edges. He started first with Joe's testimony that he hadn't placed Diane's body in the water because he hadn't wanted to let her go. "Isn't it a fact that's why you killed her?" Joseph asked. "Because you didn't want to let her go?"

Joe denied the suggestion.

"Isn't it a fact that you told her that if she left you, you would have her killed, dispose of the body so it would never be found?"

"No."

"You never told anyone that?"

"No."

"Isn't it a fact that all the verbal abuse or most of the verbal abuse in the marriage came from your end to her?"

Bekoff objected and Judge Byrne sustained. It was a question that couldn't possibly be proved or disproved.

"Isn't it a fact that the senseless arguments were the result of things you started?" asked Joseph.

"No."

"Isn't it a fact that Diane Pikul never disappeared on numerous occasions during the course of your marriage?"

"No."

"Isn't it a fact that you were the one who disappeared?"

"No."

"Isn't it a fact that you would disappear with the children without her knowledge?"

"No."

"Isn't it a fact that on the weekend of September 26 and 27, you disappeared with the children to your Rector Place apartment without her knowledge?"

Bekoff objected again and following a brief conference at the bench, Joseph moved on. Joe's behavior was still off limits.

Seeking to get certain points across to the jury through his questions, Joseph asked, and Joe denied, that his arguments with Diane were often over her being so involved in her work that she wasn't home enough, that he felt threatened by her having asserted her independence, and that he was jealous of Diane. Joe conceded he had hired a private eye to spy on Diane, and that over the years he and Diane had discussed his concerns about her having boyfriends.

Pulling out a typed record of Joe's credit calls during the key months, Alan Joseph went through a litany of toll calls between the defendant and Sandy Jarvinen, beginning with a half-hour call Joe had made to Sandy on August 17, 1987, two months before the murder.

Joe claimed he'd found their "family pictures, Sandy's and mine. . . . I said I'd been cleaning out the cellar and I found all these pictures wonderfully put together in albums and showing a lot of love and concern about our life together, and I cried, actually, because I just, you know, had a sort of sadness about that period and I realized I had most of the pictures and that I wanted to share them with her, and we had talked about other things. . . . I think I told her it's about time we settled this legal matter, that we could work it out somehow."

"Do you remember anything else you talked about during the telephone call?" Joseph asked.

"I may have said something about Diane. I don't recall, though. We weren't getting along, something like that."

Reviewing several additional calls preceding Diane's death, Joe told the prosecutor he couldn't recall what he and Sandy had discussed, but he did remember that he "became more confiding as the period went along, yes."

Seeking to spell out the motive for Diane's murder, Joseph moved to the meeting with Sandy at Hyannis Airport, and Joe admitted discussing his estate and the custody of Claudia and Blake, but not in the manner Sandy claimed.

Treading carefully under Judge Byrne's watchful glare, Joseph asked: "Now, had you discussed with Miss Jarvinen the fact that you were ill, you thought you were dying?"

"I may have told her that," said Joe.

"You told a lot of people that, didn't you?"

"I told Mr. Sawoska that."

"Did you discuss the fact that you didn't want Diane to have custody of your children?"

"No."

"Isn't it a fact you told her you didn't want Diane to have custody of your children, you were dying, and you did not want her to have custody of your children?"

Joe said the prosecutor had it all wrong. "I wanted to establish custody arrangements in the event we both died." He also denied that Sandy had told him that Diane would be the natural guardian of the children and as such would get custody if he died. "I knew that," he said.

"Isn't it a fact you then said, 'Well, she may have to have an accident'?"

"I don't remember that," Joe replied.

The prosecutor wasn't going to let go that easily, especially since Joe had acknowledged the day before that he might have said it.

Joseph pressed the point, but Joe's replies came off as ambiguous. In any case, the issue lost its umph without mention of AIDS. With Joe telling so many lies to police and then changing them on the stand, it was hard to tell if the story about him dying was true or designed to cover his tracks. Joe looked healthy and his testimony about feeling good and believing that he wasn't dying seemed plausible. Because of Judge Byrne's rulings, Joseph was stuck. There was nothing more he could do on that point.

He turned instead to Joe's death-scene scenario in the master bedroom. Joseph had the defendant acknowledge that the children had been sleeping in the next room, separated from the master bedroom by only a bathroom. The inference, of course, was how could the kids not have heard? Were they so conditioned to hearing their mother and father scream at each other that they didn't get up? Or maybe, just maybe, the murder hadn't taken place in the house at all. Maybe it occurred in the yard, while Diane was on her walk. Or at the beach, as Joe had told Tripodo Senior.

Giving Joe as much rope as he would take, Joseph asked Joe to reenact the death scene again.

As had happened so many times before, Joe couldn't keep his story straight. There were slight changes or additions from the version Joe had told just the day before. Then he'd said Diane came in through the front door, down the other end of the house from the master bedroom, where he was watching TV. Now he was saying she first entered through the side door, off the kitchen, with a couple of bags, then went outside through the side door and came back into the house with another bag through the front door. In Joe's original testimony, he hadn't explained how Diane's suitcases got into the master bedroom.

Joe now said that after the initial verbal skirmish ended with Diane calling him "a faggot" and "a creep," he figured Diane went to the kitchen to get some food. "I had bought a cheesecake and I thought maybe she was interested in dessert to calm down or something. . . . I was very tired at that point and I decided I'd go to bed and also I didn't want to argue anymore, so I started to take my shirt off."

"You're going to go to bed?" asked Joseph.

"I'm going to bed."

"In the guest room?"

"Yes," said Joe.

"And you're taking the sweatshirt off?"

"Yes."

"Where are you?" Joseph asked. Joe stuttered in response, stating that he was "by the foot of the bed, in the middle of the bed."

"The guest room?"

"In the master bedroom," said Joe.

"The bedroom *she's* going to sleep in?" asked Joseph, straining to hold back the sarcasm.

"Yes."

"Okay," said Joseph, agreeing to go along for a bit. "What are you facing?"

"I'm facing the head of the bed."

"What happened?"

"A few minutes later I felt a pain in my side."

"A pain in your side, or your back?"

"Back, from the side to the back." Joe's answers were starting to sound all-inclusive.

"What are you doing when you're feeling this pain?"

"I had just finished taking my top off and I was just standing there, you know, before—"

"Where do you put your top when you take it off, when you had taken it off?"

"Put it on the bed," Joe explained.

"What are you doing, bending over, laying it on the bed, dropping it on the bed, throwing it on the bed?"

"Throwing it," said Joe, again raising the question of why he was discarding clothing on a bed he no longer slept on, in a room he no longer slept in.

"And what happens? You feel the pain, what happens?"

"I turned and I saw she had a knife, and at this point the knife is raised in a position to stab me," said Joe.

The prosecutor wanted to make sure Joe was still relating the same scenario he'd given the day before, with Diane holding the knife up by her head, with the point facing down, in preparation of a downward thrust.

"Yes, facing toward my chest."

Joseph wanted to be sure he had it right. "Are you facing her at this point?"

"Yes, I'm facing her at that point."

"How far away from her are you?"

"A foot and a half. Two. A foot and a half—a foot."

"What do you do?" Joseph asked.

"I reached out in my hand to distance her and I grabbed her by the neck."

Which hand? "Right hand," said Joe. And Diane had the knife in her right hand. That was simple enough to visualize: face-to-face, Joe's right hand on Diane's neck, Diane's right hand with the knife raised, ready to come down on him; Diane 5-3½, Joe nearly six feet.

More difficult to imagine was how Diane had quietly approached, slashed Joe on the side, then pulled back this two feet or so, thereby giving Joe time to turn around—almost like an announcement—all before she proceeded to come toward him with the knife raised eye-high in the downward-thrust position.

"Okay, what happens?" Joseph continued.

"This is all happening very quickly, and I squeezed her neck as hard as I could. I struggled to get the knife away from her with the other hand, and that's when the knife came down and hit me in the back or hit me in the tooth."

"Hit you in the back?" said Joseph as a couple of spectators chuckled loudly.

"In the tooth," Joe corrected.

"In your tooth?"

"Yeah, in the mouth."

"What portion of the knife hit you?"

"I think it was the handle," said Joe, less sure than he'd been the day before.

"So you're struggling for the knife, you got her with your right hand around her neck, she's got the knife up with her right hand, you're warding off with your left hand?" asked Joseph.

"Yes."

"The knife then comes down and hits you on the cheek?"

"Yes, it was deflected and came down on the cheek."

"Which side?" the prosecutor wondered.

"Down here," said Joe, indicating where his right upper tooth had disappeared.

"Then what happens?"

"Then her body went limp," Joe answered irritably, as if to say, What do you think happened next?

"Let me ask you this. Were you bleeding a lot?"

"No, it was a false tooth. There was very little bleeding."

That wasn't what Joseph meant. He wanted to know about any bleeding from the back injury.

"The back, I was bleeding."

"Blood gushing out?"

"It was coming out," said Joe. "It was painful."

He said the blood got on his clothes and on the rug, "and later some by the door, I guess."

"You guess?"

"It had to be," said Joe. The prosecutor just stared at Joe, not saying a word. Joe repeated the statement. "It had to be."

"Why did it have to be?" Joseph asked.

"Because I went by that door and I brushed up against it," said Joe, his memory suddenly crystal clear about a picayune detail that occurred while he was in the depths of panic.

"You remember brushing up against that door?"

"I remember hitting something as I was moving out the door. . . . I hit the side of the wall, I think, or brushed up against it."

"Did you get blood against the side of the wall?"

"A bit."

"Did you clean it up?"

"I didn't clean that spot up, no, I didn't see it."

"But you cleaned the spot up on the side of the wall?"

"No, that was essentially the amount of blood that was on the wall," said Joe.

Under further questioning, Joe said he wasn't sure when he brushed up against the wall, but was certain it wasn't during the struggle. Joe seemed to be making the blood fit his story, since the cops had been unable to ascertain its origins.

"Did you ever move from the foot of the bed during the struggle?" Joseph asked. Joe said he had not.

"How long did the struggle take?"

"Seconds," said Joe.

"Can you give me an estimate?"

When Joe said he couldn't, Joseph suggested ten seconds, or perhaps fifteen. "I really can't, it just seemed so fast," said Joe.

"How about if I tell you to assume that the struggle is occurring right now, think back and tell me to stop when you think the length of the struggle occurred."

Worth objected, and Judge Byrne disallowed the time test.

So Joseph resumed the running story. "Okay, so she goes limp. What happens next?"

"Her bowels let go and she vomited a little bit from her mouth."

"While she's standing up?" Joseph asked incredulously.

"No, as she was going down. I mean, when her body went limp, I let go, and by the time she was on the floor her bowels let go and a little bit of vomit appeared on her mouth," Joe explained.

"While you're struggling with her and she's got the knife up and you're warding off the blow, what's she doing with her other hand?"

Joe mumbled a stream of stuttering gobbledygook. "I'm not entirely sure. This was all—I was scared and she may—the other hand—she may have been trying to get my hand off, I'm not sure. I mean it was just happening so fast, I don't know. I mean, my preoccupation was to save my life."

"All right," said Joseph, content to let Joe dig himself in deeper. "She's now on the ground. What do you do?"

"Well, I was just—I was so horrified by the whole thing I was kind of in a state of shock," said Joe, sounding heartbroken. "I lifted her up on the bed, I put her on the bed and put her head under a pillow."

Were you bleeding? Yes. Get any blood on her? No. How'd you lift her up? Pulled her by the shoulders. "I kind of lifted her under her arms and put her back on the bed." Joe said he then went to the bathroom for a towel to clean the blood off his back.

"Let me ask you this, Mr. Pikul," said Joseph. "Your wife goes limp, she goes down to the ground and you look at her and you're in a state of shock, right?"

"I thought she was dead."

"How long do you look at her?"

"I don't remember, not long."

"Five seconds, ten seconds?"

"I don't know, Mr. Joseph. It was, it was, it was an emotional—I don't know. I was in shock. I really couldn't believe what had happened and—"

"So you don't know?" asked Joseph.

"I don't know."

"How long does it take you to pick her up and put her on the bed?"

"I don't remember that either, but I don't think it was too long."

"You get the towel from the bathroom. How long does that take?"

"I don't know, thirty seconds, I'm not sure. It was just a few feet away."

The prosecutor wanted to know if Joe was bleeding a lot. "It was oozing. It wasn't a gush or anything like that. It was hurting quite a bit at this point."

"She slashed you with a knife and it was oozing out a little bit?" Joseph pressed.

"No, it had been a little heavier, and it seemed to be more oozing at that point," said Joe.

Joseph smiled. He said he wanted to make sure everyone was talking about the same injury. So he walked back to his table and selected the photo of the scab on Joe's right side. Joe said that was indeed the wound.

Asked how he stopped the bleeding, Joe said that after he wiped the wound with the towel, he wrapped the towel around himself. "I went back and looked at Diane and I thought that *we* had to—I had to get out, I was afraid the children would wake up and see, you know, see her dead and see me bleeding, and I thought I'd get her out of the house as quickly as I could."

Joe had said *we* had to, then caught himself. Bob Wayburn had warned Joseph to be on the lookout for a multiple personality. Wayburn couldn't put his finger on it, but he recalled several occasions during the custody case when he thought Joe had started talking in the third person. Perhaps Chloe or Jasmine, the two "girls" who liked to dance to Tina Turner tunes so much, was trying to make an appearance. Nonetheless, Joe had corrected himself, so the prosecutor turned to other matters—the tarp, the plastic sheets off the lawn chairs, the towels, the bathrobe, and all the ligatures.

Joe said he laid the tarp out on the floor at the foot of the bed, then cradled Diane's body, put it into the tarp, and stuffed the towels and robe and plastic sheets around the body. But he couldn't get the sequence right. He said he walked out to the Mazda to get the tarp from the cargo area, then returned to the master bedroom to lay it out on the floor. He said he turned and grabbed a bathrobe out of the closet, then went just outside the bedroom to a linen closet to grab a handful of big towels. Somewhere in there, Joe said, he picked up Diane's body off the bed, "from the feet and shoulder," and placed it on the tarp.

"Cradled the body, then?" Alan Joseph asked.

"Yes, I did," said the defendant.

When he was shown some of the towels, Joe admitted they had come from his house, as did the two matching towels he now admitted having placed in the car-wash dumpster.

Asked when he retrieved the plastic sheets, Joe said, "After the towels."

"Then what you're telling us is you went out, you got the tarp, you came in, put the tarp down, you went to the closet, you grabbed the towels—is the body on the tarp at that point in time or the body still on the bed?" Joseph asked.

"On the tarp."

"So you go out and you get the tarp, bring it in, you open it up. You take the body off of the bed, you lay it down, you then go get the towels, lay the towels on the body, you then go back out and you get the plastic tarps, those two plastic lawn-chair covers, and you come back in and you lay the plastic over the top of the body?" Joe agreed with that scenario as Judge Byrne adjourned for the day.

Out in the hallway the next morning, Barbara Martin, a longtime friend of the Pikuls, gave a few reporters her opinion of Joe's latest version. "Don't tell me that she got those head wounds from being dragged across the floor," she said. "This sure woke everybody up. You can't believe how upset everyone is." But with parenting responsibilities, jobs, indifference, and other commitments, the contingent of Diane's friends was nowhere to be seen. Martin was one of only two acquaintances to attend court that day, the first time any of them had been back since the trial began.

"What I can't understand is all this inadmissible stuff," Martin said, "like how all during that summer Diane was telling all of us how Joe told her 'I'm going to get the kids. I'll kill you and dispose of the body where no one will ever find it.' "

"He threatened her many times in the past," said Martin, who had driven more than three hours from her home on Long Island. "He said, 'I'll take the kids to Key West and become a fisherman and you'll never get any money from me.' "

Martin said she was not surprised to hear that there had been testimony about a struggle. She said Diane would have stood up to Joe and would have fought back. "She told me the week before, 'I can't take it anymore.' " She said Diane was afraid to be in the same car with Joe, and that's why she drove out to the Hamptons in the second car. But why, then, had Diane let Claudia and Blake ride out with Joe? "I don't know. I just don't know," she said.

During a recess, Alan Joseph tried to explain to Martin how the law really works—rules about admissibility of evidence, hearsay, the so-called dead man's rule preventing the introduction of statements that cannot be cross-examined because the person who supposedly made them is not alive to confirm or deny them. Joseph assured Martin that through his questioning of witnesses he was bringing out positive information about Diane and negative information about Joe's abusive behavior toward her.

These were complex issues for the uninitiated, and Joseph tried his best. He understood the frustration, the desire to help out. But he had a trial to conduct and he had to conduct it under the rules of law. He excused himself to get back to his case.

Back on the stand, Joe proceeded to change more of his prior testimony. Now he said he wasn't certain of the order in which he ran around and gathered all the towels and plastic and robe, and he wasn't certain in what order he had used each item. He was never asked why his memory had grown hazy overnight, but perhaps he had realized that he would have to explain how he had spread the plastic lawn-chair covers underneath the body if they were the last things he got. Now he was attributing his uncertainty to his state of "absolute panic."

Asked why he put the towels, the bathroom rug, and everything else on Diane's body, Joe said he wanted to "prevent her from, her body from, from any kinds of fluids that might come out."

Joseph pointed out that Diane wasn't bleeding. "What fluids might come out?"

"I don't know. She vomited," said Joe. But Joe had already cleaned that up, according to his previous testimony.

"What fluids might come out?"

"I have no idea," said Joe.

"Why did you take a rug, a bathrobe, two lawn-furniture covers—plastic, kind of big—a number of beach towels, plus a car cover? Why did you need all those other items?"

"I don't know," said Joe.

Then Joe claimed he wrapped the pink cord around Diane's neck, hands, and feet *after* he stuffed her and everything else into the tarp and wrapped it up. "So, in other words, you're telling us that the tarp is around her and you wrap the cord around her, around the tarp, the *outside* of the tarp?" asked Joseph.

"Yes, that's what I recall," said Joe, suggesting a scenario amply contradicted by several state-police photos and the autopsy report. Joe now also said he didn't think that he had tied Diane's hands with the belt from the bathrobe before he wrapped the tarp around her, when in fact he must have. Neutralizing Worth's argument that no fingerprint test had been performed, Joe then admitted he'd washed his blood off the kitchen knife.

Joseph asked Joe where Diane's hands had been while he was doing all the wrapping. "They must have been down," Joe offered. Asked how he tied the cord about Diane's neck, Joe replied: "I don't know the sequence. I don't remember that." But he was certain of one thing, the ties around the neck and the feet were on the outside of the tarp.

Shown a photo of Diane's hands tied, Joe said he couldn't recall when he did that but was certain he'd done it immediately after the killing. "So then what you're telling us is with the tarp wrapped around her hands, her hands are tied in front of her with her arms down to the sides?" Joseph asked. Joe agreed.

Finished with the packaging process, the prosecutor resumed with the reenactment, having Joe describe how he dragged Diane's body past the children's bedroom, out of the house, and into the car. "The door was closed," Joe explained.

Pressed whether he had bent over while he was pulling Diane, Joe said, "Maybe a little bit."

"You're telling us you're standing up straight?"

"Not straight, you'd be stooped a little bit. You know how people pull somebody," said Joe, again not helping his cause. Trying to complement Dr. Taff's testimony— and rule out Worth's scenario of how Diane sustained her head injuries—Joseph asked whether Diane's back, shoulders, head, and buttocks were on the ground. Joe said Diane's head and back were on the ground and thought it logical that her shoulders would have been touching, too. No, Joe said, he hadn't banged Diane against any walls on the way out, but yes, he had banged her on the sliding glass door.

"Hard?" Joseph asked.

"Well, that's as hard as a body being pulled that way would be pulled, I mean, I didn't hit her head, I was pulling her body."

Joseph now referred to the photos showing all the ligatures tied up like a handle, outside the tarp. Skeptically he inquired: "Yet you dragged her by the feet out of the house, is that what your testimony is?" Joe said it was.

The prosecutor turned to Diane's Ralph Lauren shirt, the one with the big rip and knot in it. "Now, when she was wearing this shirt, was she wearing it with this knot on her?" Joseph asked.

"I don't remember," said Joe. "I think that this shirt does tie up on the top, I don't know, I can't recall it."

"Does it tie up like *that* around the neck?" Joseph asked, displaying the ripped pieces knotted together.

"I have absolutely no idea, Mr. Joseph," Joe replied,

additionally denying that he'd put the knot in the shirt so he could carry the body and claiming not to remember even making the knot.

Joseph turned to the other ripped article of clothing. "Is that the skirt Diane Pikul was wearing the day you killed her?" Joe said it was.

So wasn't it a fact, Joseph continued, that Joe had tied the ripped shirt pieces together so he "could pick her up by the knot of the shirt and by the hem or the waistband of the skirt to take her out of the house?" No, said Joe.

"By doing so, the clips on the waistband of the skirt spread apart, isn't that true?"

"I didn't do it that way," Joe insisted.

The exercise went on for hours.

"Are you telling us that you never hit, punched, or struck Diane Pikul on Saturday, October 24, 1987?"

"Absolutely."

"There's no question in your mind about that, is there?"

"There's absolutely no question in my mind about that," said Joe, proceeding to issue a string of denials. "I didn't touch my wife. . . . I didn't hit her at all. . . . I didn't strangle her." The head wounds occurred "when I was dragging her."

Nearly every recess brought corrections in Joe's testimony. After one lunch break, Joe explained that he'd looked at some photos and now recalled that the ligatures around Diane's neck had been inside the tarp, not outside. The pictures included the grotesque close-up of Diane's neck and face that the defense had fought so long and hard to keep from the jury's eyes. So here was Joe refreshing his memory with a forbidden photo.

When Judge Byrne realized what had occurred, he angrily called a recess, stalking out of the courtroom redfaced with the attorneys in tow. When he returned, his anger still visible, the usually calm and soft-spoken judge yelled at the jury members: "Disregard anything about that picture not in evidence. I made a ruling it's not to come in. You're not to consider anything about it, not to speculate about it."

Prosecutor Joseph's tone was much stronger from that point, and he proceeded to pummel Joe, despite the extensive practice sessions with his attorneys every Sunday in the weeks leading up to his appearance on the witness stand.

"Mr. Pikul, isn't it a fact that Diane Pikul never had in her possession the knife on October 24, 1987?"

"No."

"Isn't it a fact that Diane Pikul never came at you with that knife as you testified to on October 24, 1987?"

"No."

"Isn't it a fact you were doing the same thing when you tried to cover your tracks with the condoms?"

"No."

"You're telling us that you had no conception as to what self-defense was on October 24, 1987?"

"Not during the moments of my panic, no."

"You had no conception of self-defense on Sunday, October 25, 1987?"

"No."

Joseph pointed out that Joe was fifty-four, college-educated, traveled the world, a veteran of the armed services. How could he not know about self-defense? How could he have failed to tell all those policemen about his wife's attack?

Joe had an answer for everything, or tried to provide one, but this policy only served to get him in more trouble.

Joseph asked the defendant how he was able to see at the beach when he took Diane's body there. "Well, there was plenty of moonlight and I had a flashlight. It was quite light for that time of night."

"So it wasn't dark out, it was light out?"

"It was dark," said Joe.

Joseph purposely bounced around, focusing on an issue—say the beach—then the towels, then back to the beach, or on to the knife. The back-and-forth routine was working because Joe now admitted that he had mentioned "something about peanut brittle" when he told the Sawoskas about his need for a dentist.

Joe's professed love for his children also took a beating. When he had dropped Claudia and Blake off at the Sawoskas, he had supposedly been contemplating suicide. So Joseph made sure the jury found out that neither Sawoska had ever met Claudia, and Henry had met Blake once, at a lunch in Manhattan.

Yes, Joe admitted, at the time he had a niece in New York City. Yes, the children had live-in baby-sitters in the past and live-out baby-sitters. Yes, there were Inga and Carina. Yes, there was Bernetta. "Isn't it a fact the children had baby-sitters who spent a lot of time with the children, who helped raise the children?" Joseph asked. "Yes," said Joe.

Among the swirl of half-truths, Joe acknowledged that when he called the Sawoskas the Sunday afternoon following Diane's death, he lied that he was on the Thruway and would be there shortly. "Turned out not to be true," said Joe matter-of-factly. "Maybe I meant the Massachusetts Turnpike," which made his timetable for a trip back to the Hamptons even less plausible.

Although Joe stuck to his story that he didn't have Diane's body with him, he acknowledged that he drove around Massachusetts, at least in part, to find a burial spot.

"Did you find any good locations?" Joseph asked.

"Nothing seemed to make sense to me at this point," said Joe, failing to explain why he felt the need to find a grave for a corpse supposedly buried at a beach hundreds of miles away.

Seeking to throw more mud on Joe's version of a return trip to the Hamptons, Joseph pointed out how the defendant had told Detective Composto that he left Lee, Massachusetts, at midnight and got home to New York about 1:00 A.M., and how he'd also claimed to have made the trip from the Hamptons to Boston in four hours.

Then he asked Joe if it was dark when he got back to Amagansett the Sunday in question. "I think there was still some light," said Joe. How did he get back into the house, with the new security code and all? "I must have found it by then," Joe offered. If he stopped off at the house for coffee and a bite to eat, what time did he arrive at the beach? "Anywhere from five to 6:30."

"Is it dark yet?" asked the prosecutor.

"It wasn't dark," Joe insisted, paying no heed to the time change that weekend.

"How did you know where to find this body?"

"I know that beach very well."

"You said there were no landmarks there, right?"

"No, but I know the dunes and I know where Diane was."

"Are you telling us that at six o'clock or so at night in October it's not getting dark?" Joseph asked.

"It was getting dark, but there was still light."

As for the actual retrieval, Joe said he had dragged Diane by her feet back to his car, then lifted her up—as Joseph put it: "the same way you lifted her up before, not knowing exactly how."

Then, Joe said, he went "back to the house and put some ice on her." Where had the ice been all that time? "We have a large spare refrigerator in the cellar."

Of all the tenuous claims made that day, the most difficult to imagine was Joe buying twelve bags of ice, putting them in a refrigerator—not a freezer—driving all over Massachusetts and then returning home thirty-two hours later to retrieve the ice and the body.

Joe explained that he "put the bags of ice into garbage bags which I tied so that the water wouldn't spill all over, big Glad Bags." Joseph wondered what happened to the ice bags, but Bekoff objected. Joe said he placed the bags on top of Diane's body, "on top of the tarp and around the edges." He said he didn't unwrap the tarp, he didn't untie any of the knots, and he didn't remove the ice from the bags. After putting the bags on top of the tarp, Joe said, he put "the blanket back over" the body.

"What blanket?" asked Joseph.

"I had a blanket on top of the body right along," said Joe. But what was he talking about if the body had been buried in the sand all weekend?

"Was it on top of her when she was buried then at the beach?" Joseph asked.

"No, of course not," said Joe, apparently missing the import of the prosecutor's zinger.

Alan Joseph had only started, though. Piece by piece he would reduce Joe's self-defense story to shreds.

CHAPTER · 27

Deadly
Blackmail

THE NEXT MORNING THERE WAS a new visitor in the courtroom—Mike O'Guin, research scientist and temporary
guardian. His presence reminded everyone of the two
beautiful children at the center of this tragedy, children
who were going to have to cope with their father's explanations for the rest of their lives.

O'Guin said he decided to check in on the trial out of
curiosity. "I just had to see what kind of defense a million
dollars could buy. I wanted to see what's going on because
it has some impact on my life as well as the kids." Claudia,
just ten, and Blake, six, were doing fine and being sheltered from developments as much as possible. "We have
not told the children he's admitted he killed their mother.
We've not told them that. We're trying to keep it as non-
traumatic as we can. They're in therapy. We're not going
to try to hide the truth from them. But we don't necessarily
have to walk in and say, 'Guess what's in the paper today?' " Whenever asked, O'Guin said, he and his wife
Kathy tried to respond as honestly as possible. He pointed
out that the children were speaking to their father regularly
and asking him questions about the case. "The children
actually know very little about the case. We try to shield
them from newspapers and news things. They actually
don't know a lot. They understand it's going on but they
don't know any of the specifics."

With Joe on the stand for a fourth day, Joseph revived his interest in any details concerning the icing down of Diane's body. First, Joseph established that Joe had not taken the body out of the station wagon to apply the ice; he had done it right there.

"You said you put the ice on to preserve the body," said Joseph. "Why did you want to preserve the body?" Worth objected, but Judge Byrne didn't interfere.

"I couldn't let Diane go," said Joe, mumbling. A juror motioned that he couldn't hear, so the judge instructed Joe to speak louder. "I just couldn't let Diane go. The thought of the family being broken up was just too much for me to handle," Joe said, looking and sounding quite pathetic.

Joseph wondered if Joe had had problems lifting Diane's body out of the station wagon at the Thruway site because it was wet and heavy. "I guess some water had gotten onto the tarp at the beach," Joe said.

"What did you do with the melted ice at this time?"

"The melted ice?" Joe asked back with a blank stare. "Ummm," he said, thinking about it. "I left it in the boot of the car at that point."

"Is the boot of the car wet?"

"No, not really wet," said Joe. "I mean, there was some moisture from the tarp, but it wasn't really wet. I don't know if any of the ice had leaked through, if that's what you mean."

Regardless of the question, Joe was keeping as much distance as possible between Diane's body and the ice. But his explanation for how the tarp got wet—at the beach—made no sense. He claimed that during his first visit, the time with the raft, he didn't put the body in the water. During his second visit, he supposedly went straight to the dunes to bury Diane. And during the third trip, when he supposedly went only to the sand dunes to dig up Diane and then dragged her back to the car, he again would have been nowhere near the water.

Now Joseph wanted to know what Joe did with the ice bags and the blanket in order to remove the body from the car. Had he thrown the melted ice bags to the front of the car? Joe said he'd moved them along with the blanket.

And where did the bags of water eventually end up? "I disposed of them at another dumpster," said Joe.

And where was that? "Somewhere in the vicinity by a hotel."

And when was that? "Must have been before I went to the Sawoskas." Joe said he couldn't remember the name of the hotel but was sure it was one of the big chains.

Had he thrown any credit cards away there? No. Just the bags of melted ice? "And the blanket." Why throw out the blanket? "Well, I mean, it had been on Diane's body, I just thought it would be best to throw it out."

Turning to the Monday after the murder, Joseph asked Joe why he had gone to the car wash. "I wanted to have it cleaned out to take any evidence that Diane's body had been in the car."

"What evidence?" the prosecutor asked. Joe answered that he didn't know.

"You had the tarp, two plastic lawn-furniture covers, numerous towels, large bathrobe, a rug all wrapped around her. What evidence?" Joseph asked again.

"I don't know, Mr. Joseph. The car was dirty besides," said Joe, not daring to mention the words "sand" or "melted ice."

When Joseph tried to point out the difficulty Joe would have had moving Diane's body in and out of the station wagon if the back storage area was as loaded as other witnesses claimed, Joe claimed everything was "in front of that area."

"Isn't it a fact that that stuff wasn't moved around too many times because Diane Pikul's body was in the boot area of the car when you brought the children up to the Sawoskas?"

"No."

"Those items were covering the body?"

"No."

So why throw away the credit cards? Joe said he threw them out because "I didn't think *we'd* need them any-more." He also said he thought they were incriminating.

Why throw away the knife? "Probably for the same reason. I don't recall. I just had the impulse to throw the knife out, too." Since it was washed and cleaned, why not leave the knife in the kitchen with the other knives? "I can't remember any more than I said. . . . It wasn't a lot of rhyme and reason to the things I was doing, Mr. Joseph."

Joseph asked about the air fresheners bought at the car wash, but Joe denied Claudia had complained that the car smelled. "I don't recall that," he said. "I don't think the car smelled. It just had been cleaned."

"You're saying Claudia didn't complain?"

"I don't recall that, Mr. Joseph," Joe replied, contending that he frequently bought air fresheners for his children. "They seem to love them and they came off and fell off and I didn't particularly like them but they enjoyed them." Sitting in the back row of the courtroom, Lori Mitchell wanted to jump up and scream: "He's lying," but she was forced to sit and stew.

Out of all the possible choices of persons to watch Claudia and Blake the Monday night after Diane's death, why select business associate Jean-Jacques? "I had wanted somebody at the house to watch the children in case the police came again and wanted me to go with them. . . . I thought it would be easier to have Jean-Jacques there and, you know, who I was very close to, you know, in the business, in the business. He knew the children, he was good with the children, and his presence seemed more logical than anybody else's at that point."

"More logical than the baby-sitters who were there to care for the children?" Joseph asked.

"Well, it appeared to me I wanted him there, yes," said Joe, failing to mention that he'd shown one of the baby-sitters the door for asking too many questions.

Joseph was curious why Joe hadn't told the police the truth immediately about Diane's knife attack. Joe explained that he'd been "afraid they'd arrest me and then I'd lose my children."

"You had this cut on you, right?"

"Yes, I did."

"As far as you knew that would be proof that she attacked you, right?"

Worth objected and the judge sustained.

Joseph tried it another way. "You could show them this cut to show she attacked you, right?" Worth objected again, and Judge Byrne explained to the jury that it was his job to instruct them on the defense of justification at the end of the trial. Prevented from getting his questions answered, Joseph had still made his point.

Under additional questioning, Joe acknowledged he had gone to the Greenwich Village police precinct in the middle of the night when asked so as not to raise suspicion.

"At that time you knew you had killed Diane Pikul, right?"

"That I killed Diane Pikul to save my own life, yes."

"That you knew you had killed her, right?"

"Yes," Joe conceded.

"And you didn't want the police to know that, did you?"

"Right."

Now Joseph moved back to the scratch on Joe's hand. Yes, Joe said, he'd told Composto that he got the scratch getting a ball out of the honeysuckle bushes. Yes, he does have honeysuckle bushes. Yes, he did play ball with the kids that Saturday. But it was all a lie, Joe said.

"How did you get the scratch?"

"During the struggle with Diane."

"She scratch you or you scratched against something?"

Worth tried to stop the pummeling, but Judge Byrne declined to step in.

"Did she scratch you, you scratch something, the knife?"

"I don't know exactly, Mr. Joseph. She may have scratched me with one of her hands during the fight."

"That's while she's waving this knife at you?"

"Objection," Bekoff yelled. "She has two hands, judge."

It didn't matter; Joseph had scored again.

The prosecutor next hammered away at Joe's failure to give this latest version to any of the police, seeking to turn the length of the all-night interview to his advantage. "Are you telling us that you spent five, six, maybe seven, eight hours with Detective Composto and you never told him what you told us about what happened Saturday, October 24?"

"What do you mean?" Joe asked back. "I told him a lot of things that happened."

"About the struggle with Diane?"

"No, I didn't tell him that."

"Did you ever tell him that Diane attacked you?"

"No."

"Did you ever tell him that you had to kill her in self-defense?"

"No."

"Did you ever tell him that you have a wound to prove it?"

"No."

"Isn't it a fact you never told him any of those things because it didn't even occur?"

"No," said Joe loudly and firmly.

"Isn't it a fact that wound on your side is nothing more than a scratch mark?"

"No," said Joe.

"Not made by a knife?"

"No."

Throughout the interrogation, wherever he could, Joe couldn't resist getting in his jabs at Diane. He worked in how he'd told Tripodo Junior that his "little boy loved pancakes, but that he was afraid to ask his mother to make pancakes for him because she'd probably say no." And he quoted Tripodo Junior as telling him that everyone in the barracks knew Diane "was cheating on you right from the beginning. She's a real pig."

With a weekend to reorganize, Joseph's cross-examination became even more brutal when Joe took the stand for a fifth day on Monday, March 6, 1989, the start of the trial's sixth week.

Asked why he had called New York police shortly after calling East Hampton, Joe claimed the East Hampton cops told him, "This would be a matter to report to the New York Police Department for missing persons." But on the tape already played to the jury, dispatcher Harry Field had said no such thing.

"You're saying that the East Hampton Police Department told you that on that taped telephone conversation?" Joseph asked.

"I recall that," said Joe before amending: "I'm not sure. I'm not sure."

A bit of humor dripped in while Joseph was seeking to ascertain whether Joe was treated all right at the state-police barracks after his arrest. "Had quite a number of sandwiches during the course of the evening?" Joseph asked.

"More than one I guess, yes," said Joe.

"You had drinks?"

"Well, we had soda."

"Yes, soda," said Joseph. "You were aware there was a retirement party and food had been brought in at the barracks?"

"I just thought they lived like that," said Joe, as everyone in the courtroom, especially the jurors, roared with laughter. "They never told me they had a party, no."

Pushing the testimony toward the forbidden, Joseph had Joe acknowledge that he may have told Venezia that Diane was blackmailing him with the pictures. Then Joseph asked Joe if he had told Venezia that Diane had hired a private investigator, had found out about the cross dressing, and was telling people about it.

"My wife knew that *we*— No, not that!" Joe exclaimed, cutting himself off in midsentence. Had he suppressed the appearance of one of his other personalities again?

Joseph followed with a most damaging question, one that pulled a great deal of the case together vis-à-vis the defense's allegations of police misconduct and Joe's behavior during the murder aftermath. "Up to this time, had you ever told any police officer that your wife had cut you, had attacked you with a knife, either Detective Glynn, Investigator Delaney, Detective Sergeant Bowen, Detective Composto, Detective Finelli, the East Hampton police, Investigator Probst, Investigator Oates, Investigator Tripodo, or Investigator Venezia?" Joe said he had not.

Of course, Joe had been under no obligation to tell any of those people, but all the same, he had jabbered away with every one of the officers, giving each one a different version—every version but the one being played out in court. The single most important issue, that Diane had supposedly attacked him with a knife, he had told to no one.

In his direct testimony, Joe had only touched on his version of his confession to Tripodo Senior; Alan Joseph wanted the jury to hear all of it. After all, the defense had opened the door.

Joe repeated his claim that Tripodo Senior had suggested the beach as the death site. "He asked me if I had killed Diane at the beach. He told me I had, and that's the way he said it. . . . He said, 'This is the way you did it, isn't it?' And he made a motion of strangulation and hitting her head against a rock or something."

"Wasn't 'the beach' your words?" Joseph asked.

"I don't recall that."

"He never told you it happened on a beach, did he?"

"Yes, he did say that, Mr. Joseph. He used—I think he said the Atlantic Beach," said Joe, referring to an ocean-side beach.

"Didn't he ask you, 'Where did you kill her, Joe?' "

"No."

"And you told him, 'It happened at the beach.' "

"No, I don't recall that, Mr. Joseph."

"Did you tell him it had been on Alberts Landing?"

"I told him anything he wanted to hear, I wanted to go to bed," said Joe.

"Didn't you tell Senior Investigator Tripodo, 'I went to the beach with Diane, drove out there with the Mazda about a mile away to talk'?"

"I don't recall. I may have said that," said Joe, starting to waver again.

"Wasn't it at that point that he asked you, 'How far is it, Joe, from the house to the beach?' and you told him it was about a mile?"

"I don't recall, but it could have been. It's a little more than a mile," said Joe.

"Did you tell him where on the beach this occurred?"

"I don't remember that."

"Didn't he ask you, 'Where on the beach was it then, Joe?' And didn't you tell him, 'It was to the left side of the parking area as you're looking by the water,' and that the area of the beach where you were arguing was not by the water?"

"I don't recall that. I may have said that," Joe said, acknowledging he may have said everything he had just finished denying.

Indicating a shaking two-handed choke hold, Joseph

also asked: "Didn't you tell him that she was speaking sharply and you couldn't take it anymore and you began choking her like this?"

"Absolutely not, Mr. Joseph."

"Weren't they your motions and your words, not his?"

"They were his motions, Mr. Joseph."

"Didn't you tell him several times that you left her partially buried on the beach?"

"I may have said that."

"What did you tell him after you left her partially buried on the beach?"

"I was mostly answering his questions, Mr. Joseph, I don't recall what we talked about after that."

As the questioning continued, Bekoff rose to object. "Just so we're clear, judge, we're talking about what he said to Tripodo Senior, not what happened, right?" The judge agreed. It sounded comical, but that was a key element of the defense, the need to differentiate between all those layers of lies.

"Did you tell him after you choked Diane at the beach, left her partially buried, that you went back to the house and you found condoms under her bed?"

"I think I said something to that effect, yes."

"Why did you tell him that?"

"Why did I tell him what?" asked Joe.

"That you found the condoms after the incident, not before?"

"I was just staying consistent with the other things I had told the police about the condoms at this point," Joe explained. Which of course wasn't totally correct either, since at one point he'd mentioned to the New York cops that he found the condoms after returning from his trip to Zurich.

Joseph pointed out that the condoms in question were Gold Tex, the brand that Joe said he'd never heard of during all of his intensive research of the condom market here and abroad. Backing off, Joe now said he hadn't focused that much on the foreign market. "The market had not developed that much at that point overseas. This was basically our market at that point."

"Isn't it a fact that the majority of condoms are made overseas?" Joseph asked. "Isn't it a fact, sir, that Gold

Tex for the last twenty years has been the largest manu-
facturer of condoms in Europe and you were aware of
that?"

"I wasn't aware of that."

"Isn't it a fact you were also aware that Gold Tex is not
marketed in the United States?"

"I was not aware of that. My focus on my work was
mostly in the United States."

Joseph had scored again. Not only had he shattered Joe's
story about his supposed research, but he also had pointed
out that Joe, the analyst who traveled regularly to Europe,
was the most likely purchaser of the "boyfriend's" condoms.

Finally, the prosecutor began to tie up his loose ends,
seeking to suggest that Joe had told Tripodo Senior the
real story.

"Did you tell him that you didn't know exactly when
you picked up Diane's body from the beach and put it in
the back of the station wagon?"

"I don't recall what I said about that," said Joe, again
lending credence to the scenario that he had buried Diane
very soon after the murder—regardless of precisely where
it took place—then dug her up immediately and took her
back to the house. He wouldn't have had to come back
for Diane that Sunday; he would have had her in the car
the whole time. This was the only scenario supported by
all the evidence. And Joe had offered no physical evidence
or records to support his claim of a return trip to Long
Island.

Joseph's final point of inquiry concerned the question
of the so-called slash wound. Yes, Joe said, he had been
strip-searched and photographed. Yes, he had known the
police were taking pictures of his right hand and of his
right side. "You were aware of the injury on your side?"
Joseph asked. Joe said he had been.

"Did you tell anyone at that time, 'Look, that's where
she cut me'?"

"Did I tell anybody that? No," said Joe.

Tripodo Senior had asked about where the injuries had
come from, hadn't he? Joseph inquired. Joe said he
couldn't recall. "Did he ask you if you got those marks
from the struggle with your wife on the beach?"

"I don't recall that."

"Didn't you tell him, 'No, that had nothing to do with it'?"

"I don't remember that," said Joe.

As for the fact that Joe hadn't received any medical attention for his wound, Joseph pointed out that when the nurse at the jail had asked if Joe had any medical problems requiring a doctor's attention, Joe had told her no.

The cross-examination complete, Alan Joseph sat down.

After lunch, Worth tried valiantly to plug up the most obvious holes. He asked Joe why he'd changed in the master bedroom since he'd started sleeping in the guest room. Joe said most of his clothes were still in the master bedroom, and that there was no closet in the guest room, only an armoire. This was the armoire where Joe had previously testified he kept his guns.

Worth also had Joe run through his revised explanation for perhaps his most grievous mistake on the stand—his testimony that the pink cord had been tied around Diane's neck outside the tarp. Joe had already corrected it, but Worth thought it needed another go-round. Joe now said there was no doubt in his mind that he had tied the pink cord inside the tarp, and there was no doubt that he had tied it loose.

Joe also made clear that his supposed slash wound did not actually gush blood. "Not a whole lot," said Joe.

A few points about the Gold Tex condoms needed to be cleared up, too—not the ones Joe supposedly found under the bed, but the ones the police had found in the second drawer in the master-bedroom bureau. Joe said he only learned about the condoms in the drawer from the state-police report. He had no idea they were in the house. Hadn't slept with Diane since that July, he said. "Did you have any reason to go near the condom drawer after July?" Worth asked.

"No," said Joe.

Then Joe completely changed his testimony about the tear on Diane's blouse and the stretched-out clasp on her skirt. "Was there ever a time that you moved Diane's body without benefit of the ropes that had been placed on her?" Worth asked.

"Yes," Joe now said. "When I took her off the bed and put her on the tarp."

"Do you have any explanation concerning the tears that appear in the black skirt and in the shirt?" Joe said it "could have" happened when he "lifted her off the bed by holding the waistband of her skirt and the blouse." But, he added, he still wasn't sure. The subject of the knot wasn't even raised.

Continuing with his revisions, Joe offered an alternative suggestion for the origin of the injury to Diane's left rib, given the fact that her arms were at her side as he supposedly dragged her out of the house. "Could have happened when I was lifting Diane's body into the station wagon. I could have hit on the edge of that," said Joe, again adding he was not sure.

"Did you ever punch her?" Worth asked.

"I never punched her."

Worth sought to clarify the problem of Joe having claimed he had no knowledge of the law of self-defense, despite his world travels and educational background. No, I am not an attorney, said Joe. Yes, I understand the jury will be instructed in the law of self-defense.

"That night when this incident happened, did you know what the law of self-defense was?"

"No," said Joe.

Having done all he could—after all, he was not a magician—an exhausted Steve Worth sat down.

Mercifully, Alan Joseph took even less time, focusing on the inconsistent testimony regarding the supposed blood flow from Joe's supposed wound, the supposed looseness of the pink cord, how Diane's skirt clasp had become stretched, and the guest-room armoire.

"Do you recall I asked you on cross-examination how you removed the body from the bed to the tarp and you told us you cradled it?"

"On further recollection, Mr. Joseph, I thought that lifting her by her skirt and blouse was probably the way it happened."

"I see," said Joseph. "Days later you now recall you didn't cradle the body to remove the body from the bed?"

"That's correct."

Joseph grabbed a photo of the large armoire positioned in the room Joe had been using for at least four months before Diane's death and showed it to the jury. There was plenty of room in it for clothing.

On that note, Joseph finished with the best witness his case could have ever hoped for.

Joe exited the stand and walked over to the defense table, taking his chair at the left end, facing the jury. He sat there looking nervous, his hands shaking a bit. With nothing to do, he grabbed a piece of paper, then put it down. He grabbed the tiny, clear plastic water cups, organized them in a neat row, grabbed one of them, poured a drink, then gulped it.

The lawyers walked up to the judge's bench for yet another off-the-record sidebar. Joe put his two hands together, fingers intertwined, under his chin—elbows on the defense table. Dejected, he covered the bottom of his face. Just as suddenly, he became erect, as if to show confidence.

Joe stared at the jurors; several of them stared right back.

C H A P T E R · 28

Two Over the Left Eye

THE JURY WOULD LISTEN TO several more witnesses, but for all intents and purposes, Joe Pikul's testimony was the linchpin of the case. The defense called Linda McNamara, Diane's *Harper's* colleague, who reluctantly admitted Diane had told her of the fight the night before the murder, when Diane chased Joe into the street. The testimony was designed to show Diane's "violent propensity" and corroborate Joe's version of the fight, according to Worth.

A local doctor, Jerome Quint, testified that he was 100-percent certain that the wound on Joe's side could not have been caused by a knife. Joseph also called Venezia and the two Tripodos to testify about Joe's confessions that night at the state-police barracks. Tripodo Senior said he still believed the murder occurred on the beach, just as Joe told him, but acknowledged that he wasn't sure. Though the defense tried again to impeach the police version, the tactic went nowhere. After Joe's barrage of contradictions, anyone was more believable than he.

After forty-eight prosecution witnesses, four defense witnesses, and literally garbage bags full of evidence, testimony was concluded.

Bekoff asked that the indictment be thrown out because Joseph had failed to disprove Joe's defense of self-defense beyond a reasonable doubt.

Joseph countered that his entire case disproved Joe's story, pointing specifically to Dr. Quint's rebuttal testimony. "If that wound was not caused by a knife, then Mr.

Pikul was not attacked by a knife. If Mr. Pikul was not attacked by a knife, then Diane Pikul did not attack him. If Diane Pikul did not attack him, then he killed her."

Judge Byrne denied the defense motion.

Bekoff next argued that the People had failed to prove the intent aspect of murder and asked that the charges be reduced to manslaughter. Alan Joseph said there was a wealth of information to support the charge, and Judge Byrne denied that application.

Summations were set for the morning.

Bekoff spoke for three hours, lashing out at Sandy, Dr. Taff, Dr. Quint, and the "illegal tactics and outrageous conduct by the police," especially "the lies" of Investigator Probst. As defense attorneys are prone to do in closing remarks, Bekoff filled his speech with claims that were unsupported by the testimony.

Bekoff told the jury that Joe had always planned to testify. They made Joseph prove "the who" because the defense wanted the jury to hear the rest of the story straight from Joe while learning about "the tenor of the police investigation."

Recalling the statute-of-limitations issue in Sandy Jarvinen's alimony lawsuit, the $750 bill for her trip to Manhattan, the erased answering machine tapes, and her having steered Joe to attorney Vinnie Federico, Bekoff called Joe's first wife "a manipulator," "a user," and "a conniver." Making Sandy sound like a co-defendant, Bekoff repeatedly harped on her getting immunity "like a common street criminal."

As for Sandy's claim that Joe had said, "I had to eliminate her," Bekoff retorted, "Come on, they're trying to convict a man of murder based on one word."

Because of Investigator Probst's role, Bekoff said he liked to refer to the Pikul prosecution "as the case of the phantom admission." He mocked the testimony of how Joe had interrupted the conversation in the car on the ride upstate, and "out of nowhere Joe Pikul blurts out, 'That's why I did it.' " Bekoff also emphasized that Investigator Oates had been called to the stand by the defense so that he would admit he had not heard the critical phrase uttered. "Are you happy with that testimony? One cop lies, the other cop tells the truth. It's outrageous."

The prosecution had failed to prove "the where" and "the how," Bekoff said. The only reason the jury knew "the why" was because Joe had testified that "it happened in the house, in the master bedroom."

Bekoff assaulted Dr. Taff's testimony, spending the most time on the weakest link, the claim of ligature strangulation. Admitting manual strangulation, Bekoff said the hemorrhages that were found showed "it" happened with "a straight-on blow and then a quick squeezing." The Valium in Diane's system was tossed into the mix, with Bekoff suggesting the minuscule dosage detected would have cut off oxygen much quicker during a choke hold, causing the person "to lose consciousness or die quicker."

Then Bekoff turned to the blunt-force trauma. To counter Dr. Taff's opinion that the beating came before the strangulation, Bekoff contended that the scratches on Diane's neck were self-inflicted and proved she was "involved in a struggle." Therefore, Bekoff said, Diane must have been conscious when choked.

He insisted Diane sustained the head wounds while Joe was dragging her out by the feet. There were no drag marks because the body was wrapped in the tarp stuffed with towels, the bathrobe, the throw rug, and everything else, Bekoff continued, failing to also note that there were no drag marks on the tarp either.

Then Bekoff made these evidentiary leaps of faith:

—Tripodo Senior's reasonable doubt as to where it happened "shows that Joe was truthful not only when he said it happened in the house, but when he said he lied to Tripodo Senior to get him off his back."

—The blood under Diane's fingernails had come from Joe's right hand, even though it had not been typed.

—Medical evidence proved there was a struggle.

—The police took photos of Joe's side wound because they were certain it was "related to the case," and they wouldn't have bothered to take the pictures "unless there's something there, unless there's something relevant to the case."

—Fingerprint tests on the condoms might have led police to "another suspect."

There were outright misstatements:

—Henry Sawoska had firmly ruled out the possibility that Diane's body was in the trunk, when in fact Joe's college buddy made a point of saying it had been very dark.

—Blood was found on or near the door track to the sliding glass door, when in fact it was the master-bedroom door.

—Authorities improperly failed to take a blood sample from Joe, when in fact—as was the case with the secret AIDS motion back in Manhattan—it would have required a court order to extract a sample.

—Marshall Weingarden said it was common knowledge that Diane took off occasionally for prolonged periods of time, when in fact he testified he'd been unaware of that allegation until being told about it in the aftermath of the murder.

"Have the People proved the why?" Bekoff asked next. Profiting from all of the so-called prejudicial evidence that had been barred—the AIDS, the beatings to Sandy, and the sex tapes—he sought to diminish the import of the motive-related items that had made it before the jury.

The cross dressing was mentioned "to prejudice you, to make you say, 'Holy Cow, this guy is a cross dresser, what a kook.' I hope that in this country that is not enough to get a man convicted of murder," said Bekoff.

"Stock market was down. So what? By killing your wife, it doesn't make it go back up," the defense attorney continued. "That he was terminally ill? Joe thought so and as he sits here now with his weight, he's still hopeful it's not true. But do you kill someone because you're terminally ill? Do you magnify a potential trauma to your kids, who he loves so dearly, by taking her life as well? What kind of motive is that?"

Then there was the threatened divorce. Bekoff contended that the divorce couldn't have been a motive because it had been out on the table for a year and a half. As for Joe supposedly resenting Diane's job, Bekoff mocked: "What kind of motive is that? She got a job in March and in October he decides he doesn't like her working and he kills her? What kind of motive is that?"

Bekoff couldn't leave the subject of motive without

again proffering the boyfriend theory. "We admit Joe thinks there's a boyfriend," Bekoff said. Without additional facts, he contended Prosecutor Joseph was unable to "concede the existence of a boyfriend" because the claim "fits so well with what happened that night," and then everyone would feel sorry for Joe.

As for the condoms, Bekoff said: "No question he finds those condoms under the bed. We admit that. How did he feel? He told you he was devastated. There's the proof positive there's a boyfriend and not only is there a boyfriend, that boyfriend is having sex in his bed with Diane, right next door to where the children slept."

According to Bekoff, if Joe hadn't killed Diane, she would have killed him because Diane was petrified of "being fifty, without the kids and broke."

The night before her death, Diane "went crazy" over the early release of the baby-sitter, said Bekoff. "Imagine what happened when Joe hit that raw nerve? You don't have to imagine, you know. And if Joe didn't straight-arm Diane and choke her, today in a courtroom in Suffolk County an assistant district attorney like Mr. Joseph would be arguing, 'Diane had no right to kill Joe,' and he would point to Linda McNamara and say, 'See what her violent propensities were the night before the killing?' and he'd point to Marjorie Goldsmith and say—an impartial woman with no motive to lie—'You see, you see what the motive is? When Joe said that to her, that she was going to be alone and without the kids and broke, she couldn't take it and she killed him.' If Joe didn't do that, now he'd be dead and there'd be a different trial. But he did do it. He protected himself and he saved his life."

Seeking to dispense with another problem area, Bekoff said he had given long thought to why Diane had slashed Joe rather than stab him in the back. "Maybe she tried to, but Joe moved away, causing the slash. Maybe she wanted to slash him before she killed him to disfigure him and make him hurt. Maybe she just lost control and didn't know what she was doing. . . . We're not going to speculate and we're not asking you to speculate." But Bekoff made it clear where the blame needed to be placed. *"She in essence made Joe kill her, she broke up the family unit."*

In closing, Bekoff said Joe's behavior in the aftermath

of the fatal argument was due to panic, that Joe now realized he should have called the police, shown them his
wound and the bloody knife. But that "would have been
an awful price for the kids to pay," Bekoff claimed. "He
exercised lousy judgment," but his panic didn't prove
murder.

Bekoff took one final poke at the police, saying it was
the worst investigation he'd encountered in his twenty-plus
years on both sides of the courtroom. "You got to look
at each individual and see if he's an honest cop or a dishonest cop, a good cop or a bad cop, a dedicated cop or
a lazy cop, a smart cop or a dumb cop. What irks me is
every time I hear a policeman lie—and I hope it bothers
you—and every time they violate someone's constitutional
or civil rights, it's just not right."

Then he took a final look at Joe Pikul, the man. "We
gave you everything about Joe, the good, the bad. We told
you he was alcoholic, we told you how he met Diane, we
told you it's true he's a cross dresser. That's not a reason
to convict him of murder," said Bekoff. Innocent is innocent, "no matter what kind of life he still has, no matter
what kind of clothes he wears.

"You've seen his life-style. You might not agree with
his life-style, the fact that he had a lot of money at one
point, that he was in a limo—and that's the only reason
that evidence was brought out, the credit cards—is to show
you he had a limo driver, the same reason why he got
evidence in that he went to a beach club and had a masseuse. Maybe to say, 'We don't like this guy, we don't like
the way he lives.' That's not the way we do it in this
country. We told you the bad, too, about how the house
in Amagansett is in foreclosure, the apartments in New
York City are lost.

"I'm not looking for sympathy," said Bekoff. "I'm
searching for justice. And justice demands—*demands*—a
verdict of not guilty."

After lunch, the jury sat through nearly two hours of
Alan Joseph's summation. He started by telling the jurors
that he'd delivered what he promised in his opening statement. "I told you what the witnesses would tell you."
Sandy Jarvinen was put on first not out of weakness, he

said, but "to set the stage, to give you an idea of what was to come. . . . You judge her credibility, but I submit to you, she was entirely credible."

Joseph said his witnesses, along with the physical evidence, "put the pieces of the puzzle together." He ridiculed the inconsistent statements Joe gave to police and detailed the defendant's "various efforts . . . to conceal his involvement in this crime, saying, 'Diane ran away, she's probably got a boyfriend.' And yet on the other hand you hear about how the body is discovered not more than three miles away from where he has his car washed, several miles from where he drops the kids off that weekend, 180 miles from the house in Long Island where she was last seen alive, where she ran away with this alleged boyfriend."

The prosecutor said there was no question the mass of physical evidence connected Joe with Diane's body and the car-wash dumpster—the towels made in Brazil, the rubber gloves, and the human hair on the left palm, the credit cards, the Poco Loco bag, the multicolored bathrobe, the terrycloth belt from the Hotel Ritz robe and the human hair on it, the bankbooks, the tarp that fit perfectly over Joe's sports car.

"Then the glitter. Don't forget the glitter," said Joseph, linking the glitter found by police in the Regina and Dustbuster vacuums in the Long Island home with the glitter found in the pink throw rug found with Diane's body and with the glitter found in the boot area of the station wagon. Those discoveries, Joseph said, "connected the body with the station wagon, the body with the house in Long Island, and Joseph Pikul with the body—with transporting the body, concealing the body, dumping the body." The police had made all the connections needed to link Joe with the crime, he said.

Joe had told Sandy, "I don't want Diane to get custody of the children. She may have to have an accident" and "I had to eliminate her." And he told Investigator Probst, "That's why I did it. She deserved it. She was such a bitch." Together, Joseph continued, "The final blow was landed, connecting beyond any reasonable doubt Joseph Pikul with the murder of Diane."

Joseph suggested his case had been made even easier

by the defendant's corroboration of much of what had already been proven: that he caused Diane's death, that manual strangulation was involved, that he saw Sandy before and after the crime, and that he went to Massachusetts to find a place to dispose of the body. Although there was a dispute about what was said, the prosecutor pointed out that Joe also corroborated that he had essentially told Sandy what had happened.

The defendant also corroborated that he wrapped Diane's body in the car cover, and stuffed the package with towels and the bathrobe and the lawn-chair sheets, said Joseph. And Joe also corroborated the fact that he transported Diane's body in the Buick and that he dumped the corpse alongside the New York Thruway.

But most important, Joseph said, the defendant verified the suspicions of some police "that Joseph Pikul was lying when he talked to them, he was lying when he told them about his involvement, and lying when he told them about Diane's disappearance."

As far as Joseph was concerned, the defense of self-defense—"the so-called attack" by Diane—was concocted during the trial, "born after hearing and seeing the strength of the People's case against him—born, I submit, in an attempt to tailor the facts to support a version that might aid him in beating the rap. . . . I submit to you that his version was 'the only hope of beating this thing is on a technicality.' "

The suspicions of police were well founded, Joseph said. "Defendant told you he killed her. I submit to you that the police gave the defendant every opportunity to tell the truth. It's not the police who are on trial here, not any other witnesses who are on trial. It's the defendant who's on trial—Joseph Pikul. Not Sandy Jarvinen, not the police officers, not Diane Pikul. I submit to you that the police officers' search for the truth was hampered only by the defendant's actions, by his lies to them, his cover-up, his attempts to conceal his involvement."

"Keep in mind that he never tells one—one of ten or more police officers that he speaks with—this version. Even when he says he's tired, worn down, isolated, ready to tell them anything—anything but the version we hear during this trial.

"He's with Delaney, Bowen, and Glynn for over an hour. He's with Composto for six, maybe seven hours. He's with the Newburgh investigators for six, maybe seven hours. Yet he never tells them the version we hear, although he does tell them different versions. He tells them all a different version. I submit to you, you can't have it both ways. If he's got the wherewithal to change his story and say something different, then he's not worn down. If he's so tired and worn down and he's ready to say anything, then why not as he now claims?"

Joseph said inconsistencies in Joe's statements to police had been continued on the witness stand: saying he put the ligatures outside of the tarp when some were clearly inside; saying the subject of burying something never came up, then testifying that he had made a call to Sandy saying, "The package is down." When asked about the code words with Sandy, Joseph pointed out how Joe had blurted out a new admission "like a thunderbolt from the sky. 'Oh, yes, we did discuss burial, asked about parks, went to the Berkshires, all that stuff.' Now he's got to tailor it."

Joseph lashed out at Joe's changed testimony regarding Diane's ripped clothing and whether he carried her that way. " 'No, no, never did it, never did it that way.' Five days later it's all of a sudden, 'Yes, you know, I was thinking about that, yes, that's the way I did it,' " Joseph mocked. "Think about his testimony, his specific ability to recall certain things and his total lapse of memory on others."

The jury was also asked to think about Joe's need to explain away certain things: the blood on the bedroom wall, "not the sliding glass door"; the extent of Diane's injuries supposedly sustained by dragging the body; the placement of the barbell weight; the purchase and use of "fifty to seventy-five pounds" of ice; Joe's statements to Sandy, to Tripodo Senior, to Venezia and the other cops.

"Why the need to explain all these things away? I submit to you he feels the need to explain most of this away because it would tend to incriminate him," said Joseph. "They show his intent and they disprove his claim of self-defense."

Pumping up the volume even more, Joseph battered away at Joe's trial version. For instance, Joe now claimed he found the condoms before the struggle and that his confrontation with Diane over the three-pack led to the fatal fight; in his earlier versions Joe said he found the condoms after the death, using them as proof that Diane had run off with a boyfriend.

In another instance, when Diane attacked, Joe claimed he was undressing in the master bedroom, "even though he sleeps in the guest room on the other end of the house, even though he brought his suitcase and bags . . . into the guest room. He's undressing and getting ready for bed in the bedroom, the room he hasn't slept in since July. Even though there's an armoire."

The prosecutor asked the jurors to think about Joe's version logically, starting with the differences in height and weight. "I submit to you that the wound was not made by a knife. Where did that mark come from? It could have come from anyplace. But he's got to explain it away, he's looking, he's reaching, he's groping for some corroboration. Look at that wound. Look at the photographs. I submit to you, just looking at it with logic, commonsense, day-to-day, everyday experience, you know it's not a wound that's made by a knife, definitely not made by this knife. It's a kitchen knife.

"Look at it, it's sharp, it's used to cut things. There's no slash wound. I submit to you it's a scratch, no cut, no slash. You don't need to be a doctor to know. Draw on your common experiences. You've all seen a thin cut by a knife. Think about how that cut is, it's a clean cut, skin separates, not jagged, not roughed up, scabbed over like that."

He said Sandy had no motive to lie; in fact, since Joe owed her the money from the alimony suit, she had a greater interest in seeing him acquitted. "The only witness, the only individual in this entire case who has an interest in this outcome is Joseph Pikul. I submit to you that if you disbelieve him, he's got a lot to lose. He sits through the trial, he sees how the pieces are starting to fall into place. Through the testimony he tries to change the picture. The pieces just don't fit his picture. I submit to you that his version makes no sense."

Joseph ticked off several examples: the children didn't wake up in the next room, Joe failed to call police after the supposed attack, everyone was worried about Diane's disappearance but Joe, Diane came at him from behind, missed her mark, and somehow slashed him on the side.

Joseph maintained that Diane never had the knife. He contended that Joe discarded it at the dumpster because he had used it to cut the ligatures, "and I submit to you that that was not done until Saturday afternoon, after he bought the ice."

Joseph also said he found it hard to believe that Joe had transferred all those items bought at the hardware store from the Mazda to the station wagon. "Why? I submit to you that if he had already packaged the body up, if he had already put her in the tarp, put all those things on her, tied her up, he'd have no need for the hardware store, he'd have no need for the gloves, he had no need to put them in the station wagon. I submit to you it's logical, reasonable for you to infer that the body was wrapped with ice, the ice was inside the tarp. Think about it a minute. He wants to preserve the body. Why do you put all those beach towels, big towels, the bathrobe, the rug, and two plastic lawn-furniture covers? Look how big they are. Why do you put all those things *with* the body? The body fluids? What body fluids? It doesn't make sense. I submit he put them there as a form of insulation and you don't insulate, then put ice; you put ice and then you insulate. He wants to preserve the body. And why? I submit to you because he's going on a trip, he's going to dispose of the body and he doesn't want that body detected. He's got to preserve it until he can dispose of it."

Without stating precisely where the attack had occurred, Alan Joseph proceeded to submit his favorite murder scenario: "Defendant argues with his wife, he attacks her, punches, punches her head over the eye, punches her cheek, the forehead, temple area, punches the temple area on the other side, punches her rib."

Gradually raising his voice more and more, Joseph said: "He grabs her by the neck, he chokes her, strangles her for at least forty seconds. Then he takes the pink cord—not the cord attached to the car cover—he takes the pink cord, wraps it around Diane's neck, strangling her—just to finish the job. And it causes the ligature mark on the back of her neck. I submit not self-defense. Intentional murder.

"Forty seconds," Joseph said, overestimating a bit. "Think how long forty seconds is. Let's start. Let's start now."

And so the courtroom fell silent for forty seconds, save for Joe Pikul whispering to Steve Worth at the defense table.

Joseph stared at his watch.

Forty seconds.

It was excruciatingly long.

"Forty seconds," said Joseph, breaking the silence. "And that's the minimum time. I submit that's a pretty long time. That's the minimum time he would have had to have been strangling her to cause her death."

Bekoff objected, contending that Dr. Taff had never said forty, but thirty seconds minimum. The judge said the jury's recollection would prevail.

"That act of choking, that act of strangling is an intentional act, not self-defense, not accidental," Joseph said, immediately resuming his pace. "Consider the injuries suffered by Diane Pikul. Consider their severity, consider the pattern of placement. I submit to you it sounds more like a beating, looks more like a beating, not accidental, not haphazard in placement.

"Two over the left eye—*bang, bang,*" Joseph said, bashing his right fist into his left palm. "One on the left cheek—*bang.* One on the left temple—*bang.* Two on the right temple—*bang, bang.* Three in a row in the rear scalp . . . banging her head—three in a row. You've got the diagram, you can look at it. A blow to the side of the ribs, to the left side. I submit to you, sounds like someone with a wicked right. I submit to you those are intentional injuries, they're not accidental."

Even accepting Joe's version for a minute, Joseph said, how could Diane's hip have been injured while the body was being dragged? "Think about it for a minute. She's wrapped in all these things, all this padding. She's got this tarp. She's being dragged. How does she get this bruise? Just doesn't follow, just doesn't make sense . . . If he puts stuff around her head, how does she get the head injuries? You can't have it both ways. He'd like you to."

By Joseph's figuring, Joe's version also was a mathematical impossibility. He said there were "six steps, tops" from the house to the driveway. Even with the sliding-glass-door track, it didn't add up to the ten injuries to the head. Never mind the fact that the wounds were spread out over the entire head, not just in one general area.

"How does she get the two injuries up here, right here above the left eye?" asked Joseph, pointing to the front of the face. "What's he do, pull the body around, bang it that way, then flip it around the side, get the two over here—*bang, bang*—get two more over here—*bang, bang*?" There was only one logical explanation: "an intentional beating, an intentional causing of Diane Pikul's death by Joseph Pikul."

Although he didn't have to prove it, Joseph said, he believed he knew some of Joe's motives for murder, starting with "Diane Pikul's leaving him." Joe was a self-made man "used to controlling those around him," and Diane had been gaining her independence. With the magazine job she was "struggling to get on her feet, make a life for herself, getting ready to sue for divorce, custody of the children." Joseph said Joe objected to all of that, and had told Sandy he " 'did not want Diane Pikul to have custody of those children.' "

"Yet remember Diane's ace," Joseph continued, putting Diane's dangerous game in as positive a light as possible. "Remember she acknowledged she had proof that Joseph Pikul was a transvestite and that such knowledge might prevent him from gaining custody of his children." So Joe made the decision to eliminate her in the hopes that evidence of his cross dressing would remain secret and that he would then have the children all to himself.

Joseph suggested that Joe's actions "speak louder than words—his efforts to conceal the crime, his efforts to conceal the body, his destruction of evidence, his resort to falsehood—are all, I submit, evidence of his guilty mind and further evidence of his intent.

"Yet his words also speak to us. He didn't want Diane to have custody; 'She'll have to have an accident'; 'I had to eliminate her'; 'That's why I did it, she's such a bitch, she deserved it'; 'I never did anything wrong before'; 'My only hope is to beat it on a technicality.' "

Joseph said there was no doubt that "at the time Joseph Pikul was beating Diane Pikul and strangling her, he intended to kill her. Look at his actions in causing the injuries, look at the pattern of injuries, the head injuries, the rib injuries. I submit to you those are the intentional inflicting of bruises. They're an intentional injuring of a body. It's an intentional beating, they're intentional acts. Look at strangulation, the intentional act of strangling. . . . And consider his elaborate intentional cover-up, his attempts to conceal the crime, attempts to conceal his involvement, and his efforts to conceal the body. I submit to you all of them, taken together, point undoubtedly to one conclusion, one conclusion only—the guilt of Joseph Pikul in the murder of Diane Pikul, murder in the second degree."

Don't Lead with
the Queen

THE NEXT MORNING, JUDGE BYRNE instructed the jury on the law for over an hour, telling them to consider initially a verdict of murder in the second degree, the most serious charge in New York State. If they acquitted on the murder charge, they could drop down to manslaughter in the first degree, manslaughter in the second degree, or criminally negligent homicide.

Judge Byrne also gave extensive legal direction on the defense of justification, or self-defense, which the jurors would be required to pass judgment on if and when they found Joe guilty of any of the charges. Judge Byrne explained that "use of deadly physical force" was permitted in order to save one's life.

After the jury retired to deliberate, Joe walked through the lobby with one arm around Mary, who was celebrating her birthday, and the other around "Blaze," who had by now pretty much switched over full-time to her "Samira Starr—psychic from Egypt" mode. "I'm here with my two ladies—my princess of the Nile and my princess of birthdays," said Joe. Some laughed with Joe, others at him, but everyone had a hearty laugh.

Joe said he felt good. "I think it went well. Now it's up to the Big Twelve." Drinking a large cup of coffee, he smelled of alcohol.

"Hey, you're still here!" Worth joked as he walked by his client.

The jurors first ordered lunch, since they had to wait

for a list of the exhibits to be prepared anyway. Two hours later, they asked for a rereading of Judge Byrne's explanation of the three conditions needed for a verdict of second-degree murder—that Joe had intended to kill Diane, that he strangled and beat her with the intent to cause her death, and that he actually did kill her. The intent, the method, and the who.

Joe had admitted the killing and the manual strangulation. That left the issue of intent. Half the jurors listened closely during the rereading, while the others looked as if they couldn't care less. Their minds were made up, and they were ready to go home. Judge Byrne dismissed the four alternates, and all of them said they didn't believe Joe. They would convict him of something; the question was whether it was murder. "It wasn't clear-cut," one of them said. Added another: "I don't think he really intended to kill her, just to beat the daylights out of her."

"I didn't buy the argument about the knife wound. She would have had to hold the knife like a sword," said the third. "And why couldn't the so-called boyfriend be located?"

In midafternoon, jury foreman Rick Temple, an engineer, sent out a note saying everyone wanted to take a ten-minute walk. And at 4:10, another note asked for a rereading of the technical aspect of intent. One of the jurors wanted to know if intent meant "at that moment."

Upstairs in Room 932, Joe sat around a table with Bekoff, Worth, and a couple of reporters playing hearts. Joe was horrendous, leading with the Queen of Spades early in a round he couldn't possibly win.

In between hands, Joe talked with great interest about a Chinese immigrant who had been convicted of bludgeoning his unfaithful wife to death with a hammer in Brooklyn. "Did you see that story in the paper the other day?" he asked. He explained that the husband, who was convicted of only second-degree manslaughter, was probably going to get probation despite having walloped his ninety-nine-pound wife at least eight times. The man's novel defense had included testimony from an expert in Chinese customs who said a victim of cuckoldry could be expected to be enraged at a violation of the sacred Chinese marriage.

Joe seemed fascinated that in his anger the Chinese man had thrown his wife's panties away. "Why would he throw away her underwear? I don't understand why he would do that," he said repeatedly.

The funny thing was, the Chinese guy hadn't thrown the wife's underwear out; before she had been killed, the wife had taunted her husband by telling him she had moved her underwear into her lover's apartment. Joe had misread the story.

At 6:30, the jury sent out yet another note. They wanted certain portions of Dr. Taff's medical testimony read back. The doctor had been on the stand for the better part of three days. Judge Byrne said it would take some time to find the specific passages, so he sent the now-sequestered jury to a local hotel.

There would be no verdict that night.

Everyone settled in for the possibility of a long haul. Joe used some of his spare time the next morning to listen in on another domestic murder trial across the hall. But Worth quickly put a stop to that. "You're a public figure, Joe, you can't go around visiting other trials."

Meanwhile, back in the deliberation room, the jurors had to wait until late morning for the desired portions of Dr. Taff's testimony regarding strangulation and asphyxia to be located, then read back by senior court reporter Sheila Foster.

In between Foster's recitations about "thirty seconds to two minutes," "cause of death" and "blunt-force trauma," the holdouts heard whatever it was they needed. When Judge Byrne asked if Foster should read the cross-examination on those same points, several jurors shook their heads no. "If we want it, we'll come back out and ask for it," said the foreman.

Joe, his lawyers, and several reporters resumed the card game in the upstairs conference room.

A scant fifteen minutes later, the phone rang. Worth took the call, then turned to his client. "They have a verdict. Good luck, Joe."

The reporters rushed downstairs to try to sneak an early word from one of the court officers. None of them would officially let on, but suddenly there were a whole bunch more of them around.

Mary, who'd been present earlier, was nowhere to be found.

The jury came in.

Guilty. Second-degree murder.

The guillotine of justice had fallen swiftly.

The jurors hadn't been fooled for a minute. They'd spent much of the time eating or waiting for testimony to be read back. Actual deliberations had consumed less than seven hours over the two days.

Joe stood motionless, his fingers clasped together, but certainly not as tightly as they had been when he grabbed Diane's neck the Friday night after Black Monday.

Bekoff asked that the jurors be polled individually. As each of the twelve answered yes to court clerk Dick Riker's query, Joe sat down and took a sip of water. His hands were shaking. He clenched his right fist in his lap.

Judge Byrne revoked the $350,000 bail and remanded Joe to the county jail pending sentencing. Court officers led the defendant away in manacles.

"There was an overwhelming amount of evidence," said jury foreman Rick Temple. He said the panel determined that the wounds depicted in the state-police photos had not been made by a knife. Several jurors said they also were unimpressed with the explanation about where the twelve bags of ice had been that weekend and wanted to know why Diane's boyfriend, if he existed, wasn't produced at the trial.

"There were an awful lot of discrepancies and inconsistencies regarding his own testimony," said Temple. "It was very hard for us to imagine that anyone could grab a hold—after you've beat somebody—and then grab a hold of them by the throat and constrict their windpipe for a period of thirty seconds and not know that if he persisted, it was going to cause their death."

The usual post-trial nonsense ensued. Prosecutor Joseph smiled and announced for the TV cameras that "justice has been served." The defense attorneys said they were disappointed and would appeal. Joe's guru "Samira" identified herself as Joe's niece and actually got herself on TV in New York City that night.

The news crews were getting ready to pack it in when Mary finally showed up from a shopping trip to one of the local malls. She was crying within seconds as the cameras followed her to the jail, just across the parking lot.

"I'm in shock," said Mary, tears smearing her makeup. "I honestly can't talk. Can you please understand? I'd like to grieve privately for a moment."

Reaction elsewhere also fit the expected behavioral pattern.

Raoul Felder let it be known through his high-powered and high-priced public relations consultant, Howard Rubenstein, that he was available for interviews on the verdict.

Several of Diane's friends in Greenwich Village prepared for victory parties and realized that prospects for their budding movie proposals about their "roles" in the case had improved drastically.

Down in Florida, Donald Whitmore was unsatisfied even though his former son-in-law had been convicted on the most serious charge possible. A maximum term of life in prison wasn't going to be enough. "If I was next to Joe, I'd blow his head off. He killed my daughter in cold blood," said Whitmore.

Back in Yonkers, the tangled lives of two sweet little kids had just grown considerably more complicated.

PART·VII

A POSTMORTEM

C H A P T E R • 30

Same Song, Different Melody

A MONTH AFTER JOE'S CONVICTION, everyone gathered again in Judge Byrne's courtroom for the sentencing. But as usual, court was going to start late; the attorneys and judge were in the back room having another private conference.

There didn't seem to be too much left to argue about that Tuesday morning, April 18, 1989. Under New York State law, Judge Byrne's options were limited: Joe could be given between fifteen years to life as a minimum, and twenty-five years to life as a maximum. Since he wouldn't be eligible even to apply for parole until serving the minimum, Joe would be at least sixty-nine before being released. Claudia and Blake would be young adults by then, their father's domineering influence presumably long diminished.

When Ron Bekoff and Prosecutor Joseph emerged from the judge's chambers, they spent but a few minutes speaking in open court. Their brief comments only served to deepen the latest mystery.

With a half-dozen members of the Pikul trial jury joining dozens of attorneys, spectators, TV cameras, still photographers, and reporters, Bekoff addressed Judge Byrne.

"I have this past week become aware of some potentially very important 'newly discovered evidence.' In order to make a motion to set aside the verdict based on this 'newly discovered evidence,' I need to have approximately thirty days to investigate it and provide the necessary paperwork." Under the law, any "newly discovered evidence" would have had to have been unavailable to the defense during the trial and would have to be of such importance that it would have likely changed the jury's verdict.

Alan Joseph said he was ready to proceed with the sentencing, but based on what had transpired in the back room, the prosecutor knew what was coming.

Judge Byrne noted that under state law a "set-aside motion" had to be made before sentencing and observed that Joe was in the Orange County Jail "and he's not going to go anyplace." So the judge postponed the sentencing for at least a month.

Looking disheveled and thinner than he had at the trial, Joe was quickly led from the courtroom. "Joe," Mary said in a pleading tone to her incarcerated husband. But Joe made a point of not even turning around; he was angry that Mary had been trying to peddle his and Diane's personal property, including some of his sex videotapes starring Chloe and Jasmine, for what she had dubbed "The Mary Bain Pikul Story." With an asking price of up to $100,000, Mary was a shopping mall of other people's personal belongings, including Diane's autopsy report and Joe's tax returns. She was promising to sell dozens of videotapes—from Joe's sex-filled fashion shows, to Claudia and Blake playing in the backyard in Amagansett, to secretly made tapes of Diane making love with one of her female friends—footage that Joe had told others he had in his possession for the divorce case.

Mary also let it be known she had hundreds of audiotapes for sale, nude photos of Diane, Diane's sexually explicit love letters and diaries. The audiotapes were said to be available in a wide selection: intercepted telephone calls of Diane scheming with her girlfriends for a big-money divorce settlement, Diane and Felder arguing on the phone, hours of Joe and Diane arguing, and Diane talking nice to her lovers, male and female.

Out in the lobby, Ron Bekoff said he couldn't reveal the substance of this new development, but insisted it "directly reflects on the self-defense claim. It's legitimate evidence." If true, Bekoff continued, the evidence would prove Joe had killed Diane only after she attacked him with a knife.

Mary told the TV cameras she knew the postponement was coming. "I just got back from India a week ago and I understand—" One of Bekoff's associates cut Mary off and pulled her away.

Bekoff said he had learned of the new evidence only a week ago, but contended that Mary's being away on business had nothing to do with the sentencing postponement. The defense attorney said if the new evidence panned out, there was a good chance Judge Byrne would throw out the conviction.

And how was Joe holding up? "His mood is a little bit depressed. He's away from his children. He's been convicted of murder. He's in jail. So he's depressed," said Bekoff. "Has he given up all hope? He has not."

Heading for the courtroom door, jury foreman Rick Temple, who'd taken a day off from work to see justice administered, told his colleagues: "That's it for me. That completes the amount of time I'm going to commit to Mr. Pikul. Next time, I'll read about it in the papers."

Temple's young son, excited about his father's moment of local notoriety, looked up at his dad and asked, "How can there be new evidence? They don't have the jury."

Back in Manhattan, Felder had handed off his representation of the O'Guins to Diahn McGrath, a new member of the New York bar associated with a different Madison Avenue firm.

Felder, who was still interested in pursuing a movie deal about the case, explained that McGrath was married to his law-school classmate, Thomas J. McGrath, one of the most prominent trust and estate attorneys in the country, and that she had agreed to provide her legal services on matters involving the children and Diane's estate for free. Years ago, Diahn McGrath had been a professional actress under the name Diahn Williams. She appeared on "The Tonight Show with Johnny Carson," "I Spy" and "The Andy Griffith Show." She also appeared in a feature film with James Earl Jones and played the part of Crystal Ames on the NBC soap opera "Somerset." She decided to enroll in law school when her own child started attending school. She took her task seriously.

Felder said he'd lost a bundle on the Pikul custody case,

with half his office working on it full-time at one point. Still stinging from allegations he'd overcharged and underprovided for Diane, Felder said that part of his fee from the matrimonial retainer—he repeatedly declined to say how much—was presently in an escrow account "for the children." Throughout all of 1989, he promised to give it to them "once this all clears up." (When asked about the money in mid-May 1990, Felder said he still hadn't sent the children a check. "There must have been some reason connected to the estate why I didn't send them the money," he said. That afternoon, Felder wrote two checks totaling what he would only describe as "five figures." Actually, each child was sent a check for $5,000, totaling the same $10,000 Felder had put in a special account in late 1987. Apparently the account did not immediately pay interest, at least to the children.)

Felder referred all other questions to one of his new employees, "a man who knows more about the case than anybody," one Bob Wayburn, former counsel for the New York City Human Resources Administration.

Diahn McGrath, a tall, stylish blond woman with a tenacious approach, began filing papers on behalf of her new clients with a vengeance. Mike and Kathy O'Guin were appointed temporary administrators of Diane's estate and guardians for Claudia and Blake in Surrogate's Court. As had been the case all along, Joe's relatives—the Bergelts and Pawlowskis—declined to get involved, despite being named in Diane's will.

Joe's civil attorney Paul Kurland, who had refused to turn over the official copy of Diane's will until the criminal trial ended, finally furnished it so McGrath could begin probate proceedings.

Although Diane's will named Joe as sole beneficiary, under New York law Joe could not inherit from Diane. By virtue of his conviction, Joe was not only civilly dead, but his civil death preceded his murdering of Diane. As McGrath saw it, everything flowed to Diane's next beneficiaries—Claudia and Blake.

To further guarantee that the children weren't left unprovided for, McGrath also started working on a wrongful-death suit against Joe. The plan was simple: get a multi-million-dollar judgment against Joe so that anything owned by him would be forfeited to Diane's estate and therefore to the children. "He admitted he killed her. Therefore Joe forfeits everything," McGrath said.

Initially, she was confident—as were so many of Diane's friends and advisers—that Joe had millions salted away somewhere. It was still difficult for everyone to believe that behind the Pikul facade, Joe and Diane had really been broke.

As she searched and searched, McGrath discovered only nickel-and-dime assets along with a weighty pile of bills. The Social Security Administration awarded survivor benefits of $6,021 to each child, to be followed by $421 per month each until the age of eighteen. There was a $49,000 life insurance policy from *Harper's* and a pension from the city of New York from Diane's Parks Department job. Also, the New York State Crime Victims Compensation Board had awarded each child $15,000, with about one-fourth of the money available immediately.

But that was it. The rest of the news was bad.

The house in Amagansett had no equity left in it. In addition to the $200,000 mortgage seriously in arrears, Joe had taken out several informal secondary mortgages, most notably one with his civil attorney Kurland for $80,000. The bank holding the original paper wanted to foreclose, but since Diane owned part of the house, the estate questions had to be cleared up first. The real-estate market had gone soft; perhaps the house would fetch $250,000 if sold on the open market, less than the total of the outstanding debits.

The IRS was still looking for the money owed from 1986. Joe had finally gotten around to filing the federal return for that year—just a week before Diane's murder. McGrath said an IRS official told her it appeared that Diane's signature had been forged.

Sandy still wanted her money.

Joe and Diane had never left home without their American Express cards; thousands were owed on these and other accounts.

"The bills are stacking up to the ceiling," McGrath said in frustration. "There'll be nothing left for the kids."

Two extensions and two and a half months after the verdict, Ron Bekoff finally revealed his "newly discovered evidence"—a transcript of a single microcassette tape of Joe and Diane arguing.

There in the midst of the screaming and yelling, Diane threatened Joe: "I don't care if I go to jail, I'll kill you if I have to."

In his motion papers, officially filed on May 30, 1989, Bekoff noted that Samira Starr—"a near-daily observer of the defendant's trial"—had been arrested for burglary at the Pikul residence in upstate Cuddebackville and that Mary had found "a microcassette" while conducting an inventory of the personal property in the house to determine what was missing.

"Upon listening to the microcassette, Mrs. Pikul discovered that the tape contained a lengthy conversation between the defendant, Joseph Pikul, and his deceased wife Diane Pikul," Bekoff wrote. The motion papers made no mention of any other tapes, audio or video, or of the diary in which Joe had written that his best bet might be to kill Diane.

To support his case, Bekoff cited Joe's testimony at trial, supported by Linda McNamara, about the fight Joe had with Diane the night before her death. "The defendant testified concerning his prior knowledge of his wife's violent propensities, specifically as to an incident . . . where she chased him down the street in front of their New York apartment . . . the tape is compellingly corroborative of the central issue of the defense, namely that the defendant was physically attacked by the deceased, Diane Pikul, and that it was her physical attack upon the defendant which led to her death. The tape not only proves that the deceased had previously stated her intentions to kill the defendant prior to the physical incident which led to her death, it also established her motives to do so."

Picking out the most damaging snippets, Bekoff summarized how Diane accused Joe of turning the children against her, that she wanted a divorce, that she hoped he died soon, that she was going to have to get rid of him, that she felt he'd given her AIDS, that she was too old and poor, and that no one would want to marry her. Bekoff didn't have a problem mentioning AIDS now.

"The tape, taken as a whole, shows the violent and aggressive nature which the deceased showed toward the defendant, and her willingness to engage in provocative and aggressive conduct with him," Bekoff concluded.

While the transcript provided more flavor and depth about the ugly dynamic between Diane and Joe, it was unsettling to imagine them arguing about Joe stealing her sanitary pads and underwear, Diane's ability to swear off anal sex, and who gave who AIDS. But it was more difficult to imagine any juror viewing Diane's verbal threats as proof that Joe had killed her in self-defense. Ralph Schnackenberg's story about a drunk Diane playing with a knife at the foot of their bed was much more thought provoking.

More important, the transcript raised an important legal issue: how could this conversation possibly qualify as "newly discovered evidence"? If the tape had come from a recorder concealed in Joe's shirt pocket, which it almost certainly had, then he obviously knew of the tape's existence. More to the point, he was one of the participants in the argument. He could have testified about the conversation when he took the stand during the trial, tape recording or not.

Specifically asked about the tape's origin, Bekoff replied: "We don't know who made the tape." Asked what Joe had to say on the subject, Bekoff dropped another bombshell. "I haven't spoken to Joe about it. He's not feeling too well. He's in the hospital."

Sure enough, Joe had been moved from the county jail to nearby Arden Hill Hospital. He was listed in fair condition, suffering from an undisclosed ailment.

Bekoff was asked if Joe had AIDS.

"I don't know," he replied.

Three days later, on June 2, 1989, Joe Pikul died in his sleep at age fifty-four. The motion for a new trial had been filed none too soon. But perhaps that was the idea all along.

Joe, who had lost thirty pounds since his conviction, had

been hospitalized for a week, admitted after a fainting spell. His stay in intensive care had been less than a day.

"I'm told he died of cardiac arrest, stomach cancer, and cancer of the pancreas," Bekoff explained. "I'm saddened. Joe was full of hope that the conviction was going to be stricken and that he was going to get a new trial. He was mostly concerned that he was going to get a new trial and leave the children a *legacy of truth*. And that's why he testified and hoped that they would get a trial transcript later in life and know from their dad what happened. Even last night, he spoke to Mary and he was pleased that we were going ahead."

"Did he have AIDS?" Bekoff was asked.

"I don't know if he did or didn't," Bekoff replied, his back-room conferences with Judge Byrne still under wraps.

"Perhaps God was kinder to the children," Raoul Felder said in reaction. "This way they are spared the visits in the jail. The Lord works in strange ways and this may have been the wisest possible end to this terrible tale."

Regardless of the long-range consequences, however, Claudia and Blake had just lost their only remaining natural parent.

Because Joe had died in public custody and because of persistent rumors that he had AIDS, the Orange County coroner ordered an autopsy. On Mary's behalf, though, Joe's legal team swung into action to block it. At the same time, Bekoff and Worth called a news conference with Mary in their law offices in Mineola, Long Island.

Mary tearfully told a horde of reporters that she'd been told Joe died of heart failure related to cancer of the liver. She and Bekoff talked some more about Joe leaving this *legacy of truth* "for the children"—meaning the "real story" of Diane attacking first with the knife and their father having no choice but to defend himself.

Once again Mary promised to adopt Claudia and Blake. "They should be with someone who loved their father," she said.

Pressed for more details about additional tapes, Bekoff now acknowledged that he had "a valise full of tapes, numerous tapes. They were all of the audio variety, some of the little ones, some of the big ones."

What about videotapes? "There are no videos that I observed," Bekoff replied.

As the questions grew in intensity, Mary cried louder and Bekoff grew indignant. The two of them left the room, acting as if the reporters whom they had invited for a news conference hours after Joe's death had somehow ambushed them.

Up in Goshen, state Supreme Court Justice Peter Patsalos signed a show-cause order requiring Mary to provide a legal reason why an autopsy shouldn't be performed. Geoffrey E. Chanin, an attorney for the county government, cited a "compelling public necessity" for the autopsy, namely that Joe had died while in custody. Chanin said Steve Worth had advised him that Mary objected to the autopsy for "cosmetic reasons, arguing that an autopsy was not needed because it was Mrs. Pikul's feeling that the death occurred due to cancer."

According to Anthony J. Ingrassia, the county coroner on the case, "compelling public reasons" existed not only for the autopsy to be performed, but for it to be conducted "as soon as possible to preserve the integrity of the results."

Mary had no legal ground to stand on, especially after complaining at the news conference about how bad the jail food had been for Joe. The county needed to protect itself. There was no telling what kind of lawsuit Mary might file.

Late that afternoon, Judge Patsalos signed an order directing that the autopsy be conducted "forthwith."

The call went out for Dr. Mark Taff.

That evening, Dr. Taff conducted an extensive pathological examination of Joe Pikul at Horton Memorial Hospital in Middletown. Although he made no public mention of it, Dr. Taff found a scar along the right side of Joe's waist. But it meant nothing, he later said. There was no telling where the scar had come from, he said. Or how old it was.

As for the cause of death, Dr. Taff decided that a battery of laboratory tests would have to be performed over the next few weeks. He was going to tread extra carefully on this one.

In an announcement to reporters the following morning, Ingrassia acknowledged that the lab analysis would include a serological test for the AIDS virus. "We're not saying that he did have it and we're not saying that he didn't."

The Church of St. Joseph's on Sixth Avenue, just three blocks south of the Pikul apartment, is a grand structure, built in 1833. The main body of the church is adorned with several giant chandeliers while thirteen tiny ones bedeck the balcony. The organist warns people who come to the choir loft to walk gently during services because the floorboards creak so much.

The bronze casket, decorated with a plaque reading "Joseph J. Pikul, June 2, 1989," was brought in through the front door at 9:30, the morning of the sixth. The body was wheeled down the aisle with the assistance of four surrogate pallbearers supplied by the funeral home.

Mary came next, comforted by a man with close-cropped hair, an earring, and a white sweater. He put his arm tightly around her shoulders as she began to sob.

Mike and Kathy O'Guin and the two children were forced to walk behind the spectacle. Sporting his blond bangs, blue blazer, and striped tie, Blake appeared oblivious to the unfolding events. At the wake the night before, he had poked his father's body with a finger, asking, "Why is it hard?"

Claudia was wearing a gray dress with wide white collar and a red bow. As she had done for her mother's funeral, she wore a black bow in her hair.

Attorneys Bekoff and Worth sat in a pew midway through the right side of the church. A lone woman sat in a pew on the left. A man who would only say that he'd been a friend of Joe's arrived as the service began and sat off to the right by himself.

The trickle of people continued throughout the prayers, and by ceremony's end there was a total of twenty-two churchgoers, including a plump, garish-looking, publicity seeker named Sukhreet Gabel, who had never met Joe Pikul and had known Mary only about two months.

Wearing a stained white-and-blue-trimmed sailor's

blouse, a black skirt with a large slit in the rear, and an unfashionable red wig, Gabel had gained national head-lines by secretly tape-recording her own mother, who was a judge in New York City, in a divorce-fixing scandal involving former Miss America Bess Myerson.

In the aftermath of that trial, which the government lost with the help of Gabel's zany testimony, Mary's new friend had tried a variety of schemes to remain in the public limelight, from embarking on a short-lived cabaret-singing career to allowing herself to be featured on a series of greeting cards, including one with her poised to attack with a huge knife in her hand.

So this was a small gathering, but one sprinkled with a unique breed: Sukhreet Gabel, one of those "only in New York" kind of women, coupled with Mary Eik Bain Pikul in mourning, an exacta of the bizarre. Only they were playing to an empty house—there was room for at least another 700 guests.

The Reverend Robert Norris blessed Joe's casket with holy water as Mike O'Guin held Claudia's hand. The children and the O'Guins entered the front pew, right side, followed by Mary, whose entourage settled into the second row.

The passing subway cars rattled from below as Father Norris's assistants read portions of the Letters from Paul to the Romans and the Gospel according to John. The mourners also sang the 23rd Psalm.

"We meet today to celebrate Joseph's death," said Father Norris, launching into one of those standard impersonal eulogies so frequently given when the honorer has never met the honoree. "There are many names you can call people: father, husband, friend. . . . But there is one name that is most important, the name when he was baptized, a child of God, a son of God."

A couple of truckers honked their horns outside, probably an argument over a parking space. "There is life in death. . . . No one can judge a person completely. . . . There is only One who knows who you are . . . God alone."

By now Blake had his blazer off and was getting impatient. The priest invited him to offer the bread to the altar and Blake obliged, gladly getting out of the crowded pew. But Father Norris's next offer, for Claudia to carry the chalice of wine, was met first with a cold stare, then with a forceful shaking of her head. Claudia wasn't about to budge, so Mary volunteered.

Too young to comprehend the subtleties at work, Blake carried the holy wafer and Mary carried the holy wine. Leaving the altar, Mary put her hand in Blake's hair and stroked it several times while smiling that smile of hers. Claudia sat motionlessly through it all.

Blake next watched intently as the priest waved his incense around the casket, then pinched his fingers across his nose to say "pee-you." One could only wonder how these adorable, blameless kids were ever going to pull through. If their parents had been haunted by their own childhoods, what was in store for them?

"Be merciful in judging our brother Joseph," Father Norris continued. "In baptism, he died with Christ. May he also share in the Resurrection. . . . Have mercy on us all."

Mary bent over several times during the prayers in the hopes of talking to the children. But the O'Guins just stiffened their positions as buffers, forcing Mary to turn away.

Mercifully, the service lasted only forty-five minutes.

The O'Guins and the children exited the church and quickly departed for home.

With the TV and still cameras in position, Mary readied herself behind the exiting casket. Upon reaching the front door, however, she dropped to the floor and had to be dragged back into the vestibule to be revived, not unlike her fainting spell at the custody hearing.

If Mary's collapse didn't make the perfect picture, she gave the photographers a second chance. Rejuvenated, she walked out of the church ever so slowly, clutching a bronze crucifix to scare away evil spirits. Her friend Sukhreet helped fill in the photo background by holding her up.

The two women walked to a lone waiting limo; a second car had been sent away because there wasn't anyone to fill it.

Although the burial site was supposed to be a secret, word leaked that Joe was going to be laid to rest in the cemetery next to the house on Windmill Lane in Amagansett. The price was right.

Several hours after the funeral, the hearse, the limo, and Steve Worth's car rode through Main Street and its quaint stores. One last time, Joe passed by the Amagansett Hardware Store and Tony Lupo's deli. Then it was on to tiny Oak Grove Cemetery, where Joe had purchased the last available burial plots, no more than thirty yards from the side of his house. The funeral-home crew placed Joe's casket beside the open grave. The largest bouquet was adorned with a purple ribbon that read "Beloved Husband."

Father Norris had not made the trip from the city, but a local funeral director waiting at the cemetery said a priest from a church in East Hampton was en route.

As they waited, Mary, Sukhreet, Bekoff, and Worth went into the house. The visit was Worth's and Bekoff's first into the supposed scene of the crime, made out of idle curiosity since the defense team had declined to pay a visit before the trial. For the two women, however, the tour had a more definite purpose.

Finally, at 1:20, the Reverend Vincent Hagan commenced what could generously be described as a brief service.

One of the funeral men brought eight yellow roses to the grave site so that the mourners most dear to the deceased could place them on the casket. It was part of "the package," he explained. But after Mary, Sukhreet, Bekoff, and Worth, there was no one else to give a flower to. Looking quickly to his left to ascertain that Mary wasn't watching, the man threw the remaining flowers behind a tombstone.

"Save him from eternal death," said the priest, with birds chirping in the background. "We ask you, Lord, to watch over our brother. May he rest in peace." Father Hagan expressed "sorrow in the death of our brother Joseph" and asked that "our faith be our consolation. . . . In Your mercy forgive whatever wrongs he may have done in his life. Now in Your love and mercy give him a place."

As he walked to his car, Father Hagan was asked how he'd gotten involved in the proceedings. "I never saw any of these people before. I'm from Florida. I'm just visiting," the priest said stiffly. As for Joe Pikul, Father Hagan added: "I've never heard of this man."

With that, Father Hagan got into his car and left.

Worth and Bekoff got into their car and left.

Mary and Sukhreet went back into the house.

Since the hearse driver wanted to get back to Manhattan before traffic started to back up later in the afternoon, Mary and Sukhreet stayed inside for only a few minutes. Then they exited carrying three garbage bags filled to capacity. There were several videotapes on the top of one of the two bags Mary was carrying. Sukhreet carried the third bag and a stack of photo albums.

The two women walked briskly and deposited themselves and the bags in the rear seat of the limousine, which then pulled out of the driveway.

Diahn McGrath was furious when she heard that Mary had rifled the house. She immediately consulted the East Hampton police, who immediately requested legal papers proving the O'Guins' role as guardians.

The failure to inventory and secure the Amagansett home, at least after Joe's conviction, had fallen through the cracks. But it was understandable since no one had really suspected that after all these months, incriminating sex tapes, among other things, would still be lying around the house.

McGrath said she was going to take the entire matter to court.

The next morning, a beat-up Ford Fairmont without license plates was parked in the bushes between Joe's grave and the gate leading to the Pikul backyard, about 100 feet up the cemetery's dirt road. The backseat was covered with newspaper articles about Joe's death.

The car looked abandoned, and bore a thirty-day, New Jersey nonresident registration in the name of Mary Bain Pikul, address: 224A Eden Road, Cuddebackville, New York.

The registration had expired June 5, the day before the funeral. Had Mary dumped the car? But when? She'd taken the funeral limo back to the city the afternoon before. It made no sense. Mary must have driven back; she was probably in the house.

By this time, McGrath had spoken to Detective Kenneth Brown, who had supervised the town of East Hampton's investigation of Diane's disappearance back in October 1987. She told him that Joe's 1985 will was identical to Diane's, leaving the estate to the other spouse and then to the children. McGrath also told Brown that Joe died civilly the day he was convicted and that under state law, since he stood to inherit from the person he was convicted of murdering, Joe's civil death preceded Diane's actual death.

The bottom line, McGrath explained, was that Mary had no authority under either will to take property, dispose of property, sell property, or do anything to property once owned by Joe or Diane and now owned by the children. Mary's only claim was a monetary one, McGrath said, a possible one-third share of the proceeds from the sale of any assets from Joe's estate.

Several hours later, on a request from McGrath, police found Mary inside the house. "All I want to do is get Joe's diaries and tapes," Mary told Detective Brown. Incredibly, she'd come back for more dirty laundry.

But by now Brown had heard McGrath's explanation and received her fax of the O'Guins' guardianship papers. Brown convinced Mary to leave, at least until he could get more information from the Surrogate's Court in Manhattan. A patrol car was posted in the Pikul driveway.

McGrath was understandably furious. "The kids own the house 100 percent," she said. "This is disgusting. Here comes this woman into the lives of these children and now she's attempting to profit off them."

That afternoon, less than twenty-four hours after Joe was laid to rest, McGrath filed a motion in Surrogate's Court asking that Mary and Sukhreet return "three large bags of personal effects and photo albums of the Pikul family." McGrath noted in her affidavit that she believed "most, if not all of the items in question, are photographs, diaries, videotapes, and other memorabilia of Diane, Joseph, Claudia, and Blake Pikul." In an accompanying affidavit, Mike O'Guin argued that there could be "no question" that "all the Pikul family's tangible personal property, in particular all books, diaries, audio tapes, videotapes, manuscripts, etc. belong to the Pikul children, Claudia and Blake."

Surrogate's Court Judge Marie Lambert signed a temporary restraining order barring Mary, her attorneys, and Sukhreet from entering the Windmill Lane house or removing any additional property. Mary also was ordered to prepare an inventory of what she'd removed and return everything to the court at a hearing in two weeks. In the meantime, the judge barred Mary and her cohorts from publishing, distributing, photographing, duplicating, referring to, or "using in any manner, shape, or form" any of the photographs, papers, tapes, recordings, or any other items removed.

Later that afternoon, when Mary returned to the East Hampton Police Department to inquire about being allowed back in the house, she asked to use the telephone to call Maury Povich at the Fox Network program "A Current Affair."

"Hello, this is Mary Pikul. Is Maury there?" Mary asked.

Told that Maury wasn't in, Mary then spoke to a producer, explaining that she had talked to her attorney and that she could appear for an interview the following evening but had to be picked up by limo at her office in New Jersey.

While she was at it, Mary asked Detective Brown to be on the program; he could be shown guarding the Windmill Lane property. Brown politely declined, and instead told Mary that under orders from Judge Lambert he and his men had sealed the doors and windows of the house on Windmill Lane. Brown then also took Mary's keys to the house.

As soon as she departed, Brown called McGrath to inform her of Mary's plans to go public.

The next morning, McGrath set out to serve copies of Judge Lambert's restraining order on the key parties. Fearing that Mary was going to go on the air immediately with the tapes, McGrath and Mike O'Guin staked out the Fox

Network studios on East Sixty-seventh Street in Manhattan.

The plan was to serve Mary on the way in, but she evaded the makeshift dragnet. It wasn't until 7:25 P.M., as Mary exited an elevator with two other women, that McGrath cornered her target.

"Mrs. Pikul?" McGrath asked.

Mary nodded, and McGrath handed her a copy of the judge's order. Mary looked at it and walked away.

McGrath and O'Guin quickly moved to their next subject, Sukhreet Gabel, whose apartment was nearby on East Sixty-ninth Street.

When McGrath asked the doorman for "Ms. Gabel," he called up to Apartment 7A on the house phone. With Gabel's approval, McGrath took the elevator to her floor, where another copy of the judge's order was promptly served. Gabel explained that she had no animosity toward McGrath or the O'Guins.

In the next twenty-four hours, McGrath served Bekoff by mail out in Long Island and sent "A Current Affair" a copy of the court order by fax machine.

The interview and tapes were never aired.

On June 21, 1989, nearly three weeks after Joe's death, Mary testified in Surrogate's Court that she'd taken the diaries and tapes because she wanted to write a book. "Joe didn't want his story told, but he felt it was okay if I told my story," she said.

Claiming she'd misunderstood the restraining order, Mary produced several items, including a nude photo of Diane, Diane's passport, and a couple of videotapes.

Judge Lambert angrily scolded Mary, telling her she didn't own any of the materials. The judge got especially angry when the discussion turned to items like the nude photo of Diane.

Judge Lambert ordered Mary to produce the purloined property, ruling that those in control of Diane's estate would ultimately determine what could be released to the public, if anything.

The following Monday, the day of the judge's deadline, Mary turned over additional material, but still not everything. Somehow Mary again avoided being cited for contempt.

Finally, the word came from Coroner Ingrassia on the cause of Joe's death. In a carefully worded official announcement, Ingrassia said the long-awaited results of the toxological and serological tests showed that Joe died of cancer of the lymphatic system, pneumonia, and "opportunistic infections" including adrenalitis, oral candidiasis, pneumocystis carinii pneumonia, and cytomegalovirus pneumonitis.

Joe had died of AIDS.

Reeling from another round of headlines, McGrath and the O'Guins were more concerned about Claudia and Blake and wondered whether they needed to be tested. For the O'Guins, it seemed like they never had time to come up for air. It was one problem after another.

While Kathy and Mike struggled to steady the lives of Claudia and Blake with the help of therapists, Diahn McGrath continued her search for assets to finance the children's living expenses. The search took her far and wide.

It turned out that during the summer of 1987 Joe had purchased as many term life insurance policies as he could get his hands on—more than $1.5 million worth. But following his arrest, he failed to make the next annual premiums and the policies had lapsed. Desperately exploring all angles, McGrath went so far as to consider whether she could argue the insurance policies were still valid on the grounds that the AIDS made Joe incapable of conducting his business affairs, including sending in the new premiums.

A search for secret bank accounts also turned out to be an empty basket. Joe did have a Swiss bank account—Mary had made countless inquiries about it, and Jean-Jacques, Joe's former business associate, was questioned about the account at Bank Oppenheim Pierson (Schweiz) AG in Zurich from his new address in Geneva. Because of the secrecy surrounding such accounts, McGrath experienced great difficulty obtaining information about the balance. But it appeared there was very little, if anything, left in it.

Expectations further dimmed when Bekoff's law firm revealed in court papers that Joe had used $40,000 from that account as part of his bail collateral. If there'd been more money in it, Joe would have used it for his bail rather than scrounging the final $70,000 from his friends, as he had been forced to do. In fact, McGrath said, Joe had withdrawn about $250,000 from the account just before his arrest to serve as a retainer for his first set of criminal attorneys.

Two other possibilities offered hope—a bank account uncovered in Toronto and stocks Joe held in an overseas firm. But in both instances, the funds amounted to no more than several thousand dollars.

The sad picture of poverty could no longer be disputed. If somewhere in his crazy mind Joe had a hidden account, it appeared the secret died with him, or someone got there before McGrath.

In the meantime, the bills on the house in Amagansett, from broken water pipes to local property taxes, continued to pile up against Diane's estate.

No less than six law firms, including Katzenstein's Sixth Avenue operation, inquired about the Surrogate's Court action or the house foreclosure lawsuit on Long Island. If any money was found, the attorneys wanted to be standing first in line.

The Pikul story had reached one of the inevitable nadirs of probate law: the battle of the lawyers v. the orphans. "This is a case of two little babies—motherless, fatherless, and penniless—against all these attorneys," said McGrath. "I have the feeling this will drag on for years."

The sobering realization that there had been more debits than credits on the night Joe had killed Diane only served to heighten everyone's interest in the one remaining piece of change worth fighting for: the rest of Joe's bail money.

When Joe hired Bekoff and Worth, he paid them $75,000 up front and signed over his $180,000 share of the bail—in a formal contract—as part of their $250,000 base fee.

With Bekoff getting $2,000 per trial day and Worth $1,000 per trial day, the unpaid portion of Joe's bill had swelled to $300,450, including expenses. The attorneys realized prospects weren't promising for them to get their full fee, but they figured they at least had clear title to the remaining bail money.

After Joe's conviction, though, when Bekoff and Worth called the insurance company for a check, they learned that the Internal Revenue Service had already slapped the firm with a $103,564.32 lien for Joe's back payments.

It wasn't easy, but Thomas R. Hession, another partner in the Bekoff-Worth firm, convinced the IRS that the government claim was invalid since Joe had assigned the money to the law firm prior to placement of the federal lien. In effect, the money really belonged to the Bekoff-Worth law firm as soon as Joe signed the contract for legal services. Hession again asked the insurance company to issue the check, but before that could be done, McGrath got wind of the transaction and promptly made a claim on behalf of the children.

Bekoff's firm sued the bail bondsman and the insurance company, arguing that Joe's claim to the money ceased before the trial began, when he assigned the bail collateral to the law firm. McGrath argued that part of the money, if not all of it, belonged to Diane's estate and therefore to the children, pointing out that at least part of the bail funds had come from Joe's pension fund and profit-sharing accounts, in which Diane had "at least a 50-percent interest." She further argued that Joe forfeited his share of the bail funds "when he intentionally killed Diane."

Hession replied that the remaining bail money had come entirely from Joe's personal funds and that Joe "had the absolute right to transfer his property."

Joe's share of the bail money included the $40,000 withdrawn from his personal Swiss account and a $140,000 Bank of New York check dated November 3, 1987, from Arnhold & S. Bleichroeder Inc. According to an accounting provided by Jeremy G. Epstein, an attorney who represented the brokerage house on the matter, $76,592 represented compensation still owed Joe for 1987, minus the appropriate federal, state, and local taxes. The balance, $63,408, represented the sale of twenty shares of Arnhold & S. Bleichroeder Inc. that Joe kept in his personal account.

McGrath also tried to establish that Diane would have been entitled to some of those assets as part of the dissolution of her marriage to Joe. "If Diane had lived and had seen her divorce proceeding through a conclusion, she would have been entitled to consideration of these funds as marital property subject to equitable distribution. Her entitlement in these funds cannot be extinguished by Joseph Pikul having killed her." On the other hand, McGrath argued in court papers, those funds and any other jointly owned assets "should be subject to forfeiture in favor of Diane's estate because of the intentional killing."

Hession called those claims frivolous, pointing out that Diane had never filed for divorce, "and therefore no claim existed by Diane Pikul against the assets solely owned by Joseph Pikul."

Diane's failure to file for divorce was still causing problems.

Epilogue

ON AND ON, THE COURT battles continued.

—As 1989 drew to a close, McGrath asked that the lawsuit against the bail company be transferred from Nassau County, the home turf of Bekoff and Worth, to Surrogate's Court in Manhattan, her home turf. Sometimes in the game of courts, it matters where the game is played.

As best she could tell, McGrath wrote in a legal brief, the estates of both Diane and Joe would very well assert rights to the same assets, "and both estates bear some of the liabilities—which exceed assets by at least $300,000 and possibly as much as $600,000." She said that Hession, Bekoff, and Worth were attempting to remove from Surrogate's Court "an integral part of the administration" of Diane's estate, namely "an asset that represents more than half of the combined value of Diane's and Joe's estates."

—Depositions were taken from Mary and the bail bondsman for McGrath's estate case. Mary showed up with a curious choice of a new attorney: Paul Kurland, the guy who quit representing Joe and Mary in the custody case after Mary confirmed Joe's dress-slashing attack.

—Bekoff and Worth then hired attorney Armand D'Amato, the brother of Senator Alphonse D'Amato, to fight their bail battle, despite the fact that both D'Amato brothers were in the midst of a burgeoning HUD scandal.

—Served with a subpoena to appear in Surrogate's Court, Samira the psychic delivered some property to the judge's chambers, including some tapes. It turned out that

Joe's "Princess of the Nile" was really one Marian Elma Rose, born August 15, 1924, in Beacon, New York, across the river from Newburgh, and that she was on five-years probation after being charged with grand larceny–welfare fraud for collecting public funds while employed by the county government.

—Raoul Felder had Wayburn file a motion seeking to unseal the entire custody-case file. Despite the fact that deadlines had long passed, Felder cited requests from the authors of two books about the Pikul case as a main reason for unsealing the hearing material. In a compromise, Judge Glen agreed to release the transcripts, but not the video-tape and photos of Joe prancing around in women's lingerie. According to McGrath, Judge Glen made that decision "for the children." Following an inquiry, Felder turned over his copies of Joe's sex photos and tapes from the custody hearing—two years after the completion of the proceedings.

—Felder had taken to advertising himself while selling a legal handbook as a child's rights advocate, based on his work on "the Pikul case."

—After about a year "together," Wayburn and Felder had a parting of the ways. "It didn't work out," said Felder. "He's talented. I thought his talents were suited in other directions." More to the point, the two men were at odds over their clashing recollections of their respective roles on the Pikul-O'Guin matters.

—Sandy's attorneys filed an official claim against Joe's estate for her $45,192 judgment, including interest. One way or the other, Sandy still wanted her piece of the action.

—On behalf of Diane's estate, McGrath responded by filing a wrongful-death suit against Joe's estate and Sandy. According to McGrath, Sandy was culpable since she "had prior knowledge of Joseph Pikul's intent to kill Diane. She had a duty to disclose this information. However, she did not act to prevent Joseph Pikul from accomplishing his plan."

"Geez, what a scenario," said Sandy when informed of the lawsuit. "How'd I get into this? What the hell could I do even if I did know?"

Under McGrath's strategy, Joe's estate would have the unpaid bills and Diane's estate would have any assets.

———

The wrongful-death suit sought tens of millions of dollars.

In typical estate-law strategy of "build up the victim's lost income," McGrath argued that at the time of her death Diane was "in good health and was employed at *Harper's* magazine, receiving a salary of $23,000 annually, with benefits and opportunity for increases in salary, and she contributed monetarily to the support and comfort of Claudia and Blake. Diane Pikul was also a writer of fiction with a promising future and the possibility of great financial success."

McGrath also alleged that "because of the wanton way" in which Joe killed Diane, "and the notoriety occurring thereby," Claudia and Blake have "suffered psychological distress," requiring costly counseling expenses to be incurred "and requiring continued visitation to the counselors in the future."

In Sandy's case, the wrongful-death action was more designed to keep her from easily getting ahead of the children in securing her alimony judgment. If followed through until the end, the wrongful-death suit would essentially require a second murder trial, only in civil court, where Joe's admission that he killed Diane—even in self-defense—would work against him. This legal battle, like the Surrogate's Court wrangling, figured to take years to unravel.

Mary, who continued to insist that Claudia and Blake call her "Mommy," never filed to adopt or to obtain custody under any other legal maneuver. Instead, the gossip columns reported that Mary was now dating one of Sukhreet Gabel's old roommates. Sukhreet told reporters that she'd served as matchmaker, but rumors were rampant that she was steaming over having lost her beau. A spring 1990 wedding was said to be in the works.

"Doesn't this shit ever end?" asked Diane's first husband, Ralph Schnackenberg, when he read about Mary and Sukhreet. "I just feel offended by it. There's a strong sleaze factor to this whole goddamn thing and it never ends. It goes on and on and on, these vultures out there."

As lawyer McGrath continued to fight for the Pikul orphans, Claudia and Blake continued on an intensive therapy program, with their future in the prayers of many. In the wake of their father's death, they were both tested for AIDS; the results in each case were negative. The O'Guins began the formal process to adopt, and the children began to settle into their new stable surroundings. "Everything is fine. They talk about it. We don't try to suppress anything. They just don't talk about it nearly as much because it's not in the forefront. They're concentrating on their school work and their friends. They're looking to the future," said Kathy O'Guin. "They're resilient. They're bent on surviving, on living."

With the help of Judge Lambert, McGrath was able to keep almost all of the audiotapes and videotapes out of the public limelight. Several people, from different well-to-do walks of life, were no doubt resting easier.

In the meantime, Joe's lawyers helped their client strike one more technical blow against justice from his grave.

On December 6, 1989, the *New York Times* ran the following story on the bottom of page B5, an abbreviated version of a dispatch from the Associated Press:

GOSHEN, N.Y., Dec. 5 (AP)—A judge has cleared Joseph Pikul's name because the former Wall Street securities analyst died before an appeal of his conviction on charges of murdering his wife was decided, a lawyer said today.

The lawyer, Ronald Bekoff of Mineola, said that Judge Thomas Byrne of Orange County Court signed an order on Aug. 22 erasing Mr. Pikul's conviction from court records.

"There's nothing else to do," Mr. Bekoff said. "He's dead. The case is over."

Under New York State law, a conviction must be vacated if the defendant dies while an appeal is pending. The State Court of Appeals, New York's highest court, has agreed to hear a case over whether that policy is fair.

Mr. Pikul, who died in June, was convicted on March 16 of second-degree murder in connection with the 1987 death of his estranged wife Diane Pikul, an assistant to the publisher of Harper's magazine.

Acknowledgments

Thanks to the scores of people who were willing to talk without making demands for large sums of money as others were so quick to do. Special appreciation is due the state and local police officers, attorneys, members of the prosecution team, and most importantly the friends, associates, and colleagues of Diane and Joseph Pikul who gave freely of their time and information. I am particularly grateful to Diahn McGrath, attorney for the Pikul children and their guardians, for her fairness and time, and to Investigator John N. Knight of the Orange County District Attorney's office for helping facilitate a review of the public evidence in the case.

My agent David Vigliano, who created the project, performed yeoman service guiding me through the mine field of hucksters and the guilt-ridden. His encouragement in times of need was invaluable.

At Dutton, I owe a special debt of gratitude to executive editor Kevin Mulroy for providing direction and advice, and to senior manuscript editor John Paine for an excellent job at keeping the story moving and focused.

Several colleagues in the world of daily journalism need to be thanked—Frances McMorris and photographer Dan Cronin of the New York *Daily News*, freelancer Joan Ullman, and Carolyn Colwell of *Newsday*.

None of this would have been possible without the diligent tutoring and nurturing more than twenty years ago by Willard E. Lally, my mentor and college professor. To him, I am eternally grateful.

Finally, I never would have completed this endeavor without the unswerving persistence and assistance of my wife, Cheryl, whose hard work and perspective helped shepherd the project through its roughest moments. Our two sons, Ryan and Adam, also are to be commended for understanding and accepting the countless hours stolen from their lives. Ultimately, it is to my family that I am most grateful, especially given the book's tragic subject matter.